THE

		DATE DUE		

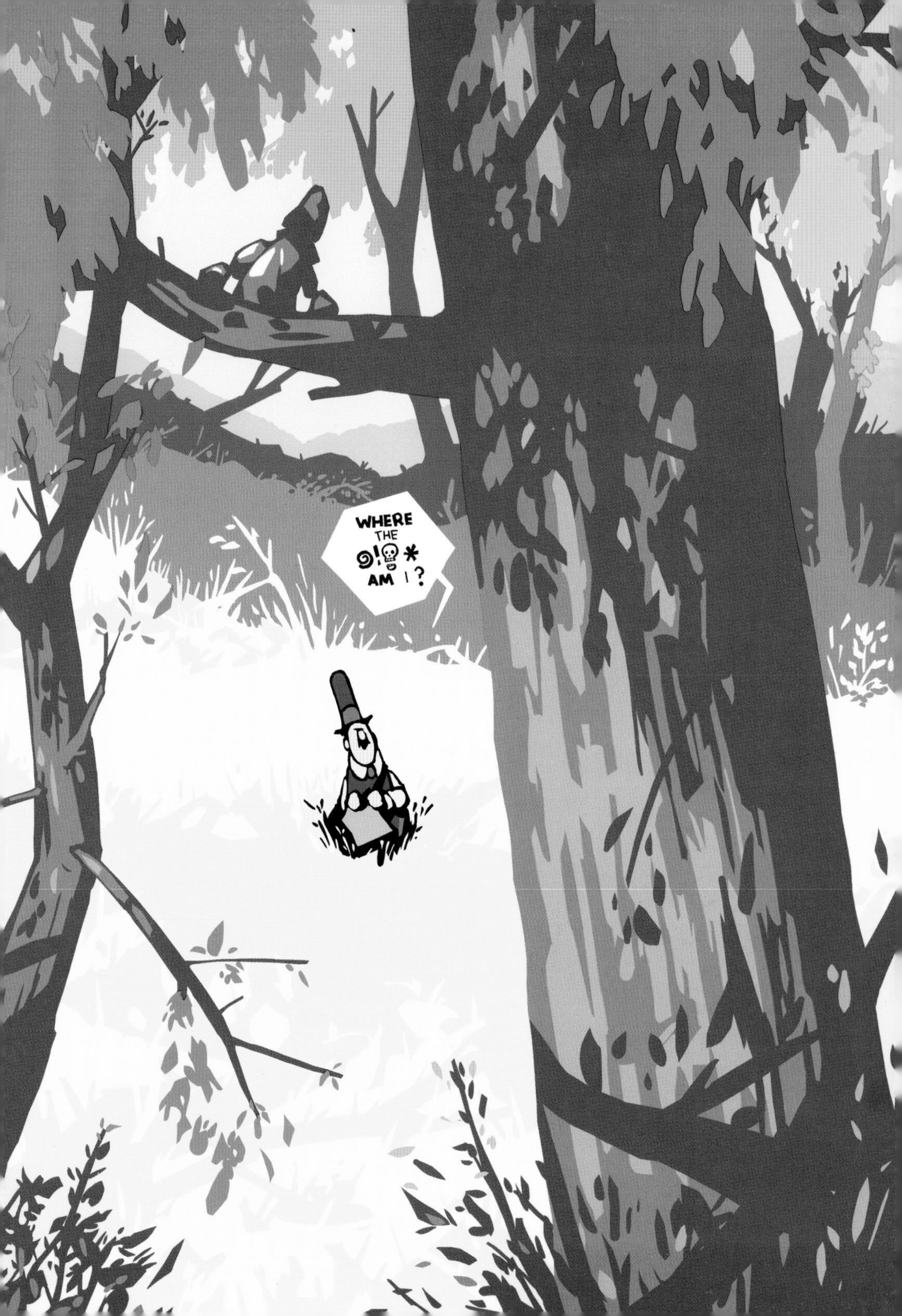
WHERE THE 9!☠* AM I?

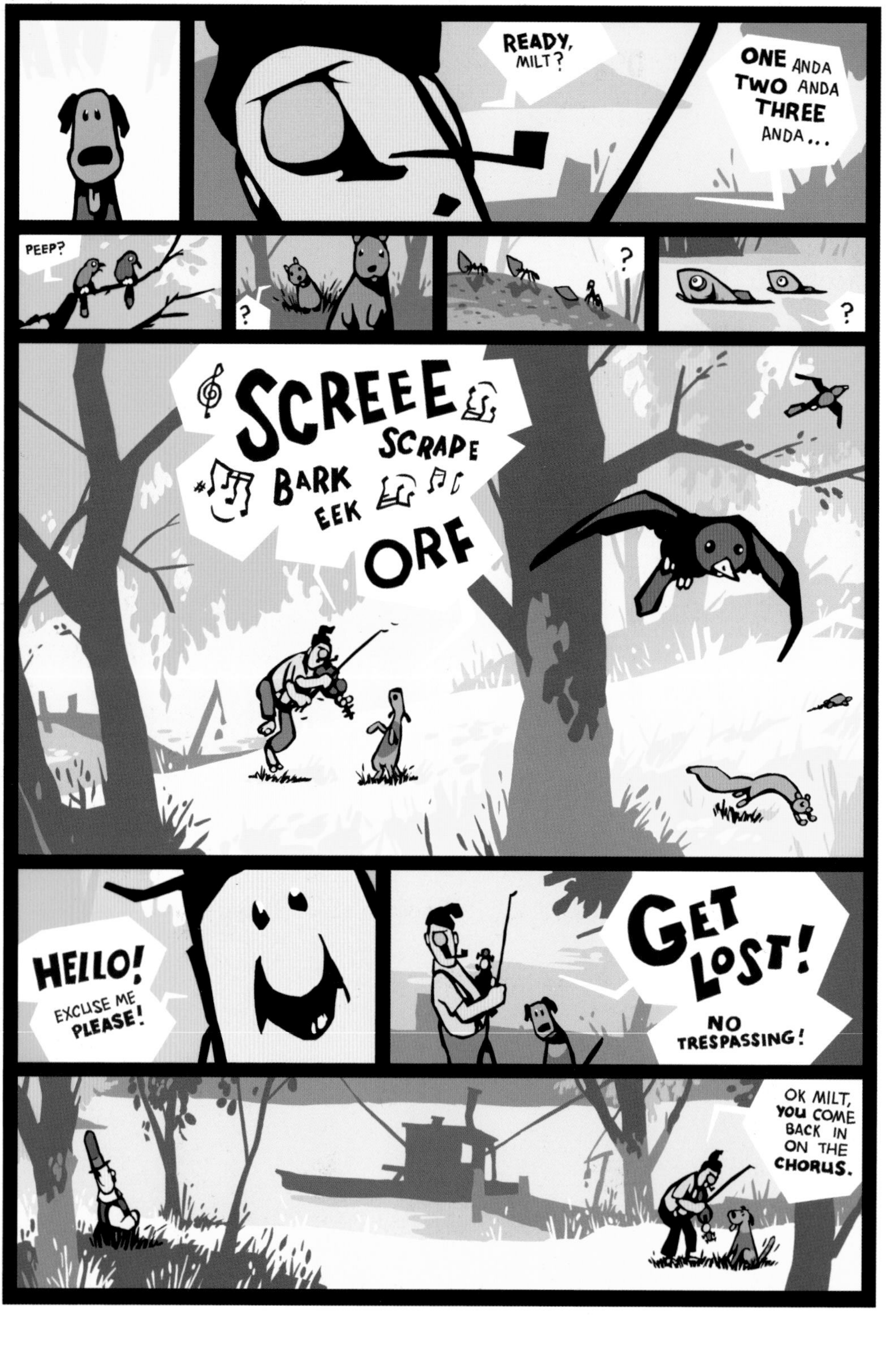
READY, MILT?
ONE ANDA TWO ANDA THREE ANDA...
PEEP?
?
?
?
SCREEE
SCRAPE
BARK
EEK
ORF
HELLO! EXCUSE ME PLEASE!
GET LOST!
NO TRESPASSING!
OK MILT, YOU COME BACK IN ON THE CHORUS.

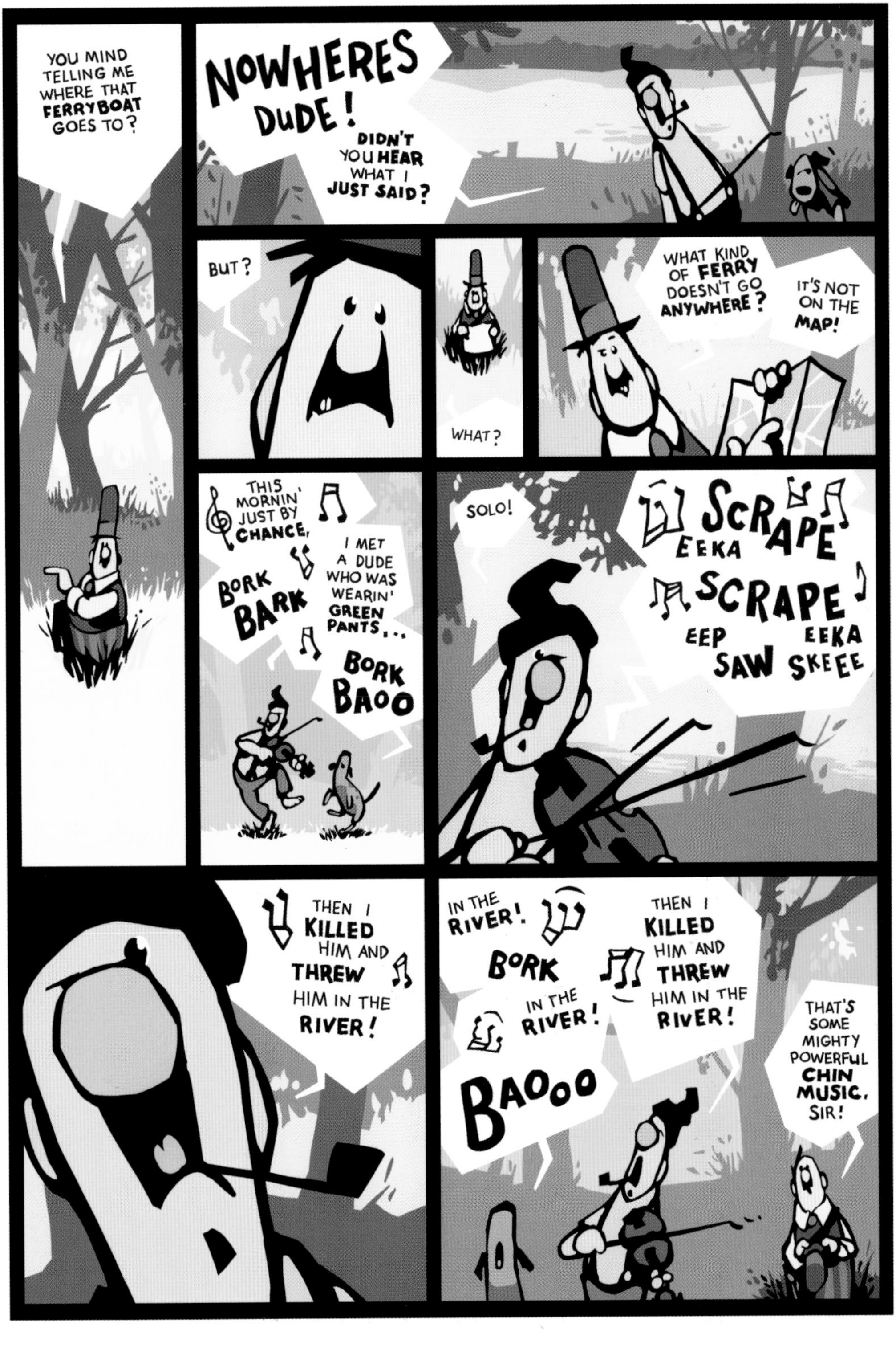
YOU MIND TELLING ME WHERE THAT FERRYBOAT GOES TO?
NOWHERES DUDE!
DIDN'T YOU HEAR WHAT I JUST SAID?
BUT?
WHAT?
WHAT KIND OF FERRY DOESN'T GO ANYWHERE?
IT'S NOT ON THE MAP!
THIS MORNIN' JUST BY CHANCE,
I MET A DUDE WHO WAS WEARIN' GREEN PANTS...
BORK BARK
BORK BAOO
SOLO!
SCRAPE EEKA
SCRAPE
EEP SAW
EEKA SKEEE
THEN I KILLED HIM AND THREW HIM IN THE RIVER!
IN THE RIVER!
BORK
IN THE RIVER!
THEN I KILLED HIM AND THREW HIM IN THE RIVER!
BAOOO
THAT'S SOME MIGHTY POWERFUL CHIN MUSIC, SIR!

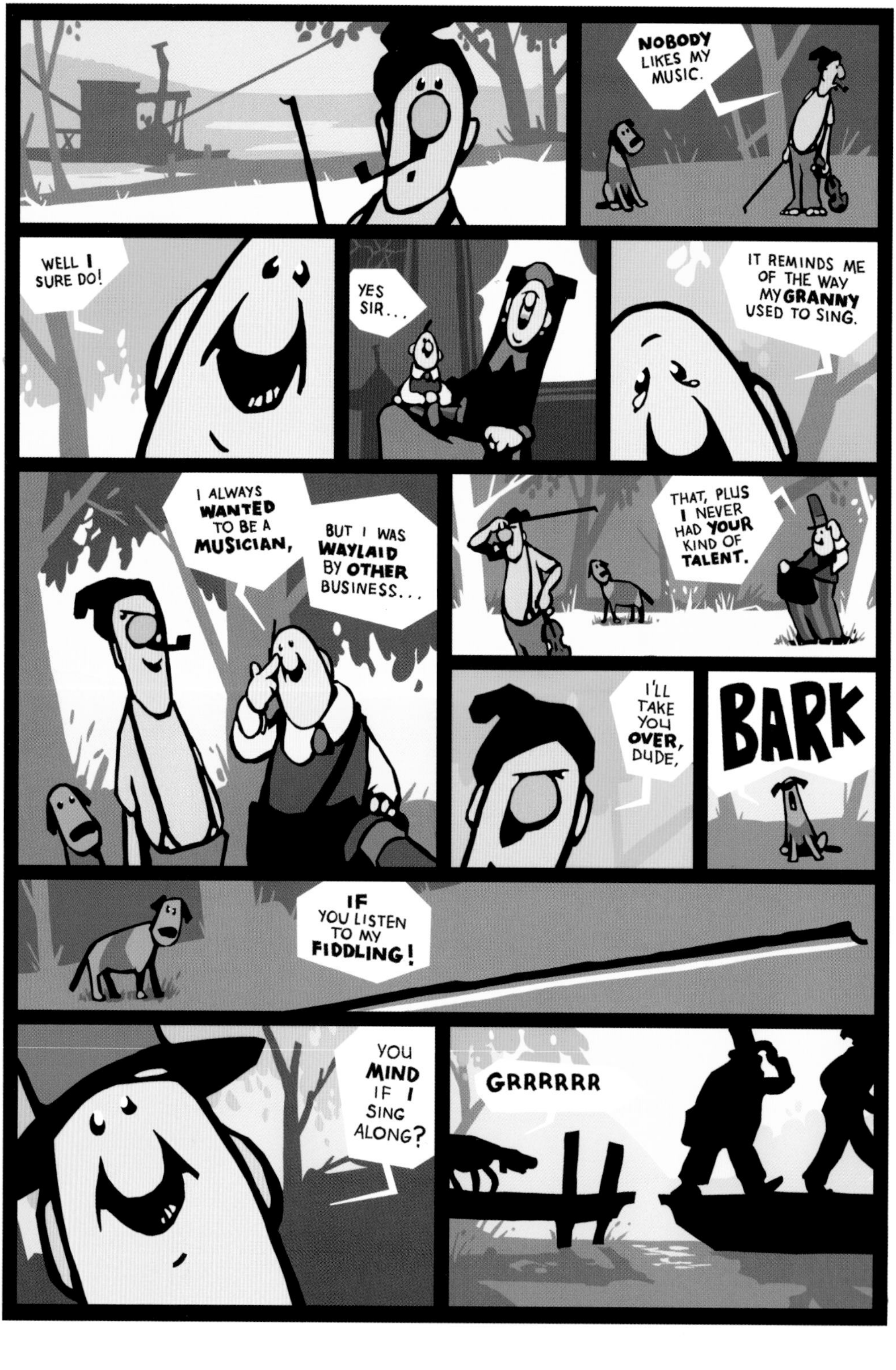
NOBODY LIKES MY MUSIC.
WELL I SURE DO!
YES SIR...
IT REMINDS ME OF THE WAY MY GRANNY USED TO SING.
I ALWAYS WANTED TO BE A MUSICIAN,
BUT I WAS WAYLAID BY OTHER BUSINESS...
THAT, PLUS I NEVER HAD YOUR KIND OF TALENT.
I'LL TAKE YOU OVER, DUDE,
BARK
IF YOU LISTEN TO MY FIDDLING!
YOU MIND IF I SING ALONG?
GRRRRRR

THE
L·O·S·T
COLONY

ADMIT ONE
BEGRUDGINGLY
READER
NO. 1

BOOK NO. 1
THE Snodgrass CONSPIRACY

Grady Klein

DO NOT TRESSPASS

First Second

NEW YORK & LONDON

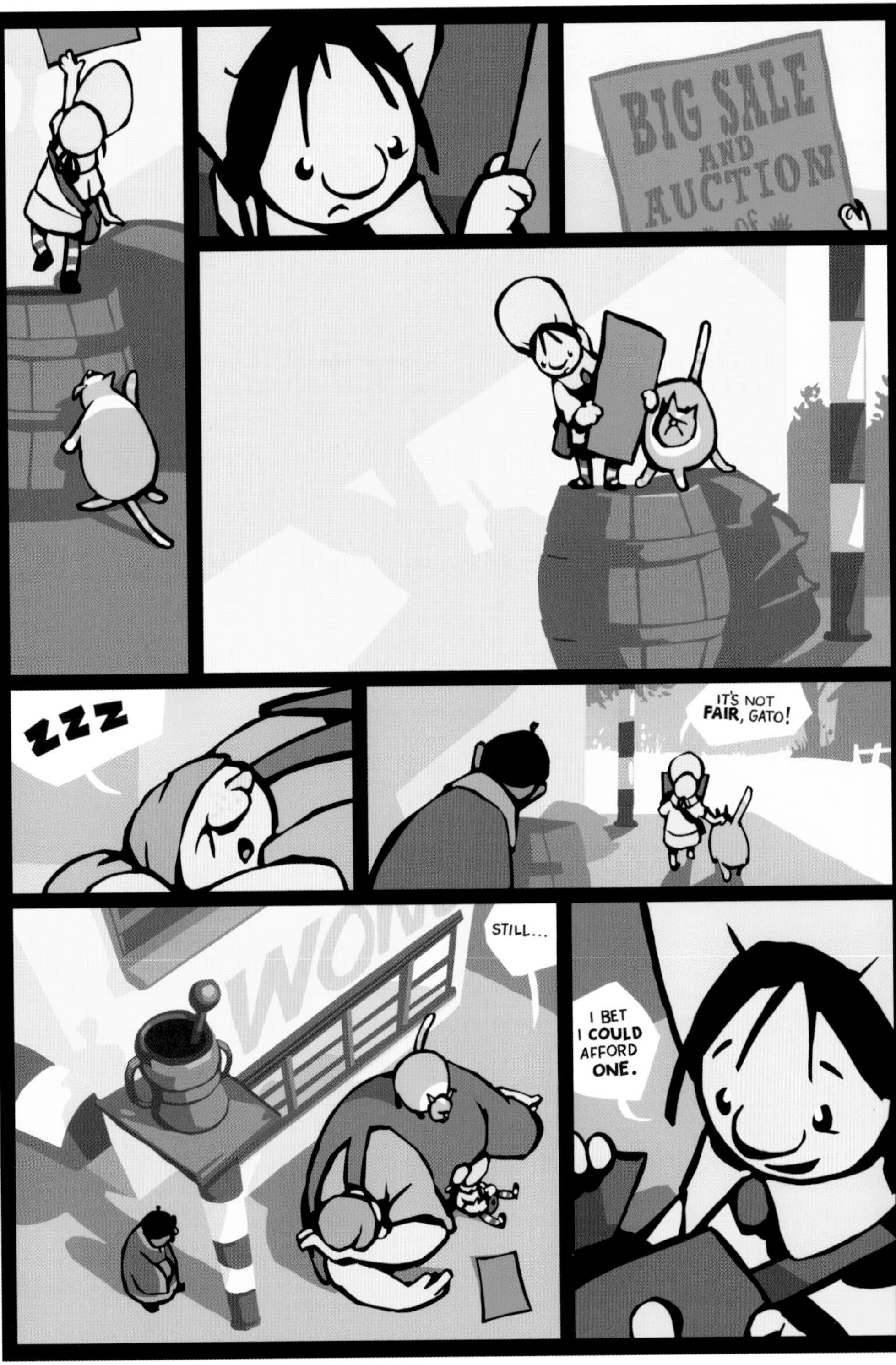
BIG SALE
AND
AUCTION
OF
ZZZ
IT'S NOT FAIR, GATO!
STILL...
I BET I COULD AFFORD ONE.

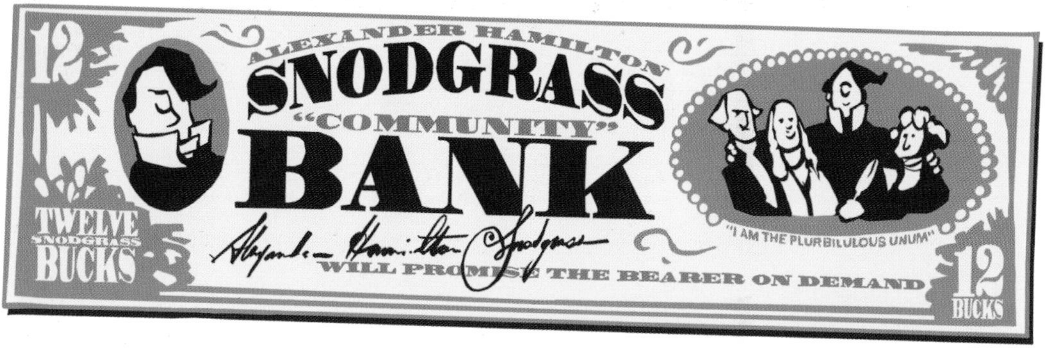

12
ALEXANDER HAMILTON
SNODGRASS
"COMMUNITY"
BANK
TWELVE SNODGRASS BUCKS
"I AM THE PLURBILULOUS UNUM"
WILL PROMISE THE BEARER ON DEMAND
12 BUCKS

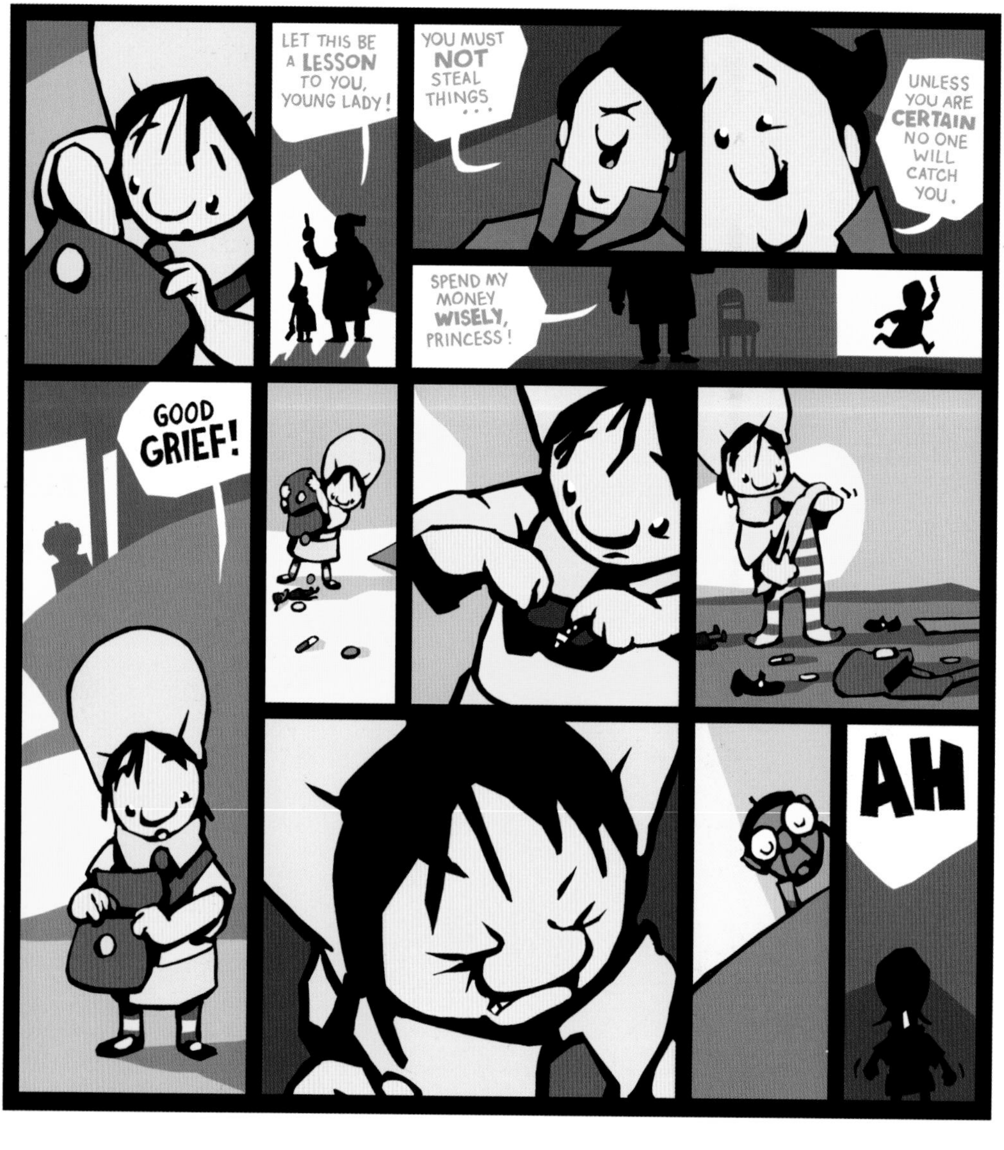

LET THIS BE A LESSON TO YOU, YOUNG LADY!
YOU MUST NOT STEAL THINGS . . .
UNLESS YOU ARE CERTAIN NO ONE WILL CATCH YOU.
SPEND MY MONEY WISELY, PRINCESS!
GOOD GRIEF!
AH

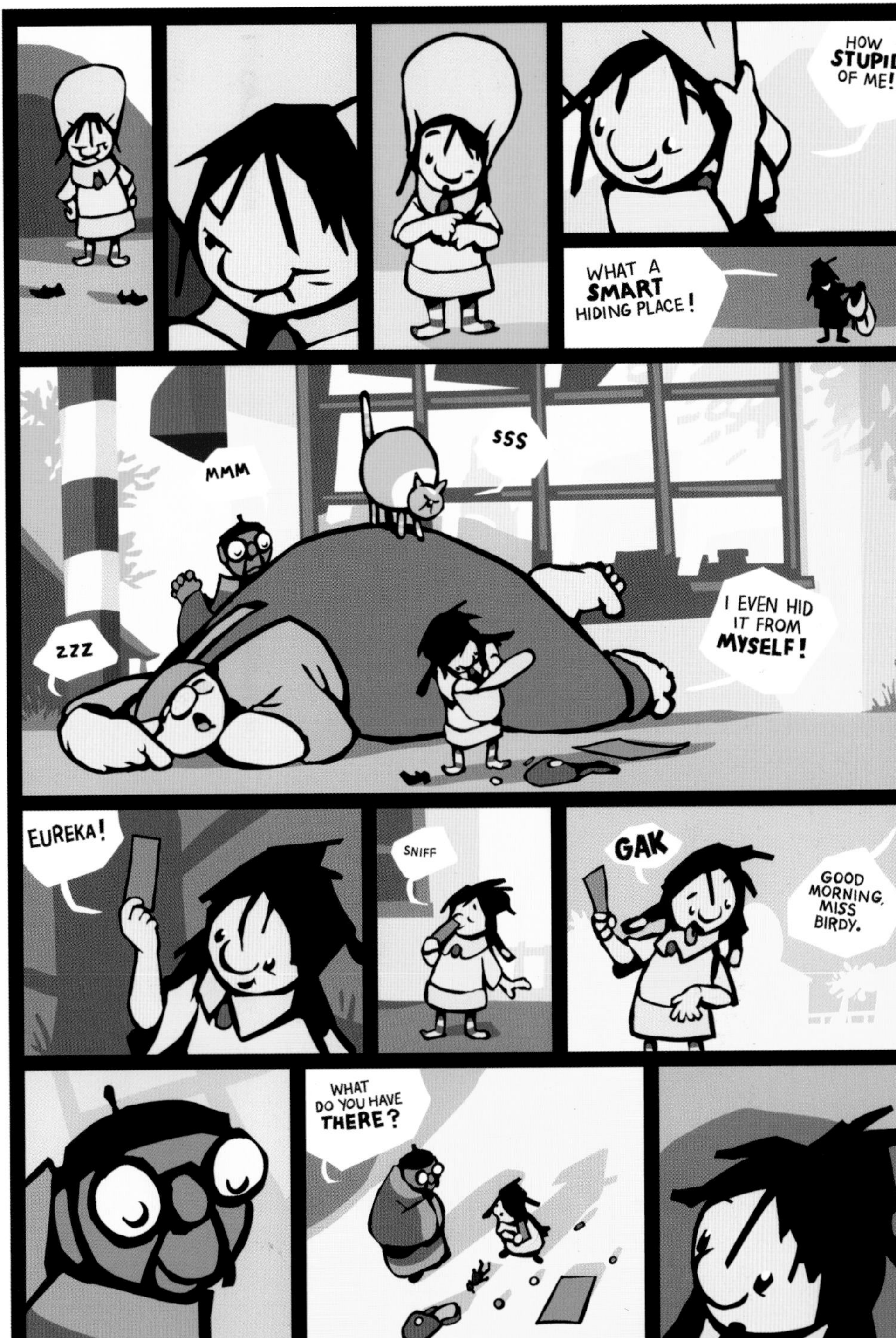
HOW STUPID OF ME!
WHAT A SMART HIDING PLACE!
MMM
SSS
ZZZ
I EVEN HID IT FROM MYSELF!
EUREKA!
SNIFF
GAK
GOOD MORNING, MISS BIRDY.
WHAT DO YOU HAVE THERE?

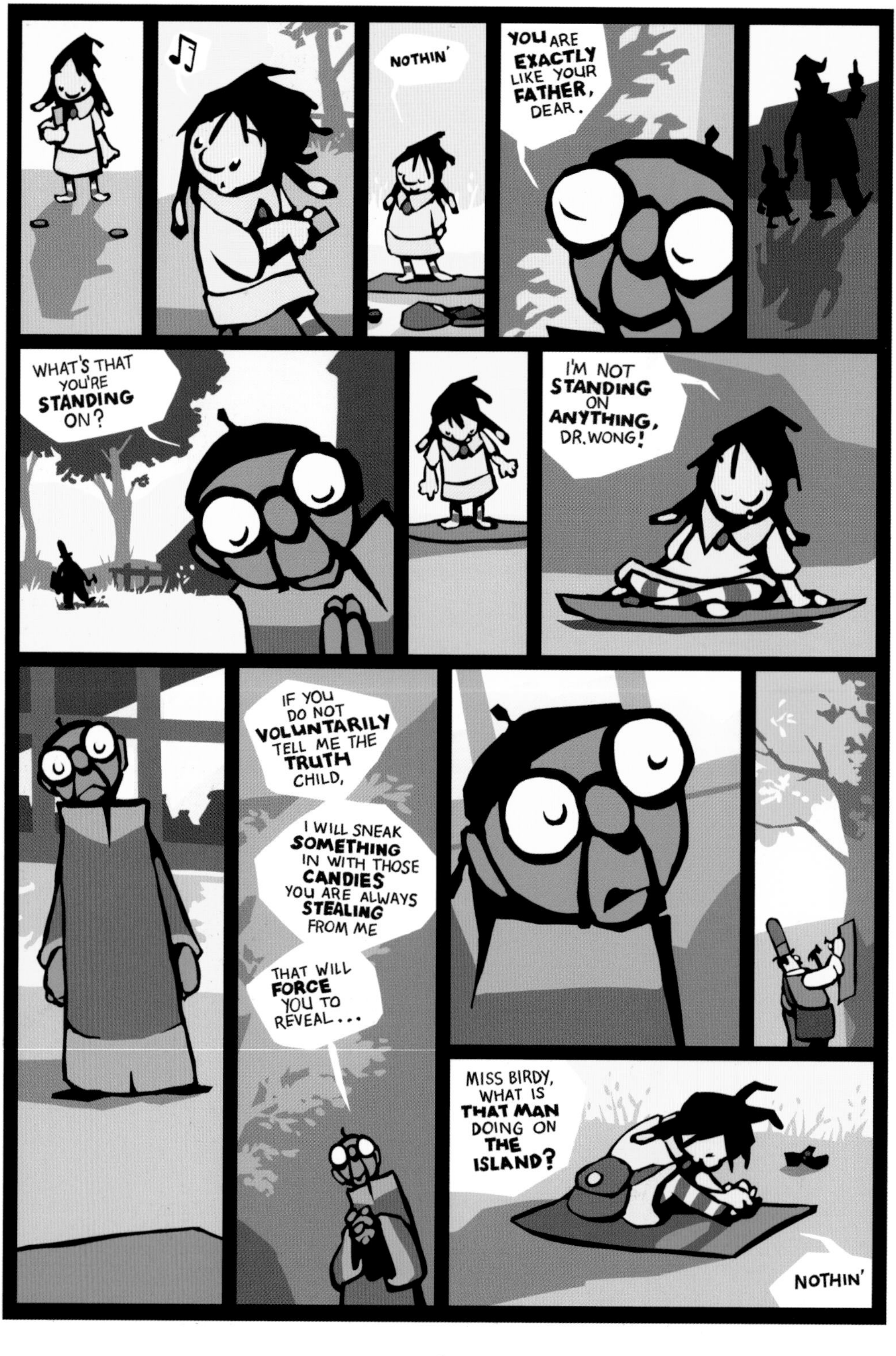
NOTHIN'
YOU ARE EXACTLY LIKE YOUR FATHER, DEAR.
WHAT'S THAT YOU'RE STANDING ON?
I'M NOT STANDING ON ANYTHING, DR. WONG!
IF YOU DO NOT VOLUNTARILY TELL ME THE TRUTH CHILD,
I WILL SNEAK SOMETHING IN WITH THOSE CANDIES YOU ARE ALWAYS STEALING FROM ME
THAT WILL FORCE YOU TO REVEAL...
MISS BIRDY, WHAT IS THAT MAN DOING ON THE ISLAND?
NOTHIN'

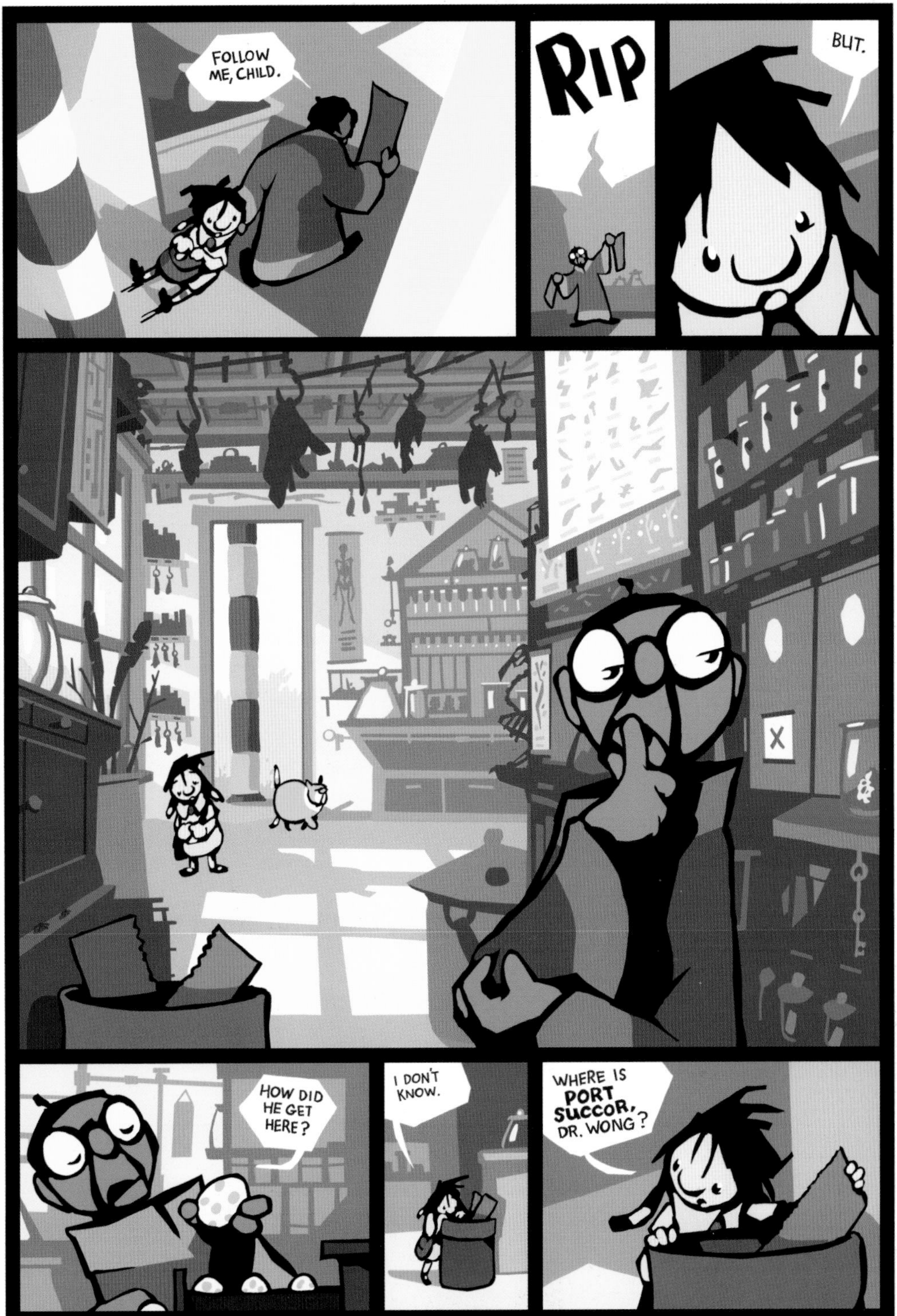
FOLLOW ME, CHILD.
RIP
BUT.
HOW DID HE GET HERE?
I DON'T KNOW.
WHERE IS PORT SUCCOR, DR. WONG?

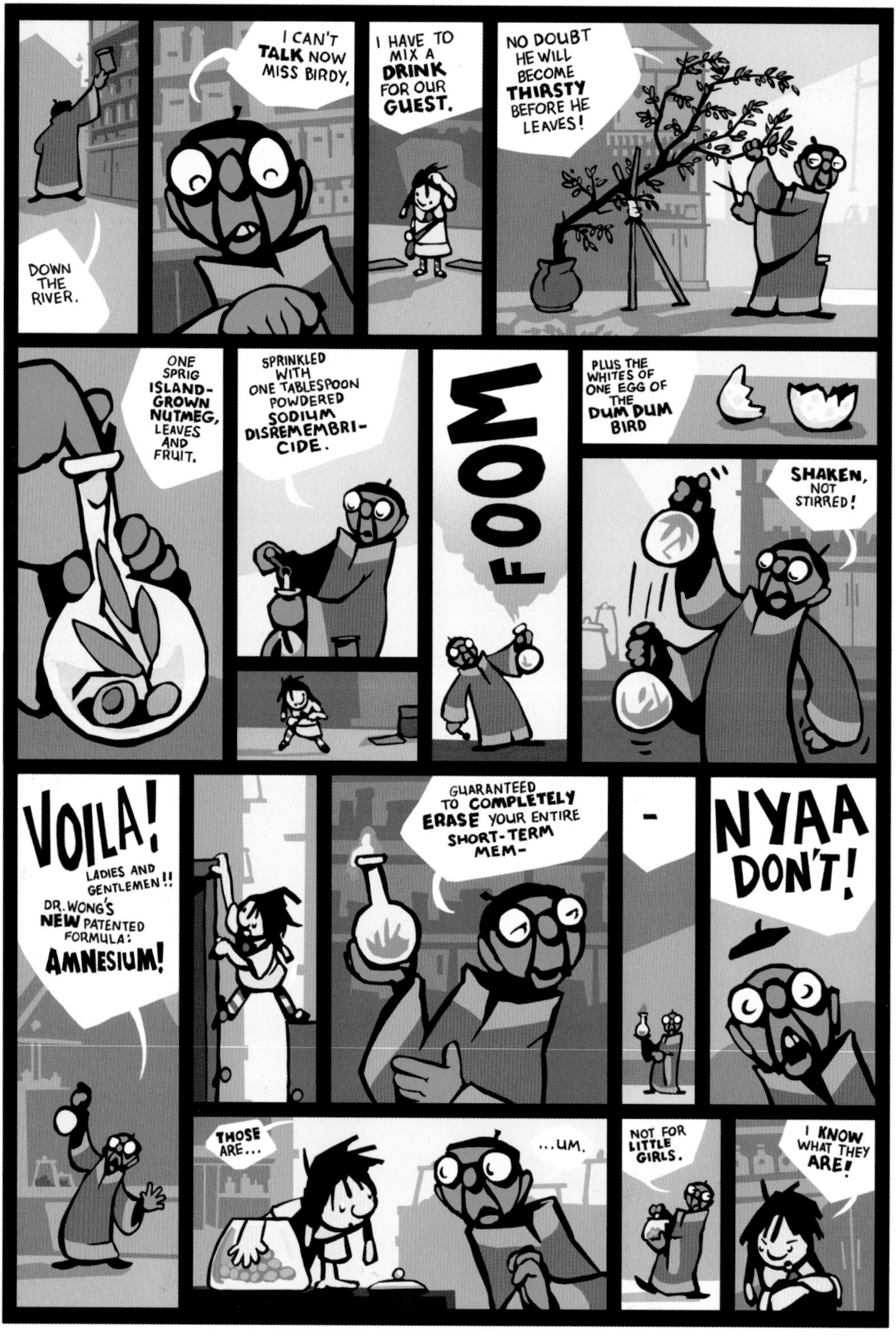
DOWN THE RIVER.
I CAN'T TALK NOW MISS BIRDY,
I HAVE TO MIX A DRINK FOR OUR GUEST.
NO DOUBT HE WILL BECOME THIRSTY BEFORE HE LEAVES!
ONE SPRIG ISLAND-GROWN NUTMEG, LEAVES AND FRUIT,
SPRINKLED WITH ONE TABLESPOON POWDERED SODIUM DISREMEMBRI-CIDE.
FOOOM
PLUS THE WHITES OF ONE EGG OF THE DUM DUM BIRD
SHAKEN, NOT STIRRED!
VOILA!
LADIES AND GENTLEMEN!!
DR. WONG'S NEW PATENTED FORMULA: AMNESIUM!
GUARANTEED TO COMPLETELY ERASE YOUR ENTIRE SHORT-TERM MEM-
-
NYAA DON'T!
THOSE ARE...
...UM.
NOT FOR LITTLE GIRLS.
I KNOW WHAT THEY ARE!

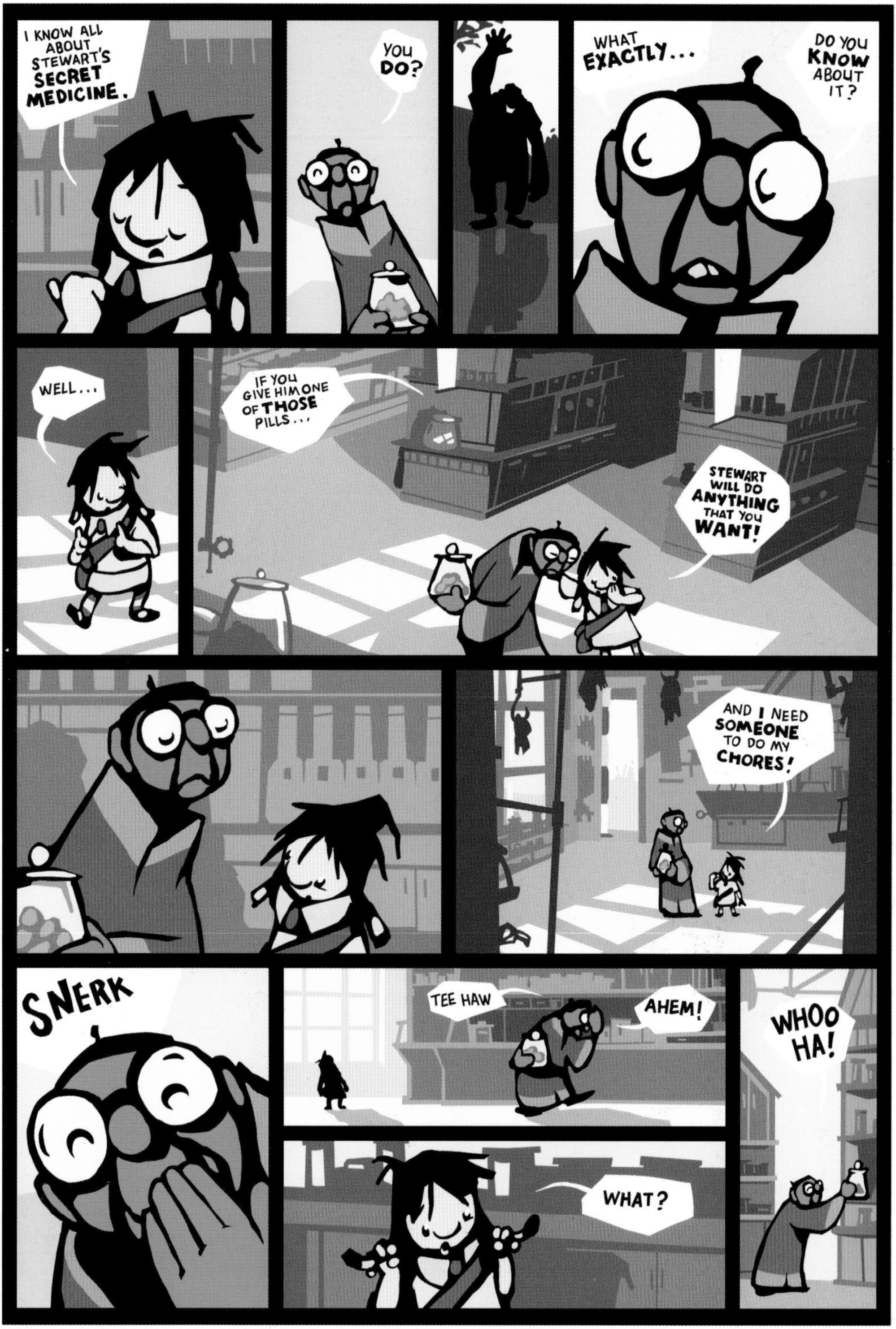
I KNOW ALL ABOUT STEWART'S SECRET MEDICINE.
YOU DO?
WHAT EXACTLY...
DO YOU KNOW ABOUT IT?
WELL...
IF YOU GIVE HIM ONE OF THOSE PILLS...
STEWART WILL DO ANYTHING THAT YOU WANT!
AND I NEED SOMEONE TO DO MY CHORES!
SNERK
TEE HAW
AHEM!
WHAT?
WHOO HA!

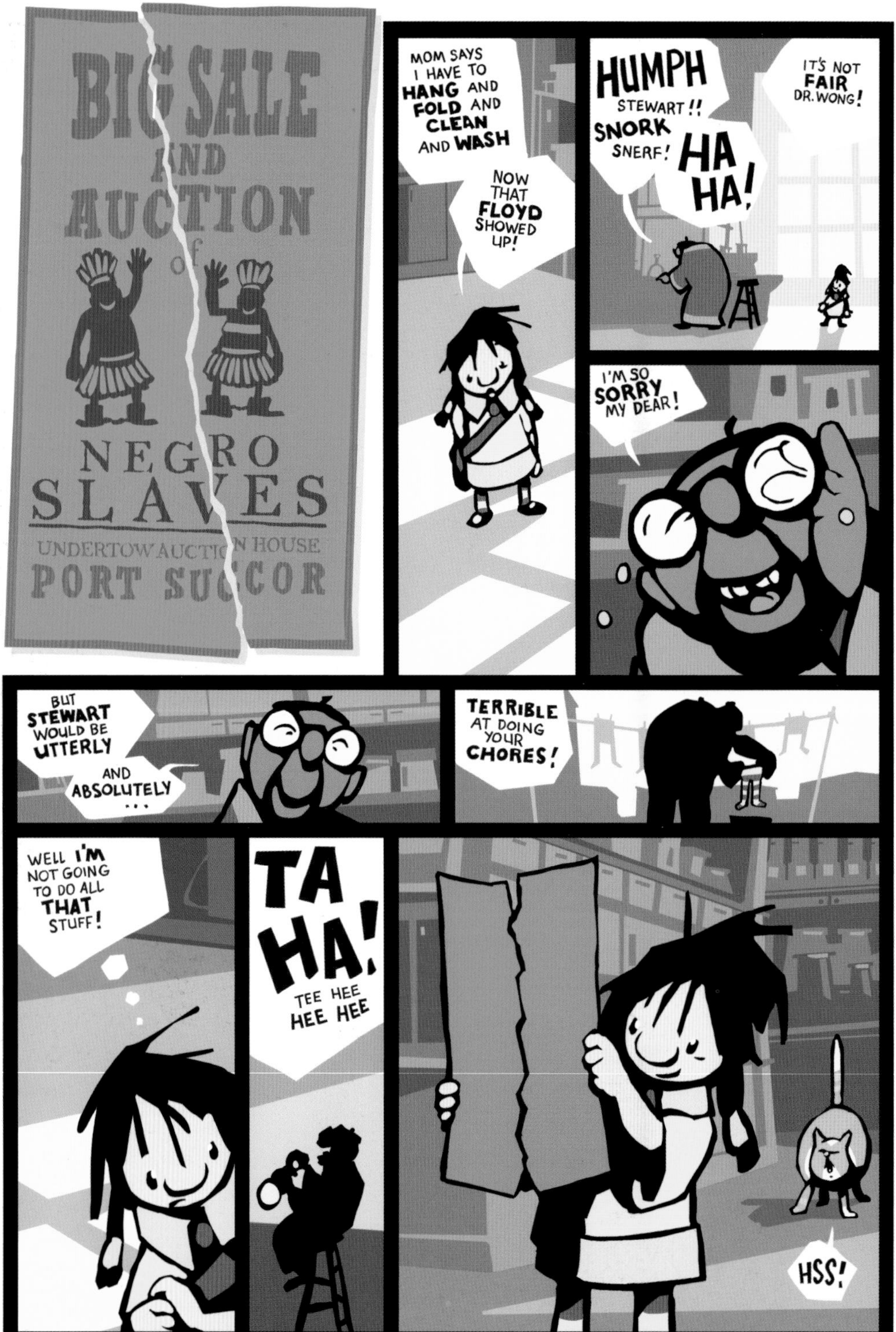
BIG SALE AND AUCTION of NEGRO SLAVES
UNDERTOW AUCTION HOUSE
PORT SUCCOR
MOM SAYS I HAVE TO HANG AND FOLD AND CLEAN AND WASH
NOW THAT FLOYD SHOWED UP!
HUMPH
STEWART!!
SNORK SNERF!
HA HA!
IT'S NOT FAIR DR. WONG!
I'M SO SORRY MY DEAR!
BUT STEWART WOULD BE UTTERLY
AND ABSOLUTELY ...
TERRIBLE AT DOING YOUR CHORES!
WELL I'M NOT GOING TO DO ALL THAT STUFF!
TA HA!
TEE HEE HEE HEE
HSS!

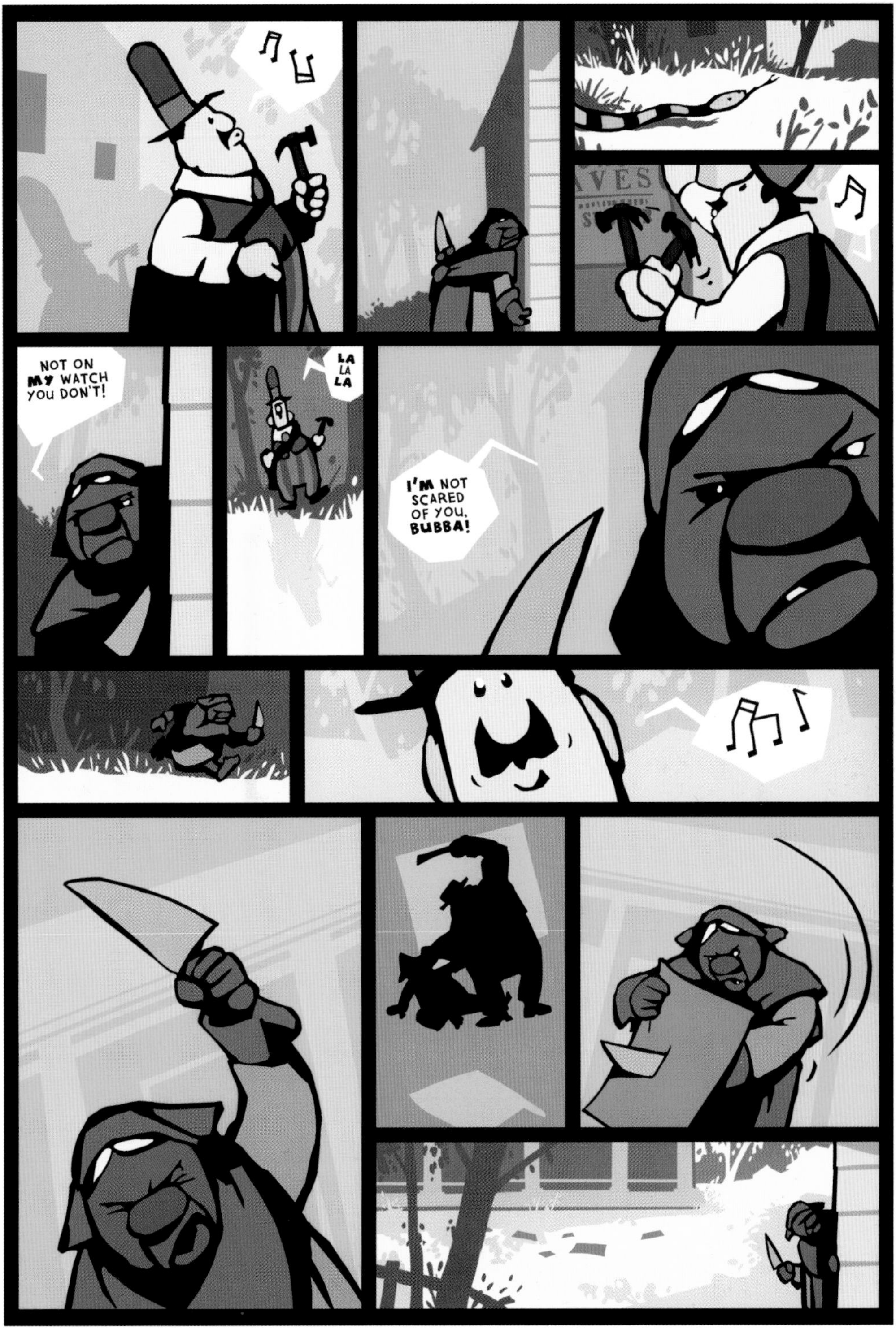
NOT ON MY WATCH YOU DON'T!
LA LA LA
I'M NOT SCARED OF YOU, BUBBA!

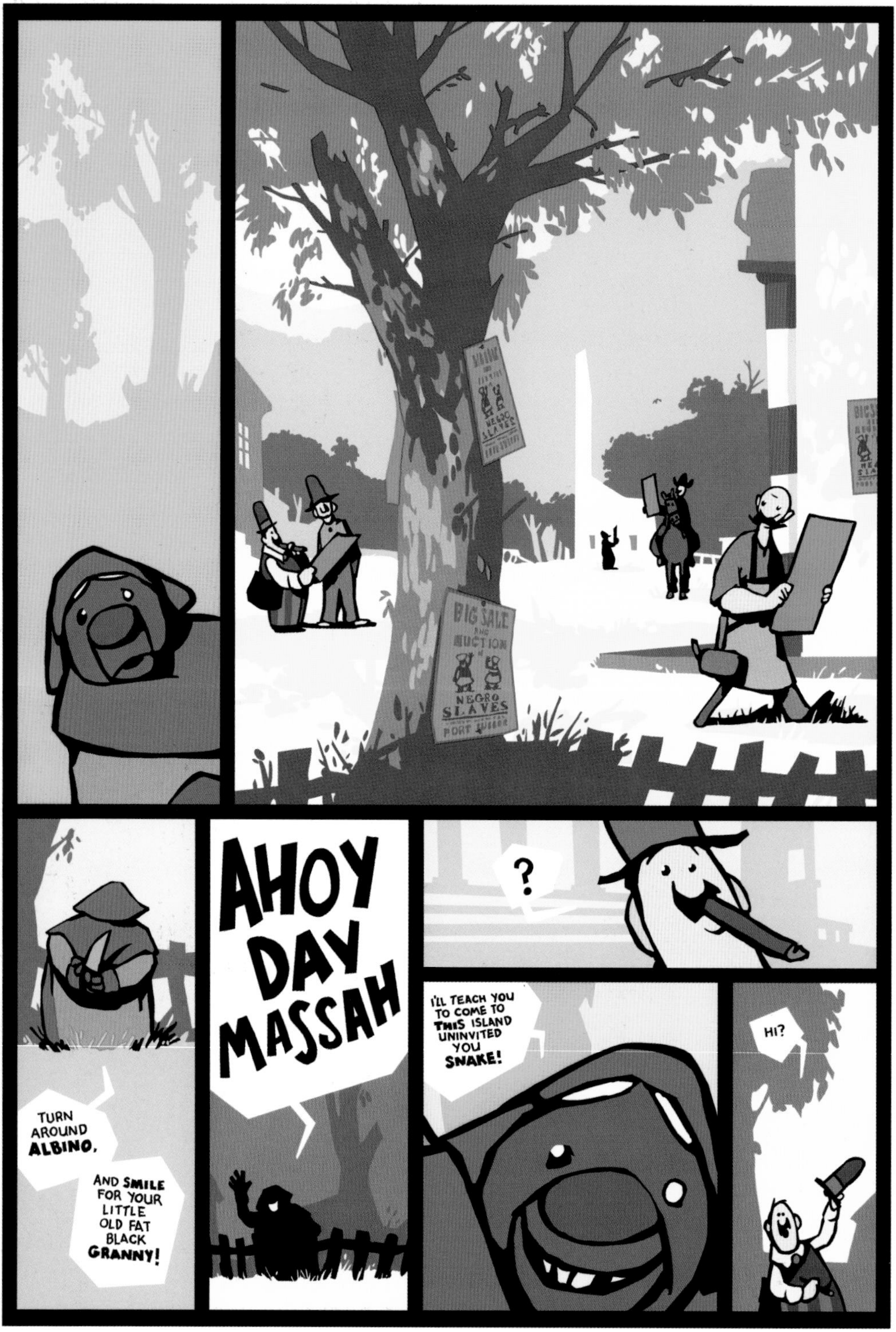
BIG SALE AND AUCTION
NEGRO SLAVES
AHOY DAY MASSAH
?
TURN AROUND ALBINO,
AND SMILE FOR YOUR LITTLE OLD FAT BLACK GRANNY!
I'LL TEACH YOU TO COME TO THIS ISLAND UNINVITED YOU SNAKE!
HI?

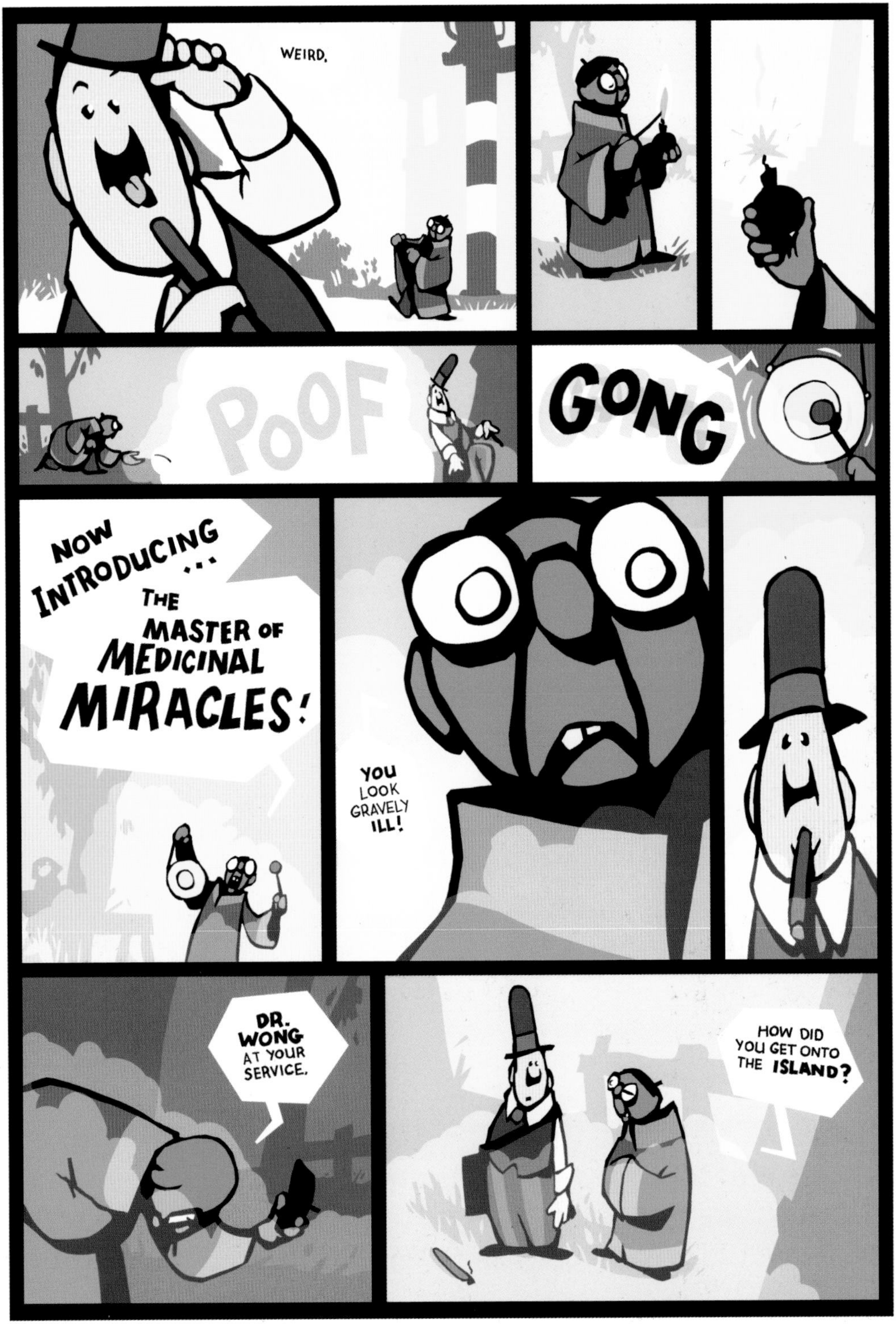
WEIRD.
POOF
GONG
NOW INTRODUCING . . . THE MASTER OF MEDICINAL MIRACLES!
YOU LOOK GRAVELY ILL!
DR. WONG AT YOUR SERVICE.
HOW DID YOU GET ONTO THE ISLAND?

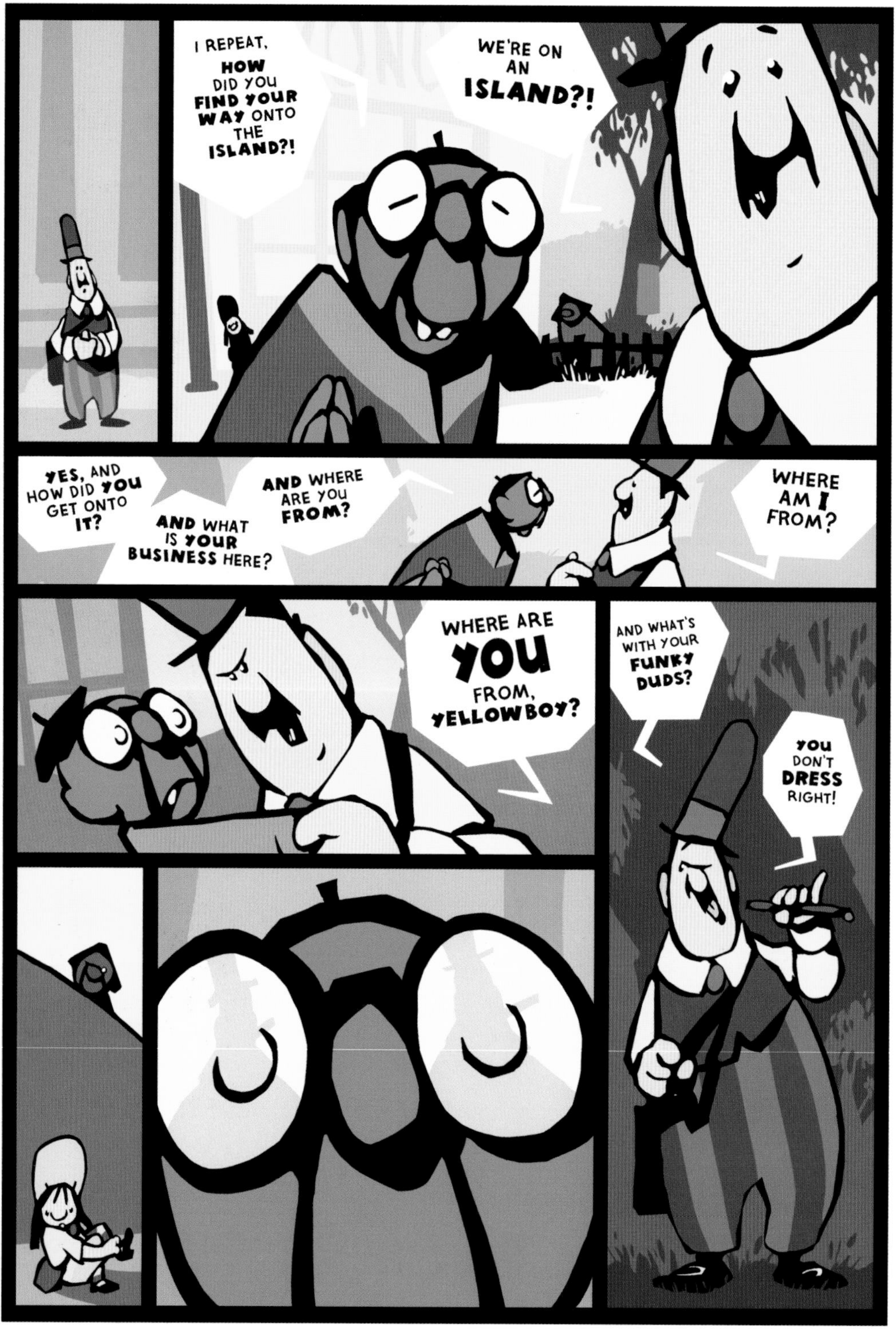
I REPEAT, HOW DID YOU FIND YOUR WAY ONTO THE ISLAND?!
WE'RE ON AN ISLAND?!
YES, AND HOW DID YOU GET ONTO IT?
AND WHAT IS YOUR BUSINESS HERE?
AND WHERE ARE YOU FROM?
WHERE AM I FROM?
WHERE ARE YOU FROM, YELLOWBOY?
AND WHAT'S WITH YOUR FUNKY DUDS?
YOU DON'T DRESS RIGHT!

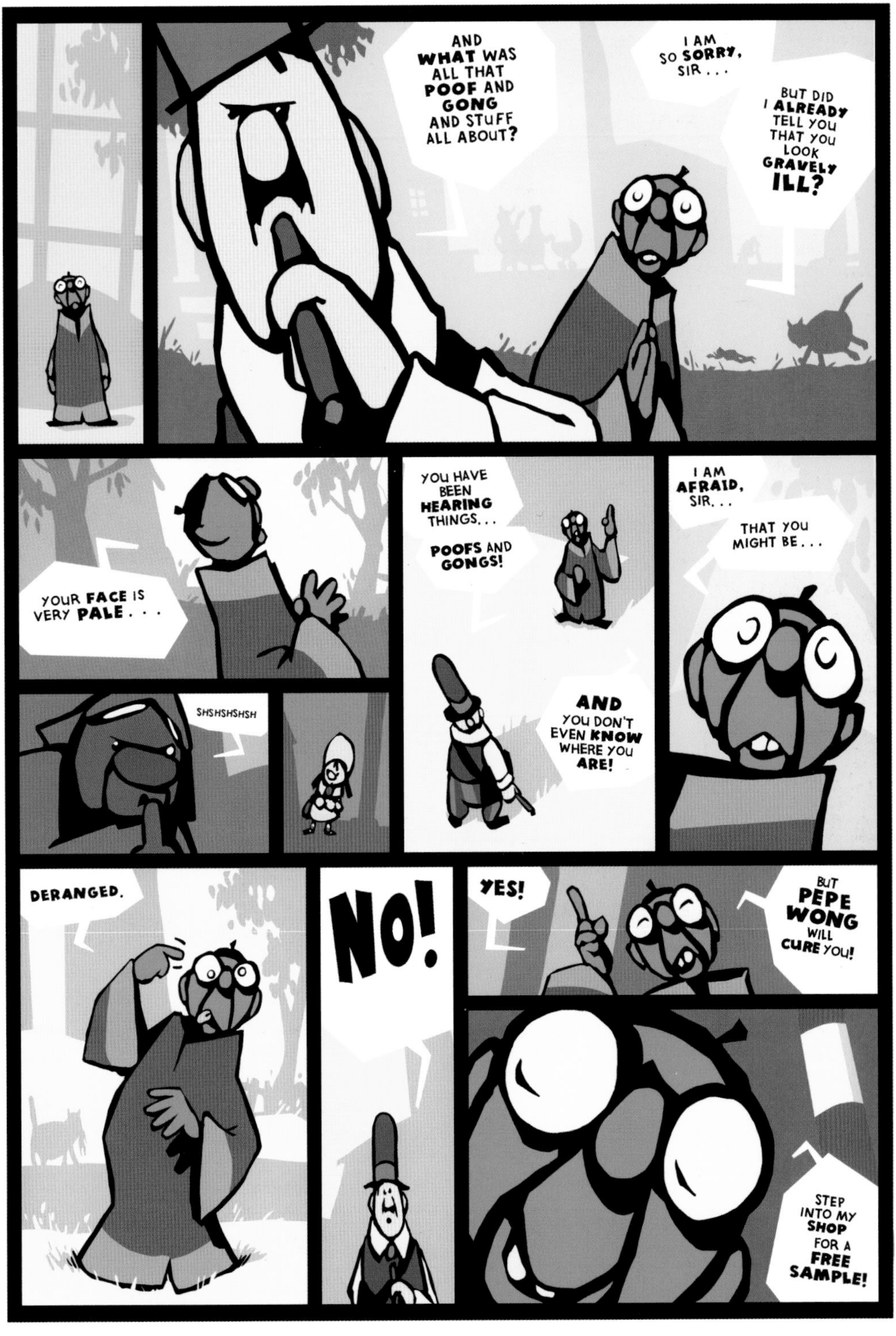
AND WHAT WAS ALL THAT POOF AND GONG AND STUFF ALL ABOUT?
I AM SO SORRY, SIR . . .
BUT DID I ALREADY TELL YOU THAT YOU LOOK GRAVELY ILL?
YOUR FACE IS VERY PALE . . .
SHSHSHSHSH
YOU HAVE BEEN HEARING THINGS. . .
POOFS AND GONGS!
AND YOU DON'T EVEN KNOW WHERE YOU ARE!
I AM AFRAID, SIR. . .
THAT YOU MIGHT BE . . .
DERANGED.
NO!
YES!
BUT PEPE WONG WILL CURE YOU!
STEP INTO MY SHOP FOR A FREE SAMPLE!

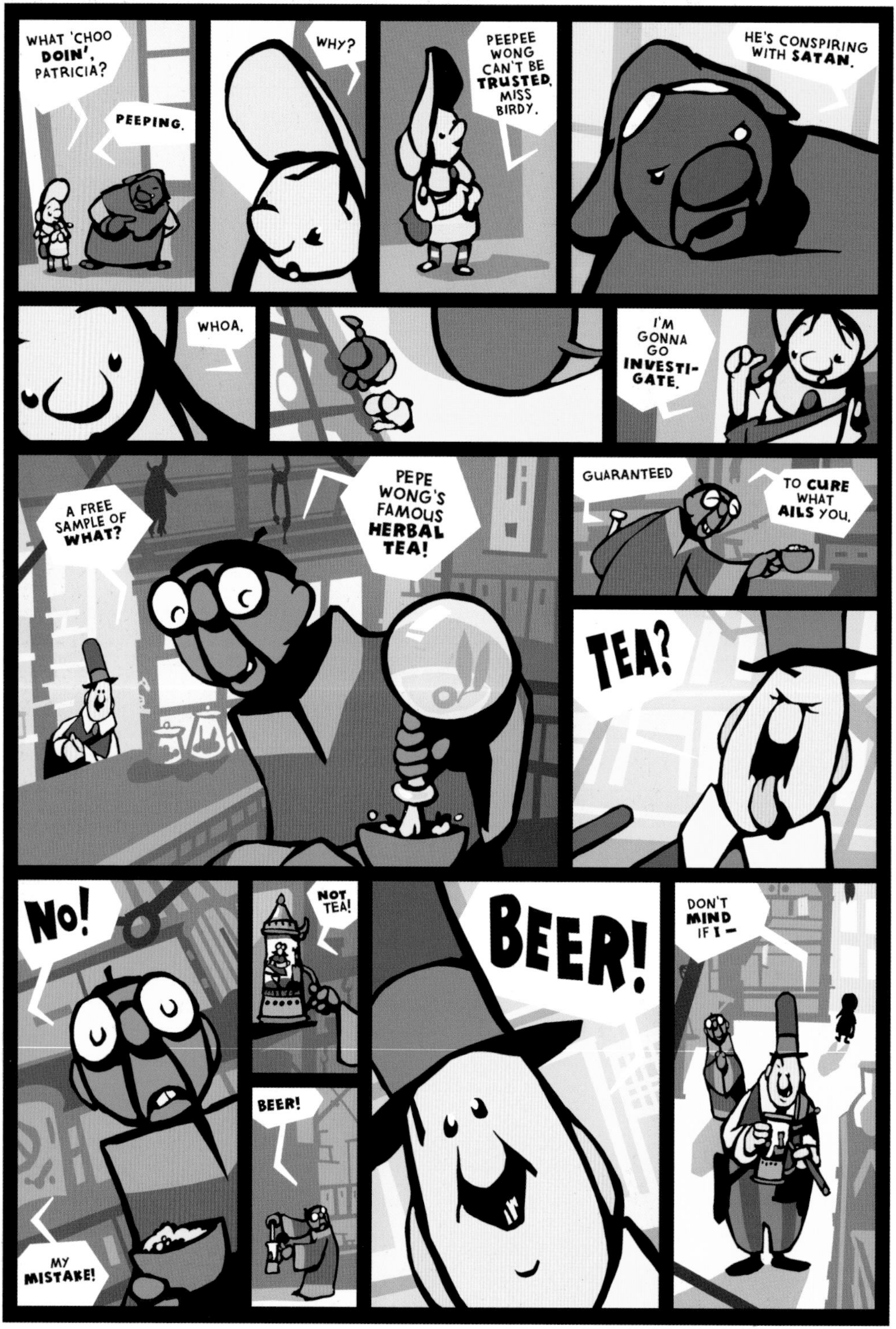

WHAT 'CHOO DOIN', PATRICIA?
PEEPING.
WHY?
PEEPEE WONG CAN'T BE TRUSTED, MISS BIRDY.
HE'S CONSPIRING WITH SATAN.
WHOA.
I'M GONNA GO INVESTI-GATE.
A FREE SAMPLE OF WHAT?
PEPE WONG'S FAMOUS HERBAL TEA!
GUARANTEED
TO CURE WHAT AILS YOU.
TEA?
NO!
MY MISTAKE!
NOT TEA!
BEER!
BEER!
DON'T MIND IF I—

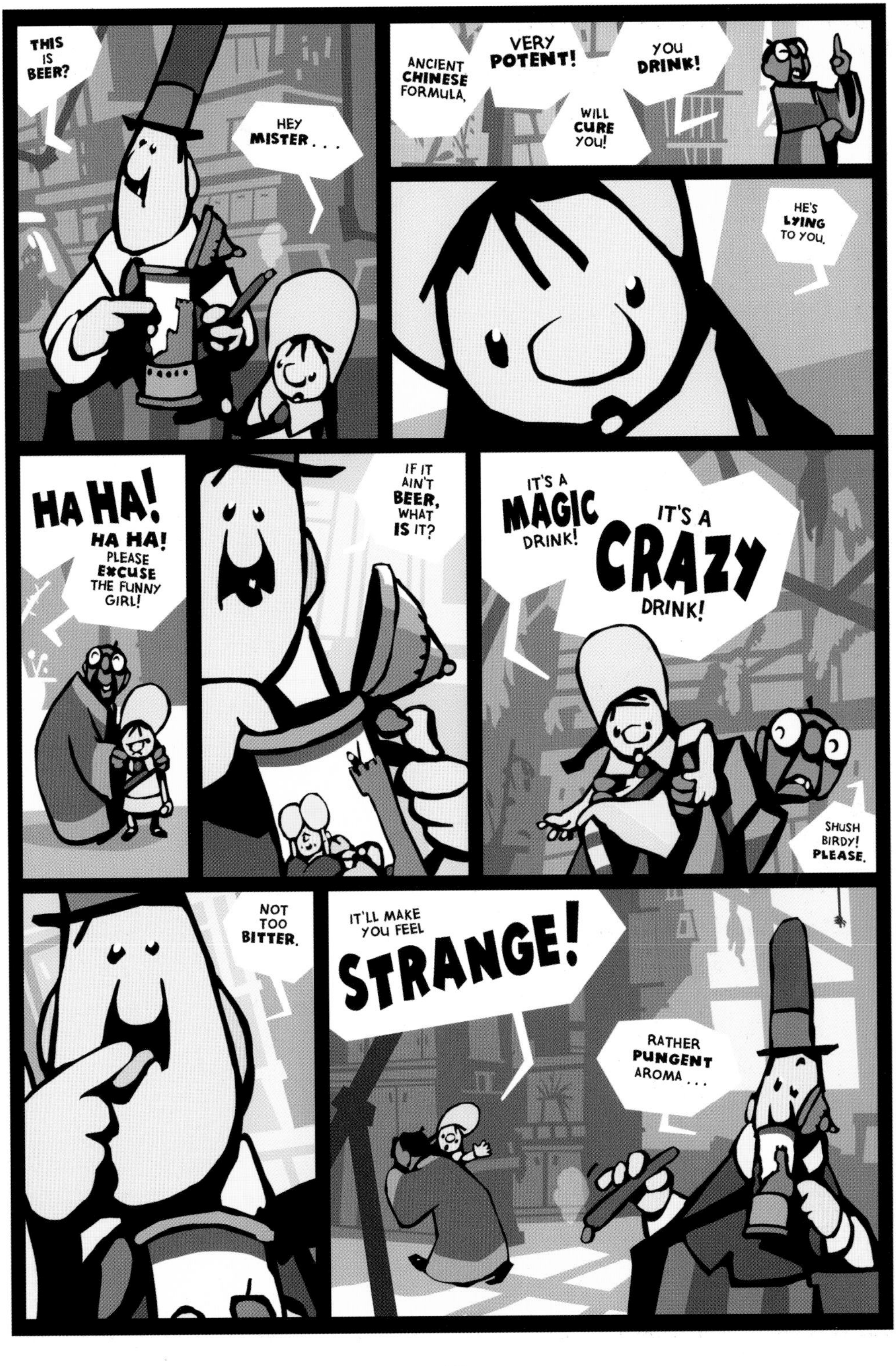
THIS IS BEER?
HEY MISTER . . .
ANCIENT CHINESE FORMULA,
VERY POTENT!
WILL CURE YOU!
YOU DRINK!
HE'S LYING TO YOU.
HA HA! HA HA! PLEASE EXCUSE THE FUNNY GIRL!
IF IT AIN'T BEER, WHAT IS IT?
IT'S A MAGIC DRINK!
IT'S A CRAZY DRINK!
SHUSH BIRDY! PLEASE.
NOT TOO BITTER.
IT'LL MAKE YOU FEEL STRANGE!
RATHER PUNGENT AROMA . . .

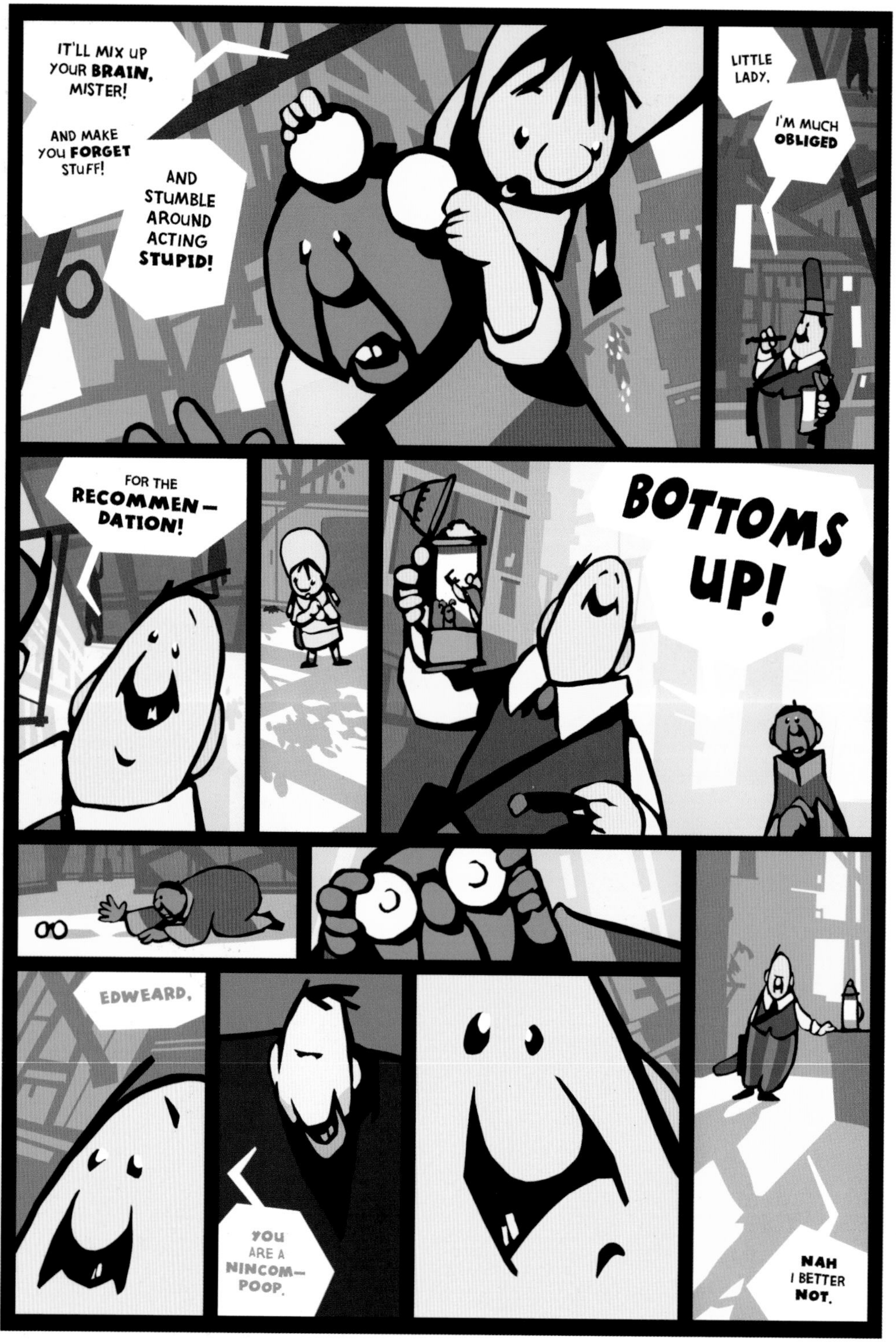
IT'LL MIX UP YOUR BRAIN, MISTER!
AND MAKE YOU FORGET STUFF!
AND STUMBLE AROUND ACTING STUPID!
LITTLE LADY,
I'M MUCH OBLIGED
FOR THE RECOMMEN-DATION!
BOTTOMS UP!
EDWEARD,
YOU ARE A NINCOM-POOP.
NAH I BETTER NOT.

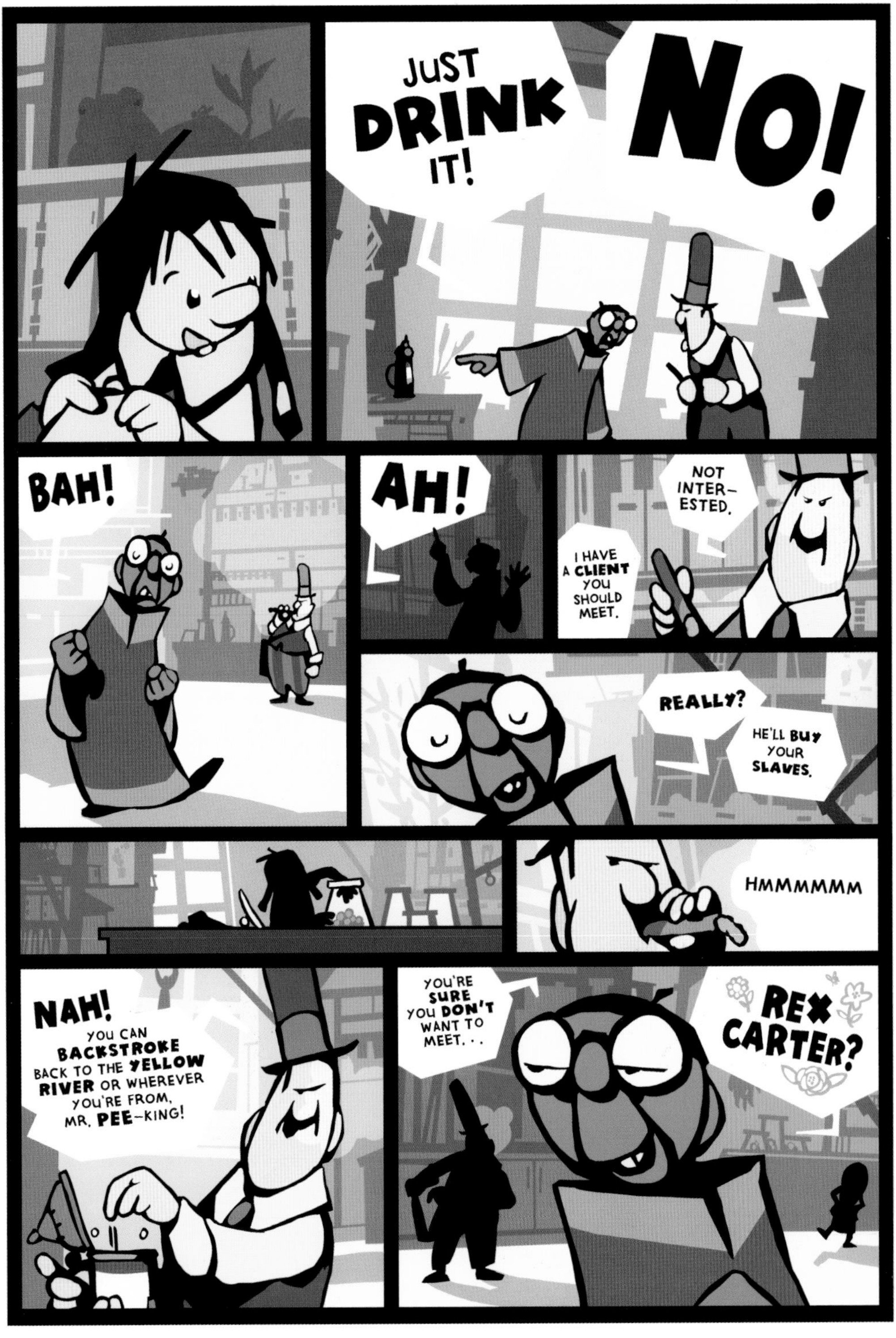
JUST DRINK IT!
NO!
BAH!
AH!
I HAVE A CLIENT YOU SHOULD MEET.
NOT INTER-ESTED.
REALLY?
HE'LL BUY YOUR SLAVES.
HMMMMMM
NAH! YOU CAN BACKSTROKE BACK TO THE YELLOW RIVER OR WHEREVER YOU'RE FROM, MR. PEE-KING!
YOU'RE SURE YOU DON'T WANT TO MEET. . .
REX CARTER?

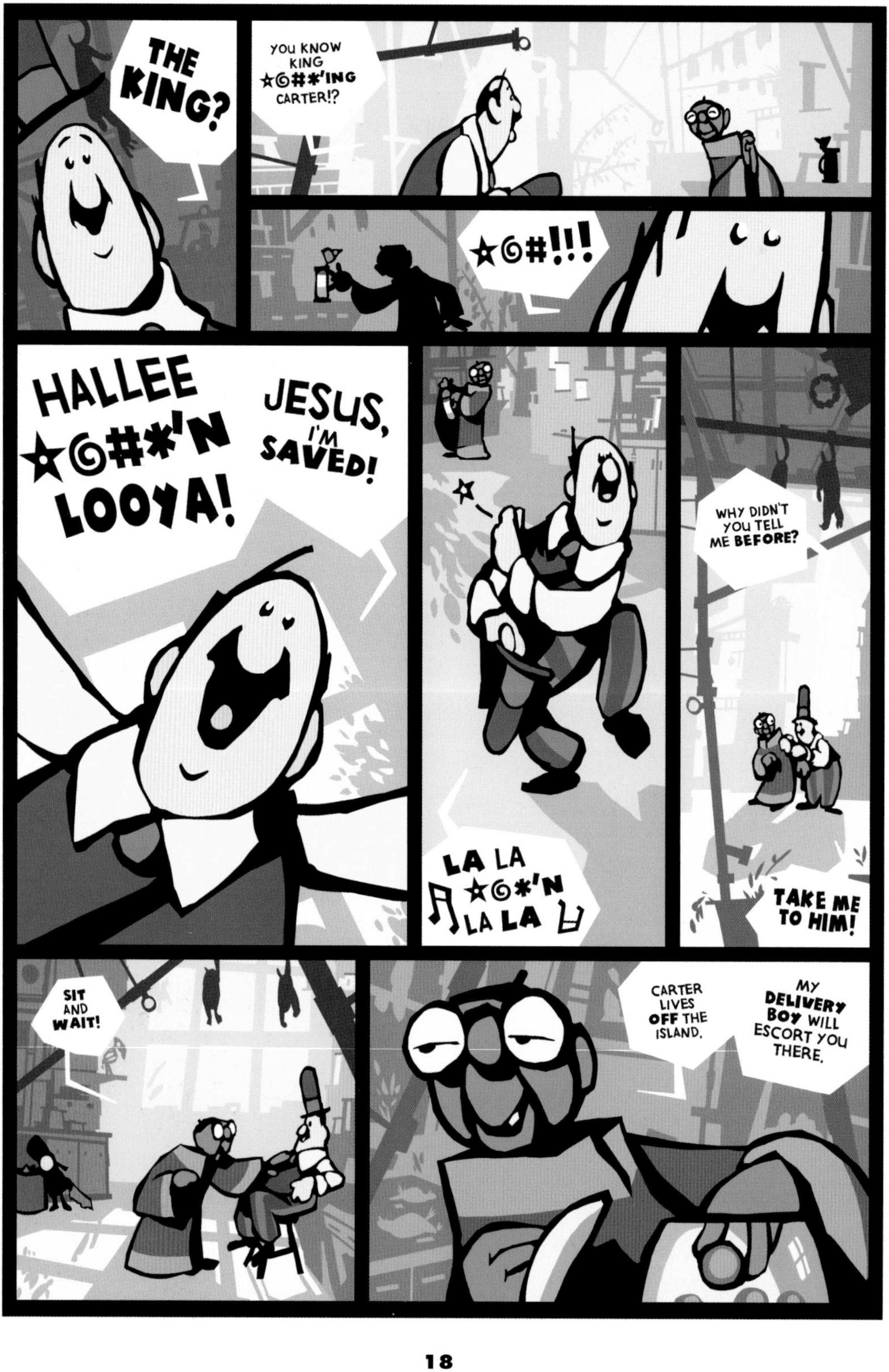
THE KING?
YOU KNOW KING ☆@#*'ING CARTER!?
☆@#!!!
HALLEE ☆@#*'N LOOYA!
JESUS, I'M SAVED!
LA LA ☆@*'N LA LA
WHY DIDN'T YOU TELL ME BEFORE?
TAKE ME TO HIM!
SIT AND WAIT!
CARTER LIVES OFF THE ISLAND.
MY DELIVERY BOY WILL ESCORT YOU THERE.

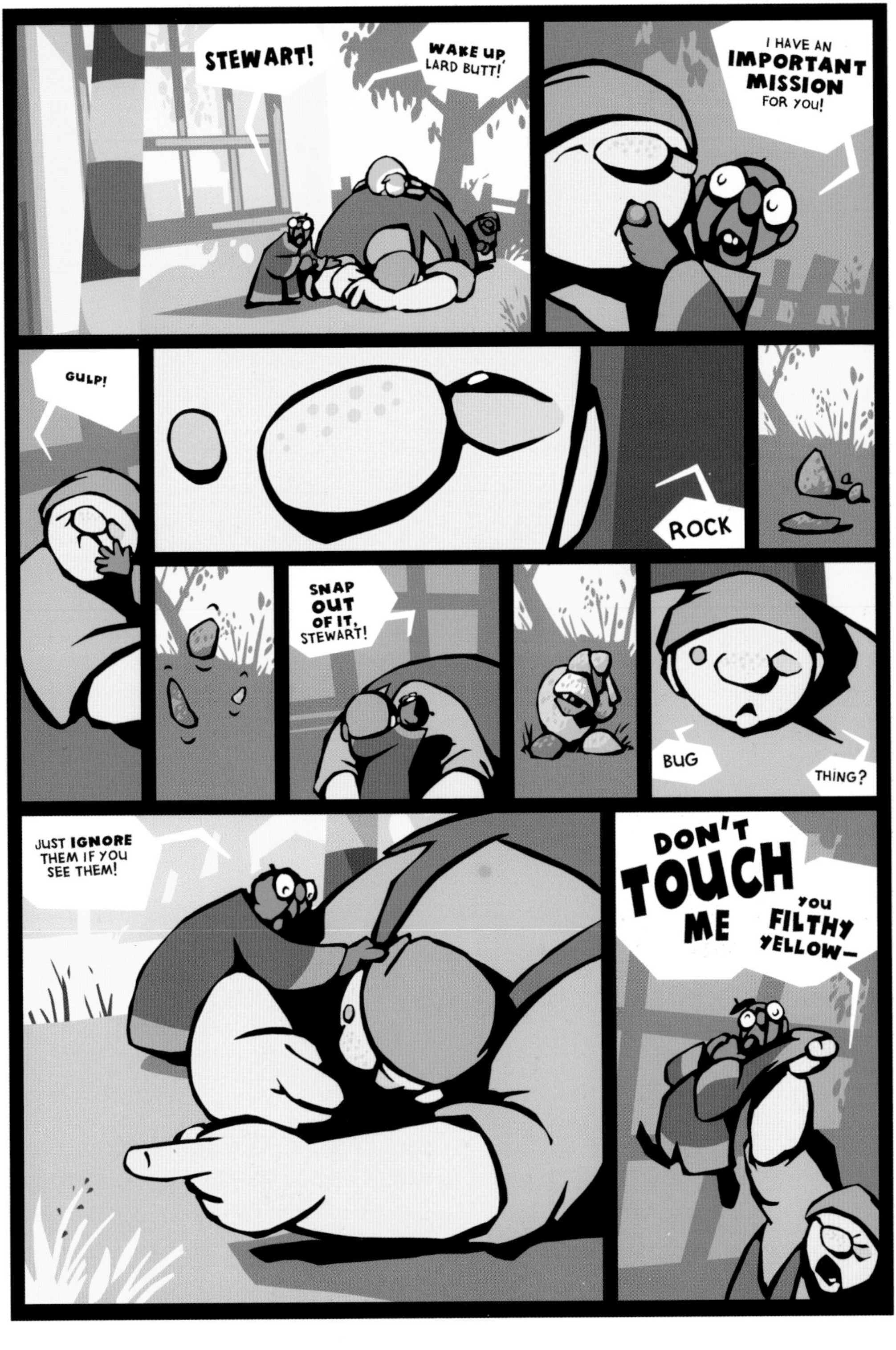

STEWART!
WAKE UP, LARD BUTT!
I HAVE AN IMPORTANT MISSION FOR YOU!
GULP!
ROCK
SNAP OUT OF IT, STEWART!
BUG
THING?
JUST IGNORE THEM IF YOU SEE THEM!
DON'T TOUCH ME you FILTHY YELLOW—

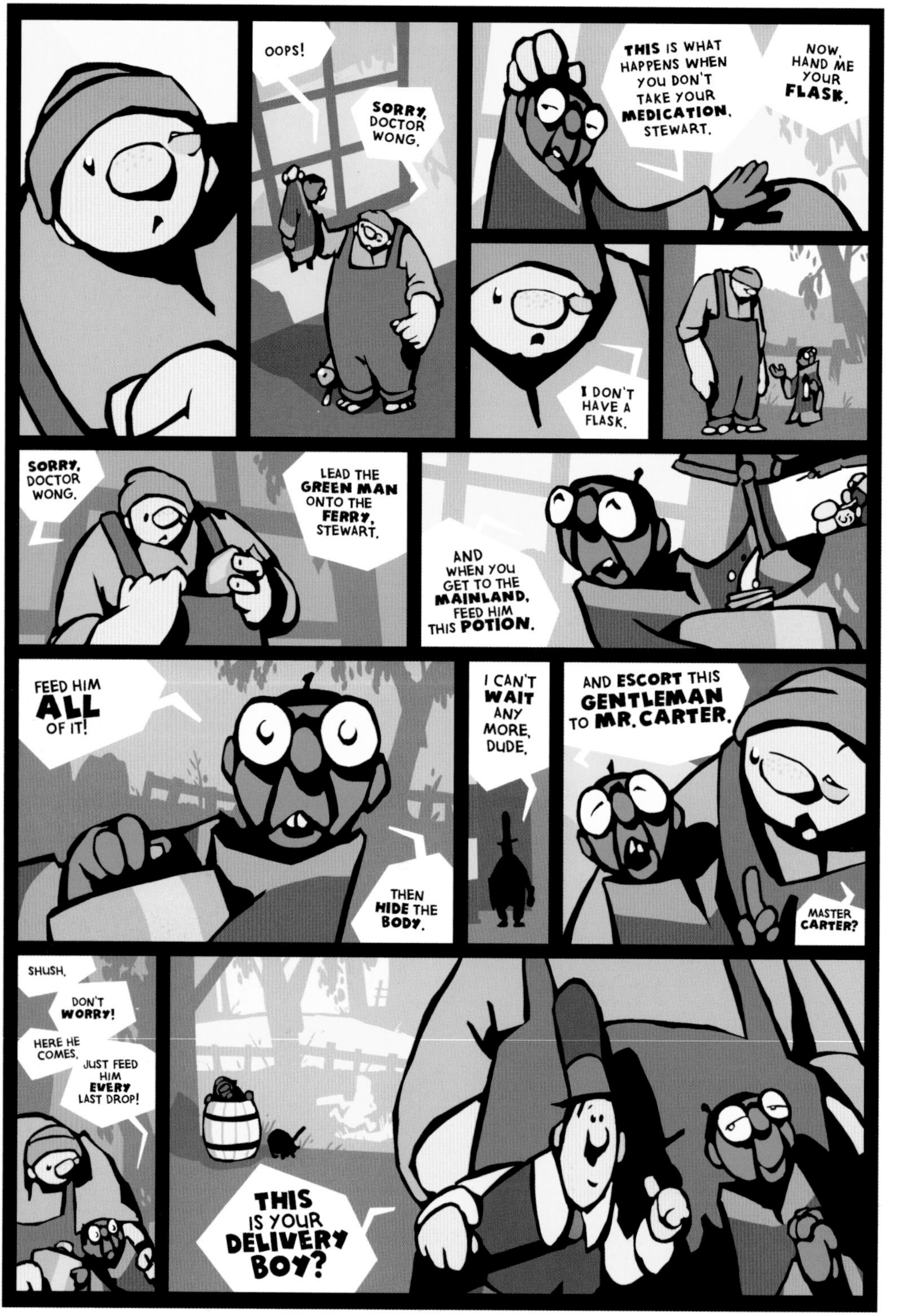
OOPS!
SORRY, DOCTOR WONG.
THIS IS WHAT HAPPENS WHEN YOU DON'T TAKE YOUR MEDICATION, STEWART.
NOW, HAND ME YOUR FLASK.
I DON'T HAVE A FLASK.
SORRY, DOCTOR WONG.
LEAD THE GREEN MAN ONTO THE FERRY, STEWART.
AND WHEN YOU GET TO THE MAINLAND, FEED HIM THIS POTION.
FEED HIM ALL OF IT!
THEN HIDE THE BODY.
I CAN'T WAIT ANY MORE, DUDE.
AND ESCORT THIS GENTLEMAN TO MR. CARTER.
MASTER CARTER?
SHUSH.
DON'T WORRY!
HERE HE COMES.
JUST FEED HIM EVERY LAST DROP!
THIS IS YOUR DELIVERY BOY?

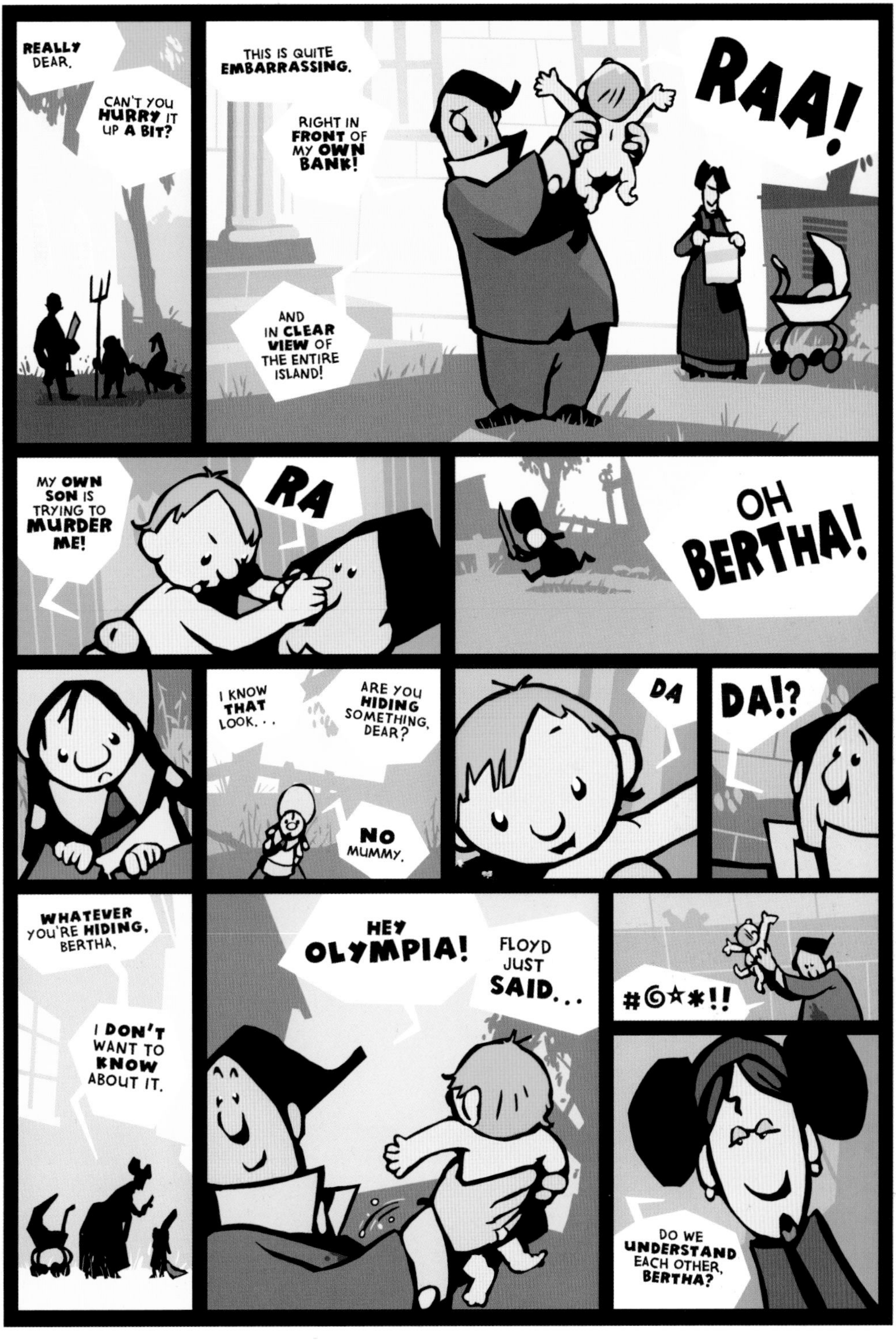

REALLY DEAR.
CAN'T YOU HURRY IT UP A BIT?
THIS IS QUITE EMBARRASSING.
RIGHT IN FRONT OF MY OWN BANK!
AND IN CLEAR VIEW OF THE ENTIRE ISLAND!
RAA!
MY OWN SON IS TRYING TO MURDER ME!
RA
OH BERTHA!
I KNOW THAT LOOK. . .
ARE YOU HIDING SOMETHING, DEAR?
NO MUMMY.
DA
DA!?
WHATEVER YOU'RE HIDING, BERTHA,
I DON'T WANT TO KNOW ABOUT IT.
HEY OLYMPIA!
FLOYD JUST SAID. . .
#@☆✱!!
DO WE UNDERSTAND EACH OTHER, BERTHA?

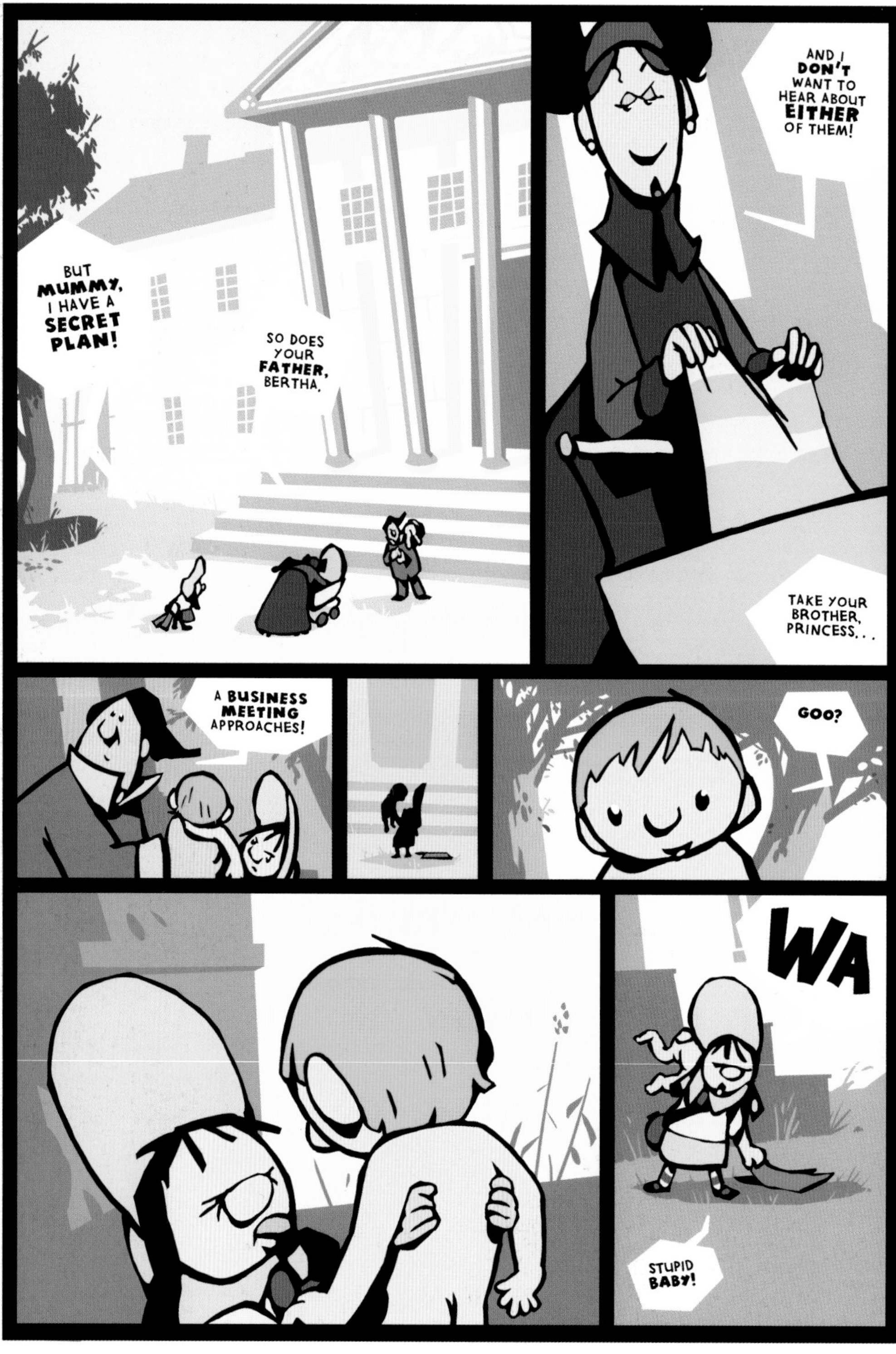

BUT MUMMY, I HAVE A SECRET PLAN!
SO DOES YOUR FATHER, BERTHA.
AND I DON'T WANT TO HEAR ABOUT EITHER OF THEM!
TAKE YOUR BROTHER, PRINCESS. . .
A BUSINESS MEETING APPROACHES!
GOO?
WA
STUPID BABY!

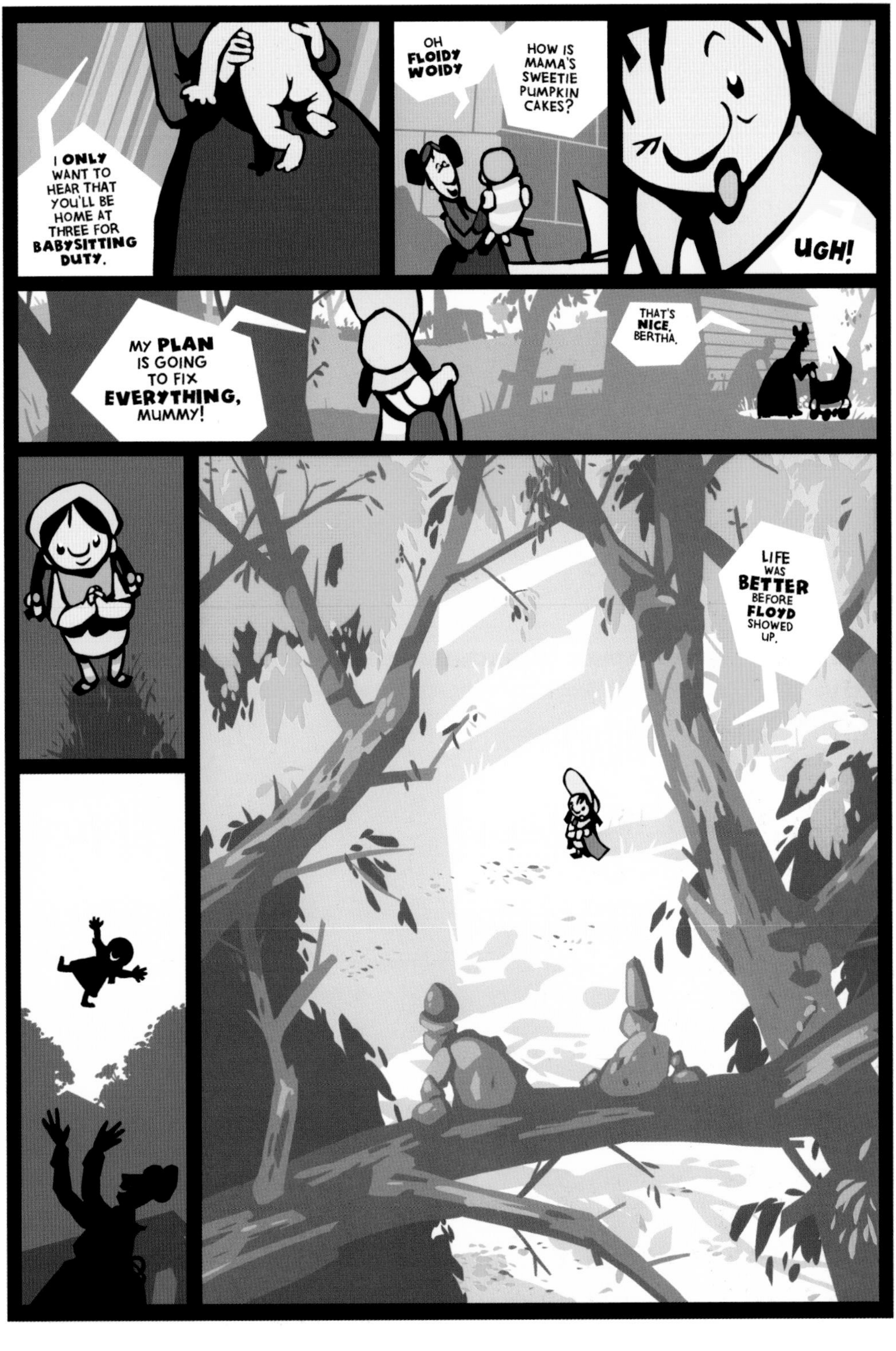
I ONLY WANT TO HEAR THAT YOU'LL BE HOME AT THREE FOR BABYSITTING DUTY.
OH FLOIDY WOIDY
HOW IS MAMA'S SWEETIE PUMPKIN CAKES?
UGH!
MY PLAN IS GOING TO FIX EVERYTHING, MUMMY!
THAT'S NICE, BERTHA.
LIFE WAS BETTER BEFORE FLOYD SHOWED UP.

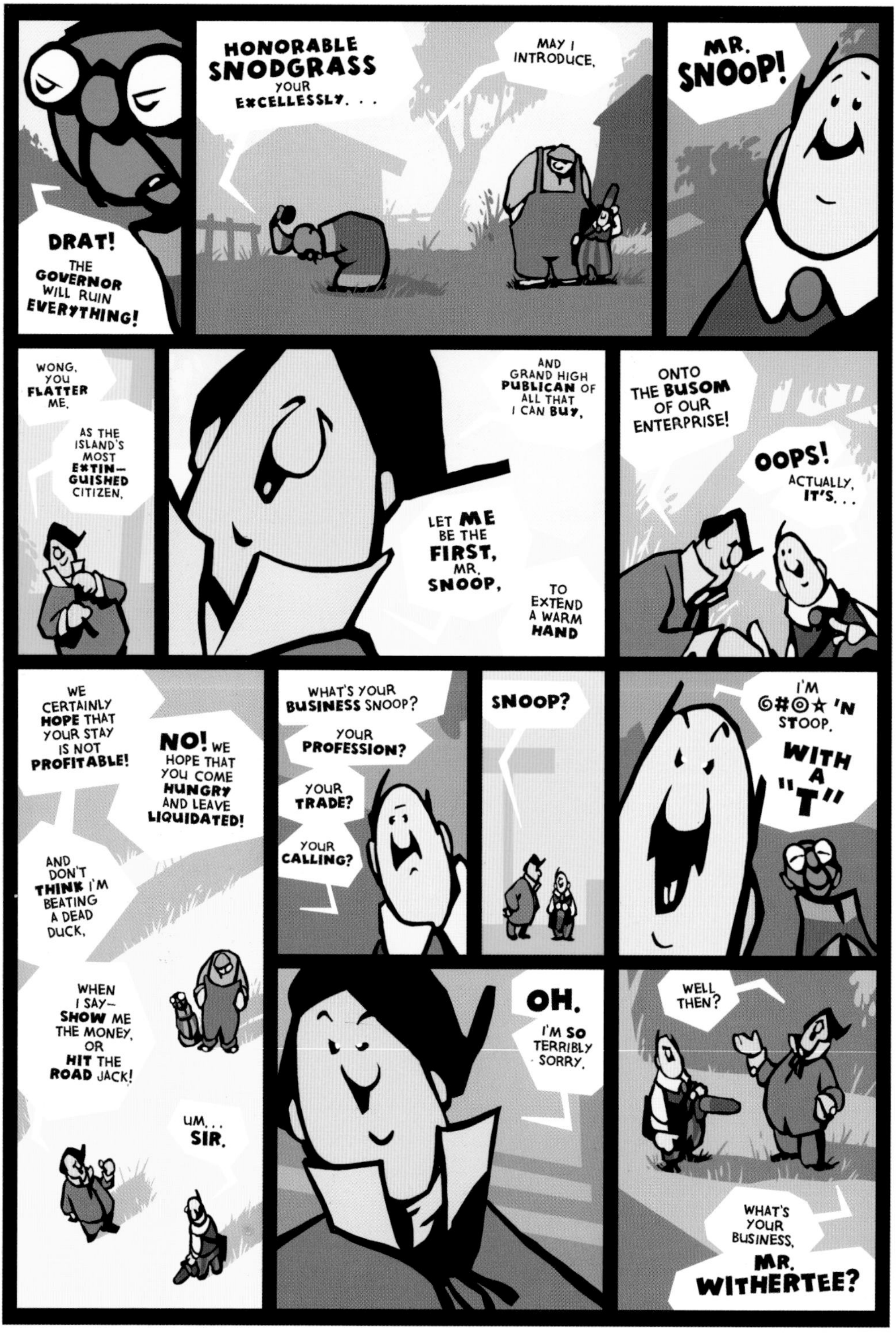

DRAT! THE GOVERNOR WILL RUIN EVERYTHING!
HONORABLE SNODGRASS YOUR EXCELLESSLY. . .
MAY I INTRODUCE,
MR. SNOOP!
WONG, YOU FLATTER ME.
AS THE ISLAND'S MOST EXTIN-GUISHED CITIZEN,
AND GRAND HIGH PUBLICAN OF ALL THAT I CAN BUY,
LET ME BE THE FIRST, MR. SNOOP,
TO EXTEND A WARM HAND
ONTO THE BUSOM OF OUR ENTERPRISE!
OOPS! ACTUALLY, IT'S. . .
WE CERTAINLY HOPE THAT YOUR STAY IS NOT PROFITABLE!
NO! WE HOPE THAT YOU COME HUNGRY AND LEAVE LIQUIDATED!
AND DON'T THINK I'M BEATING A DEAD DUCK,
WHEN I SAY— SHOW ME THE MONEY, OR HIT THE ROAD JACK!
UM. . . SIR.
WHAT'S YOUR BUSINESS SNOOP?
YOUR PROFESSION?
YOUR TRADE?
YOUR CALLING?
SNOOP?
I'M &#@☆ 'N STOOP.
WITH A "T"
OH.
I'M SO TERRIBLY SORRY.
WELL THEN?
WHAT'S YOUR BUSINESS, MR. WITHERTEE?

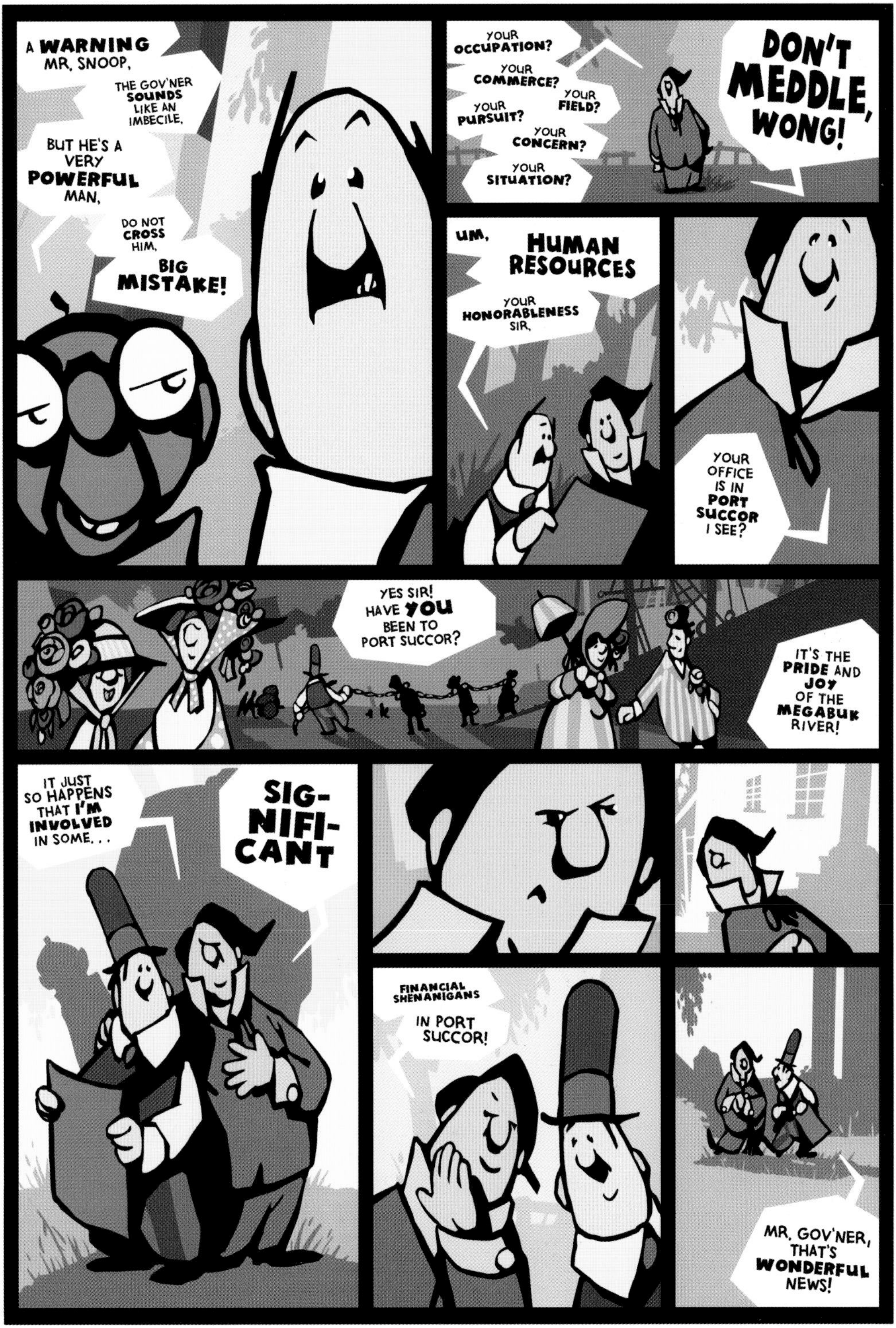
A WARNING MR. SNOOP,
THE GOV'NER SOUNDS LIKE AN IMBECILE,
BUT HE'S A VERY POWERFUL MAN,
DO NOT CROSS HIM,
BIG MISTAKE!
YOUR OCCUPATION?
YOUR COMMERCE?
YOUR FIELD?
YOUR PURSUIT?
YOUR CONCERN?
YOUR SITUATION?
DON'T MEDDLE, WONG!
UM,
HUMAN RESOURCES
YOUR HONORABLENESS SIR,
YOUR OFFICE IS IN PORT SUCCOR I SEE?
YES SIR! HAVE YOU BEEN TO PORT SUCCOR?
IT'S THE PRIDE AND JOY OF THE MEGABUK RIVER!
IT JUST SO HAPPENS THAT I'M INVOLVED IN SOME. . .
SIG-NIFI-CANT
FINANCIAL SHENANIGANS
IN PORT SUCCOR!
MR. GOV'NER, THAT'S WONDERFUL NEWS!

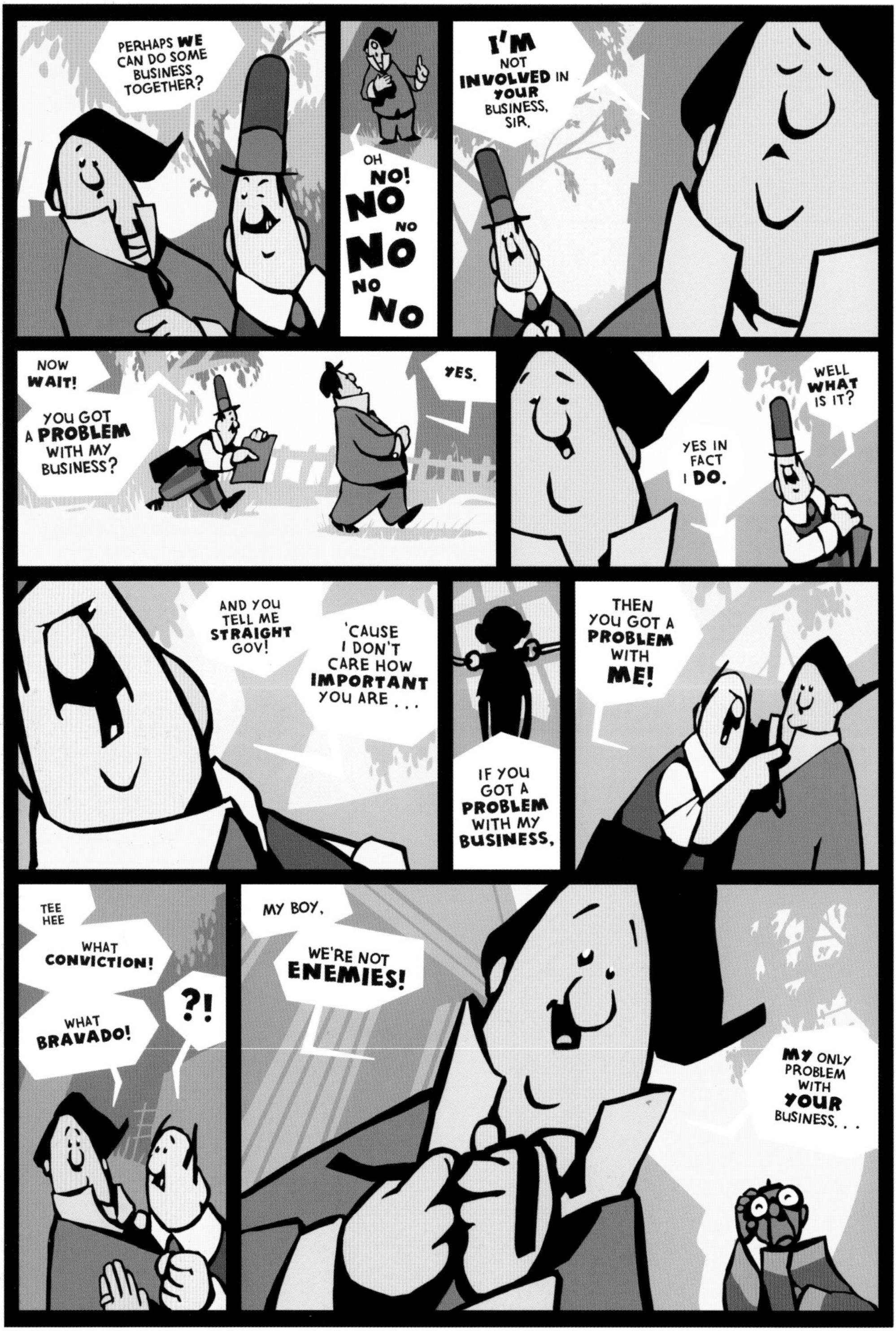

PERHAPS WE CAN DO SOME BUSINESS TOGETHER?
OH NO! NO NO NO NO NO
I'M NOT INVOLVED IN YOUR BUSINESS, SIR.
NOW WAIT!
YOU GOT A PROBLEM WITH MY BUSINESS?
YES.
WELL WHAT IS IT?
YES IN FACT I DO.
AND YOU TELL ME STRAIGHT GOV!
'CAUSE I DON'T CARE HOW IMPORTANT YOU ARE . . .
IF YOU GOT A PROBLEM WITH MY BUSINESS,
THEN YOU GOT A PROBLEM WITH ME!
TEE HEE
WHAT CONVICTION!
WHAT BRAVADO!
?!
MY BOY,
WE'RE NOT ENEMIES!
MY ONLY PROBLEM WITH YOUR BUSINESS. . .

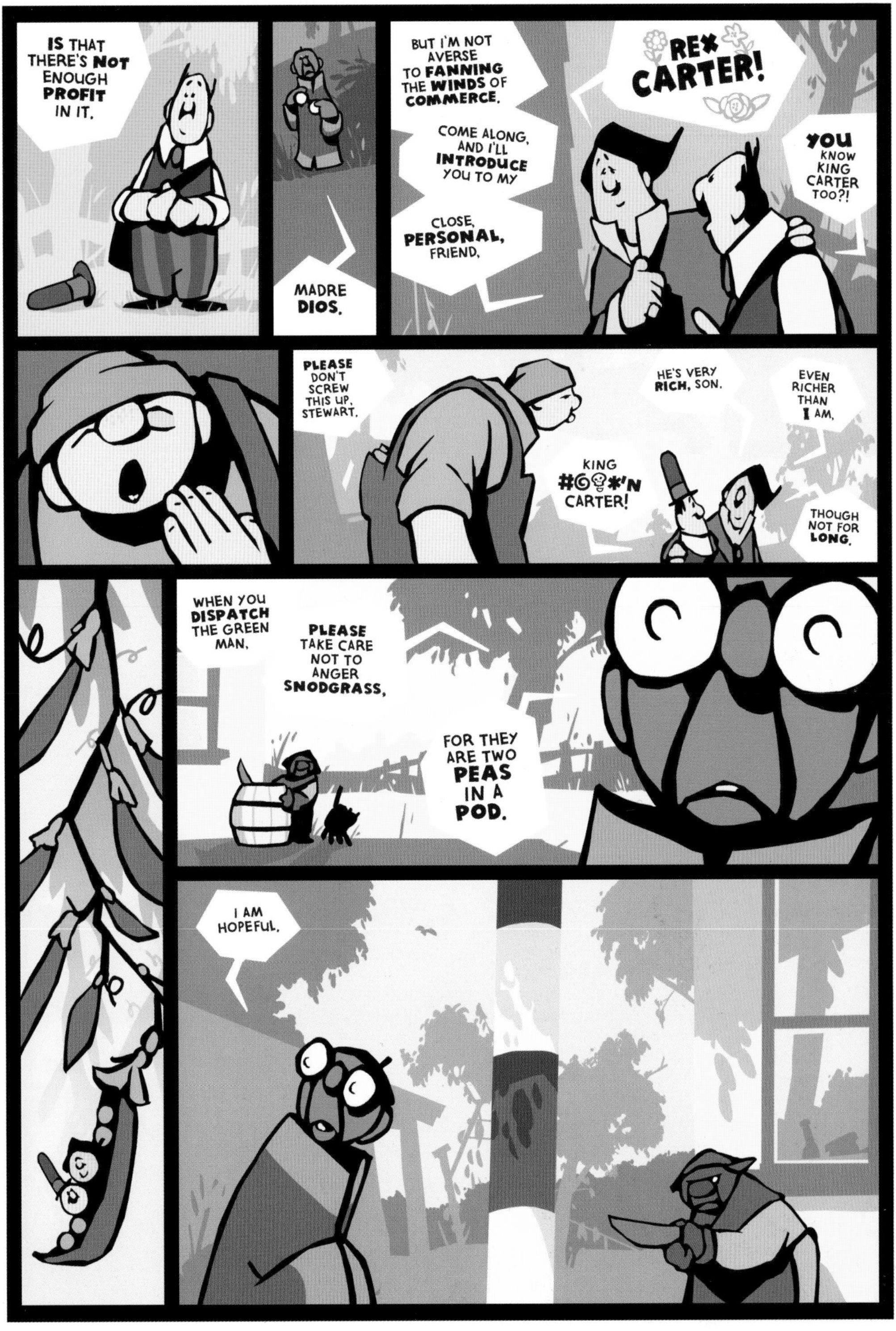
IS THAT THERE'S NOT ENOUGH PROFIT IN IT.
MADRE DIOS.
BUT I'M NOT AVERSE TO FANNING THE WINDS OF COMMERCE.
COME ALONG, AND I'LL INTRODUCE YOU TO MY
CLOSE, PERSONAL, FRIEND.
REX CARTER!
YOU KNOW KING CARTER TOO?!
PLEASE DON'T SCREW THIS UP, STEWART.
HE'S VERY RICH, SON.
EVEN RICHER THAN I AM.
KING #@☠*'N CARTER!
THOUGH NOT FOR LONG.
WHEN YOU DISPATCH THE GREEN MAN,
PLEASE TAKE CARE NOT TO ANGER SNODGRASS,
FOR THEY ARE TWO PEAS IN A POD.
I AM HOPEFUL.

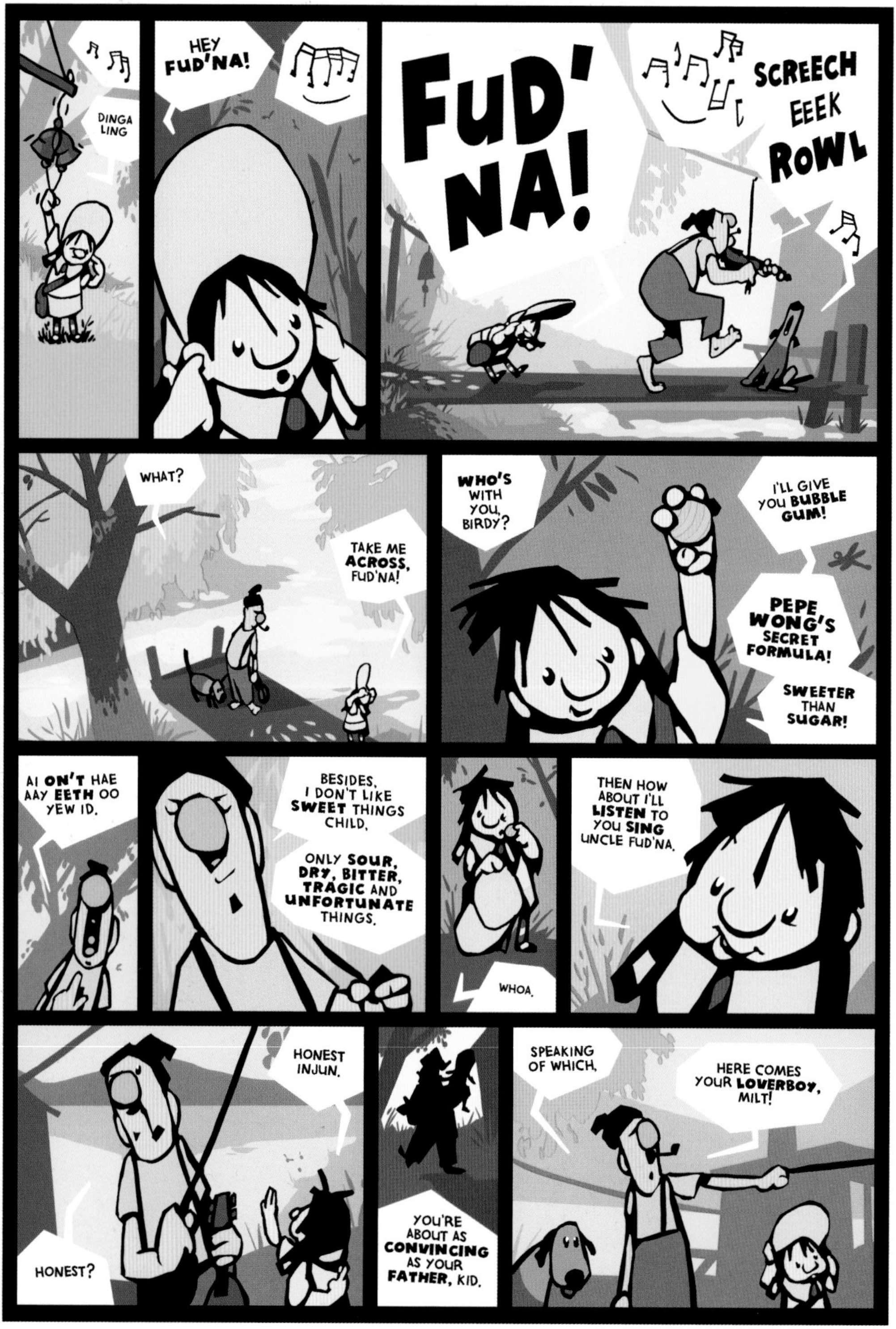
DINGA LING
HEY FUD'NA!
FUD'NA!
SCREECH EEEK ROWL
WHAT?
TAKE ME ACROSS, FUD'NA!
WHO'S WITH YOU, BIRDY?
I'LL GIVE YOU BUBBLE GUM!
PEPE WONG'S SECRET FORMULA!
SWEETER THAN SUGAR!
AI ON'T HAE AAY EETH OO YEW ID.
BESIDES, I DON'T LIKE SWEET THINGS CHILD.
ONLY SOUR, DRY, BITTER, TRAGIC AND UNFORTUNATE THINGS.
WHOA.
THEN HOW ABOUT I'LL LISTEN TO YOU SING UNCLE FUD'NA.
HONEST INJUN.
HONEST?
YOU'RE ABOUT AS CONVINCING AS YOUR FATHER, KID.
SPEAKING OF WHICH,
HERE COMES YOUR LOVERBOY, MILT!

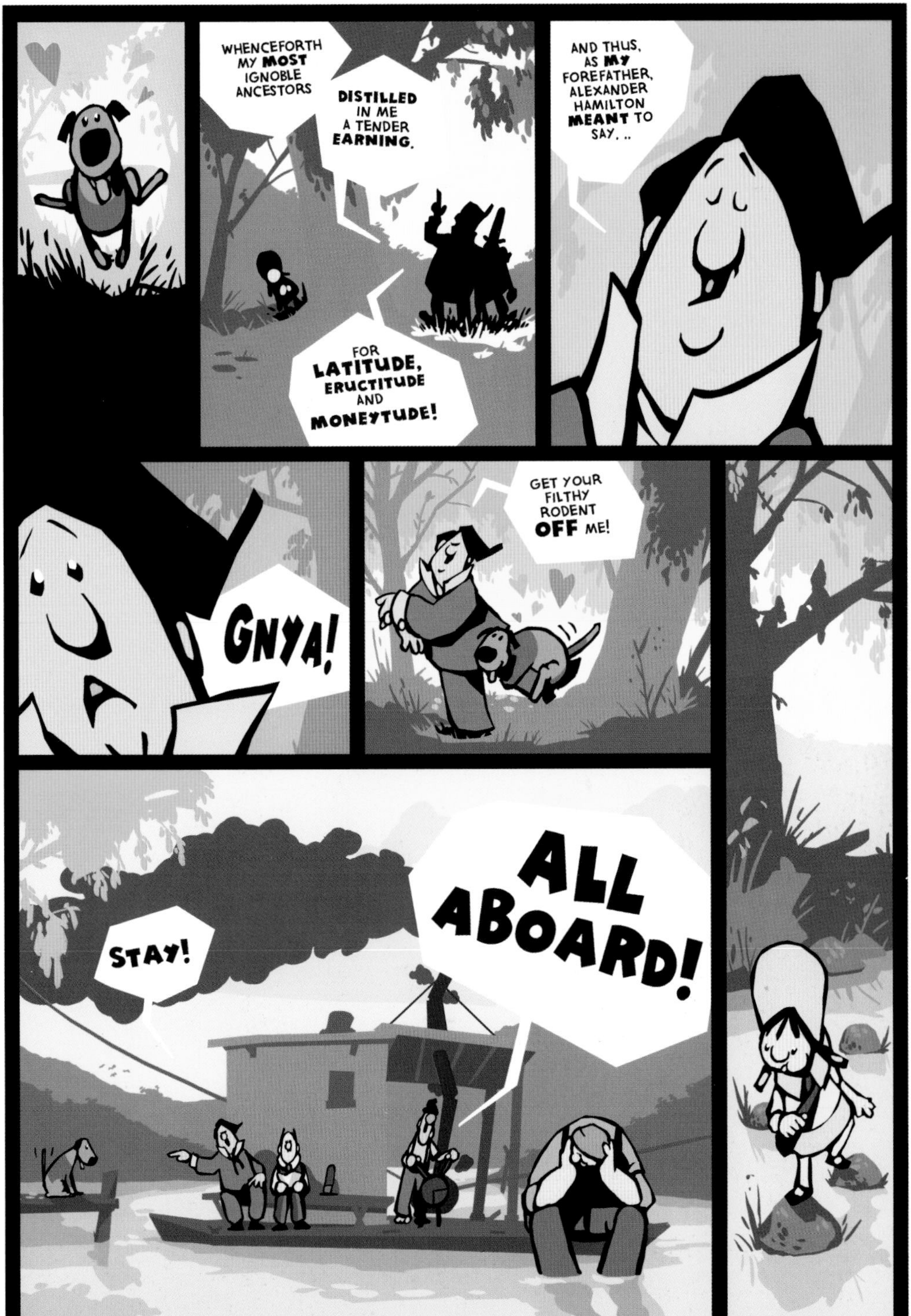
WHENCEFORTH MY MOST IGNOBLE ANCESTORS
DISTILLED IN ME A TENDER EARNING.
FOR LATITUDE, ERUCTITUDE AND MONEYTUDE!
AND THUS, AS MY FOREFATHER, ALEXANDER HAMILTON MEANT TO SAY. ..
GNYA!
GET YOUR FILTHY RODENT OFF ME!
STAY!
ALL ABOARD!

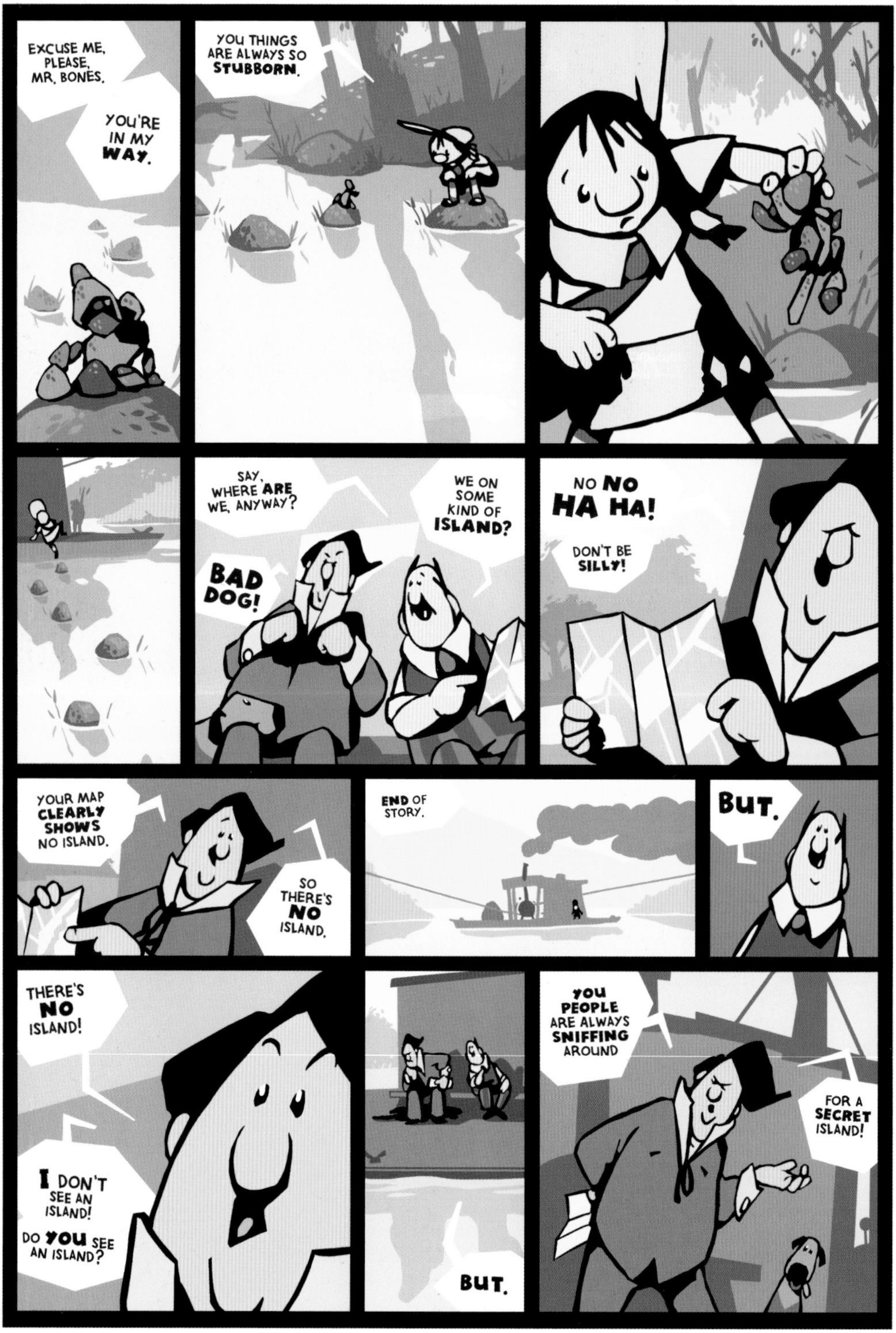
EXCUSE ME, PLEASE, MR. BONES.
YOU'RE IN MY WAY.
YOU THINGS ARE ALWAYS SO STUBBORN.
SAY, WHERE ARE WE, ANYWAY?
WE ON SOME KIND OF ISLAND?
BAD DOG!
NO NO HA HA!
DON'T BE SILLY!
YOUR MAP CLEARLY SHOWS NO ISLAND.
SO THERE'S NO ISLAND.
END OF STORY.
BUT.
THERE'S NO ISLAND!
I DON'T SEE AN ISLAND!
DO YOU SEE AN ISLAND?
BUT.
YOU PEOPLE ARE ALWAYS SNIFFING AROUND
FOR A SECRET ISLAND!

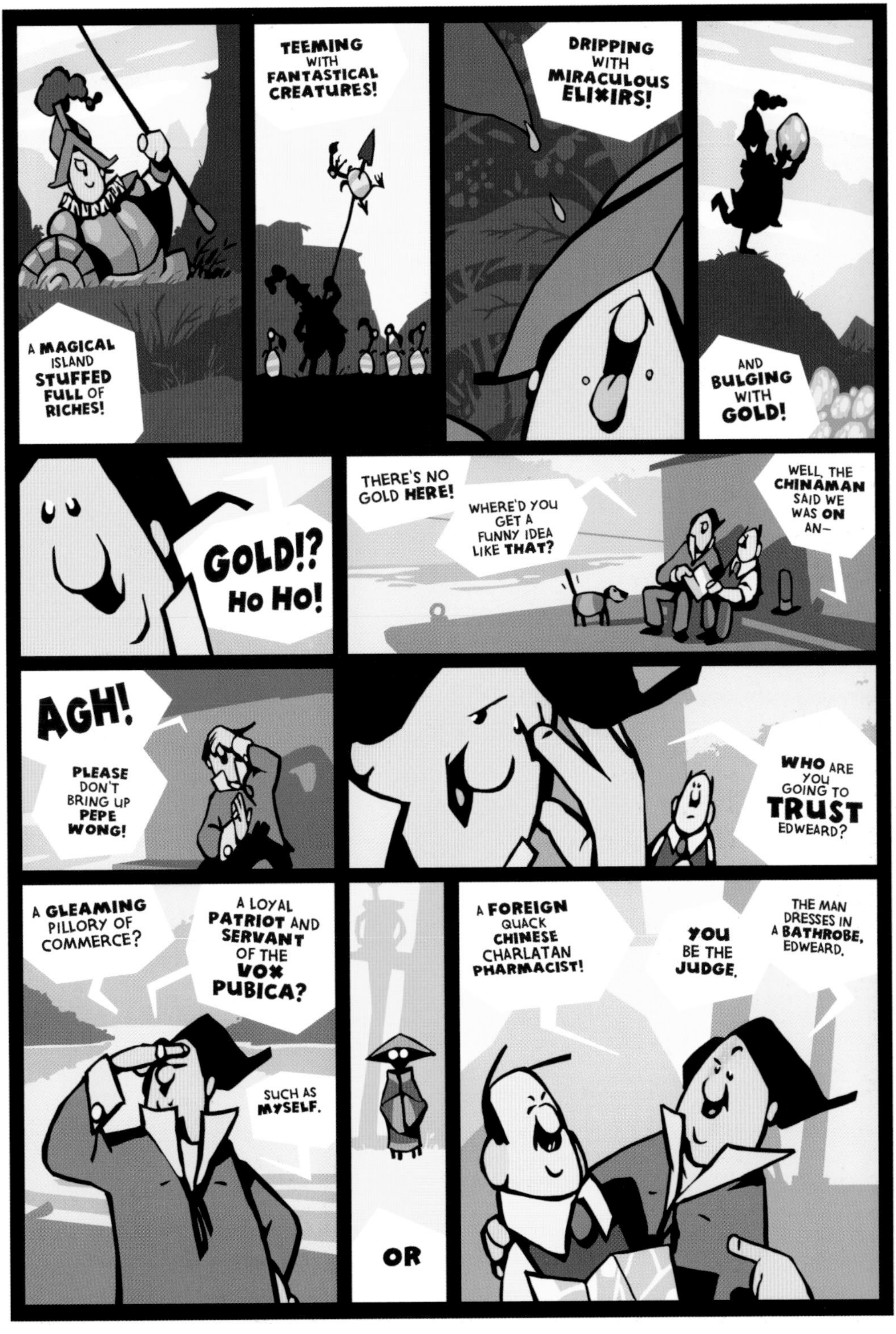

A MAGICAL ISLAND STUFFED FULL OF RICHES!
TEEMING WITH FANTASTICAL CREATURES!
DRIPPING WITH MIRACULOUS ELIXIRS!
AND BULGING WITH GOLD!
GOLD!? Ho Ho!
THERE'S NO GOLD HERE!
WHERE'D YOU GET A FUNNY IDEA LIKE THAT?
WELL, THE CHINAMAN SAID WE WAS ON AN—
AGH!
PLEASE DON'T BRING UP PEPE WONG!
WHO ARE YOU GOING TO TRUST EDWEARD?
A GLEAMING PILLORY OF COMMERCE?
A LOYAL PATRIOT AND SERVANT OF THE VOX PUBICA?
SUCH AS MYSELF.
OR
A FOREIGN QUACK CHINESE CHARLATAN PHARMACIST!
YOU BE THE JUDGE.
THE MAN DRESSES IN A BATHROBE, EDWEARD.

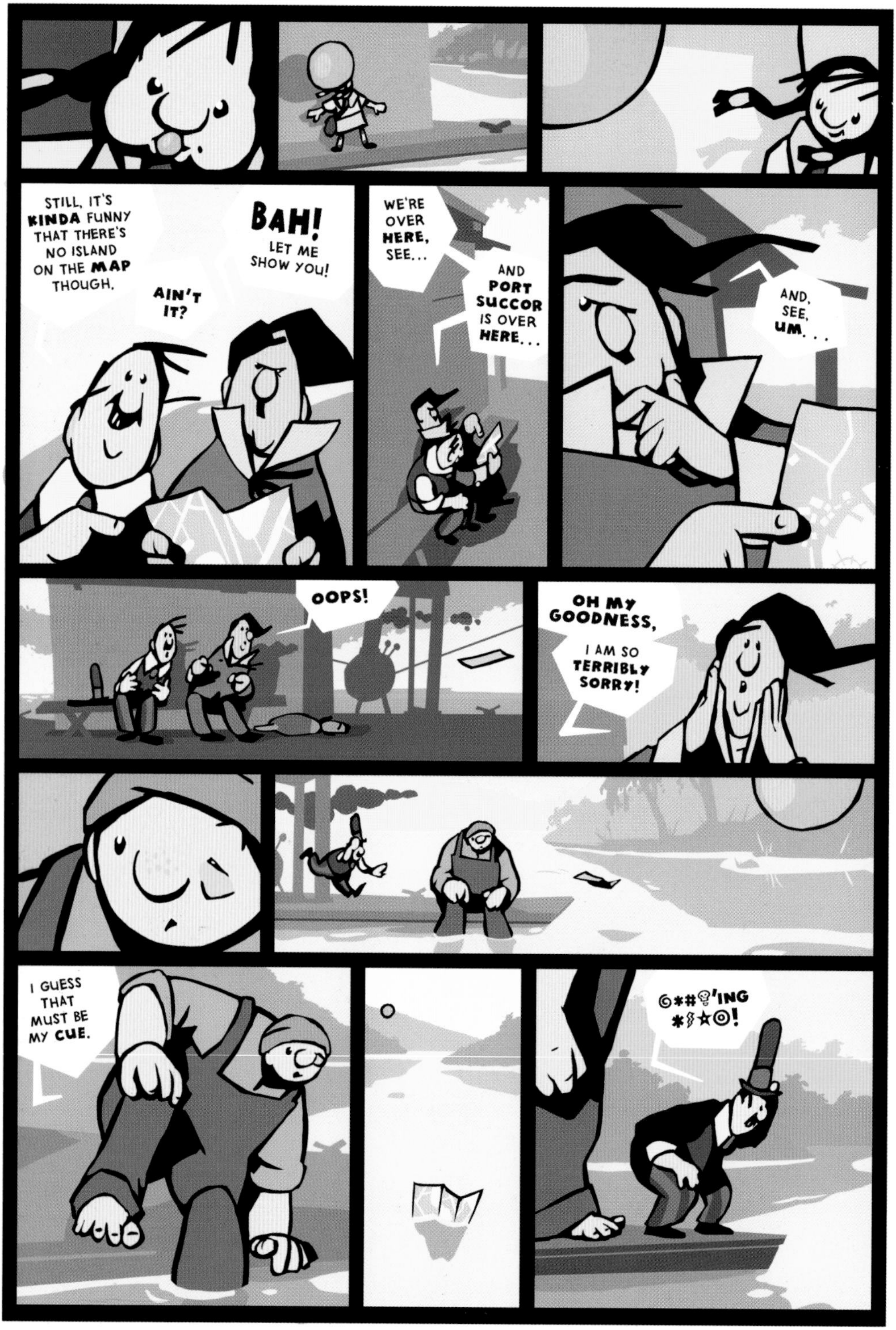
STILL, IT'S KINDA FUNNY THAT THERE'S NO ISLAND ON THE MAP THOUGH.
AIN'T IT?
BAH! LET ME SHOW YOU!
WE'RE OVER HERE, SEE...
AND PORT SUCCOR IS OVER HERE...
AND, SEE, UM...
OOPS!
OH MY GOODNESS,
I AM SO TERRIBLY SORRY!
I GUESS THAT MUST BE MY CUE.

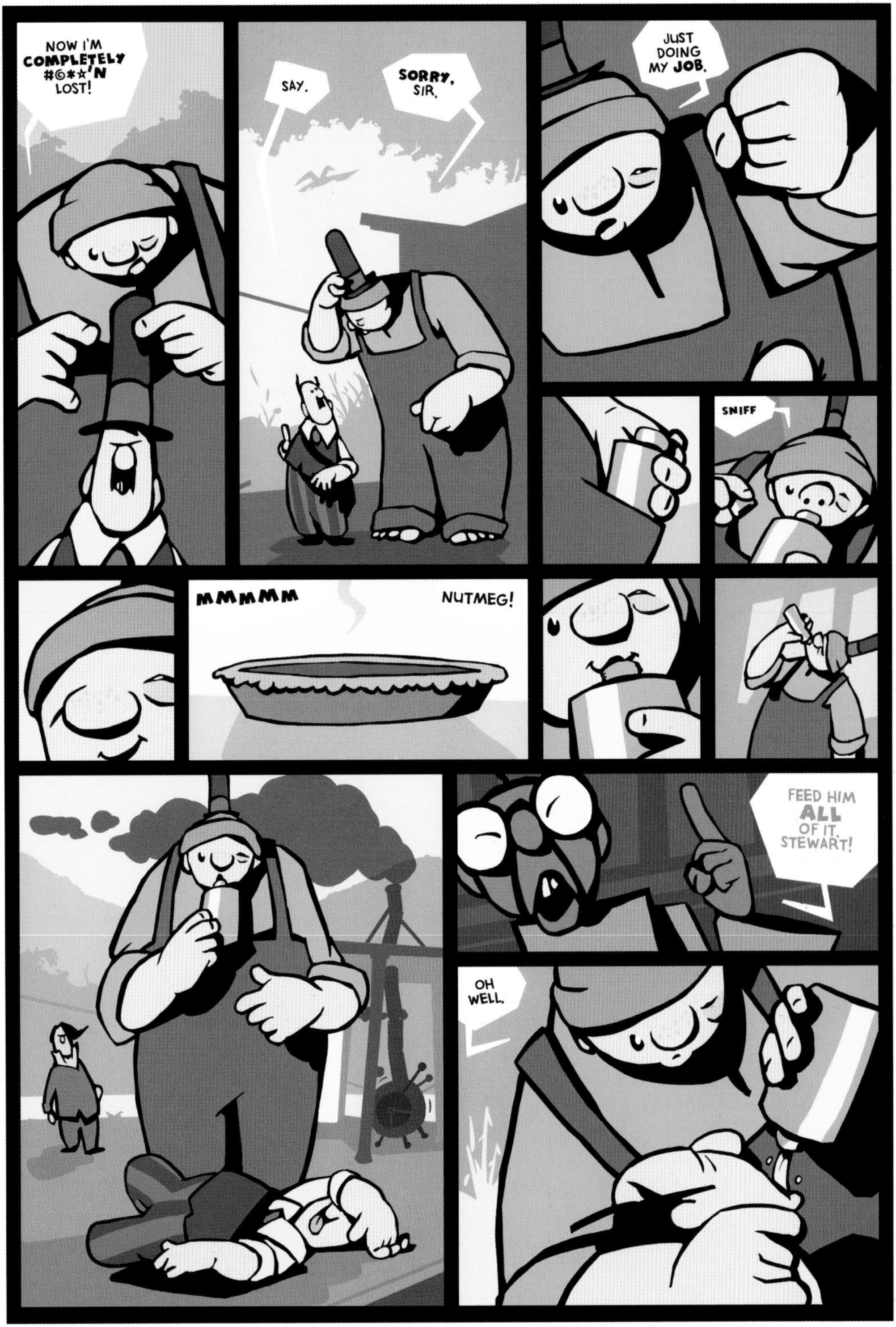
NOW I'M COMPLETELY #©*☆'N LOST!
SAY.
SORRY, SIR.
JUST DOING MY JOB.
SNIFF
MMMMM
NUTMEG!
FEED HIM ALL OF IT, STEWART!
OH WELL.

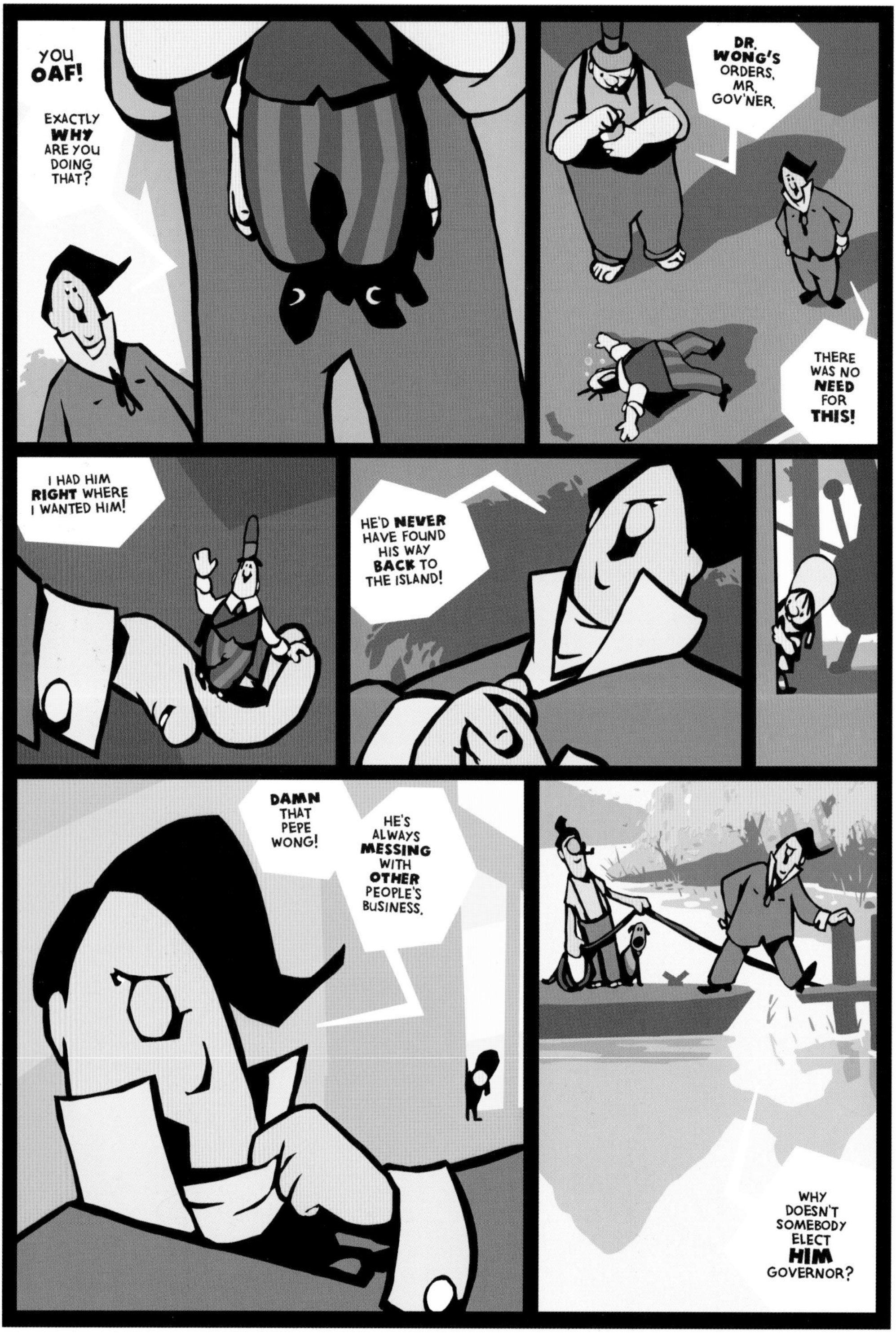
YOU OAF!
EXACTLY WHY ARE YOU DOING THAT?
DR. WONG'S ORDERS, MR. GOV'NER.
THERE WAS NO NEED FOR THIS!
I HAD HIM RIGHT WHERE I WANTED HIM!
HE'D NEVER HAVE FOUND HIS WAY BACK TO THE ISLAND!
DAMN THAT PEPE WONG!
HE'S ALWAYS MESSING WITH OTHER PEOPLE'S BUSINESS.
WHY DOESN'T SOMEBODY ELECT HIM GOVERNOR?

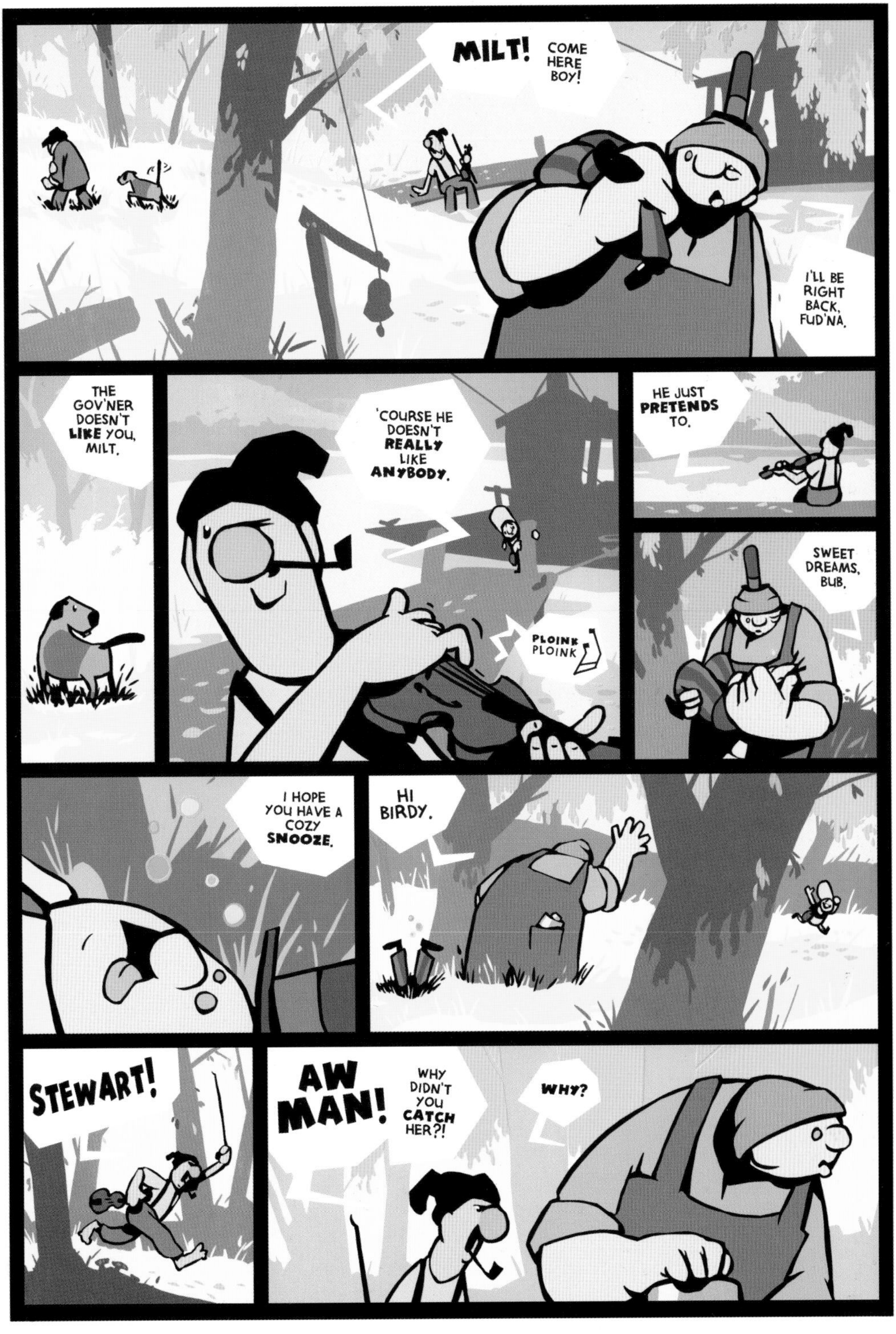
MILT! COME HERE BOY!
I'LL BE RIGHT BACK, FUD'NA.
THE GOV'NER DOESN'T LIKE YOU, MILT.
'COURSE HE DOESN'T REALLY LIKE ANYBODY.
PLOINK PLOINK
HE JUST PRETENDS TO.
SWEET DREAMS, BUB.
I HOPE YOU HAVE A COZY SNOOZE.
HI BIRDY.
STEWART!
AW MAN!
WHY DIDN'T YOU CATCH HER?!
WHY?

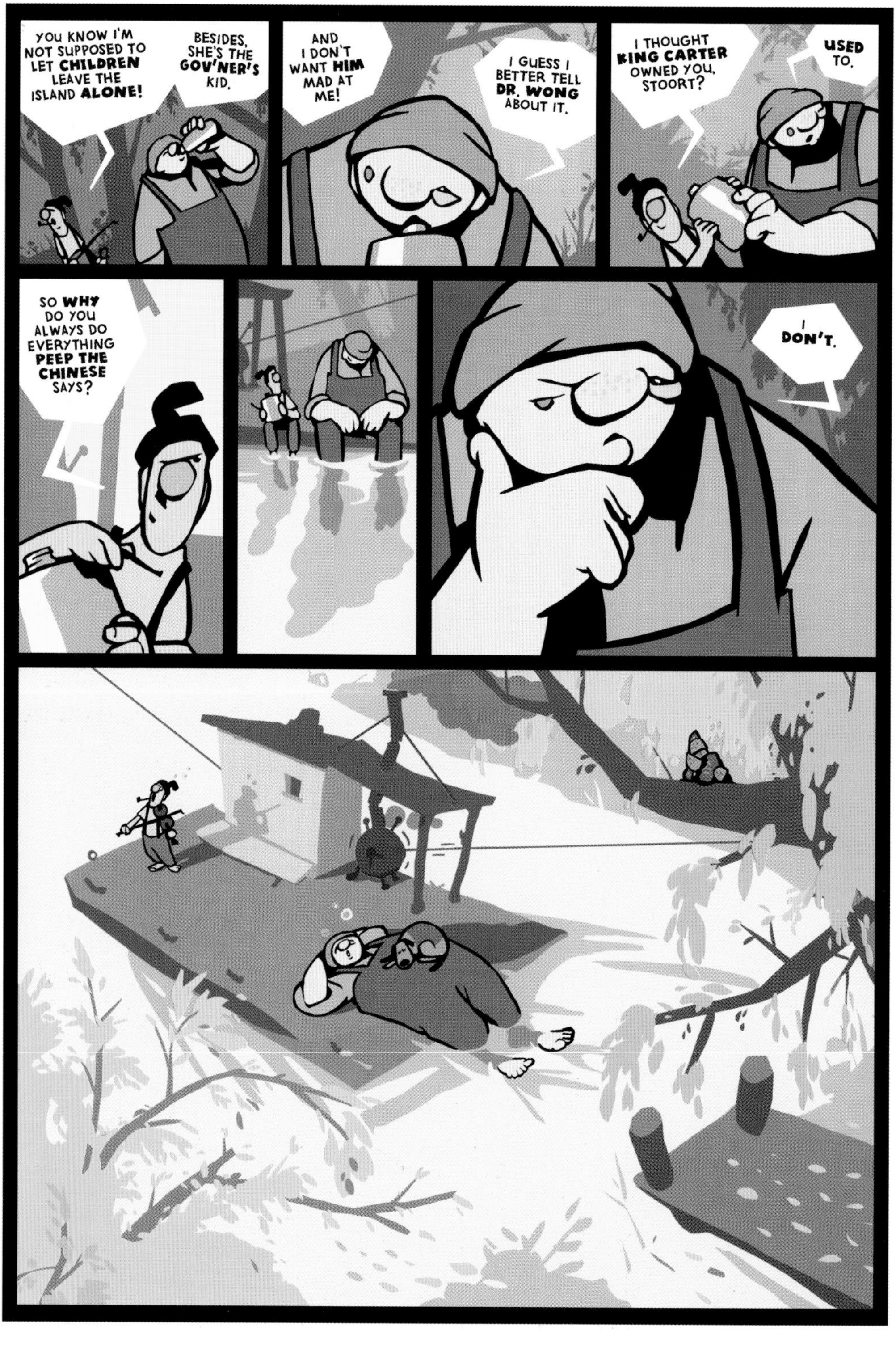
YOU KNOW I'M NOT SUPPOSED TO LET **CHILDREN** LEAVE THE ISLAND **ALONE!**
BESIDES, SHE'S THE **GOV'NER'S** KID.
AND I DON'T WANT **HIM** MAD AT ME!
I GUESS I BETTER TELL **DR. WONG** ABOUT IT.
I THOUGHT **KING CARTER** OWNED YOU, STOORT?
USED TO.
SO **WHY** DO YOU ALWAYS DO EVERYTHING **PEEP THE CHINESE** SAYS?
I **DON'T.**

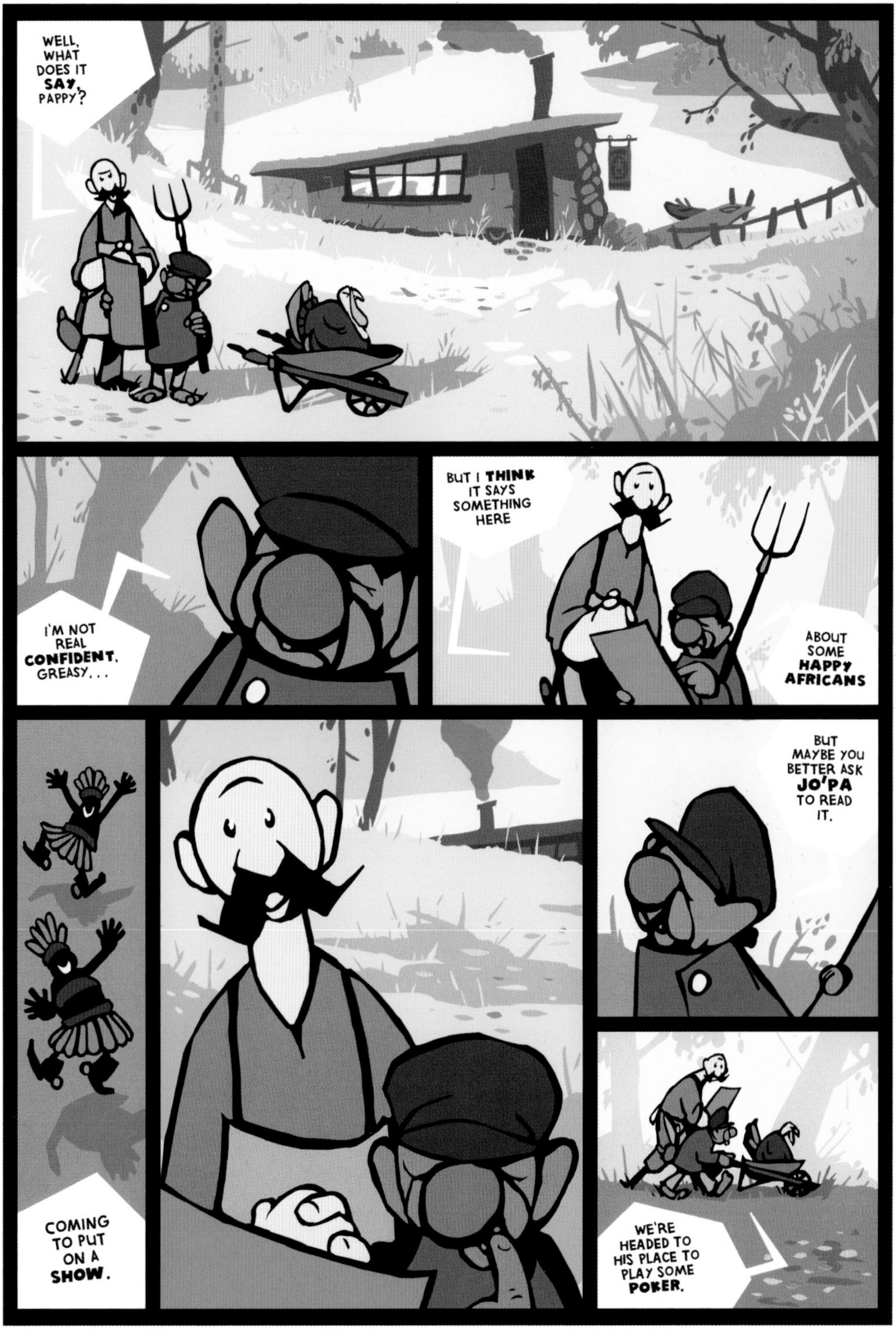

WELL, WHAT DOES IT **SAY**, PAPPY?
I'M NOT REAL **CONFIDENT**, GREASY. . .
BUT I **THINK** IT SAYS SOMETHING HERE
ABOUT SOME **HAPPY AFRICANS**
COMING TO PUT ON A **SHOW**.
BUT MAYBE YOU BETTER ASK **JO'PA** TO READ IT.
WE'RE HEADED TO HIS PLACE TO PLAY SOME **POKER**.

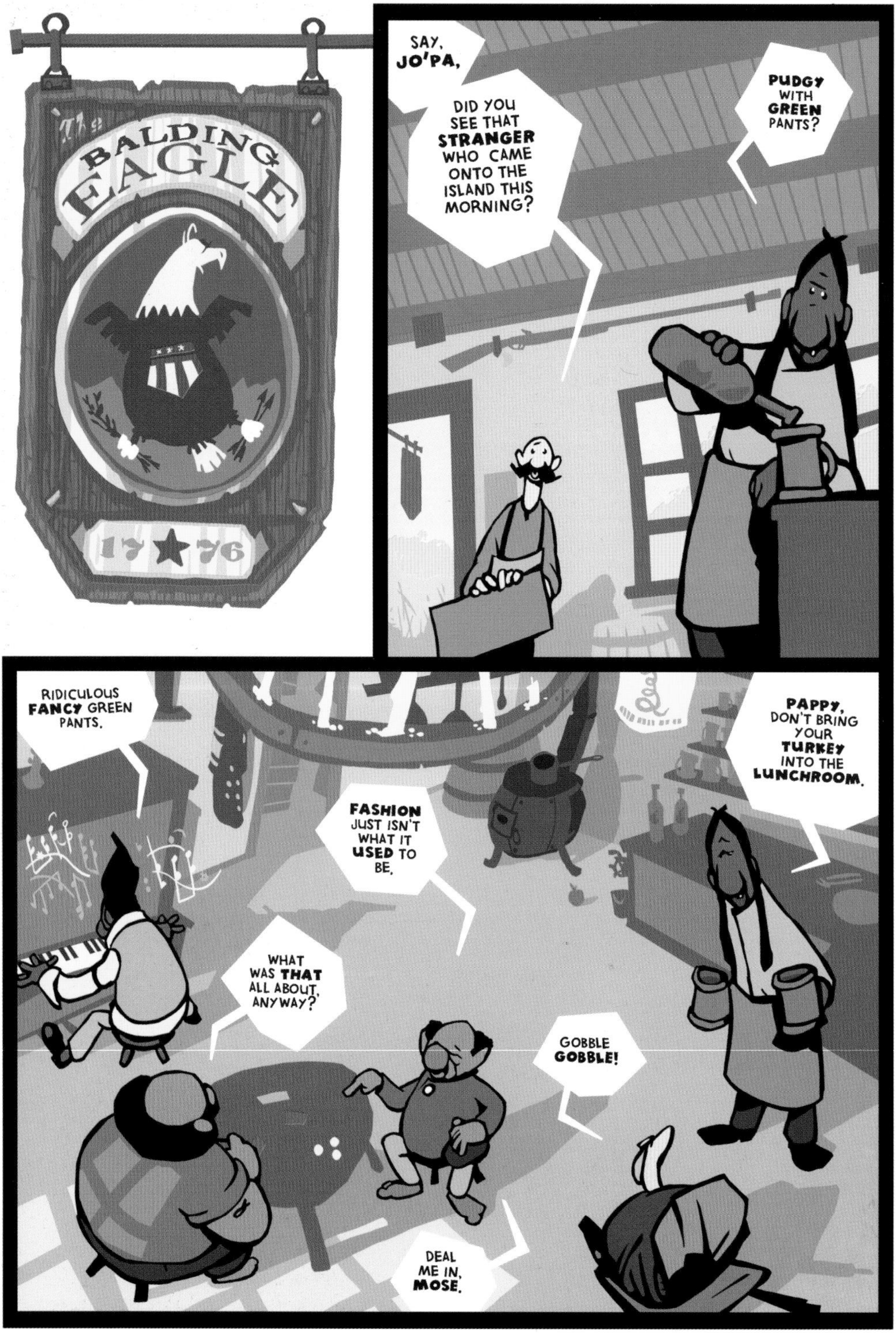
The BALDING EAGLE
17 ★ 76
SAY, JO'PA,
DID YOU SEE THAT STRANGER WHO CAME ONTO THE ISLAND THIS MORNING?
PUDGY WITH GREEN PANTS?
RIDICULOUS FANCY GREEN PANTS.
FASHION JUST ISN'T WHAT IT USED TO BE.
PAPPY, DON'T BRING YOUR TURKEY INTO THE LUNCHROOM.
WHAT WAS THAT ALL ABOUT, ANYWAY?
GOBBLE GOBBLE!
DEAL ME IN, MOSE.

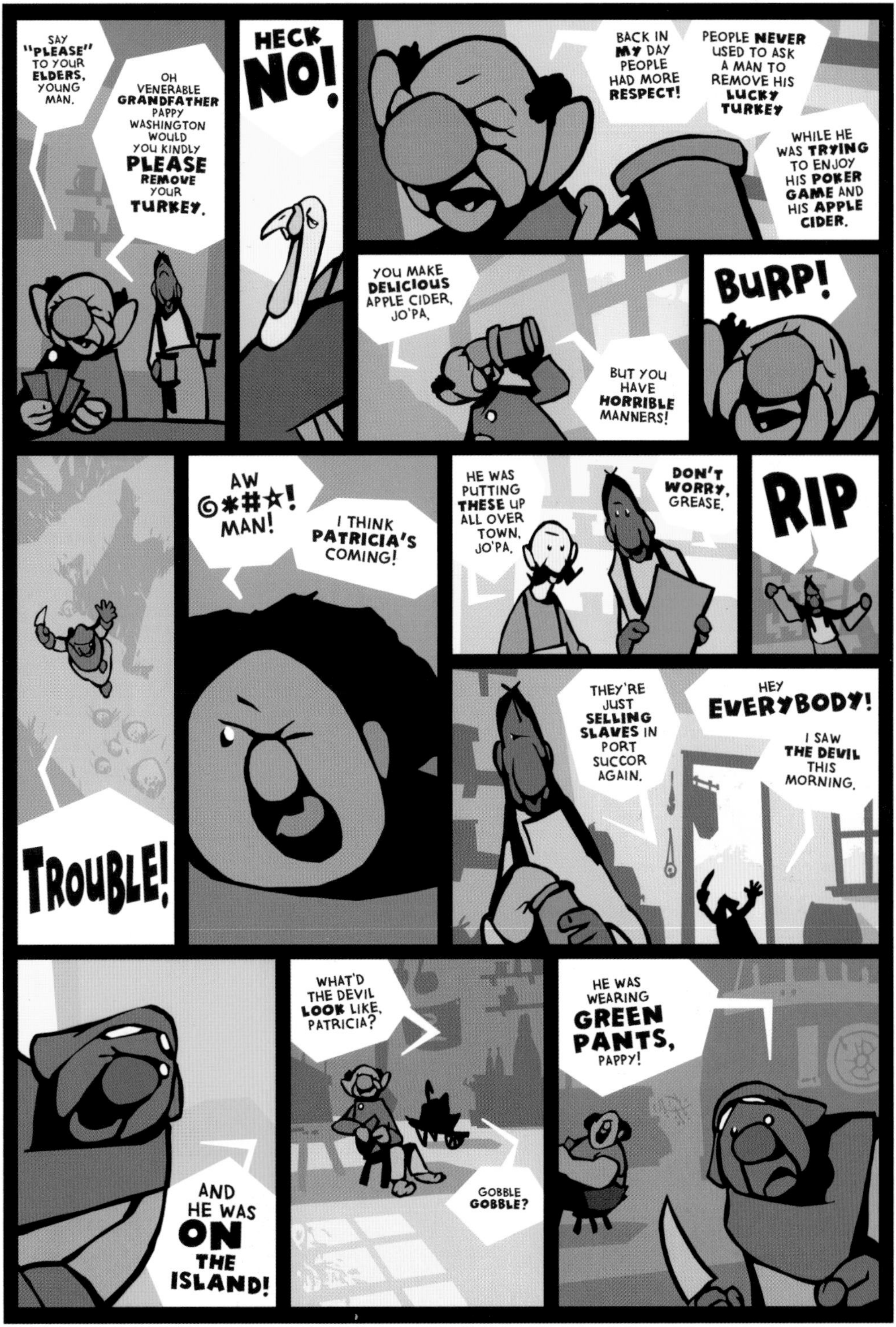
SAY "PLEASE" TO YOUR ELDERS, YOUNG MAN.
OH VENERABLE GRANDFATHER PAPPY WASHINGTON WOULD YOU KINDLY PLEASE REMOVE YOUR TURKEY.
HECK NO!
BACK IN MY DAY PEOPLE HAD MORE RESPECT!
PEOPLE NEVER USED TO ASK A MAN TO REMOVE HIS LUCKY TURKEY
WHILE HE WAS TRYING TO ENJOY HIS POKER GAME AND HIS APPLE CIDER.
YOU MAKE DELICIOUS APPLE CIDER, JO'PA,
BUT YOU HAVE HORRIBLE MANNERS!
BURP!
TROUBLE!
AW @*#☆! MAN!
I THINK PATRICIA'S COMING!
HE WAS PUTTING THESE UP ALL OVER TOWN, JO'PA.
DON'T WORRY, GREASE.
RIP
THEY'RE JUST SELLING SLAVES IN PORT SUCCOR AGAIN.
HEY EVERYBODY!
I SAW THE DEVIL THIS MORNING.
AND HE WAS ON THE ISLAND!
WHAT'D THE DEVIL LOOK LIKE, PATRICIA?
GOBBLE GOBBLE?
HE WAS WEARING GREEN PANTS, PAPPY!

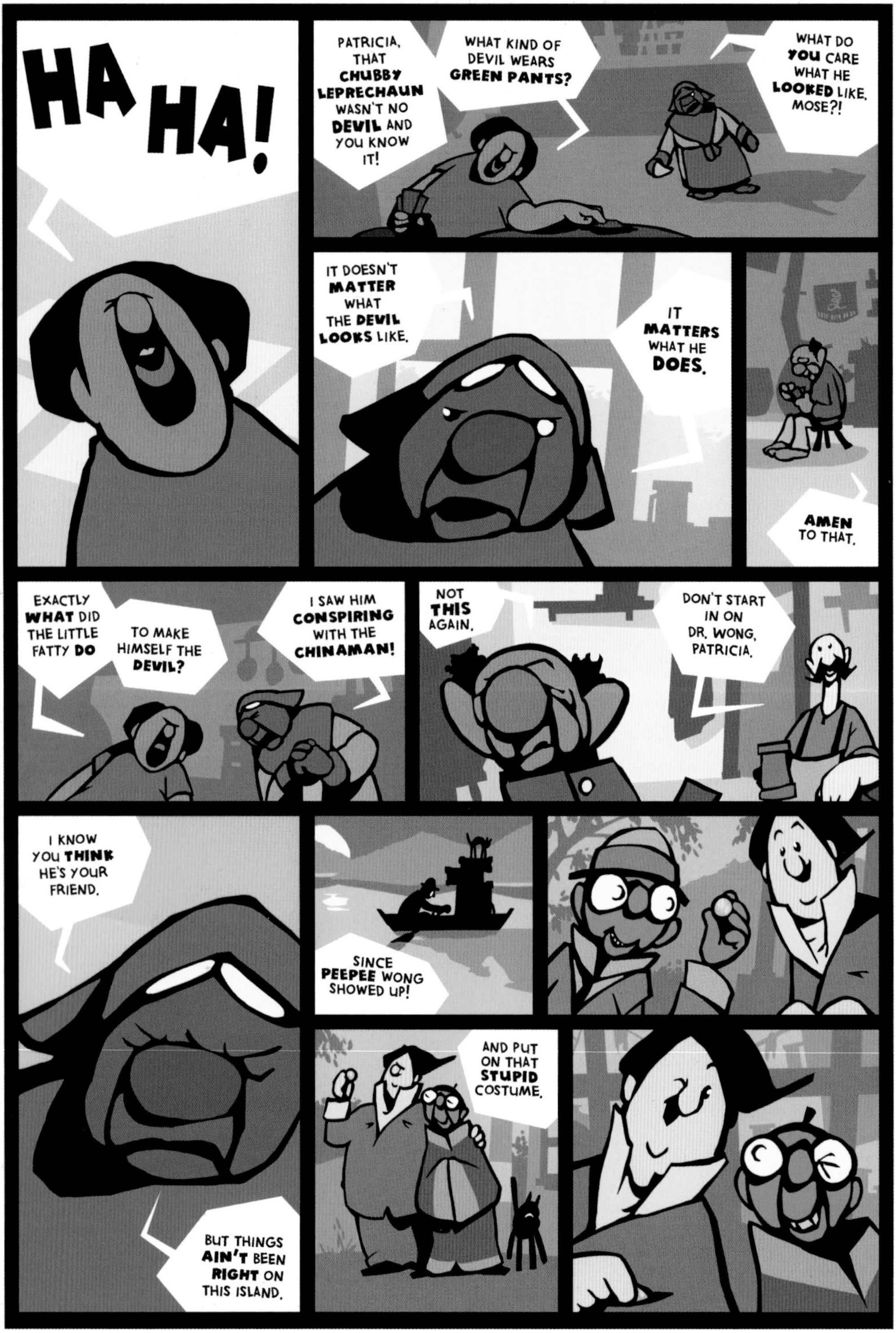

HA HA!
PATRICIA, THAT CHUBBY LEPRECHAUN WASN'T NO DEVIL AND YOU KNOW IT!
WHAT KIND OF DEVIL WEARS GREEN PANTS?
WHAT DO YOU CARE WHAT HE LOOKED LIKE, MOSE?!
IT DOESN'T MATTER WHAT THE DEVIL LOOKS LIKE.
IT MATTERS WHAT HE DOES.
AMEN TO THAT.
EXACTLY WHAT DID THE LITTLE FATTY DO
TO MAKE HIMSELF THE DEVIL?
I SAW HIM CONSPIRING WITH THE CHINAMAN!
NOT THIS AGAIN.
DON'T START IN ON DR. WONG, PATRICIA.
I KNOW YOU THINK HE'S YOUR FRIEND.
BUT THINGS AIN'T BEEN RIGHT ON THIS ISLAND.
SINCE PEEPEE WONG SHOWED UP!
AND PUT ON THAT STUPID COSTUME.

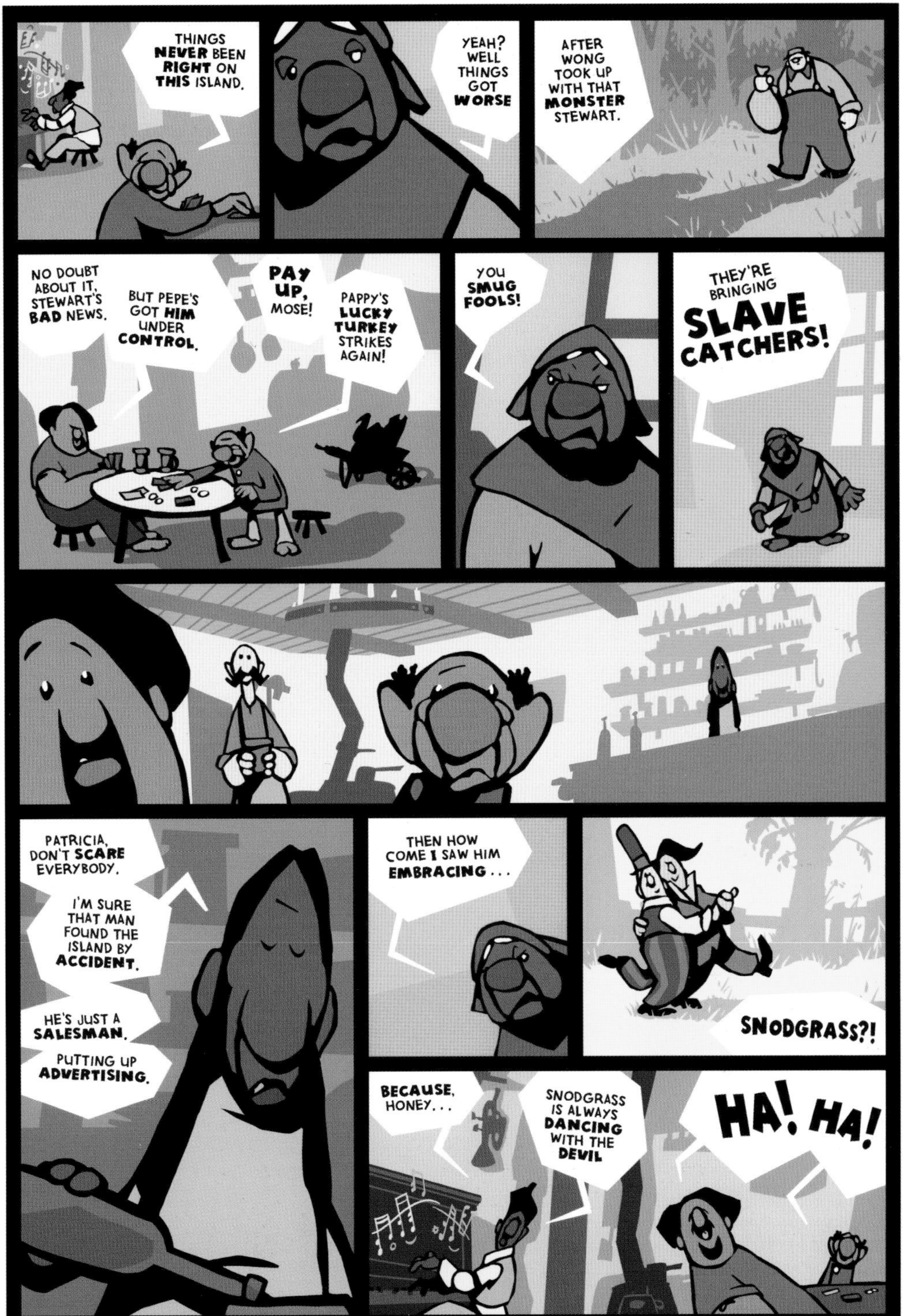
THINGS NEVER BEEN RIGHT ON THIS ISLAND.
YEAH? WELL THINGS GOT WORSE
AFTER WONG TOOK UP WITH THAT MONSTER STEWART.
NO DOUBT ABOUT IT, STEWART'S BAD NEWS.
BUT PEPE'S GOT HIM UNDER CONTROL.
PAY UP, MOSE!
PAPPY'S LUCKY TURKEY STRIKES AGAIN!
YOU SMUG FOOLS!
THEY'RE BRINGING SLAVE CATCHERS!
PATRICIA, DON'T SCARE EVERYBODY.
I'M SURE THAT MAN FOUND THE ISLAND BY ACCIDENT.
HE'S JUST A SALESMAN.
PUTTING UP ADVERTISING.
THEN HOW COME I SAW HIM EMBRACING . . .
SNODGRASS?!
BECAUSE, HONEY. . .
SNODGRASS IS ALWAYS DANCING WITH THE DEVIL
HA! HA!

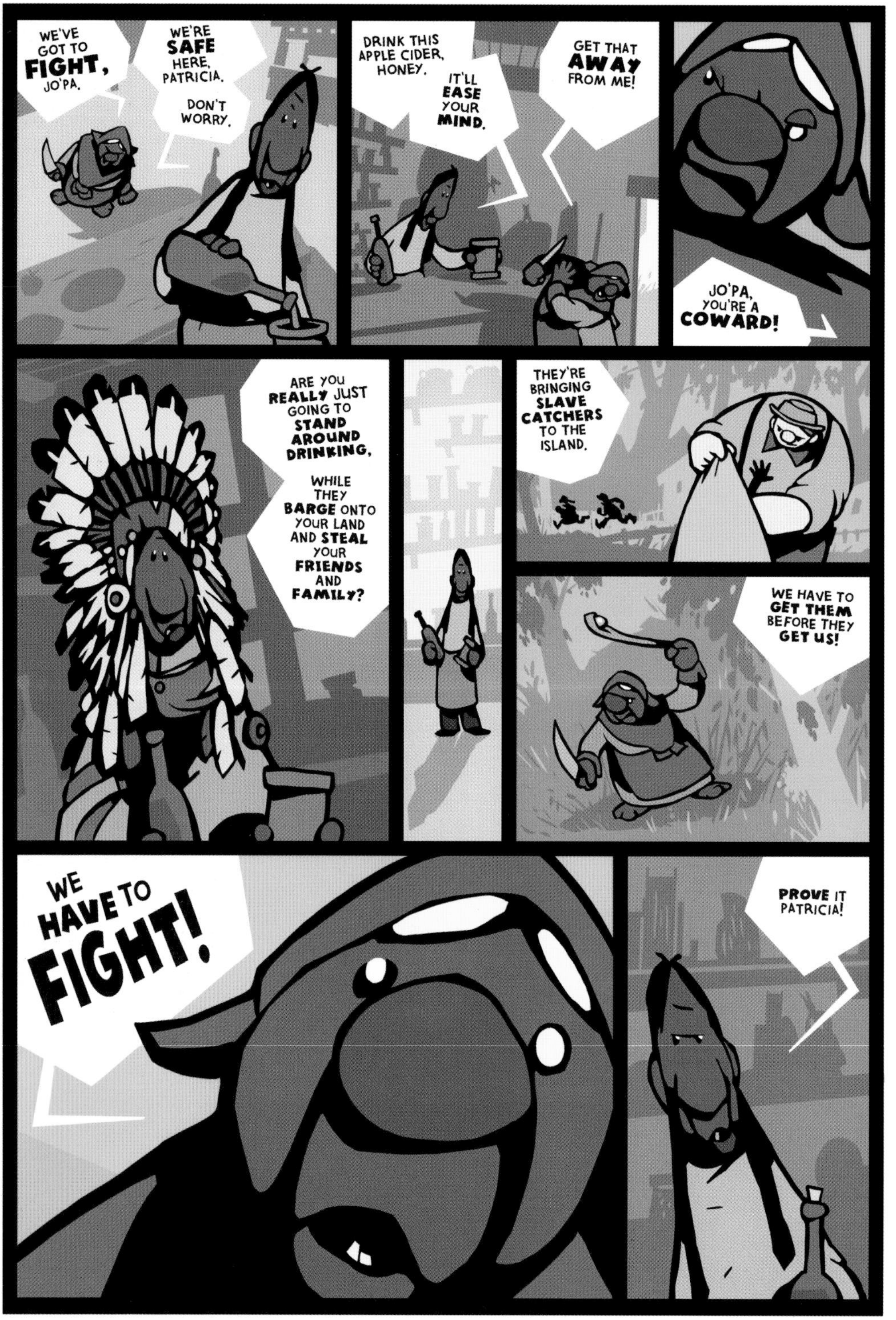
WE'VE GOT TO FIGHT, JO'PA.
WE'RE SAFE HERE, PATRICIA.
DON'T WORRY.
DRINK THIS APPLE CIDER, HONEY.
IT'LL EASE YOUR MIND.
GET THAT AWAY FROM ME!
JO'PA, YOU'RE A COWARD!
ARE YOU REALLY JUST GOING TO STAND AROUND DRINKING,
WHILE THEY BARGE ONTO YOUR LAND AND STEAL YOUR FRIENDS AND FAMILY?
THEY'RE BRINGING SLAVE CATCHERS TO THE ISLAND.
WE HAVE TO GET THEM BEFORE THEY GET US!
WE HAVE TO FIGHT!
PROVE IT PATRICIA!

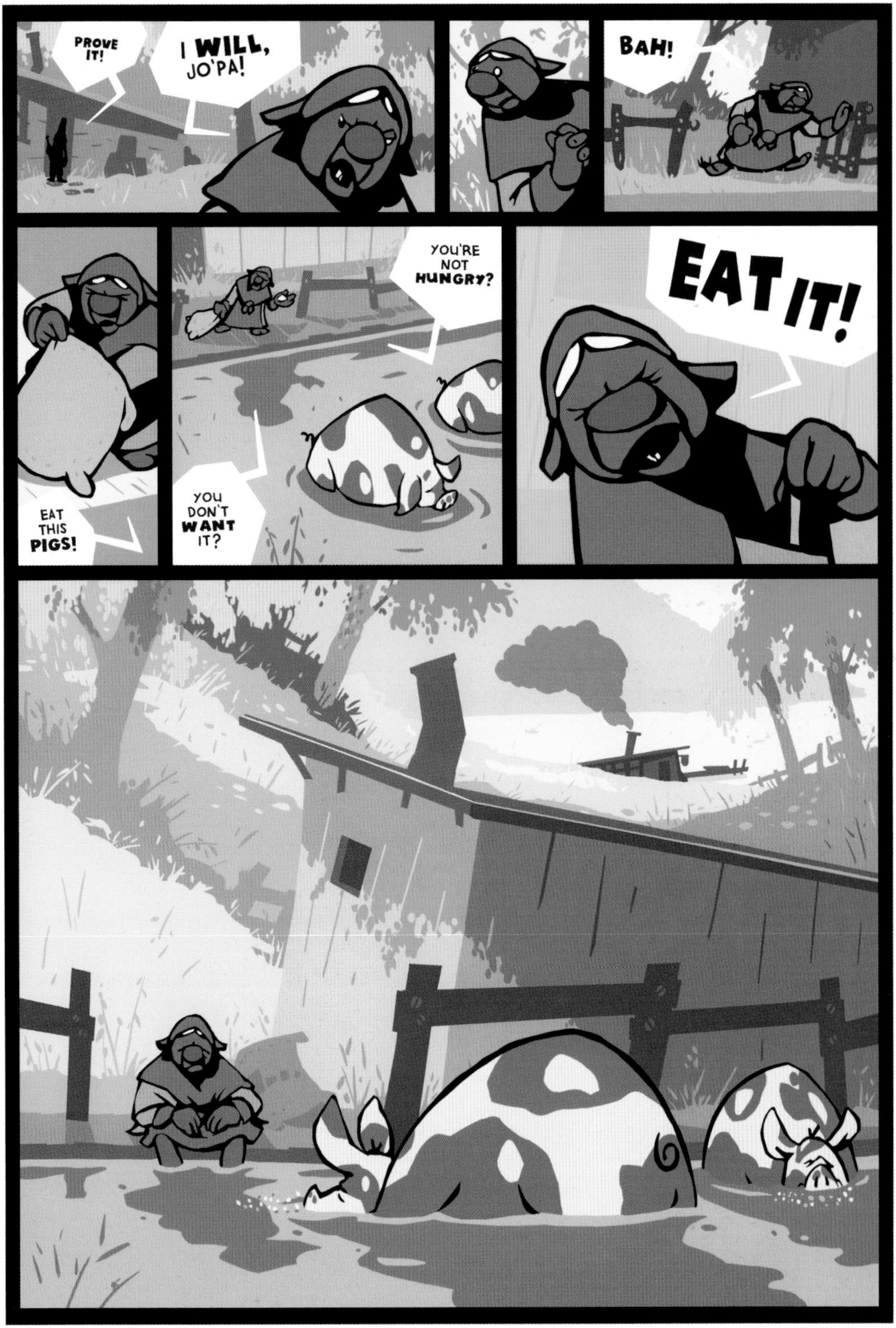
PROVE IT!
I WILL, JO'PA!
BAH!
EAT THIS PIGS!
YOU'RE NOT HUNGRY?
YOU DON'T WANT IT?
EAT IT!

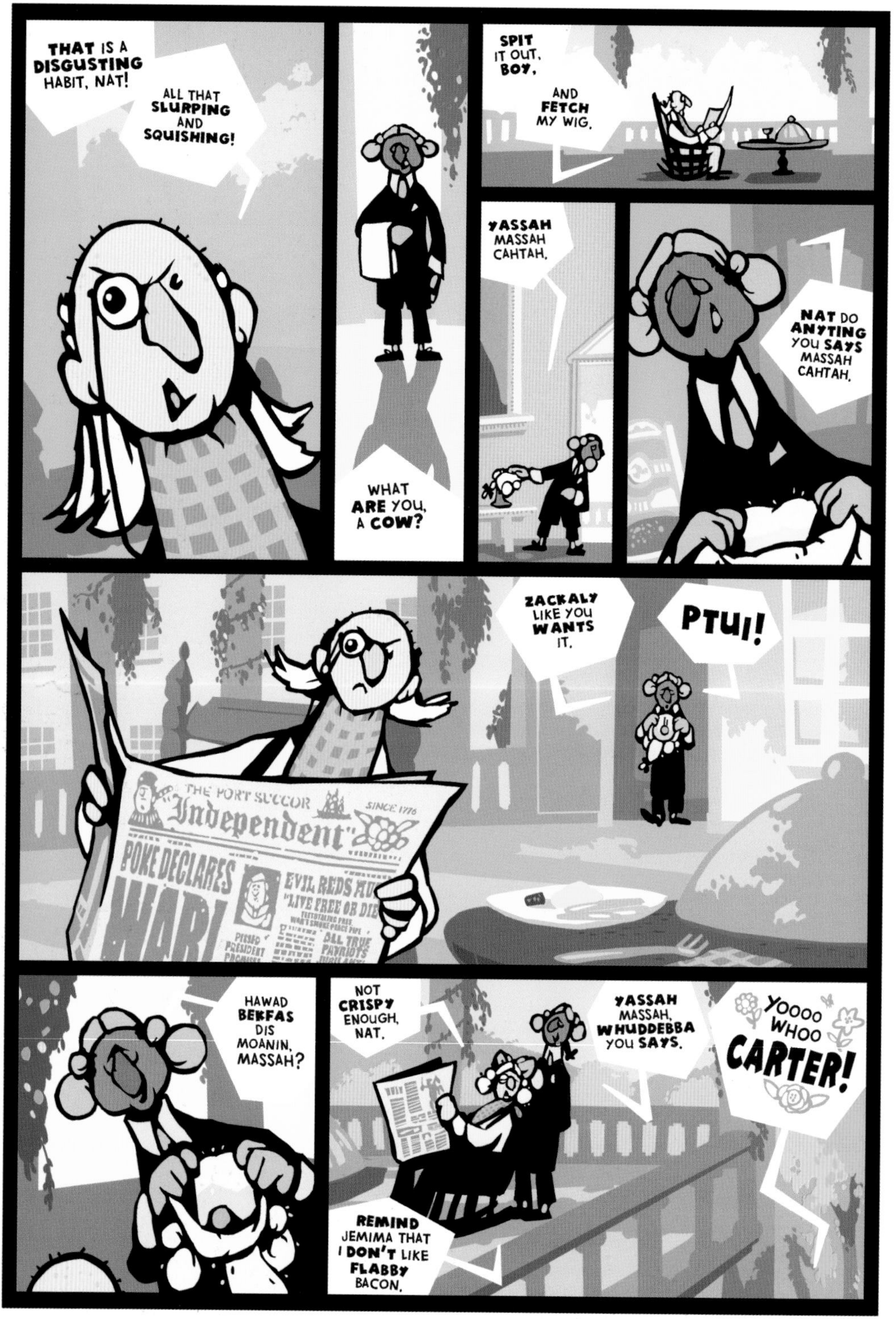
THAT IS A DISGUSTING HABIT, NAT!
ALL THAT SLURPING AND SQUISHING!
WHAT ARE YOU, A COW?
SPIT IT OUT, BOY,
AND FETCH MY WIG.
YASSAH MASSAH CAHTAH.
NAT DO ANYTING YOU SAYS MASSAH CAHTAH.
THE PORT SUCCOR Independent SINCE 1776
POKE DECLARES WAR!
EVIL REDS ...
"LIVE FREE OR DIE"
ALL TRUE PATRIOTS
ZACKALY LIKE YOU WANTS IT.
PTUI!
HAWAD BEKFAS DIS MOANIN, MASSAH?
NOT CRISPY ENOUGH, NAT.
YASSAH MASSAH, WHUDDEBBA YOU SAYS.
YOOOO WHOO CARTER!
REMIND JEMIMA THAT I DON'T LIKE FLABBY BACON.

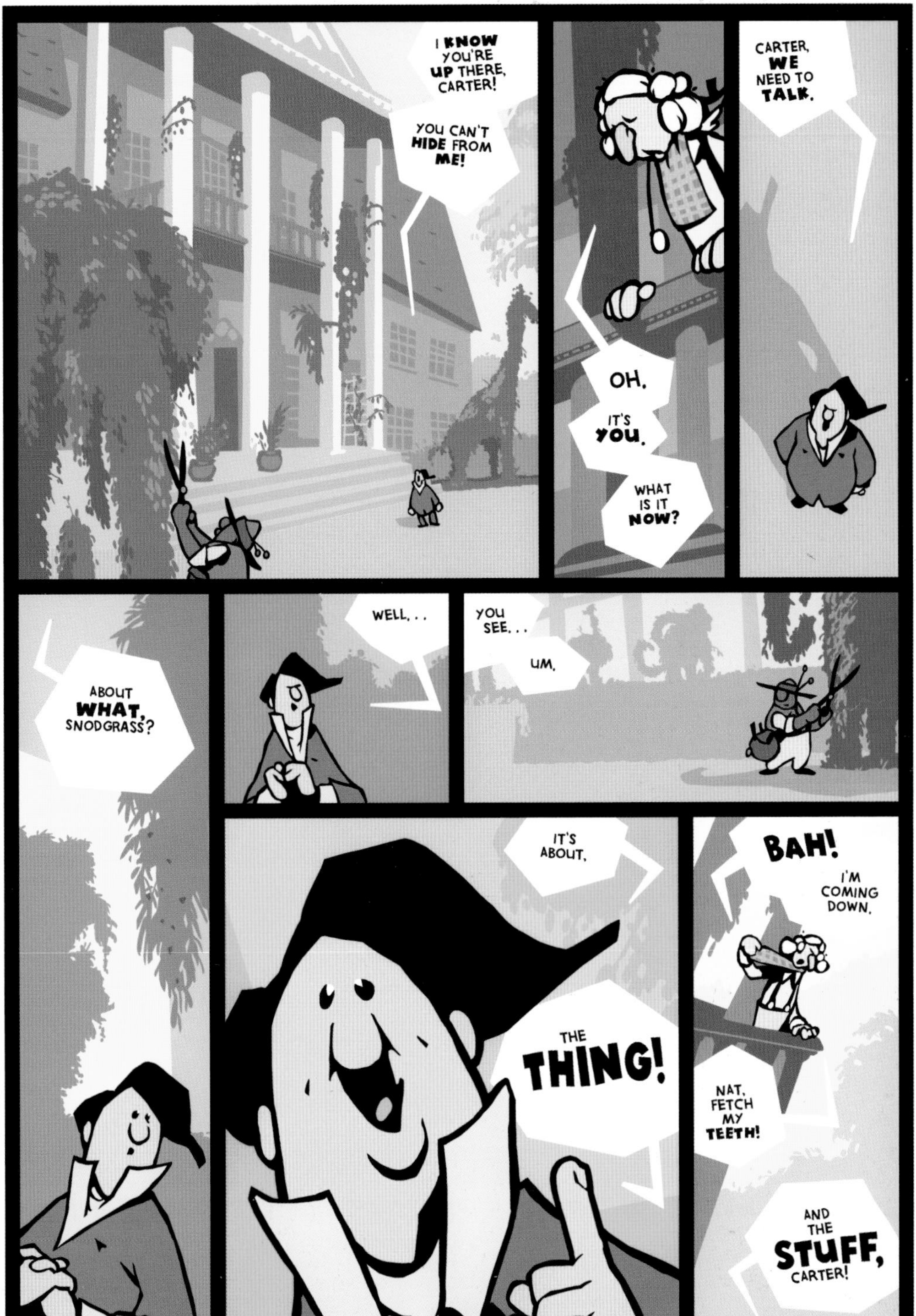
I KNOW YOU'RE UP THERE, CARTER!
YOU CAN'T HIDE FROM ME!
OH.
IT'S YOU.
WHAT IS IT NOW?
CARTER, WE NEED TO TALK.
ABOUT WHAT, SNODGRASS?
WELL, . .
YOU SEE, . .
UM.
IT'S ABOUT.
THE THING!
BAH!
I'M COMING DOWN.
NAT, FETCH MY TEETH!
AND THE STUFF, CARTER!

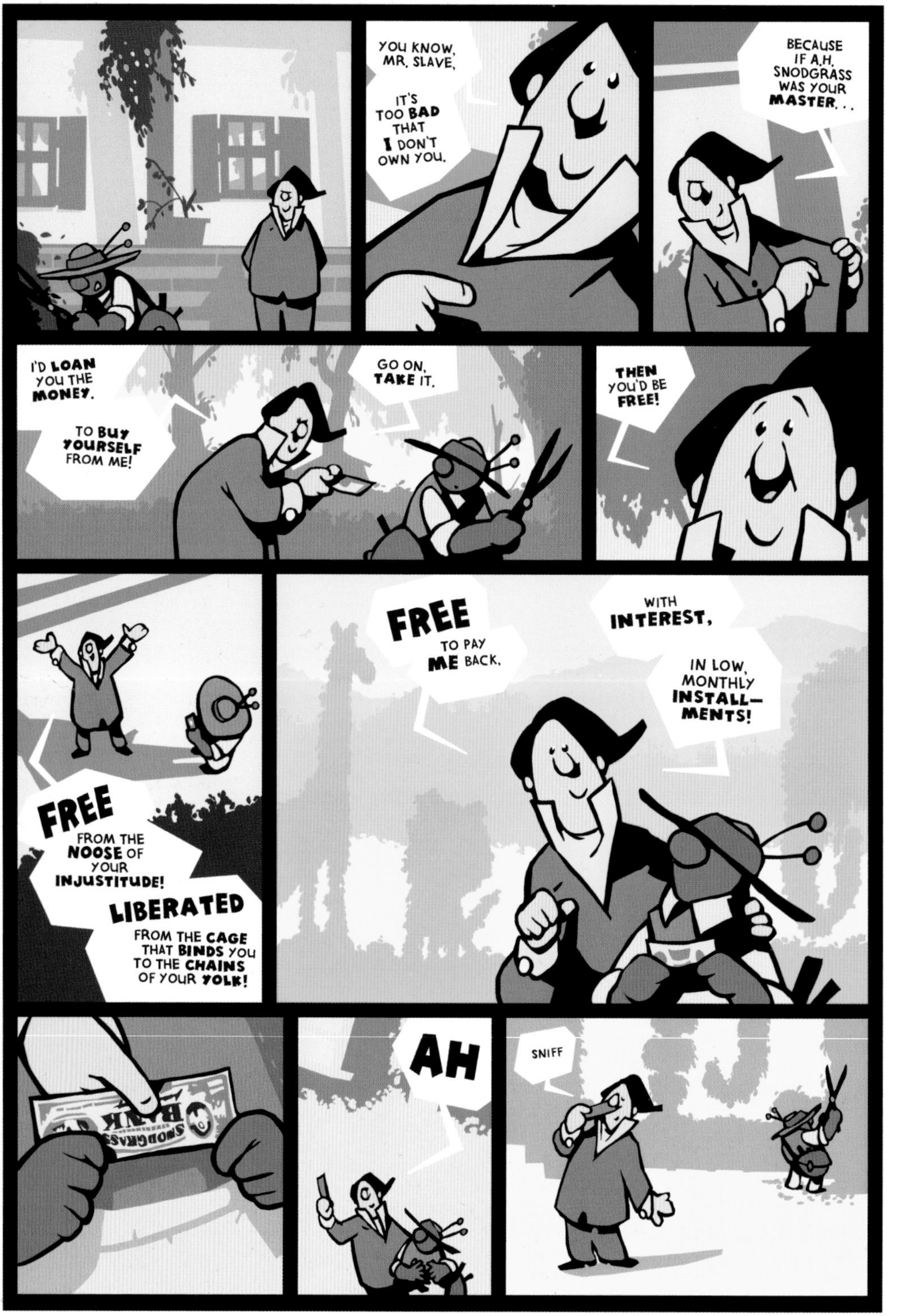
YOU KNOW, MR. SLAVE,
IT'S TOO BAD THAT I DON'T OWN YOU.
BECAUSE IF A.H. SNODGRASS WAS YOUR MASTER. . .
I'D LOAN YOU THE MONEY.
TO BUY YOURSELF FROM ME!
GO ON, TAKE IT.
THEN YOU'D BE FREE!
FREE FROM THE NOOSE OF YOUR INJUSTITUDE!
LIBERATED FROM THE CAGE THAT BINDS YOU TO THE CHAINS OF YOUR YOLK!
FREE TO PAY ME BACK,
WITH INTEREST,
IN LOW, MONTHLY INSTALL–MENTS!
BANK
SNODGRASS
AH
SNIFF

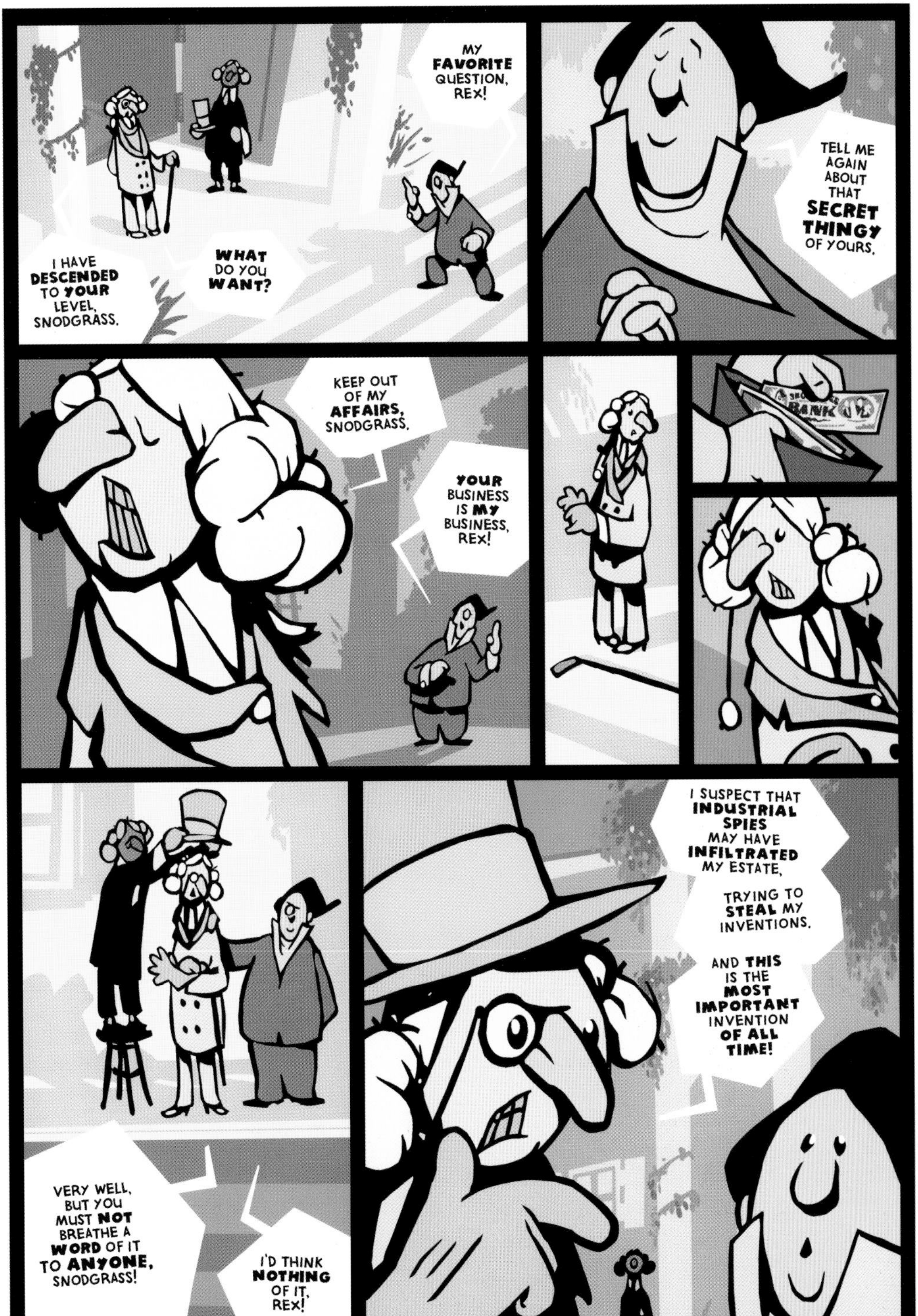
I HAVE DESCENDED TO YOUR LEVEL, SNODGRASS.
WHAT DO YOU WANT?
MY FAVORITE QUESTION, REX!
TELL ME AGAIN ABOUT THAT SECRET THINGY OF YOURS.
KEEP OUT OF MY AFFAIRS, SNODGRASS.
YOUR BUSINESS IS MY BUSINESS, REX!
VERY WELL, BUT YOU MUST NOT BREATHE A WORD OF IT TO ANYONE, SNODGRASS!
I'D THINK NOTHING OF IT, REX!
I SUSPECT THAT INDUSTRIAL SPIES MAY HAVE INFILTRATED MY ESTATE,
TRYING TO STEAL MY INVENTIONS.
AND THIS IS THE MOST IMPORTANT INVENTION OF ALL TIME!

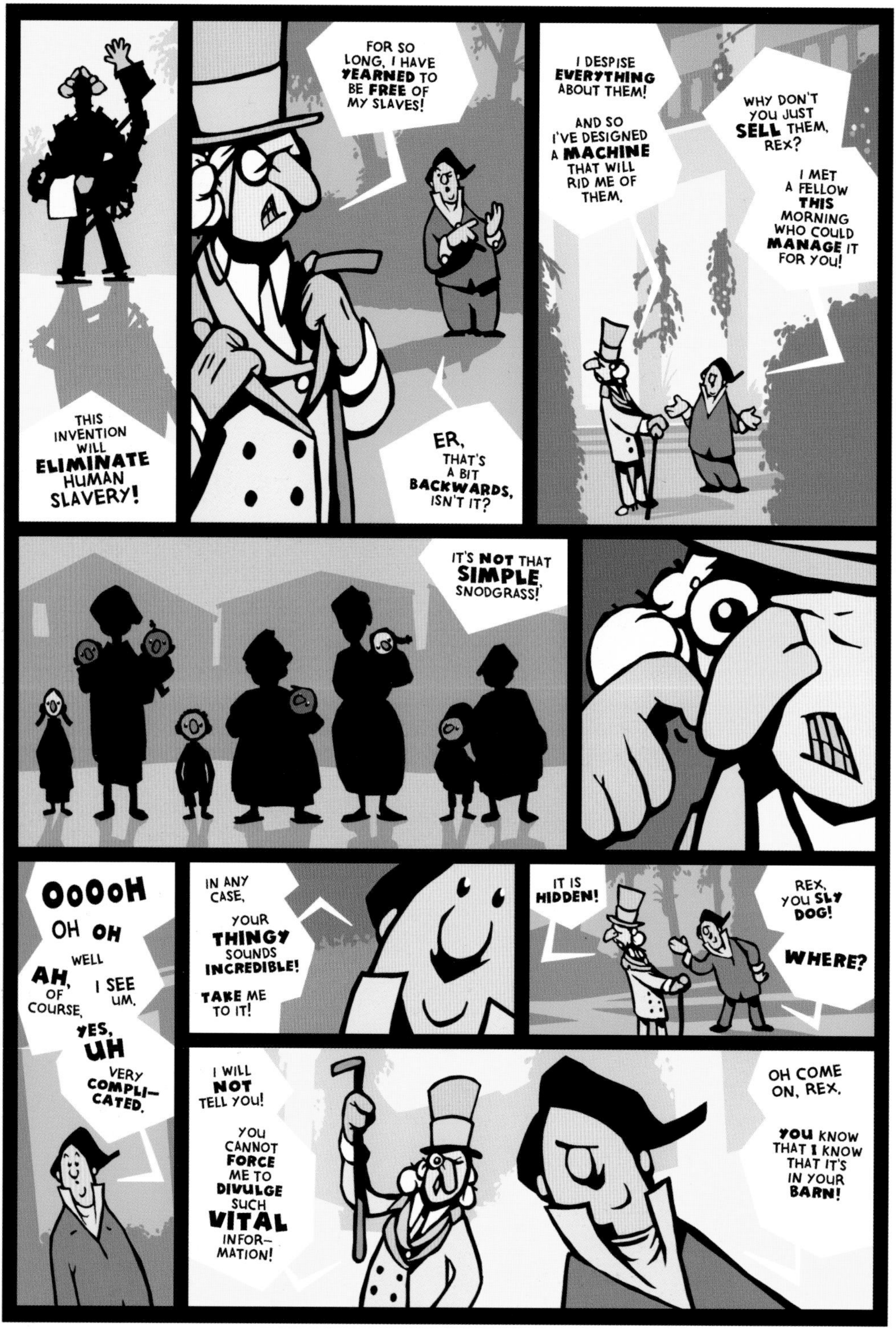
THIS INVENTION WILL ELIMINATE HUMAN SLAVERY!
FOR SO LONG, I HAVE YEARNED TO BE FREE OF MY SLAVES!
ER, THAT'S A BIT BACKWARDS, ISN'T IT?
I DESPISE EVERYTHING ABOUT THEM!
AND SO I'VE DESIGNED A MACHINE THAT WILL RID ME OF THEM.
WHY DON'T YOU JUST SELL THEM, REX?
I MET A FELLOW THIS MORNING WHO COULD MANAGE IT FOR YOU!
IT'S NOT THAT SIMPLE, SNODGRASS!
OOOOH OH OH WELL AH, I SEE UM, OF COURSE, YES, UH VERY COMPLI- CATED.
IN ANY CASE, YOUR THINGY SOUNDS INCREDIBLE!
TAKE ME TO IT!
IT IS HIDDEN!
REX, YOU SLY DOG!
WHERE?
I WILL NOT TELL YOU!
YOU CANNOT FORCE ME TO DIVULGE SUCH VITAL INFOR- MATION!
OH COME ON, REX.
YOU KNOW THAT I KNOW THAT IT'S IN YOUR BARN!

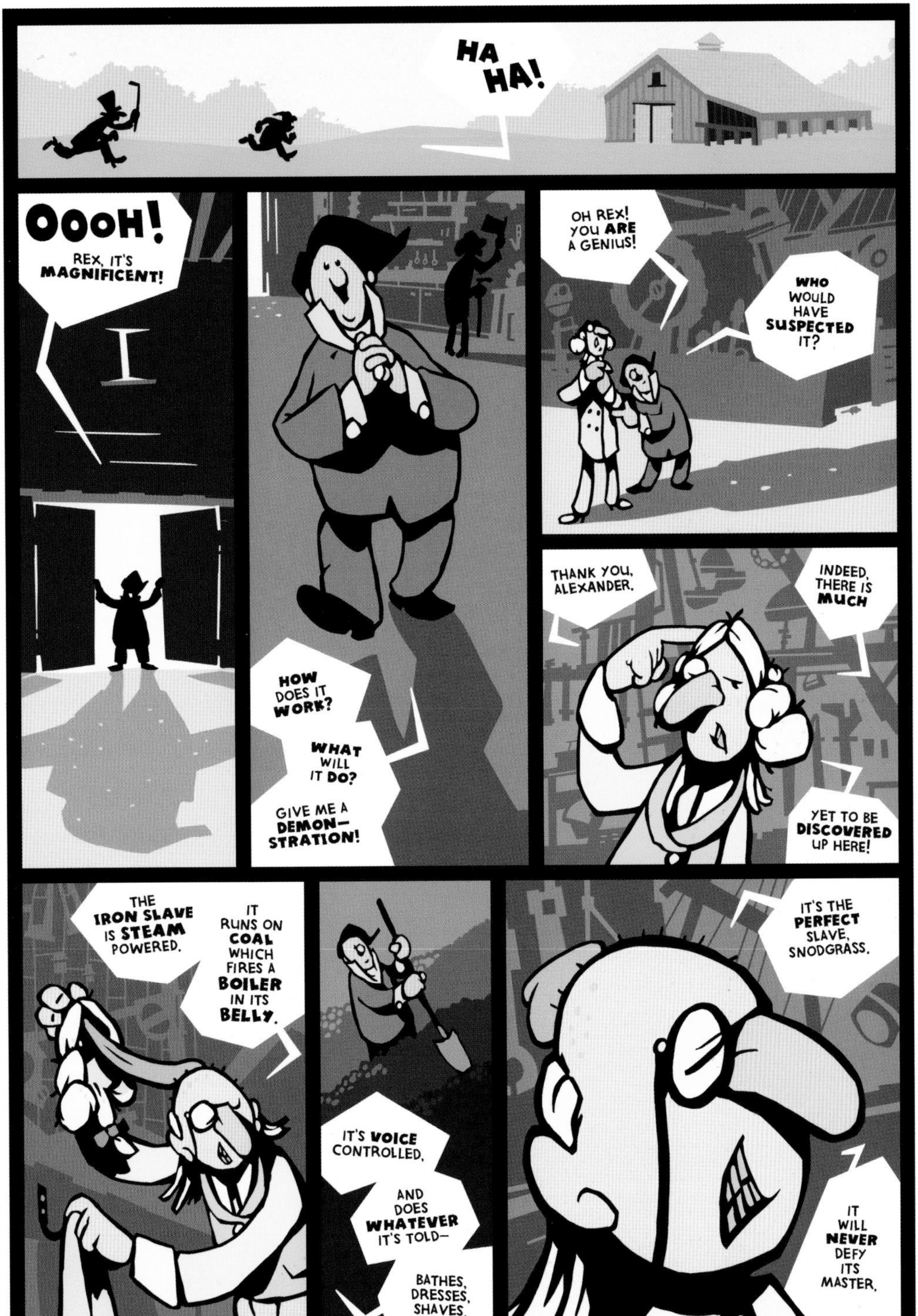

HA HA!
OOOH!
REX, IT'S MAGNIFICENT!
HOW DOES IT WORK?
WHAT WILL IT DO?
GIVE ME A DEMON-STRATION!
OH REX! YOU ARE A GENIUS!
WHO WOULD HAVE SUSPECTED IT?
THANK YOU, ALEXANDER.
INDEED, THERE IS MUCH
YET TO BE DISCOVERED UP HERE!
THE IRON SLAVE IS STEAM POWERED.
IT RUNS ON COAL WHICH FIRES A BOILER IN ITS BELLY.
IT'S VOICE CONTROLLED,
AND DOES WHATEVER IT'S TOLD—
BATHES, DRESSES, SHAVES.
IT'S THE PERFECT SLAVE, SNODGRASS.
IT WILL NEVER DEFY ITS MASTER.

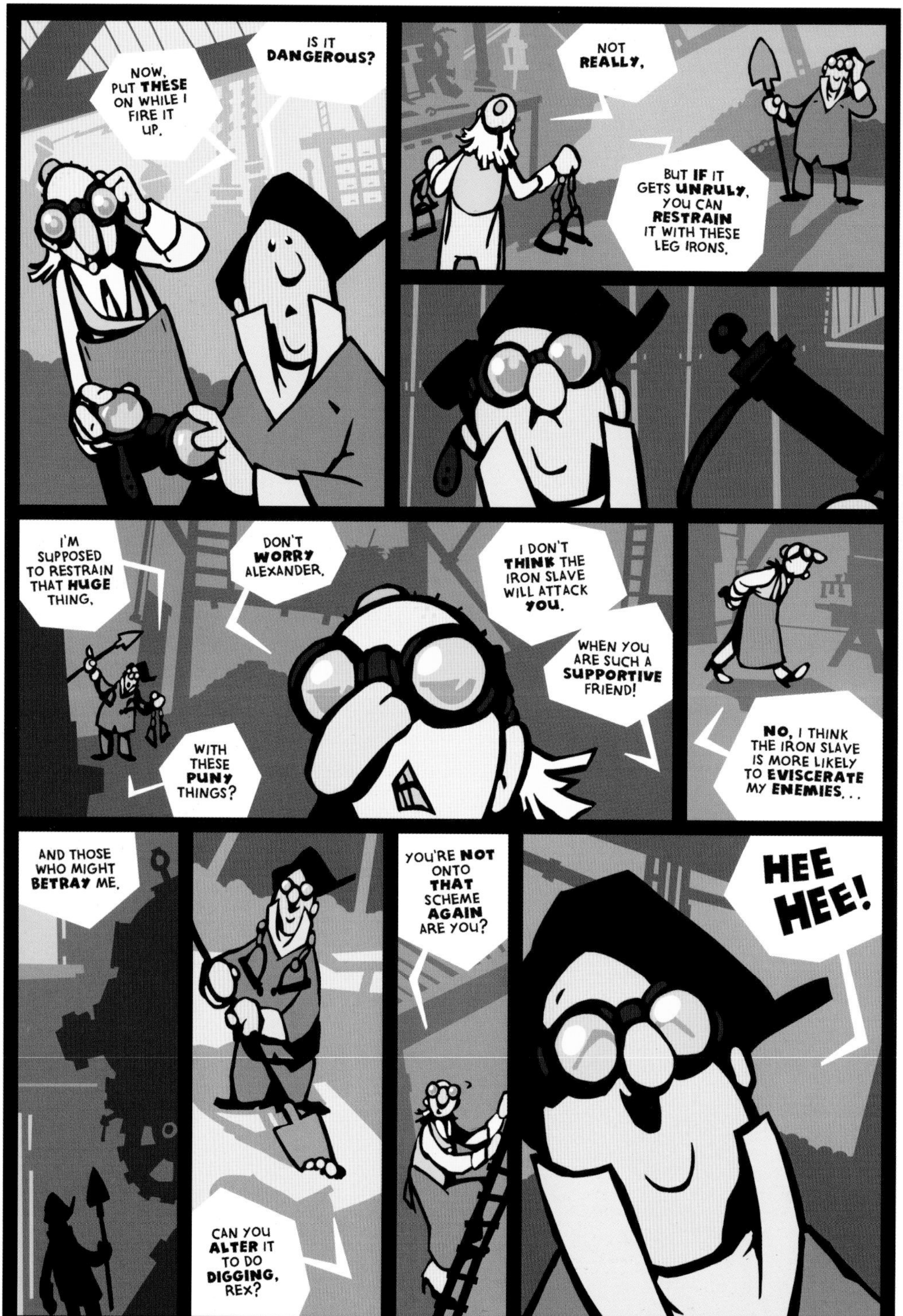
NOW, PUT THESE ON WHILE I FIRE IT UP.
IS IT DANGEROUS?
NOT REALLY.
BUT IF IT GETS UNRULY, YOU CAN RESTRAIN IT WITH THESE LEG IRONS.
I'M SUPPOSED TO RESTRAIN THAT HUGE THING.
WITH THESE PUNY THINGS?
DON'T WORRY ALEXANDER.
I DON'T THINK THE IRON SLAVE WILL ATTACK YOU.
WHEN YOU ARE SUCH A SUPPORTIVE FRIEND!
NO, I THINK THE IRON SLAVE IS MORE LIKELY TO EVISCERATE MY ENEMIES. . .
AND THOSE WHO MIGHT BETRAY ME.
CAN YOU ALTER IT TO DO DIGGING, REX?
YOU'RE NOT ONTO THAT SCHEME AGAIN ARE YOU?
HEE HEE!

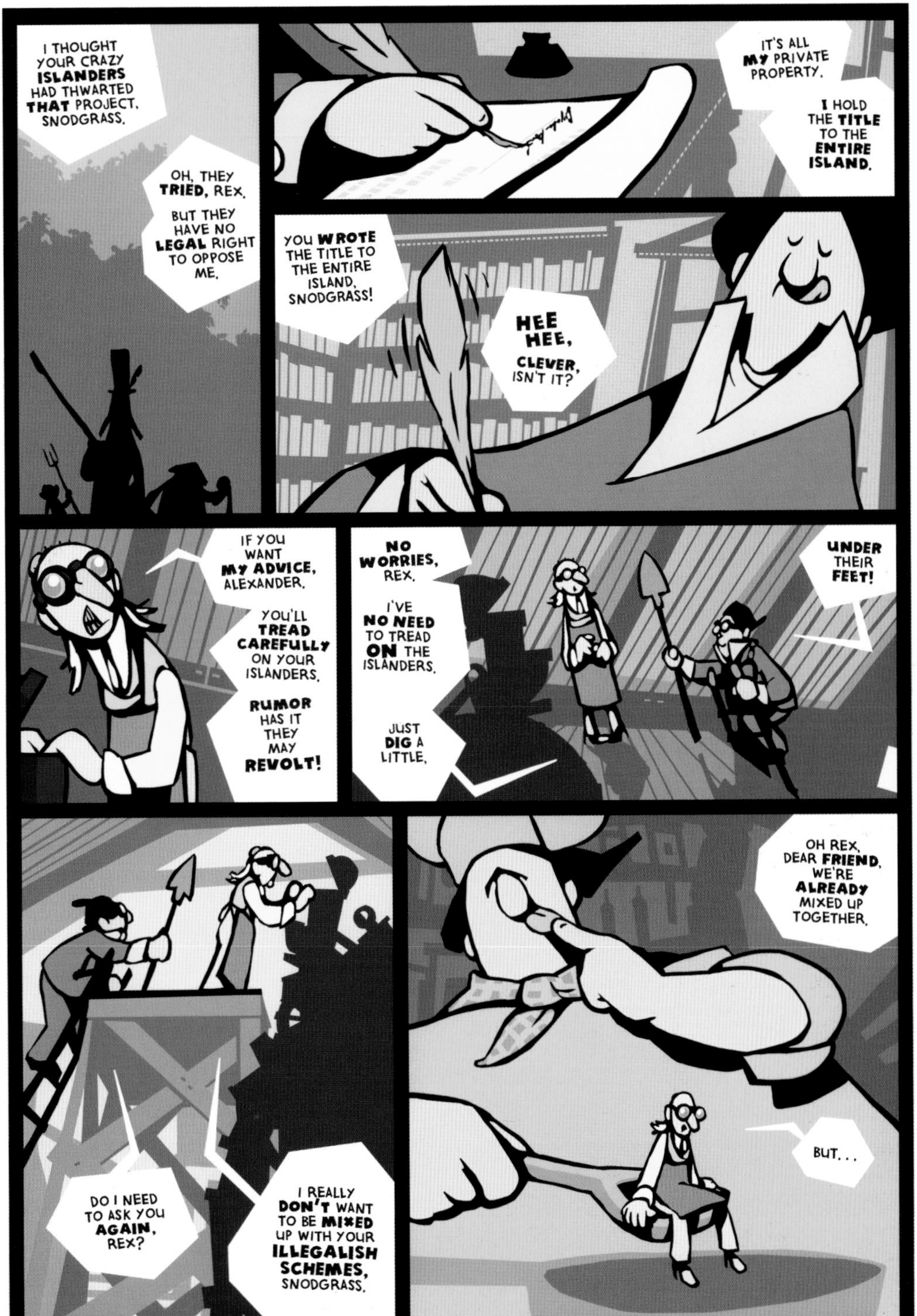

I THOUGHT YOUR CRAZY ISLANDERS HAD THWARTED THAT PROJECT, SNODGRASS.
OH, THEY TRIED, REX.
BUT THEY HAVE NO LEGAL RIGHT TO OPPOSE ME.
IT'S ALL MY PRIVATE PROPERTY.
I HOLD THE TITLE TO THE ENTIRE ISLAND.
YOU WROTE THE TITLE TO THE ENTIRE ISLAND, SNODGRASS!
HEE HEE, CLEVER, ISN'T IT?
IF YOU WANT MY ADVICE, ALEXANDER,
YOU'LL TREAD CAREFULLY ON YOUR ISLANDERS.
RUMOR HAS IT THEY MAY REVOLT!
NO WORRIES, REX.
I'VE NO NEED TO TREAD ON THE ISLANDERS.
JUST DIG A LITTLE,
UNDER THEIR FEET!
DO I NEED TO ASK YOU AGAIN, REX?
I REALLY DON'T WANT TO BE MIXED UP WITH YOUR ILLEGALISH SCHEMES, SNODGRASS.
OH REX, DEAR FRIEND, WE'RE ALREADY MIXED UP TOGETHER.
BUT. . .

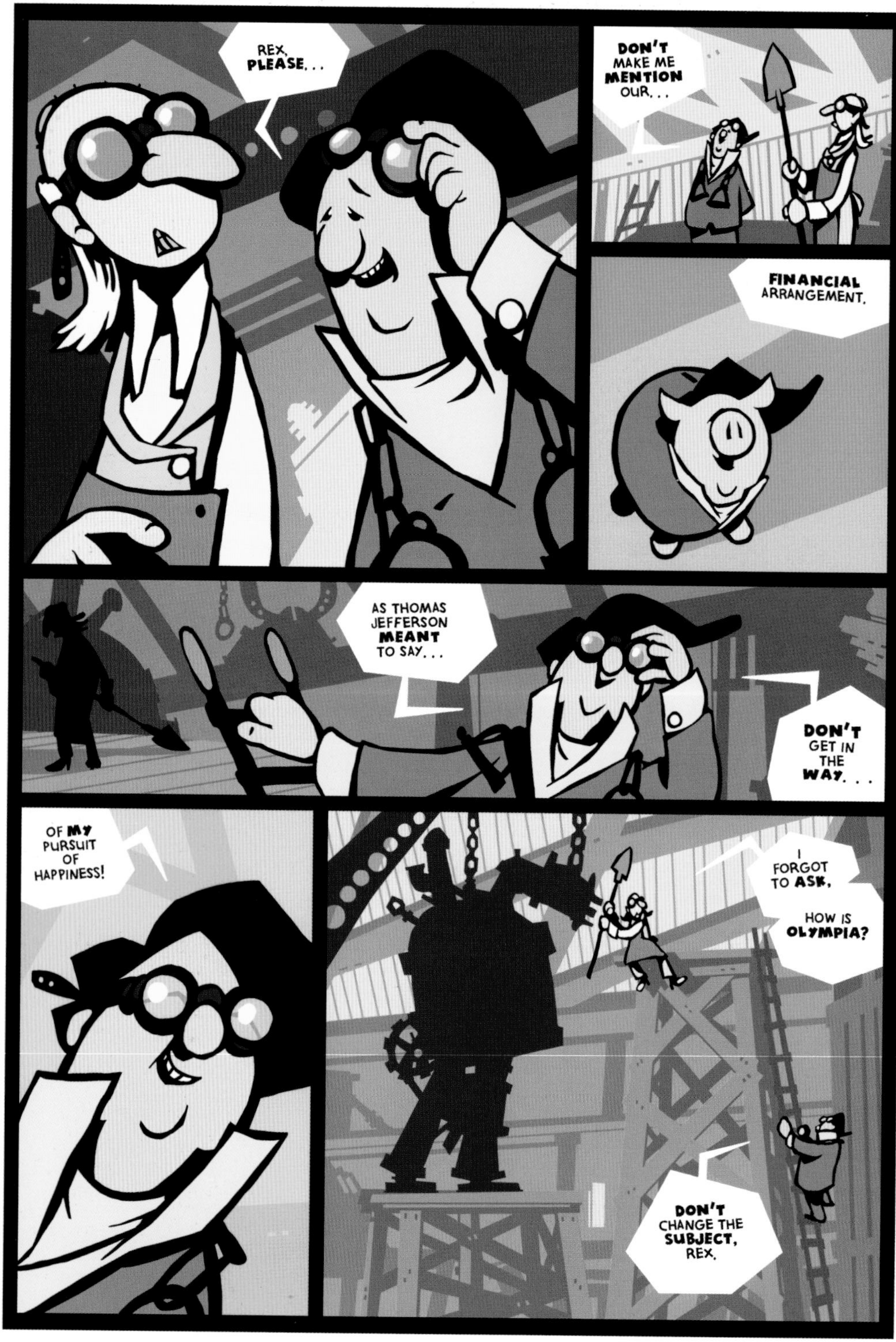
REX, PLEASE. . .
DON'T MAKE ME MENTION OUR. . .
FINANCIAL ARRANGEMENT.
AS THOMAS JEFFERSON MEANT TO SAY. . .
DON'T GET IN THE WAY. . .
OF MY PURSUIT OF HAPPINESS!
I FORGOT TO ASK,
HOW IS OLYMPIA?
DON'T CHANGE THE SUBJECT, REX.

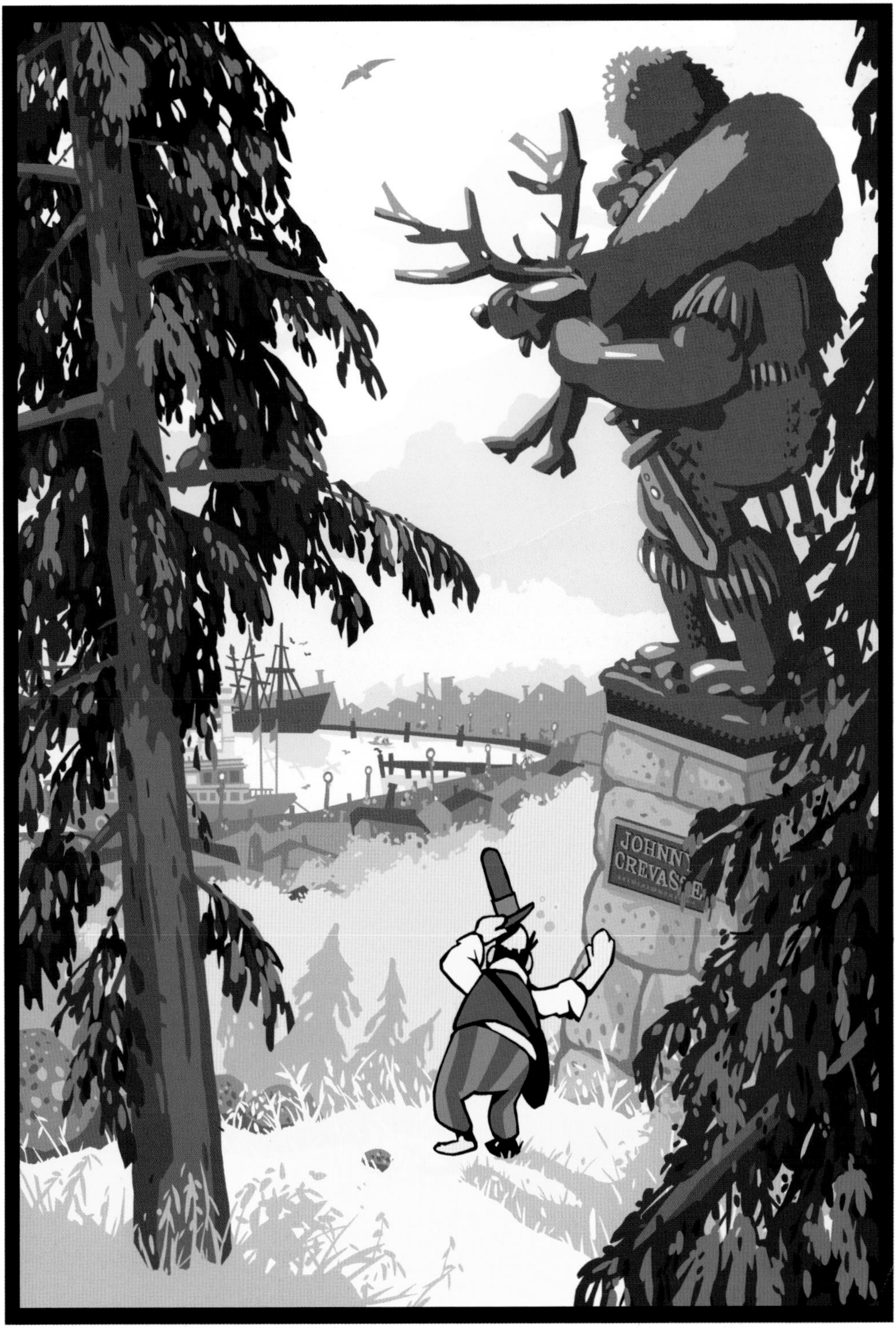
JOHNN
CREVASSE

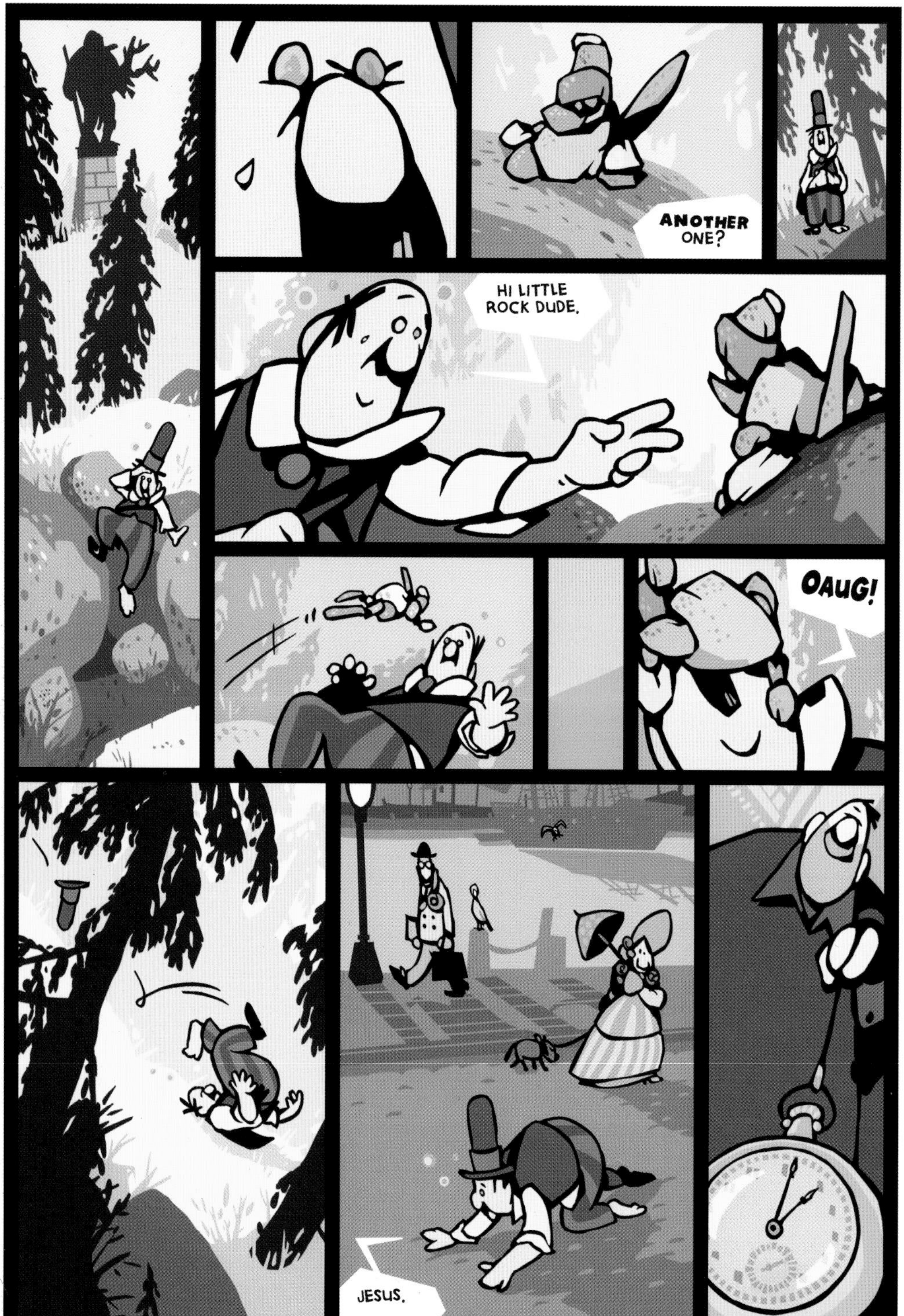
ANOTHER ONE?
HI LITTLE ROCK DUDE.
OAUG!
JESUS.

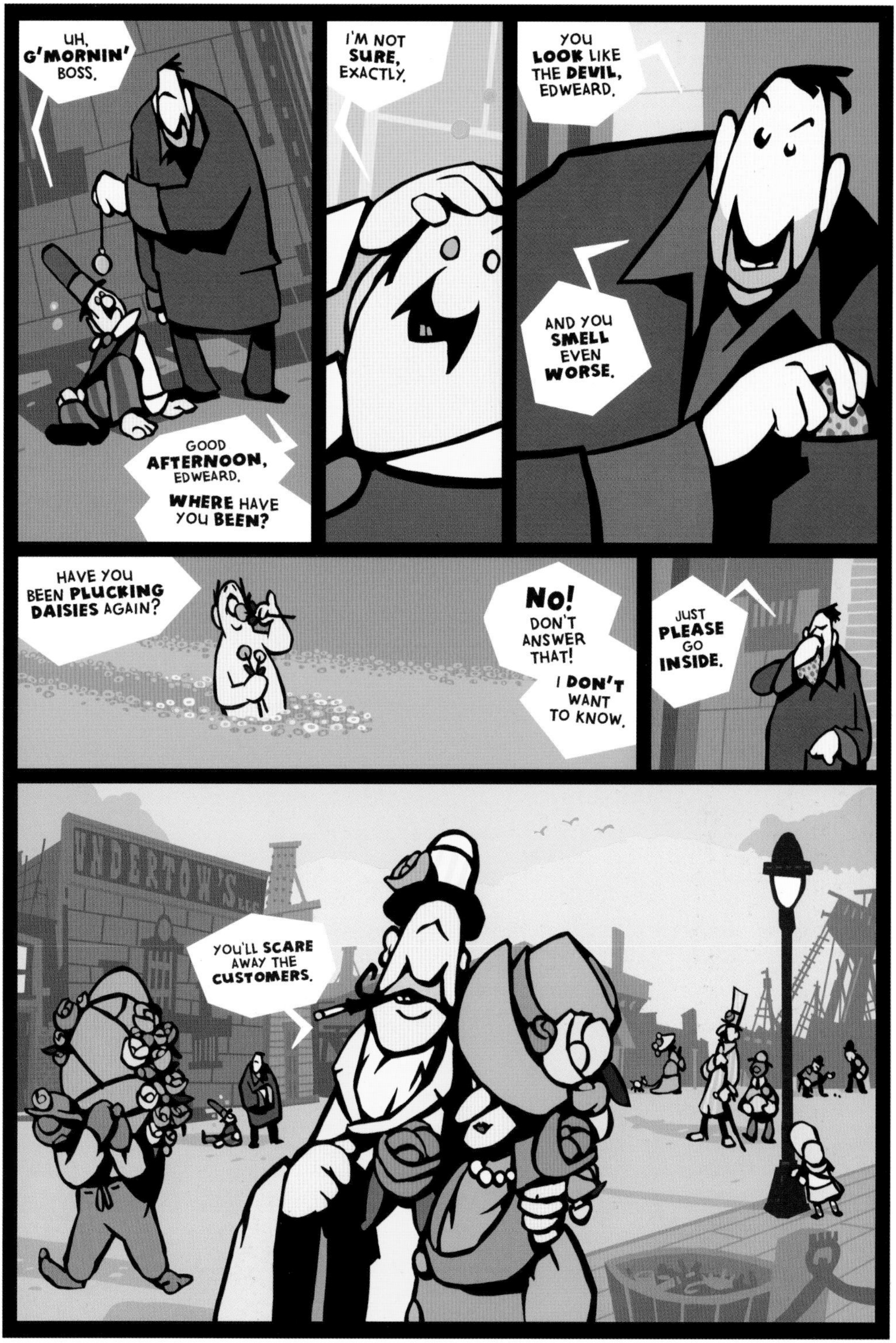
UH, G'MORNIN' BOSS.
GOOD AFTERNOON, EDWEARD.
WHERE HAVE YOU BEEN?
I'M NOT SURE, EXACTLY.
YOU LOOK LIKE THE DEVIL, EDWEARD.
AND YOU SMELL EVEN WORSE.
HAVE YOU BEEN PLUCKING DAISIES AGAIN?
NO! DON'T ANSWER THAT!
I DON'T WANT TO KNOW.
JUST PLEASE GO INSIDE.
UNDERTOW'S
YOU'LL SCARE AWAY THE CUSTOMERS.

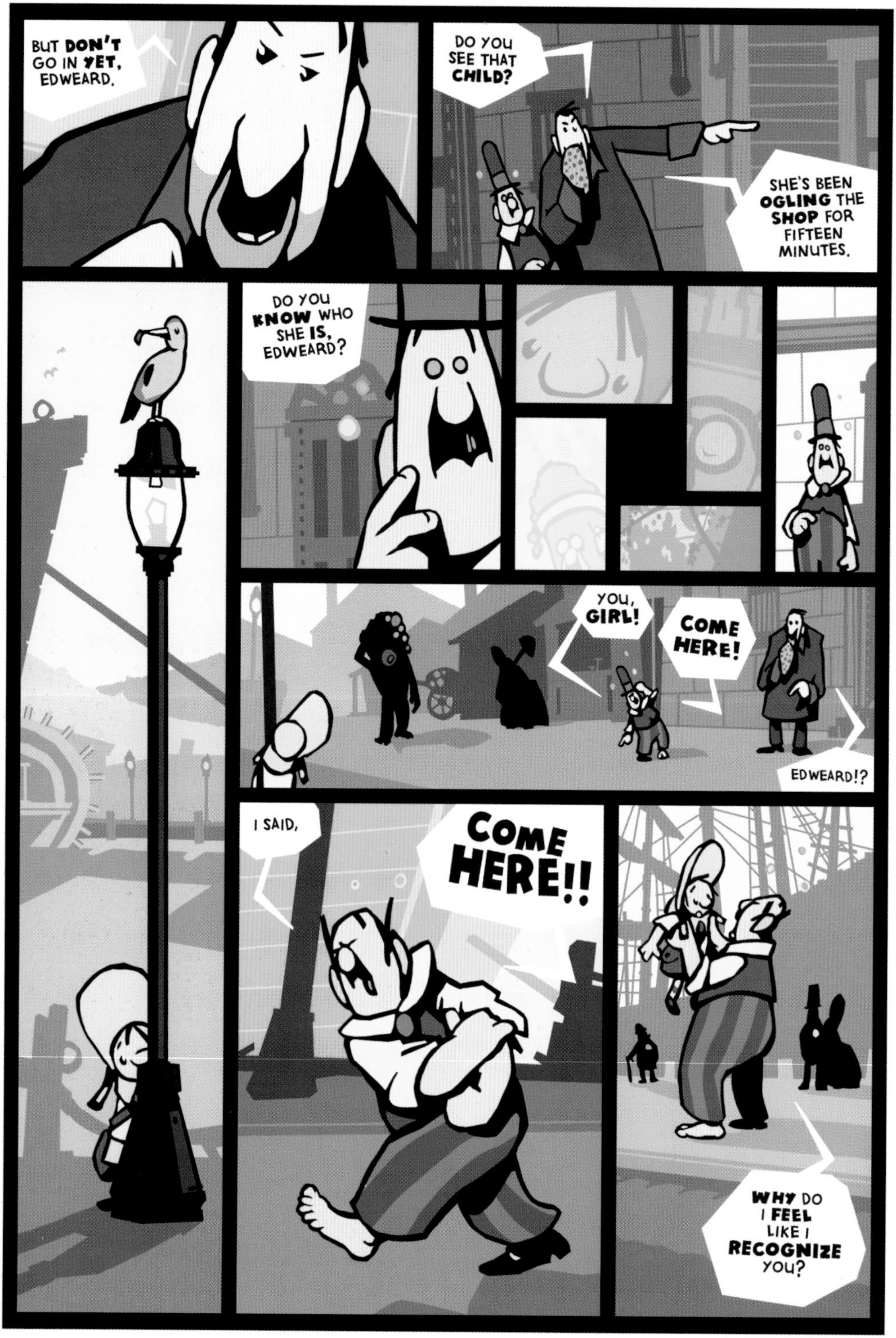
BUT DON'T GO IN YET, EDWEARD.
DO YOU SEE THAT CHILD?
SHE'S BEEN OGLING THE SHOP FOR FIFTEEN MINUTES.
DO YOU KNOW WHO SHE IS, EDWEARD?
YOU, GIRL!
COME HERE!
EDWEARD!?
I SAID,
COME HERE!!
WHY DO I FEEL LIKE I RECOGNIZE YOU?

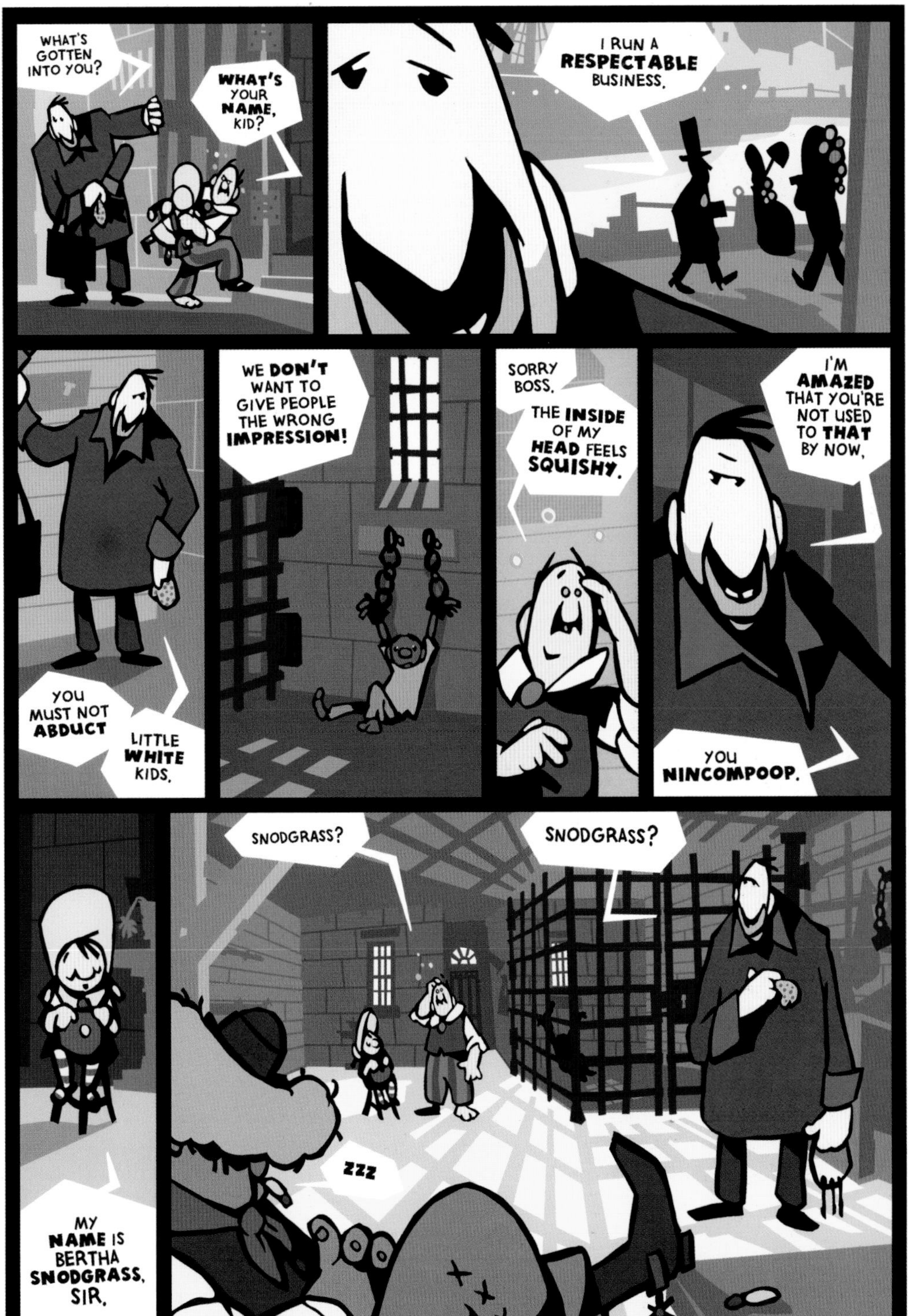
WHAT'S GOTTEN INTO YOU?
WHAT'S YOUR NAME, KID?
I RUN A RESPECTABLE BUSINESS.
YOU MUST NOT ABDUCT
LITTLE WHITE KIDS.
WE DON'T WANT TO GIVE PEOPLE THE WRONG IMPRESSION!
SORRY BOSS.
THE INSIDE OF MY HEAD FEELS SQUISHY.
I'M AMAZED THAT YOU'RE NOT USED TO THAT BY NOW.
YOU NINCOMPOOP.
MY NAME IS BERTHA SNODGRASS, SIR.
SNODGRASS?
SNODGRASS?
ZZZ

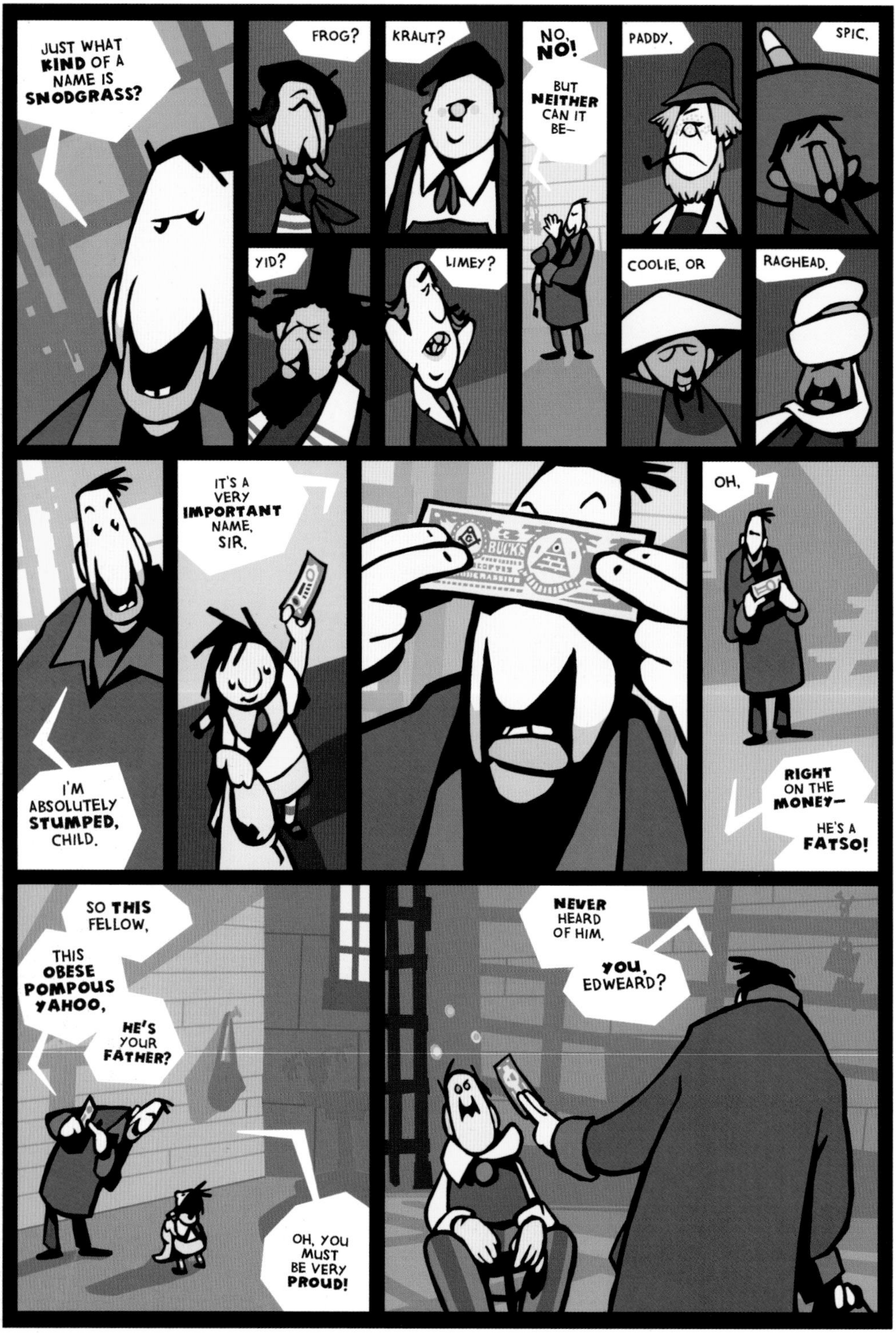
JUST WHAT KIND OF A NAME IS SNODGRASS?
FROG?
KRAUT?
NO, NO!
BUT NEITHER CAN IT BE–
PADDY,
SPIC,
YID?
LIMEY?
COOLIE, OR
RAGHEAD,
I'M ABSOLUTELY STUMPED, CHILD.
IT'S A VERY IMPORTANT NAME, SIR.
OH,
RIGHT ON THE MONEY–
HE'S A FATSO!
SO THIS FELLOW,
THIS OBESE POMPOUS YAHOO,
HE'S YOUR FATHER?
OH, YOU MUST BE VERY PROUD!
NEVER HEARD OF HIM.
YOU, EDWEARD?

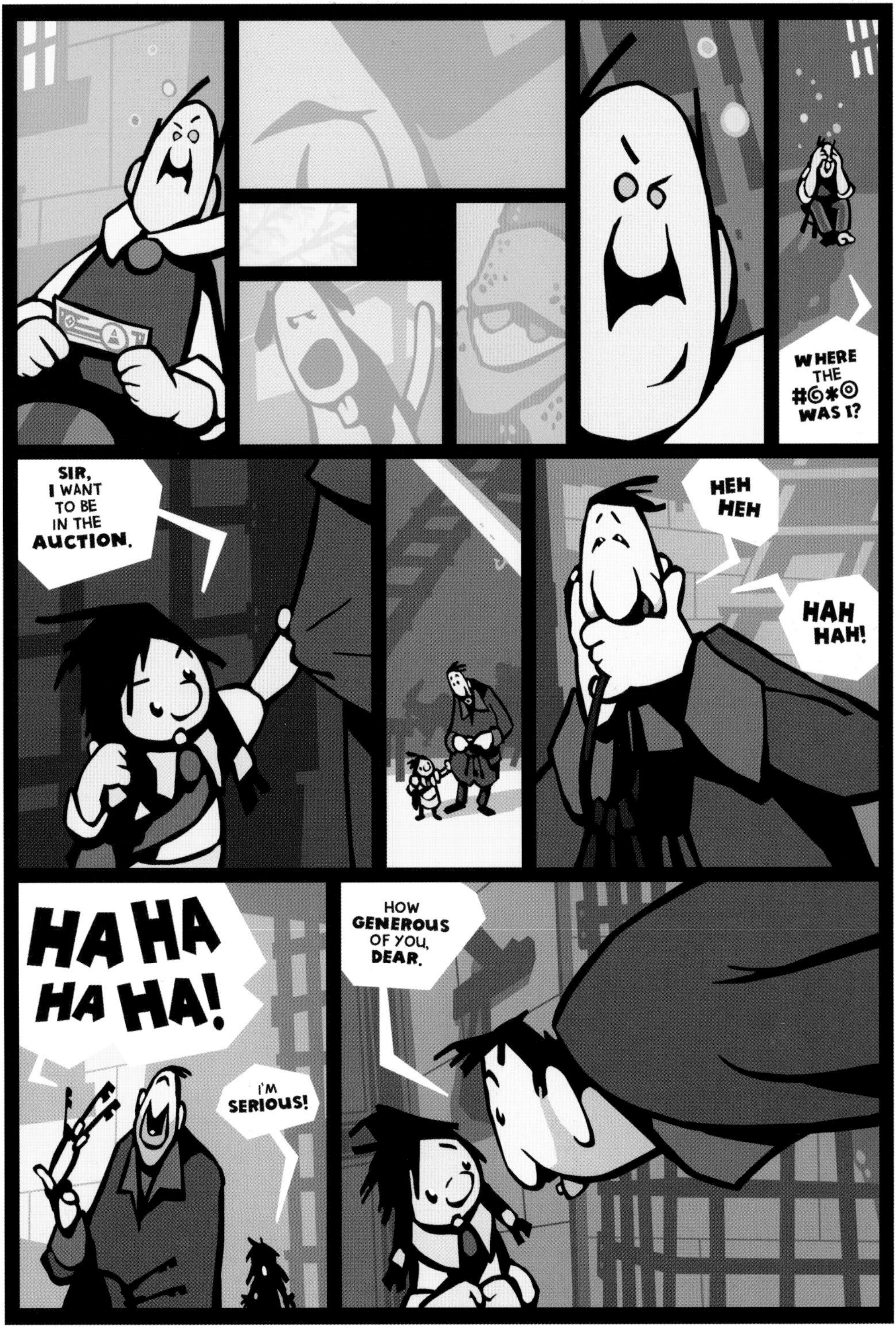
WHERE THE #@*@ WAS I?
SIR, I WANT TO BE IN THE AUCTION.
HEH HEH
HAH HAH!
HA HA HA HA!
I'M SERIOUS!
HOW GENEROUS OF YOU, DEAR.

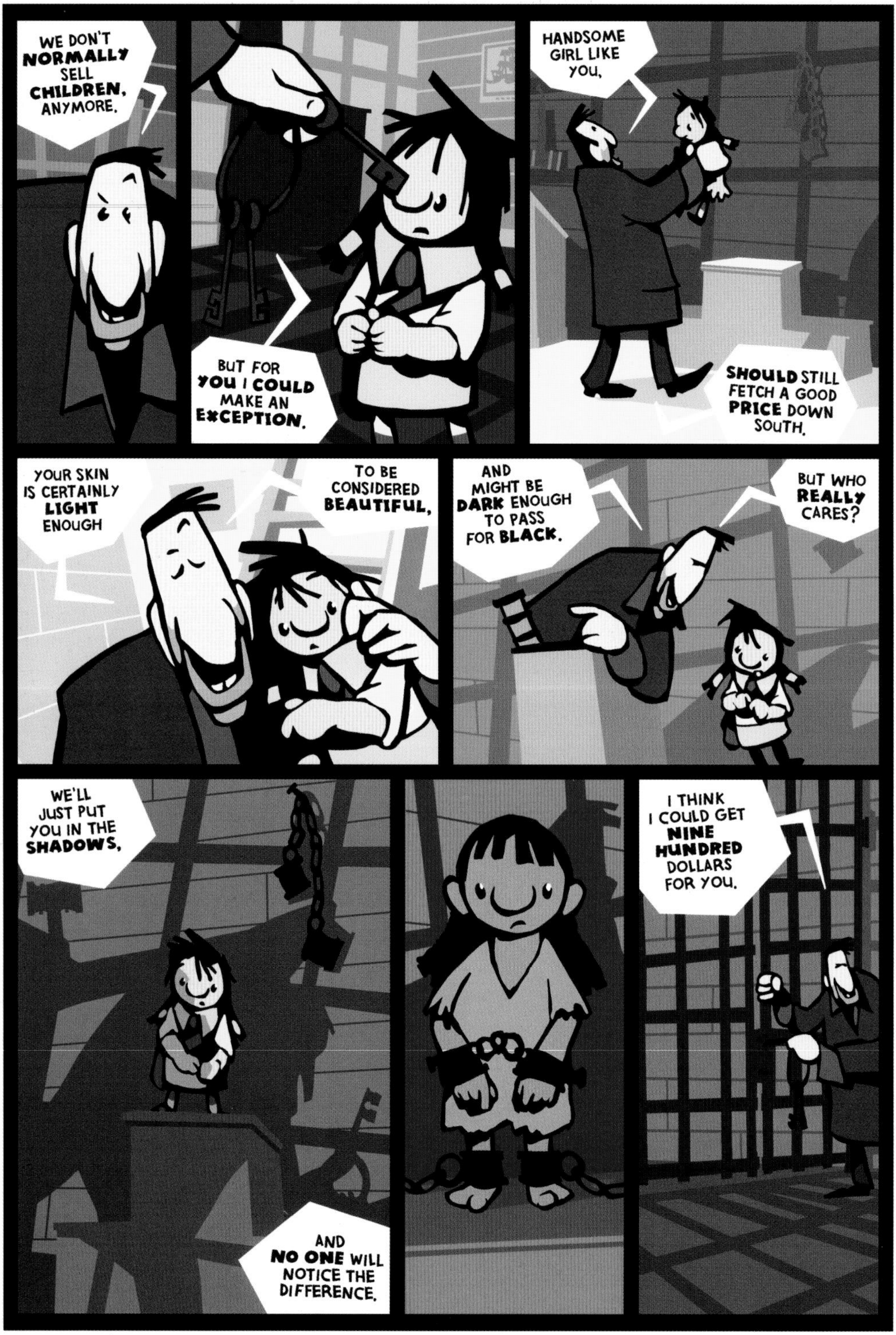
WE DON'T NORMALLY SELL CHILDREN, ANYMORE.
BUT FOR YOU I COULD MAKE AN EXCEPTION.
HANDSOME GIRL LIKE YOU,
SHOULD STILL FETCH A GOOD PRICE DOWN SOUTH.
YOUR SKIN IS CERTAINLY LIGHT ENOUGH
TO BE CONSIDERED BEAUTIFUL,
AND MIGHT BE DARK ENOUGH TO PASS FOR BLACK.
BUT WHO REALLY CARES?
WE'LL JUST PUT YOU IN THE SHADOWS,
AND NO ONE WILL NOTICE THE DIFFERENCE.
I THINK I COULD GET NINE HUNDRED DOLLARS FOR YOU.

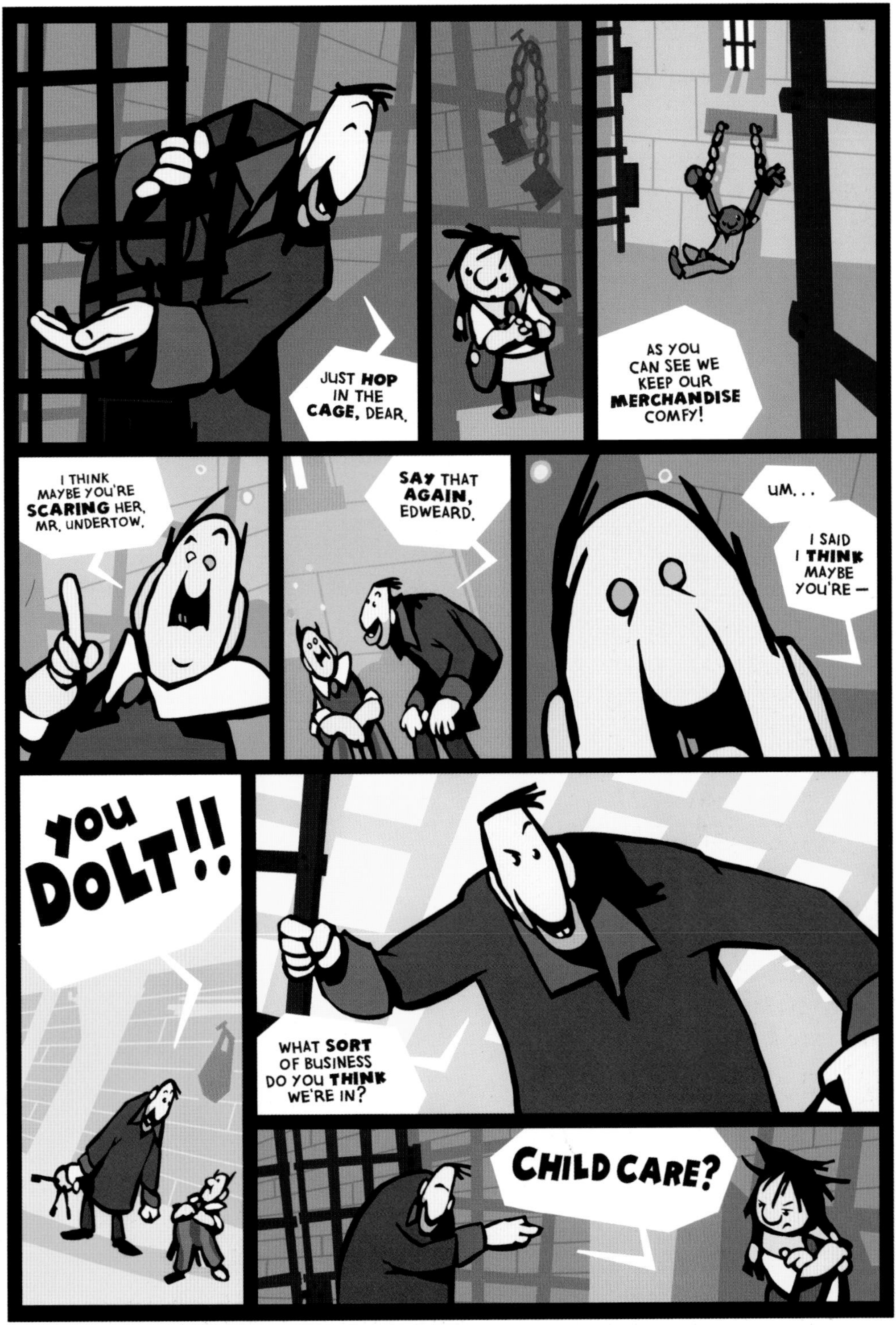
JUST **HOP** IN THE **CAGE**, DEAR.
AS YOU CAN SEE WE KEEP OUR **MERCHANDISE** COMFY!
I THINK MAYBE YOU'RE **SCARING** HER, MR. UNDERTOW.
SAY THAT **AGAIN**, EDWEARD.
UM. . .
I SAID I **THINK** MAYBE YOU'RE —
YOU DOLT!!
WHAT **SORT** OF BUSINESS DO YOU **THINK** WE'RE IN?
CHILD CARE?

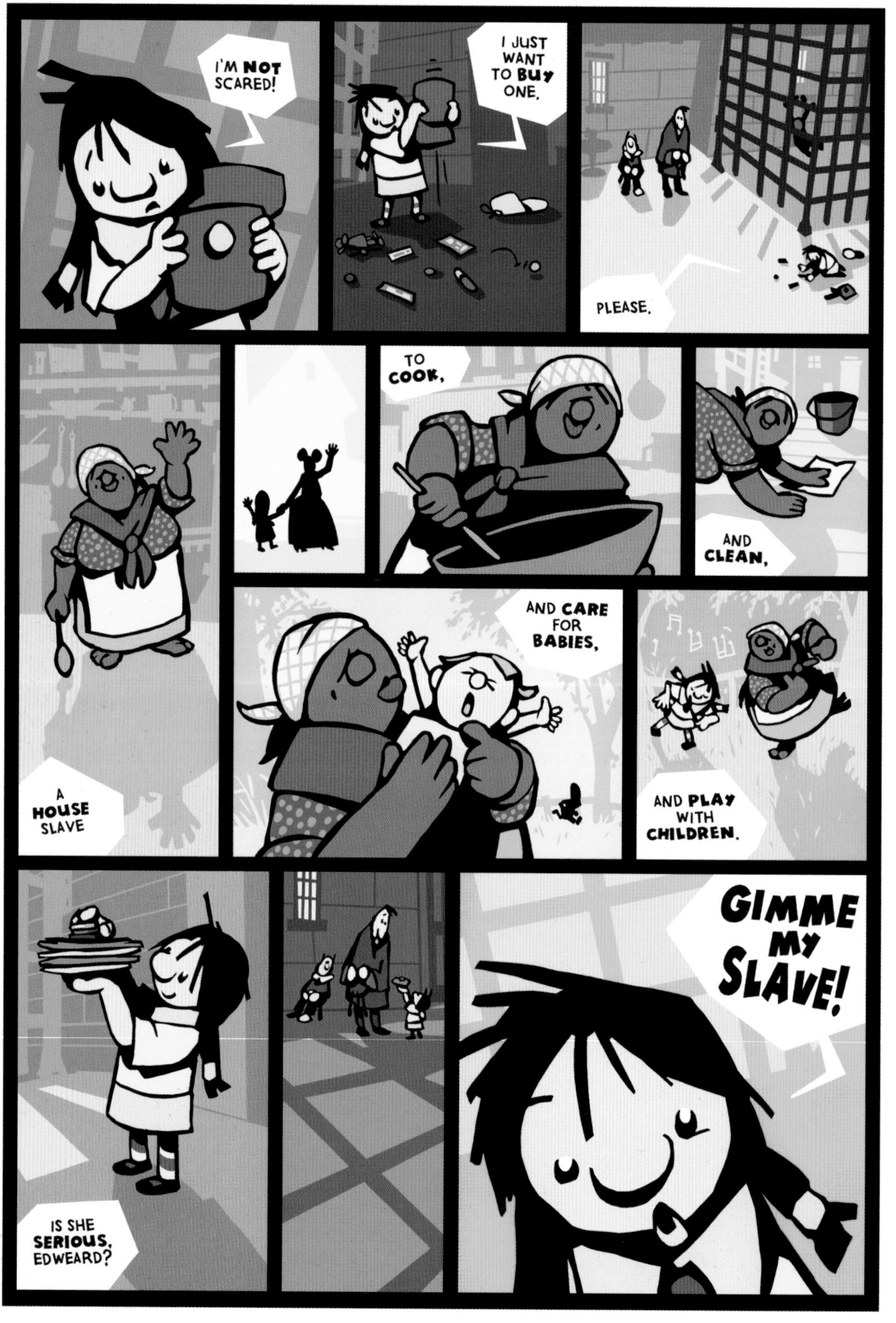
I'M NOT SCARED!
I JUST WANT TO BUY ONE.
PLEASE.
A HOUSE SLAVE
TO COOK,
AND CLEAN,
AND CARE FOR BABIES,
AND PLAY WITH CHILDREN.
IS SHE SERIOUS, EDWEARD?
GIMME MY SLAVE!

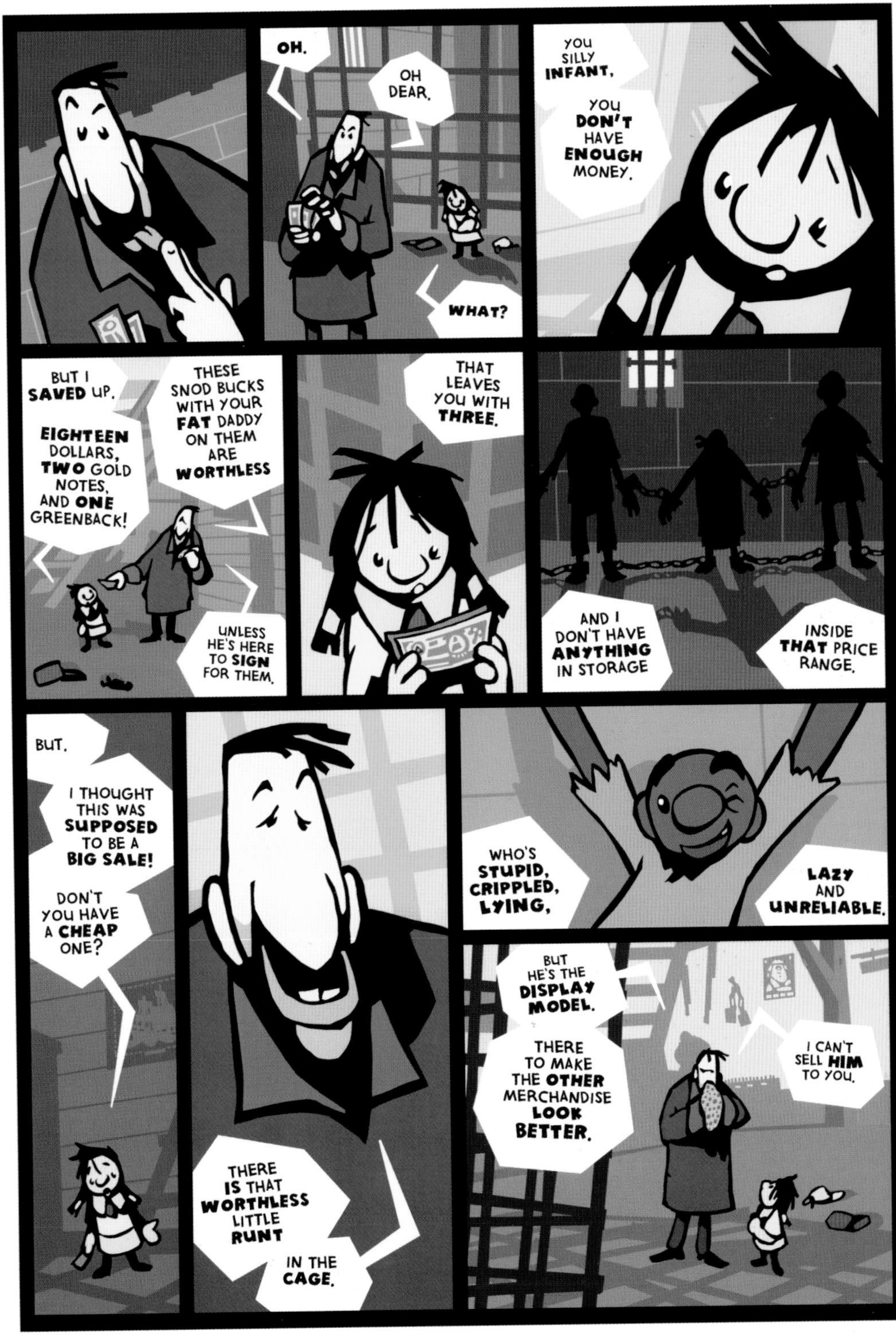
OH.
OH DEAR.
WHAT?
YOU SILLY INFANT,
YOU DON'T HAVE ENOUGH MONEY.
BUT I SAVED UP.
EIGHTEEN DOLLARS, TWO GOLD NOTES, AND ONE GREENBACK!
THESE SNOD BUCKS WITH YOUR FAT DADDY ON THEM ARE WORTHLESS
UNLESS HE'S HERE TO SIGN FOR THEM.
THAT LEAVES YOU WITH THREE.
AND I DON'T HAVE ANYTHING IN STORAGE
INSIDE THAT PRICE RANGE.
BUT.
I THOUGHT THIS WAS SUPPOSED TO BE A BIG SALE!
DON'T YOU HAVE A CHEAP ONE?
THERE IS THAT WORTHLESS LITTLE RUNT
IN THE CAGE.
WHO'S STUPID, CRIPPLED, LYING,
LAZY AND UNRELIABLE.
BUT HE'S THE DISPLAY MODEL.
THERE TO MAKE THE OTHER MERCHANDISE LOOK BETTER.
I CAN'T SELL HIM TO YOU.

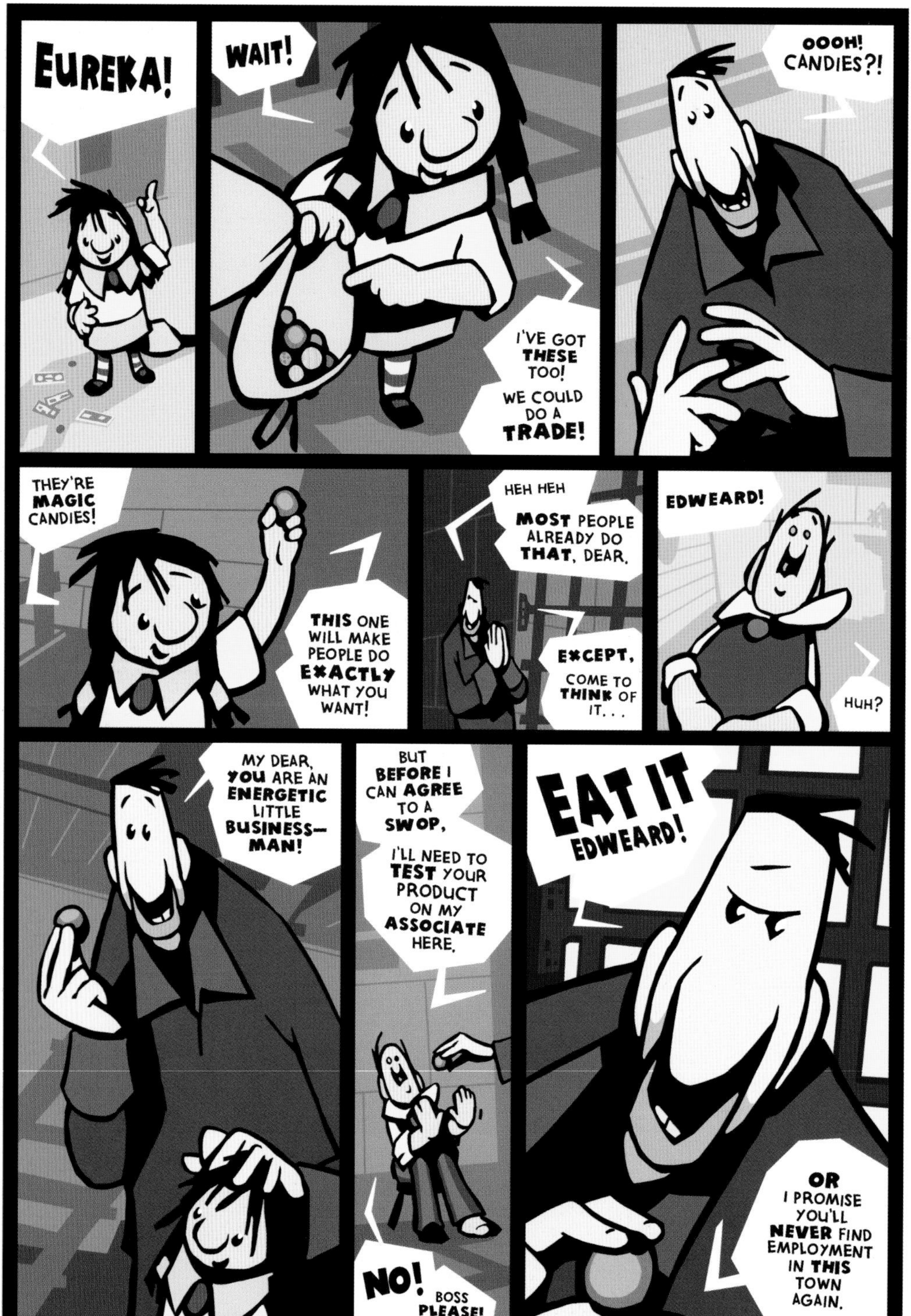
EUREKA!
WAIT!
I'VE GOT THESE TOO!
WE COULD DO A TRADE!
OOOH! CANDIES?!
THEY'RE MAGIC CANDIES!
THIS ONE WILL MAKE PEOPLE DO EXACTLY WHAT YOU WANT!
HEH HEH
MOST PEOPLE ALREADY DO THAT, DEAR.
EXCEPT,
COME TO THINK OF IT. . .
EDWEARD!
HUH?
MY DEAR, YOU ARE AN ENERGETIC LITTLE BUSINESS-MAN!
BUT BEFORE I CAN AGREE TO A SWOP,
I'LL NEED TO TEST YOUR PRODUCT ON MY ASSOCIATE HERE.
NO! BOSS PLEASE!
EAT IT EDWEARD!
OR I PROMISE YOU'LL NEVER FIND EMPLOYMENT IN THIS TOWN AGAIN.

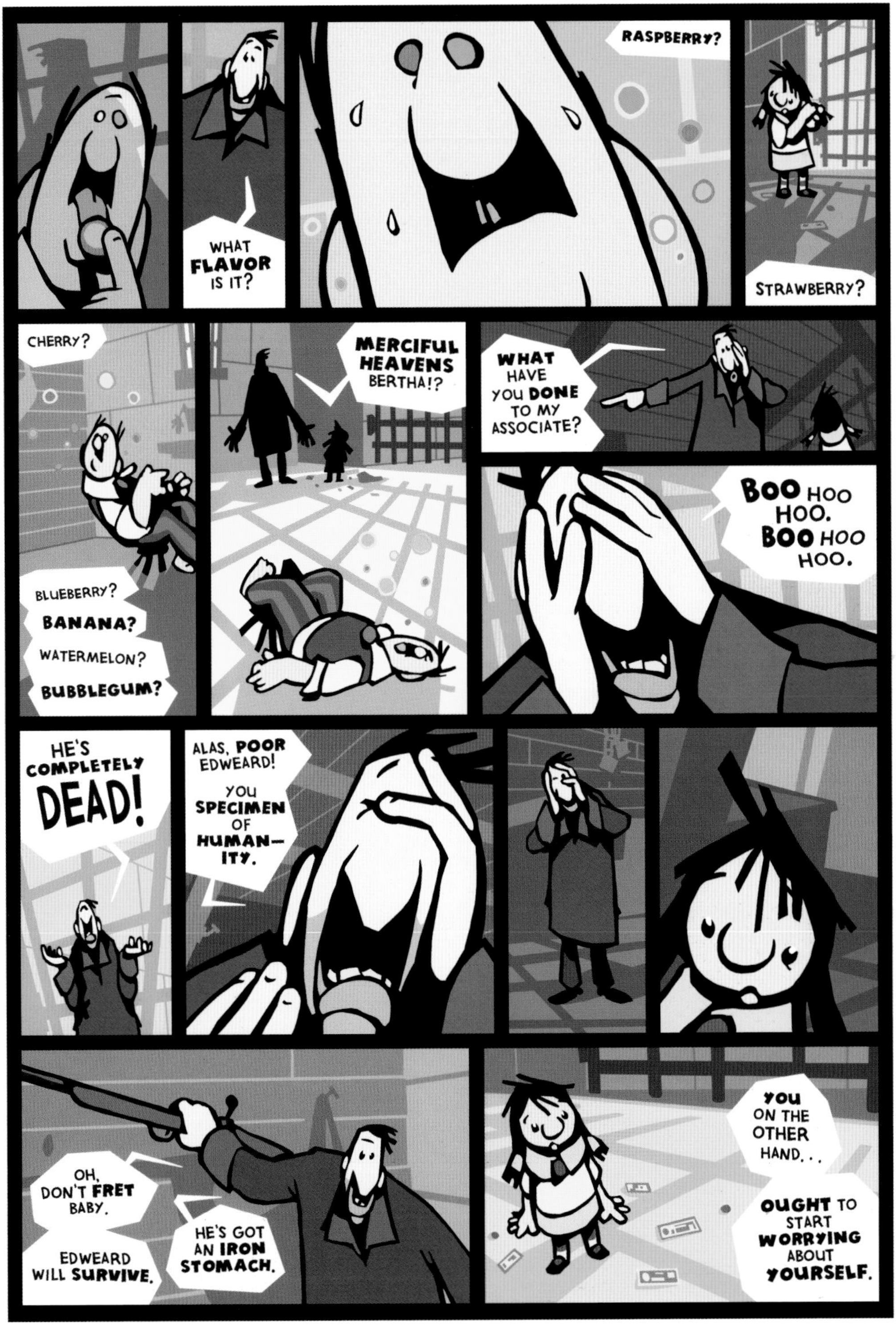
RASPBERRY?
WHAT FLAVOR IS IT?
STRAWBERRY?
CHERRY?
BLUEBERRY?
BANANA?
WATERMELON?
BUBBLEGUM?
MERCIFUL HEAVENS BERTHA!?
WHAT HAVE YOU DONE TO MY ASSOCIATE?
BOO HOO HOO. BOO HOO HOO.
HE'S COMPLETELY DEAD!
ALAS, POOR EDWEARD!
YOU SPECIMEN OF HUMAN-ITY.
OH, DON'T FRET BABY.
EDWEARD WILL SURVIVE.
HE'S GOT AN IRON STOMACH.
YOU ON THE OTHER HAND. . .
OUGHT TO START WORRYING ABOUT YOURSELF.

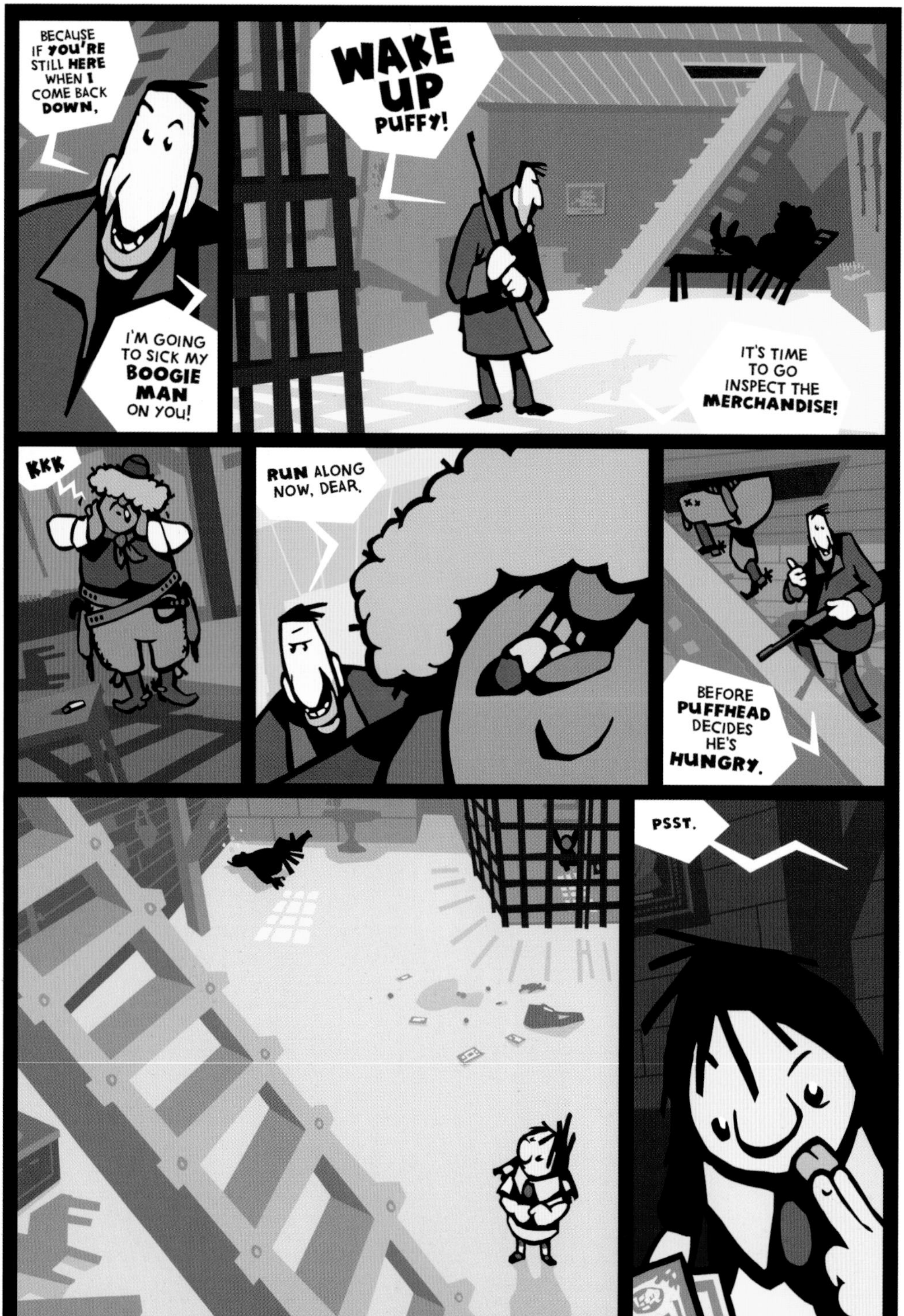
BECAUSE IF YOU'RE STILL HERE WHEN I COME BACK DOWN,
I'M GOING TO SICK MY BOOGIE MAN ON YOU!
WAKE UP PUFFY!
IT'S TIME TO GO INSPECT THE MERCHANDISE!
KKK
RUN ALONG NOW, DEAR.
BEFORE PUFFHEAD DECIDES HE'S HUNGRY.
PSST.

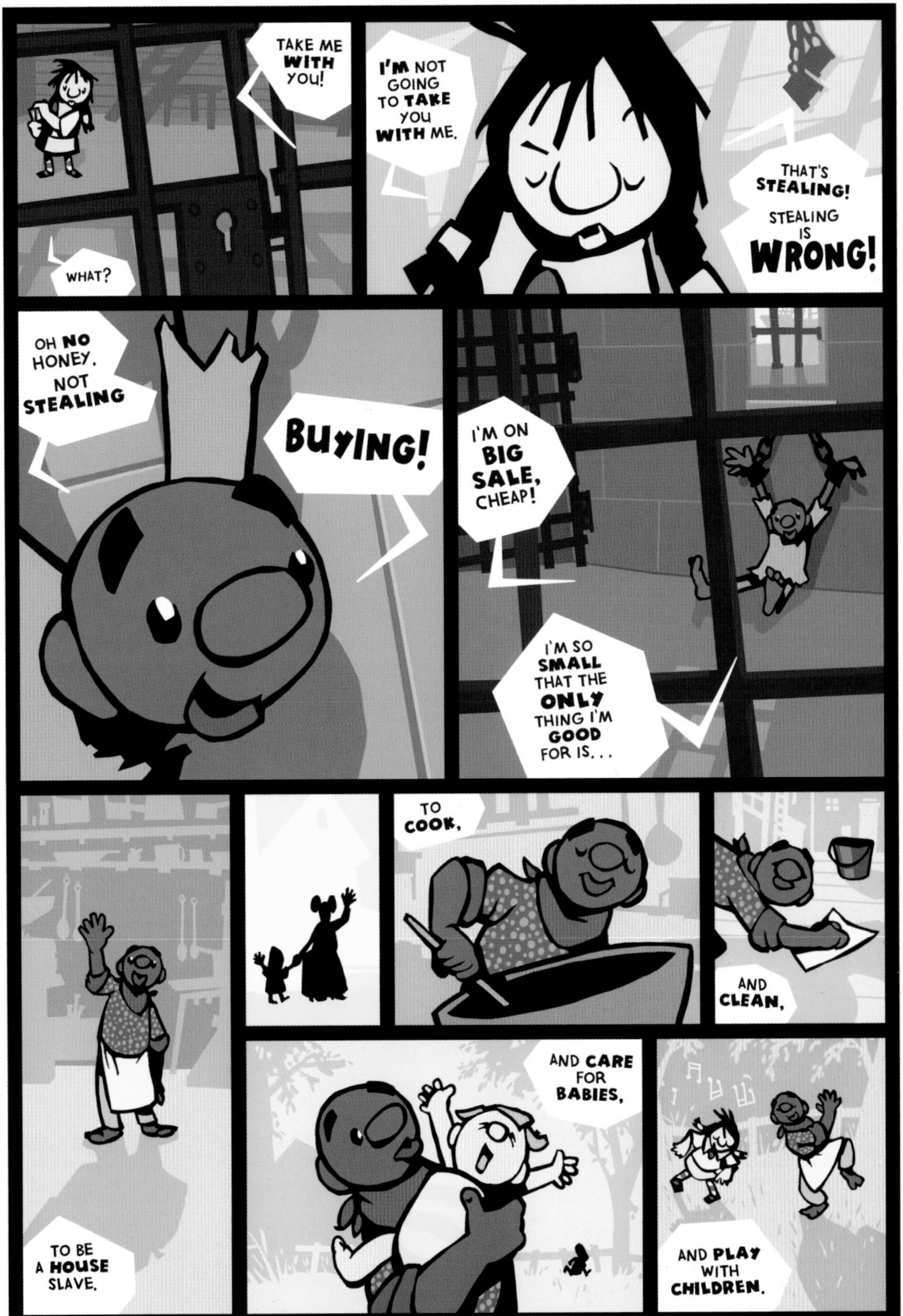

TAKE ME WITH YOU!
WHAT?
I'M NOT GOING TO TAKE YOU WITH ME.
THAT'S STEALING! STEALING IS WRONG!
OH NO HONEY. NOT STEALING
BUYING!
I'M ON BIG SALE, CHEAP!
I'M SO SMALL THAT THE ONLY THING I'M GOOD FOR IS. . .
TO BE A HOUSE SLAVE.
TO COOK,
AND CLEAN,
AND CARE FOR BABIES,
AND PLAY WITH CHILDREN.

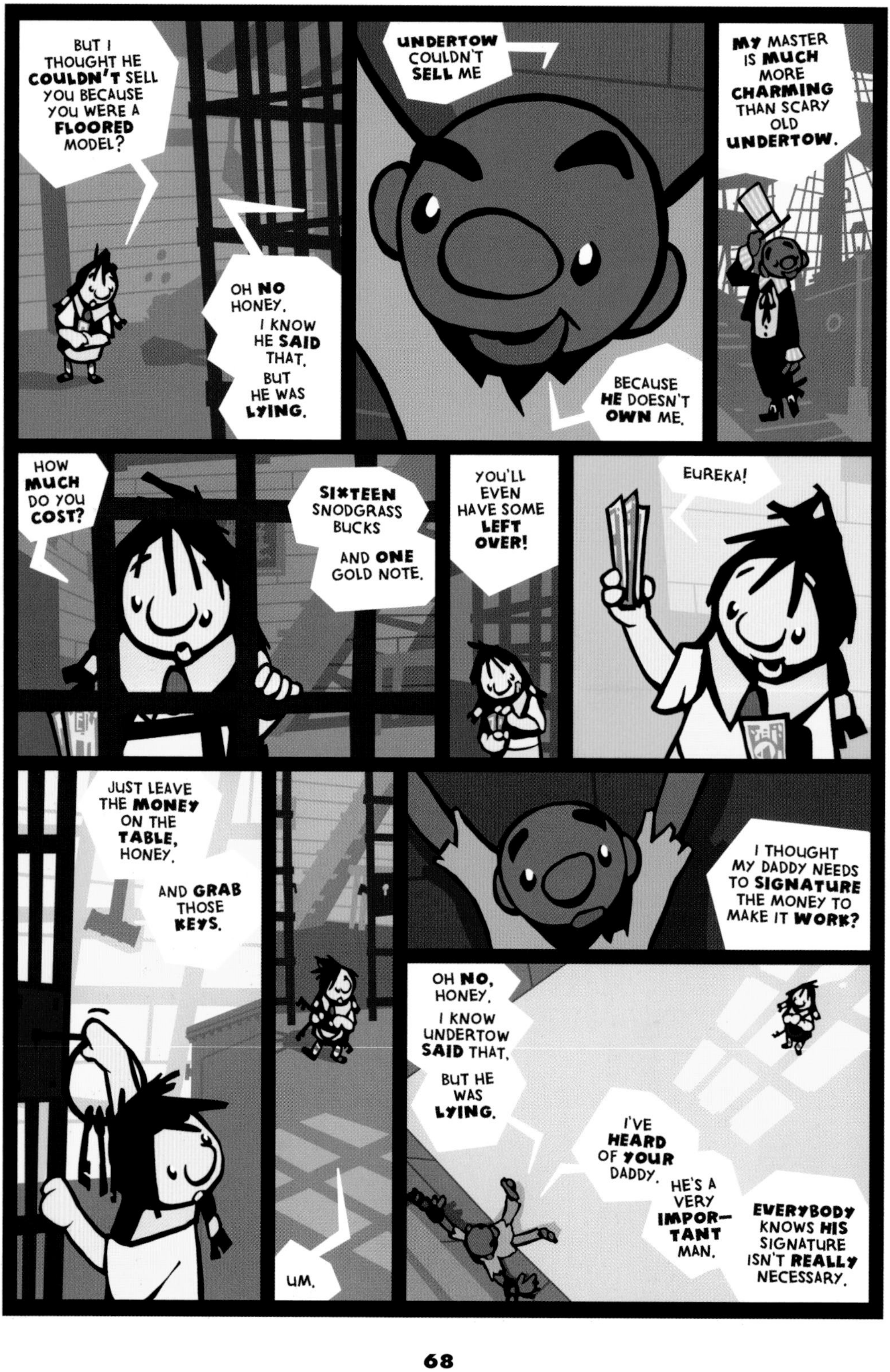

BUT I THOUGHT HE COULDN'T SELL YOU BECAUSE YOU WERE A FLOORED MODEL?
OH NO HONEY.
I KNOW HE SAID THAT.
BUT HE WAS LYING.
UNDERTOW COULDN'T SELL ME
BECAUSE HE DOESN'T OWN ME.
MY MASTER IS MUCH MORE CHARMING THAN SCARY OLD UNDERTOW.
HOW MUCH DO YOU COST?
SIXTEEN SNODGRASS BUCKS
AND ONE GOLD NOTE.
YOU'LL EVEN HAVE SOME LEFT OVER!
EUREKA!
JUST LEAVE THE MONEY ON THE TABLE, HONEY.
AND GRAB THOSE KEYS.
UM.
I THOUGHT MY DADDY NEEDS TO SIGNATURE THE MONEY TO MAKE IT WORK?
OH NO, HONEY.
I KNOW UNDERTOW SAID THAT,
BUT HE WAS LYING.
I'VE HEARD OF YOUR DADDY.
HE'S A VERY IMPOR-TANT MAN.
EVERYBODY KNOWS HIS SIGNATURE ISN'T REALLY NECESSARY.

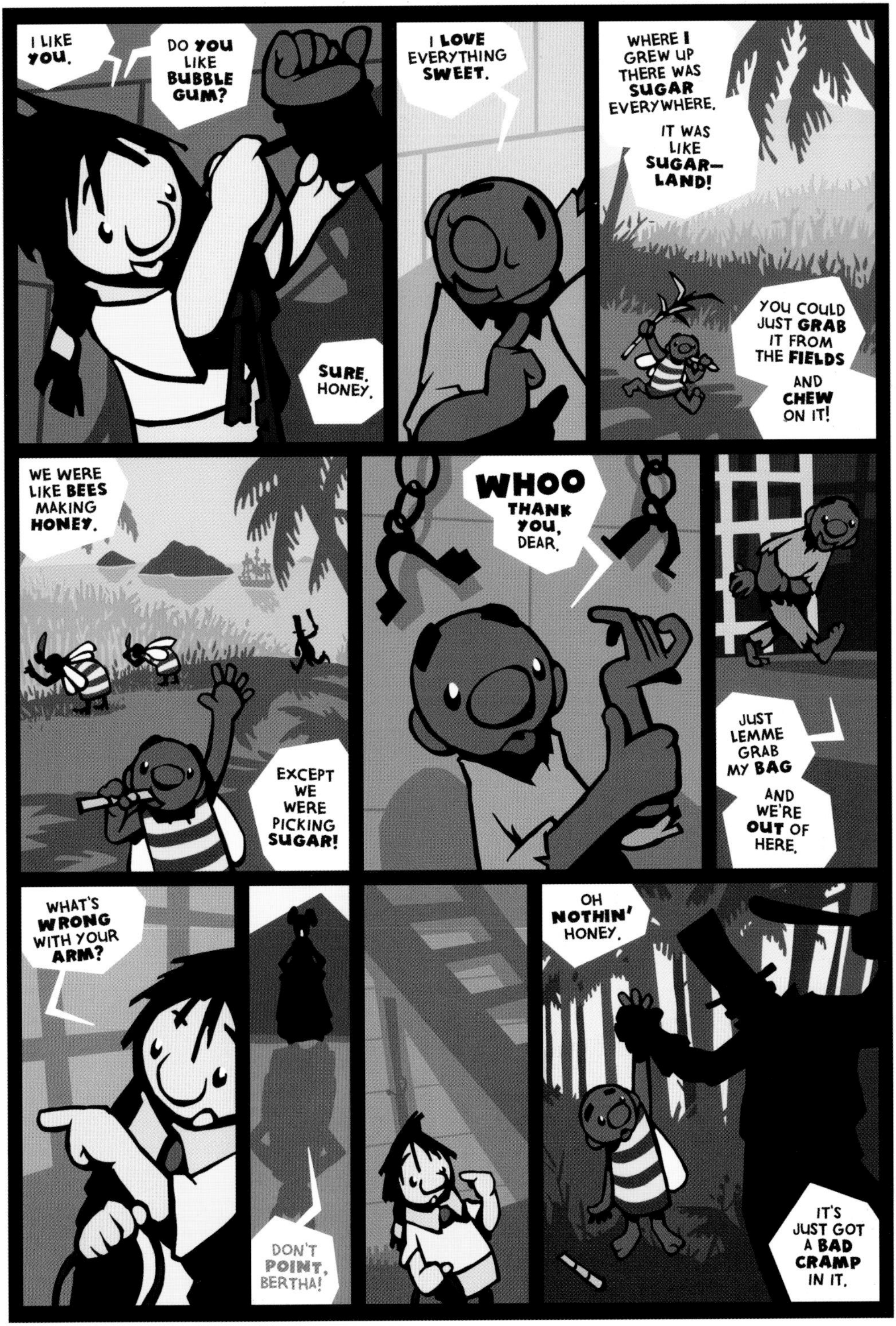

I LIKE YOU.
DO YOU LIKE BUBBLE GUM?
SURE. HONEY.
I LOVE EVERYTHING SWEET.
WHERE I GREW UP THERE WAS SUGAR EVERYWHERE.
IT WAS LIKE SUGAR-LAND!
YOU COULD JUST GRAB IT FROM THE FIELDS
AND CHEW ON IT!
WE WERE LIKE BEES MAKING HONEY.
EXCEPT WE WERE PICKING SUGAR!
WHOO
THANK YOU, DEAR.
JUST LEMME GRAB MY BAG
AND WE'RE OUT OF HERE.
WHAT'S WRONG WITH YOUR ARM?
DON'T POINT, BERTHA!
OH NOTHIN' HONEY.
IT'S JUST GOT A BAD CRAMP IN IT.

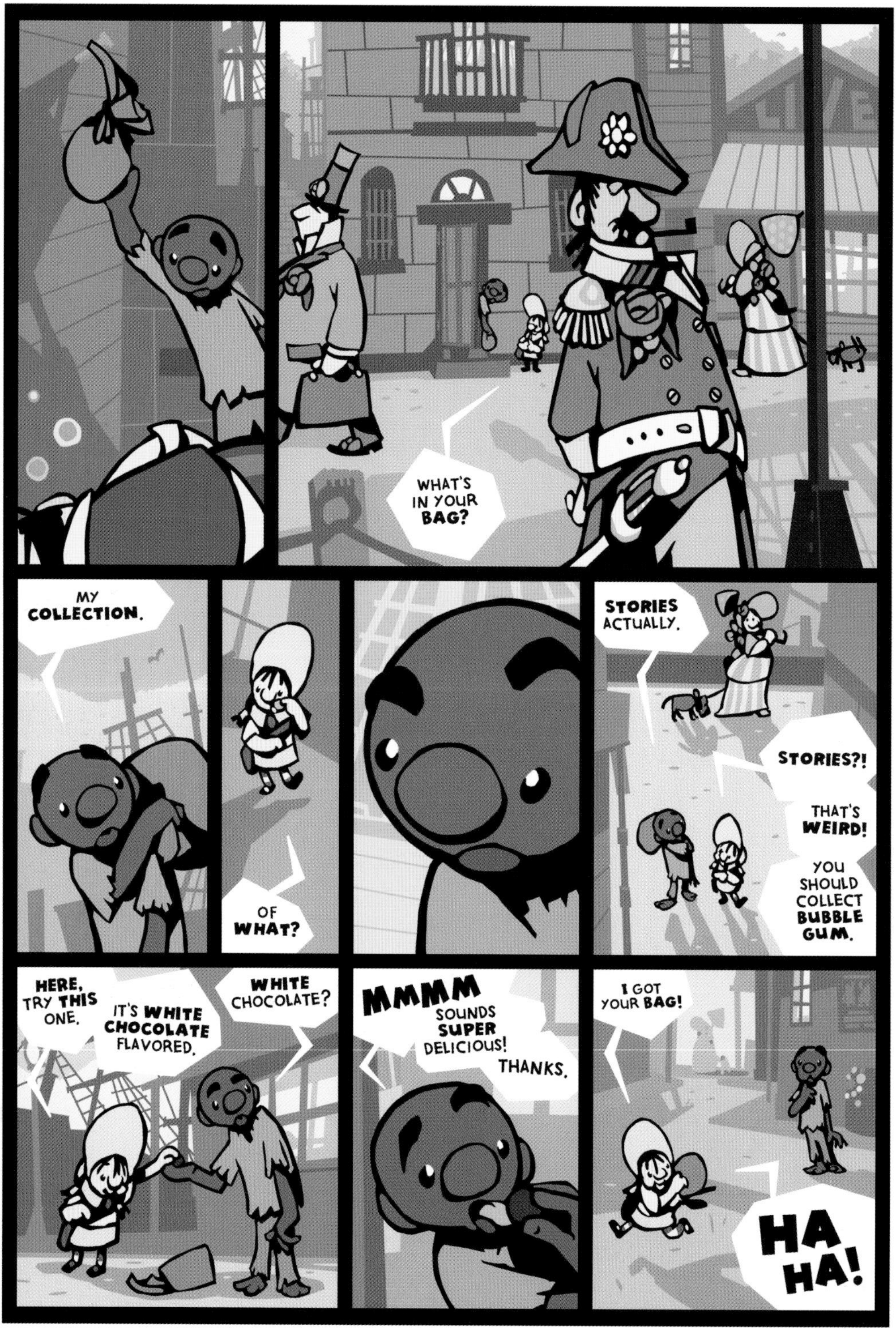
WHAT'S IN YOUR BAG?
MY COLLECTION.
OF WHAT?
STORIES ACTUALLY.
STORIES?!
THAT'S WEIRD!
YOU SHOULD COLLECT BUBBLE GUM.
HERE, TRY THIS ONE.
IT'S WHITE CHOCOLATE FLAVORED.
WHITE CHOCOLATE?
MMMM
SOUNDS SUPER DELICIOUS!
THANKS.
I GOT YOUR BAG!
HA HA!

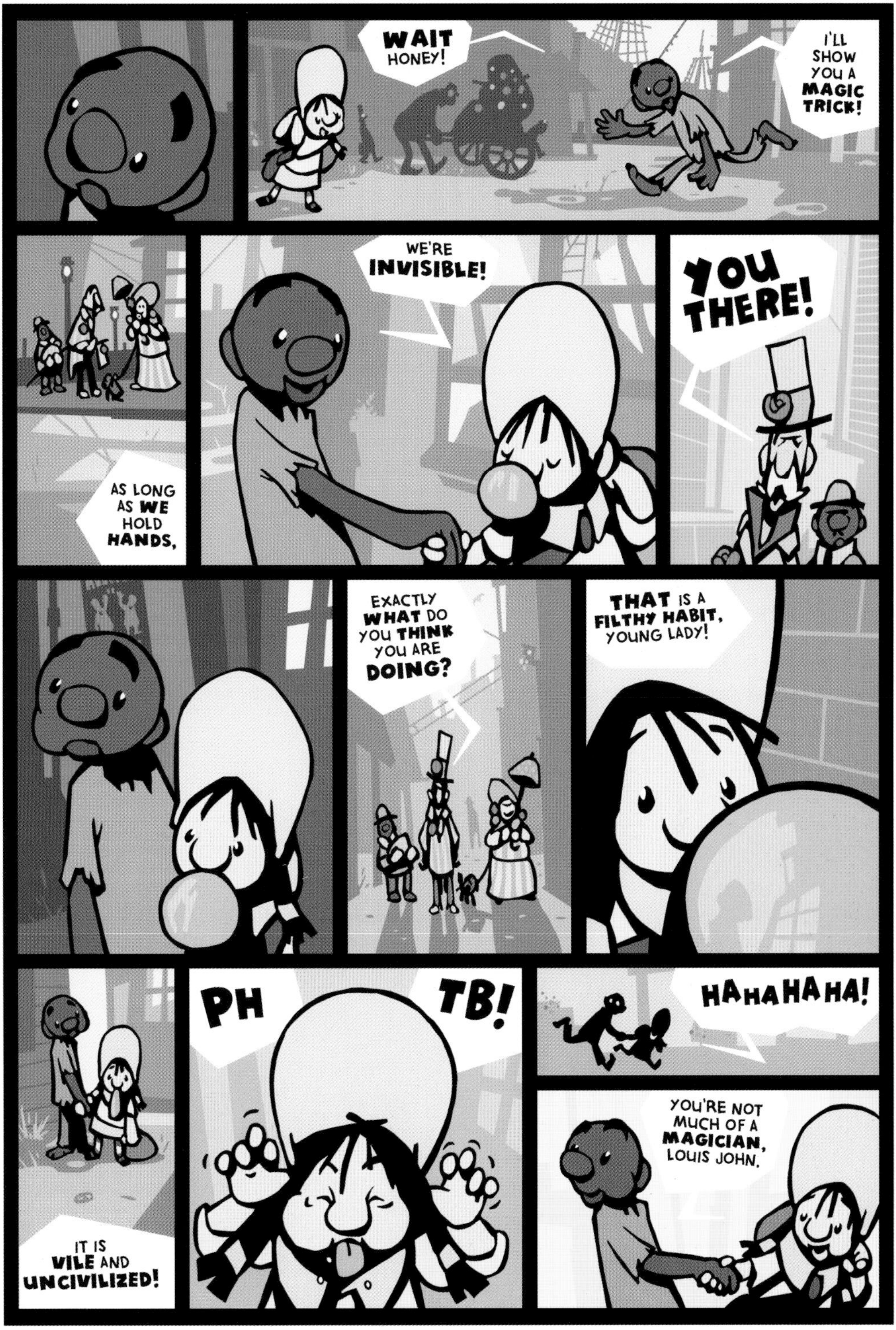

WAIT HONEY!
I'LL SHOW YOU A MAGIC TRICK!
AS LONG AS WE HOLD HANDS,
WE'RE INVISIBLE!
YOU THERE!
EXACTLY WHAT DO YOU THINK YOU ARE DOING?
THAT IS A FILTHY HABIT, YOUNG LADY!
IT IS VILE AND UNCIVILIZED!
PH
TB!
HAHAHAHAHA!
YOU'RE NOT MUCH OF A MAGICIAN, LOUIS JOHN.

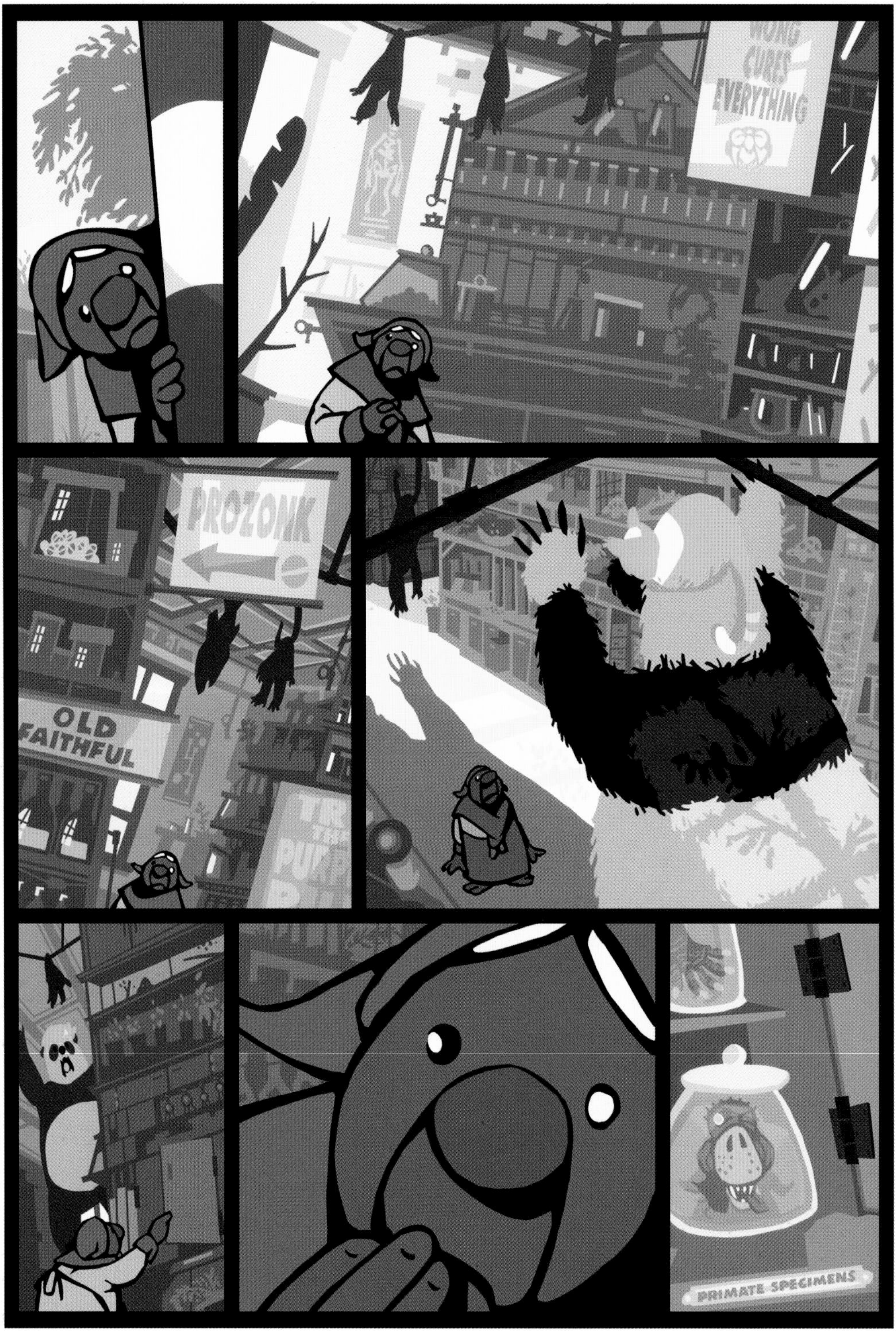
WONG CURES EVERYTHING
PROZONK
OLD FAITHFUL
PRIMATE SPECIMENS

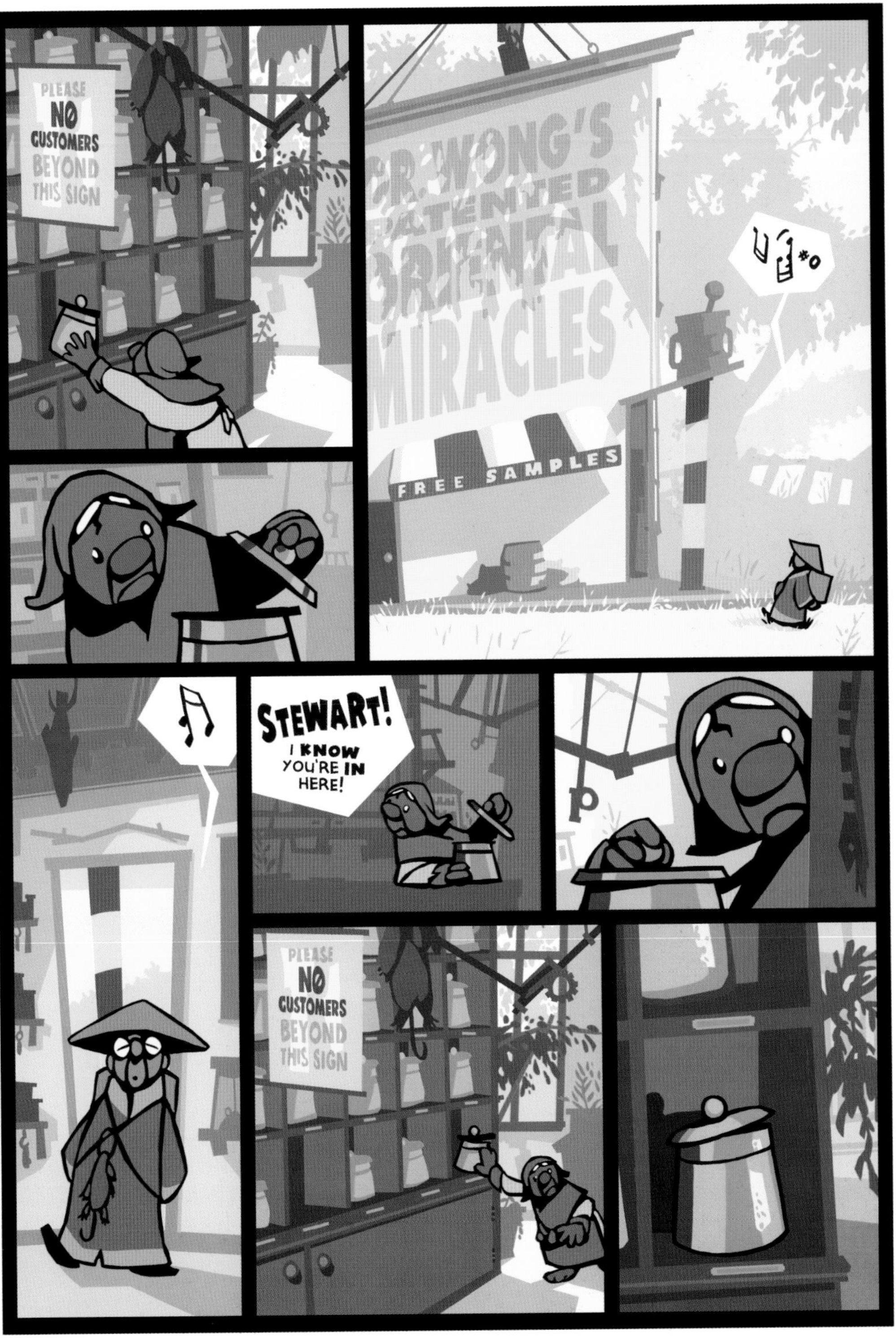
PLEASE
NO
CUSTOMERS
BEYOND
THIS SIGN
DR. WONG'S
PATENTED
ORIENTAL
MIRACLES
FREE SAMPLES
STEWART!
I KNOW YOU'RE IN HERE!
PLEASE
NO
CUSTOMERS
BEYOND
THIS SIGN

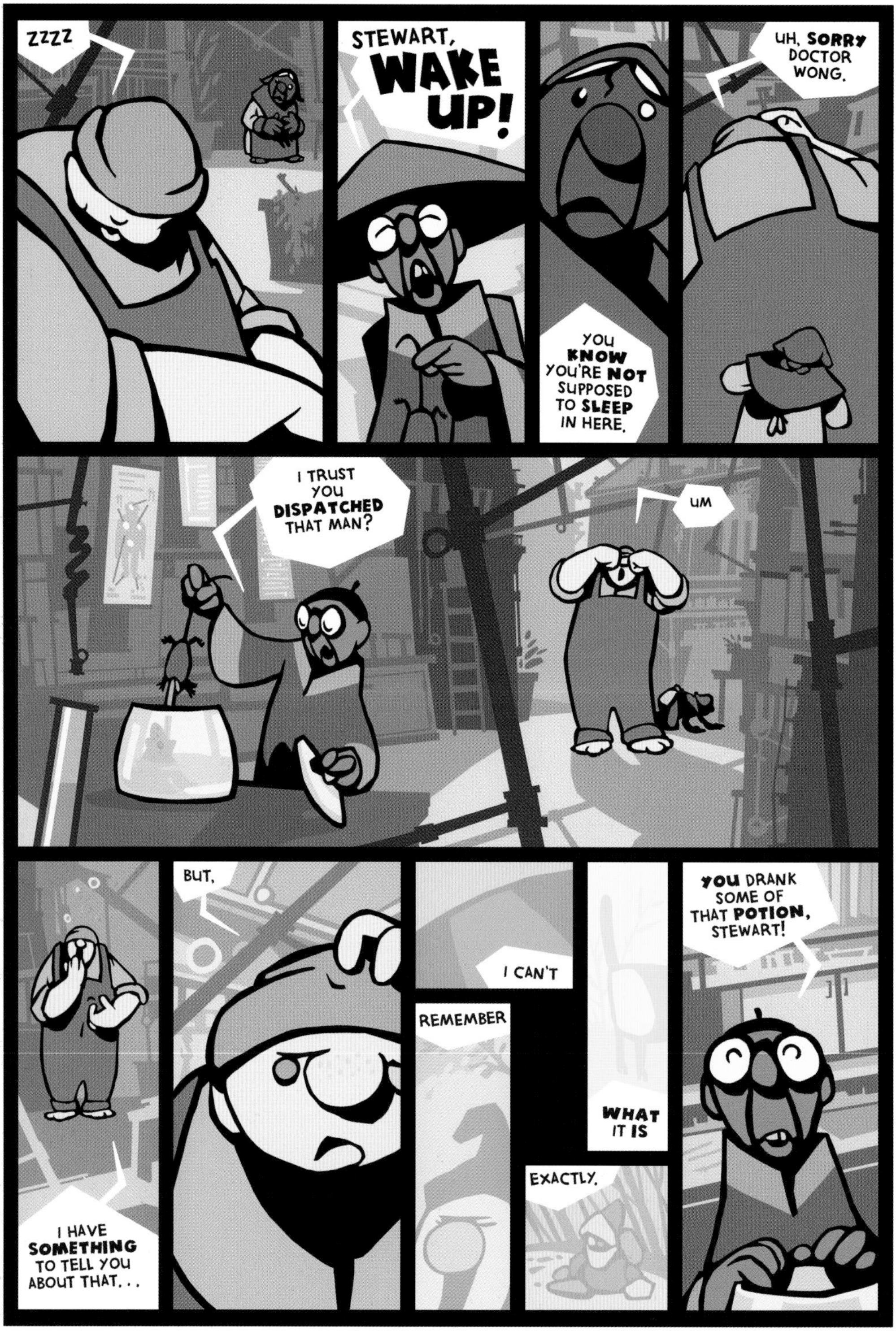
ZZZZ
STEWART, WAKE UP!
YOU KNOW YOU'RE NOT SUPPOSED TO SLEEP IN HERE.
UH, SORRY DOCTOR WONG.
I TRUST YOU DISPATCHED THAT MAN?
UM
I HAVE SOMETHING TO TELL YOU ABOUT THAT. . .
BUT,
I CAN'T
REMEMBER
WHAT IT IS
EXACTLY.
YOU DRANK SOME OF THAT POTION, STEWART!

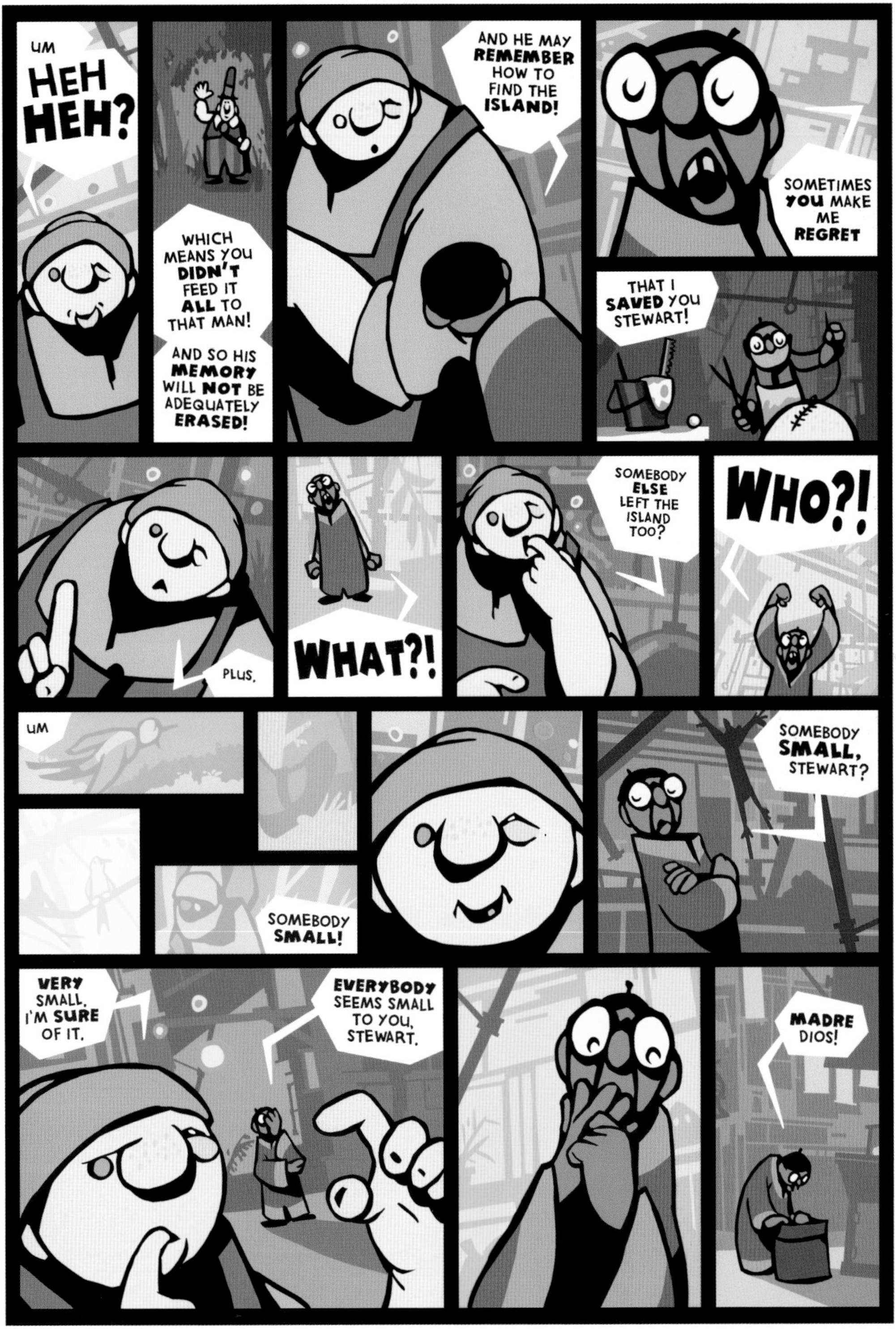
UM
HEH HEH?
WHICH MEANS YOU DIDN'T FEED IT ALL TO THAT MAN!
AND SO HIS MEMORY WILL NOT BE ADEQUATELY ERASED!
AND HE MAY REMEMBER HOW TO FIND THE ISLAND!
SOMETIMES YOU MAKE ME REGRET
THAT I SAVED YOU STEWART!
PLUS,
WHAT?!
SOMEBODY ELSE LEFT THE ISLAND TOO?
WHO?!
UM
SOMEBODY SMALL!
SOMEBODY SMALL, STEWART?
VERY SMALL, I'M SURE OF IT.
EVERYBODY SEEMS SMALL TO YOU, STEWART.
MADRE DIOS!

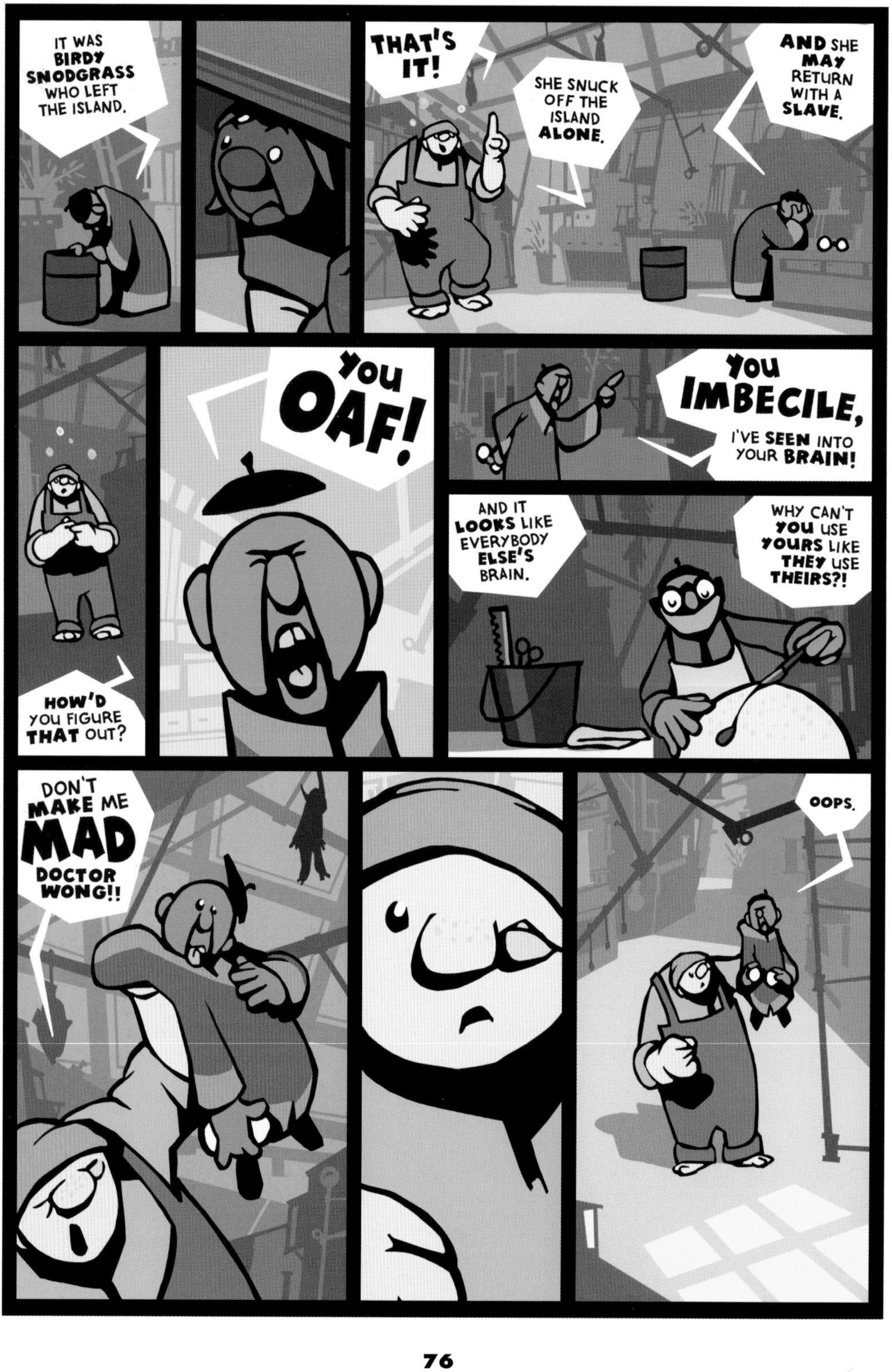
IT WAS BIRDY SNODGRASS WHO LEFT THE ISLAND.
THAT'S IT!
SHE SNUCK OFF THE ISLAND ALONE.
AND SHE MAY RETURN WITH A SLAVE.
YOU OAF!
YOU IMBECILE,
I'VE SEEN INTO YOUR BRAIN!
AND IT LOOKS LIKE EVERYBODY ELSE'S BRAIN.
WHY CAN'T YOU USE YOURS LIKE THEY USE THEIRS?!
HOW'D YOU FIGURE THAT OUT?
DON'T MAKE ME MAD DOCTOR WONG!!
OOPS.

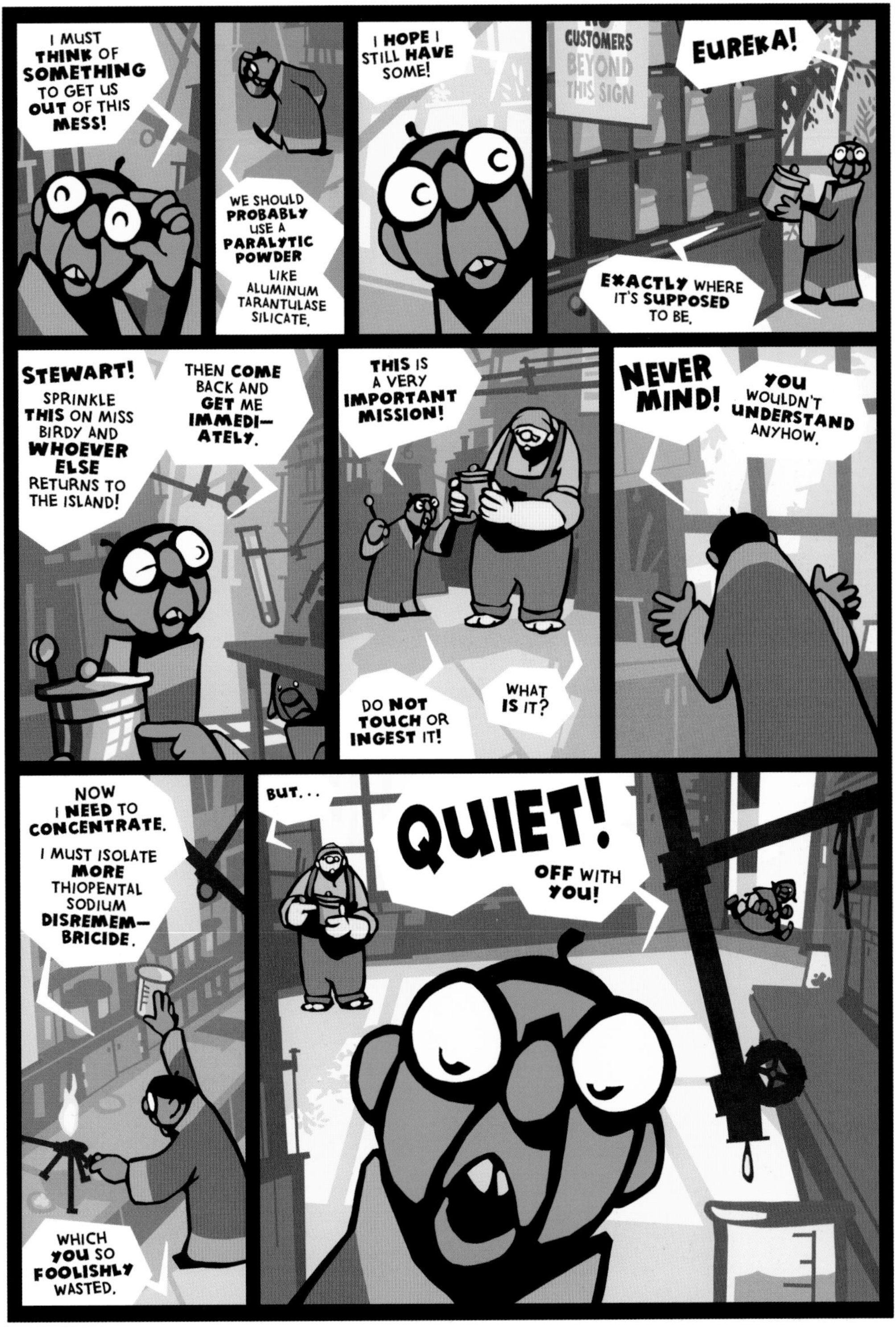
I MUST THINK OF SOMETHING TO GET US OUT OF THIS MESS!
WE SHOULD PROBABLY USE A PARALYTIC POWDER
LIKE ALUMINUM TARANTULASE SILICATE.
I HOPE I STILL HAVE SOME!
NO CUSTOMERS BEYOND THIS SIGN
EUREKA!
EXACTLY WHERE IT'S SUPPOSED TO BE.
STEWART!
SPRINKLE THIS ON MISS BIRDY AND WHOEVER ELSE RETURNS TO THE ISLAND!
THEN COME BACK AND GET ME IMMEDI- ATELY.
THIS IS A VERY IMPORTANT MISSION!
DO NOT TOUCH OR INGEST IT!
WHAT IS IT?
NEVER MIND!
YOU WOULDN'T UNDERSTAND ANYHOW.
NOW I NEED TO CONCENTRATE.
I MUST ISOLATE MORE THIOPENTAL SODIUM DISREMEM- BRICIDE.
WHICH YOU SO FOOLISHLY WASTED.
BUT...
QUIET!
OFF WITH YOU!

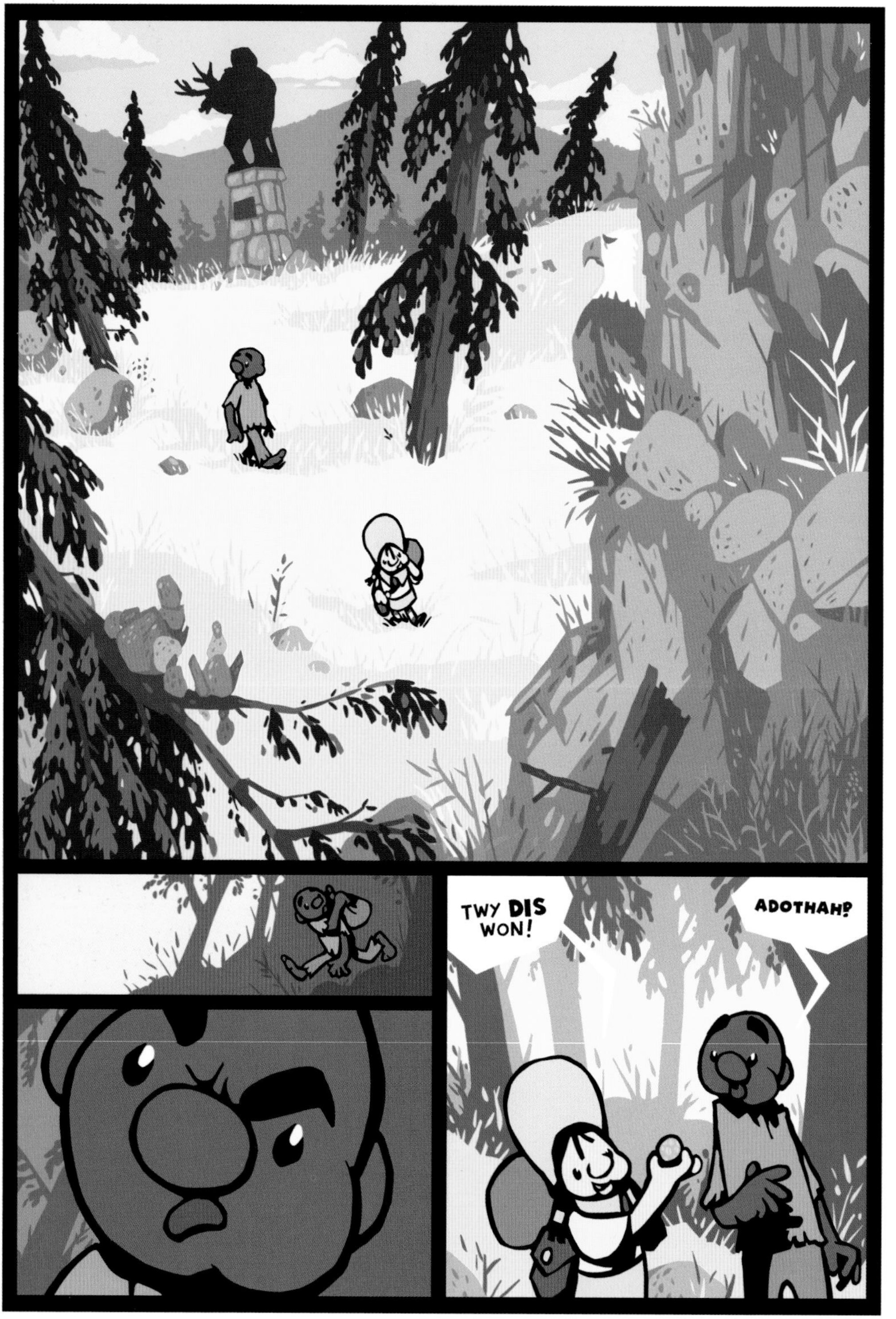
TWY DIS WON!
ADOTHAH?

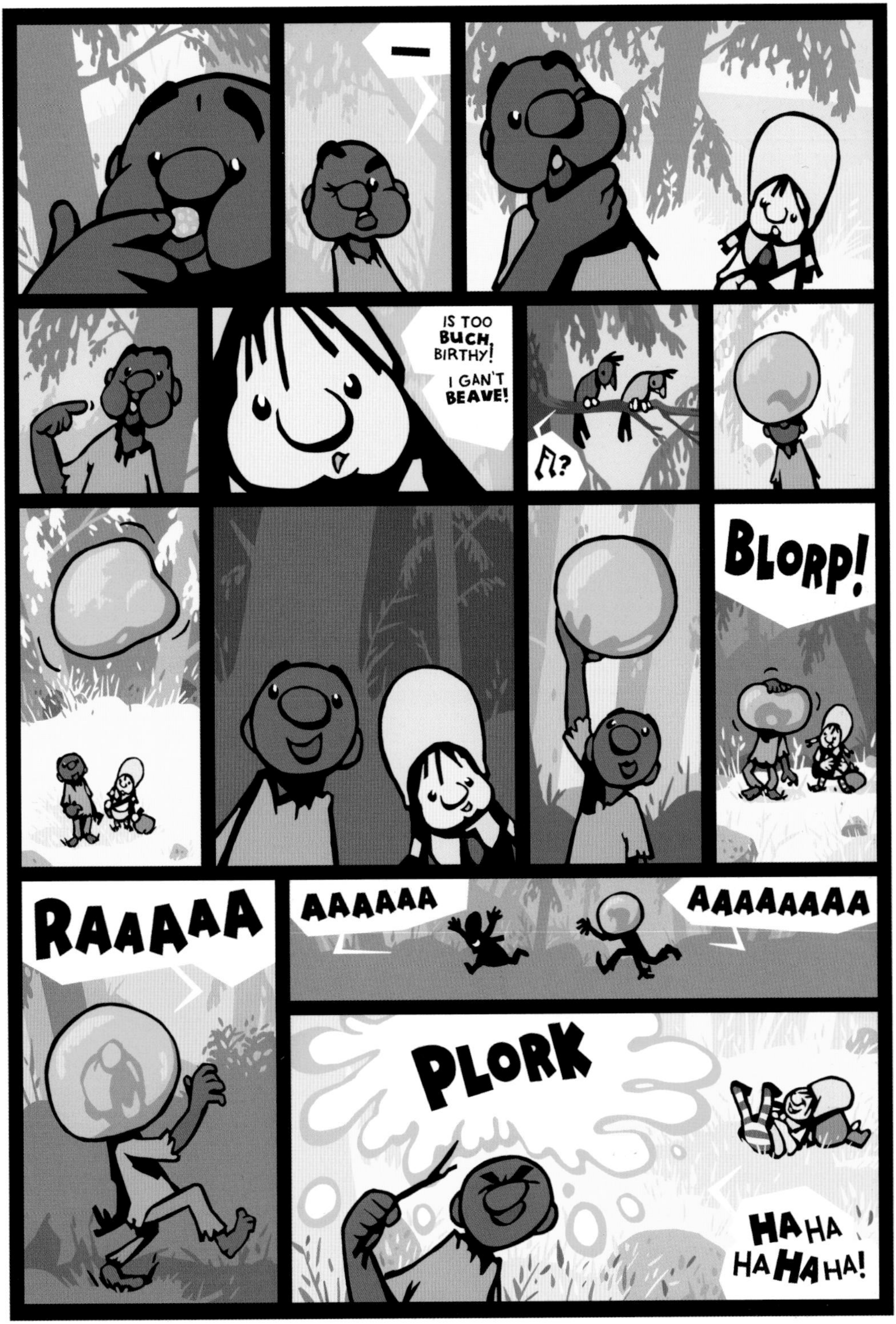
–
IS TOO BUCH, BIRTHY!
I GAN'T BEAVE!
?
BLORP!
RAAAAA
AAAAAA
AAAAAAAA
PLORK
HAHA HAHAHA!

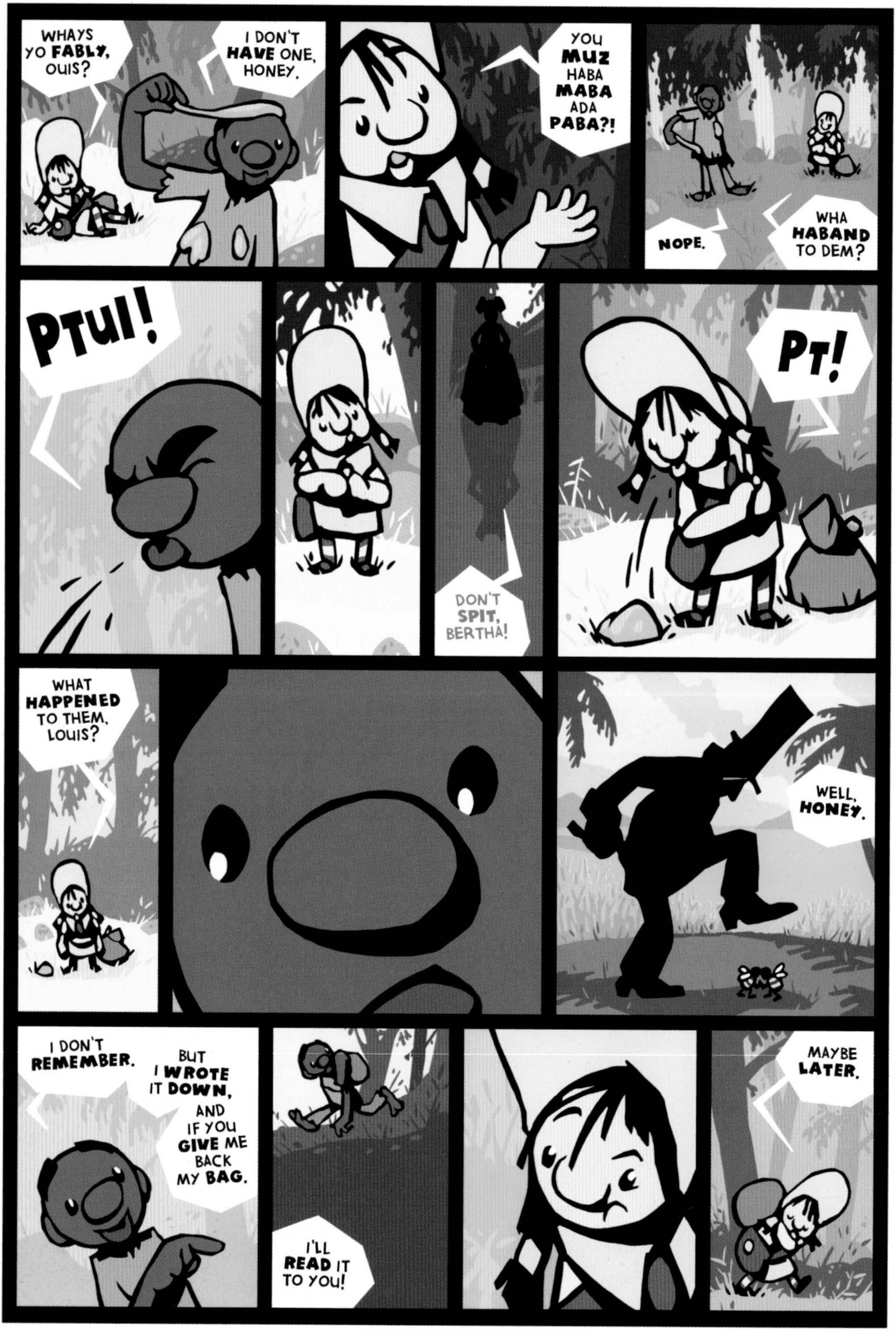
WHAYS YO FABLY, OUIS?
I DON'T HAVE ONE, HONEY.
YOU MUZ HABA MABA ADA PABA?!
NOPE.
WHA HABAND TO DEM?
PTUI!
DON'T SPIT, BERTHA!
PT!
WHAT HAPPENED TO THEM, LOUIS?
WELL, HONEY.
I DON'T REMEMBER.
BUT I WROTE IT DOWN,
AND IF YOU GIVE ME BACK MY BAG.
I'LL READ IT TO YOU!
MAYBE LATER.

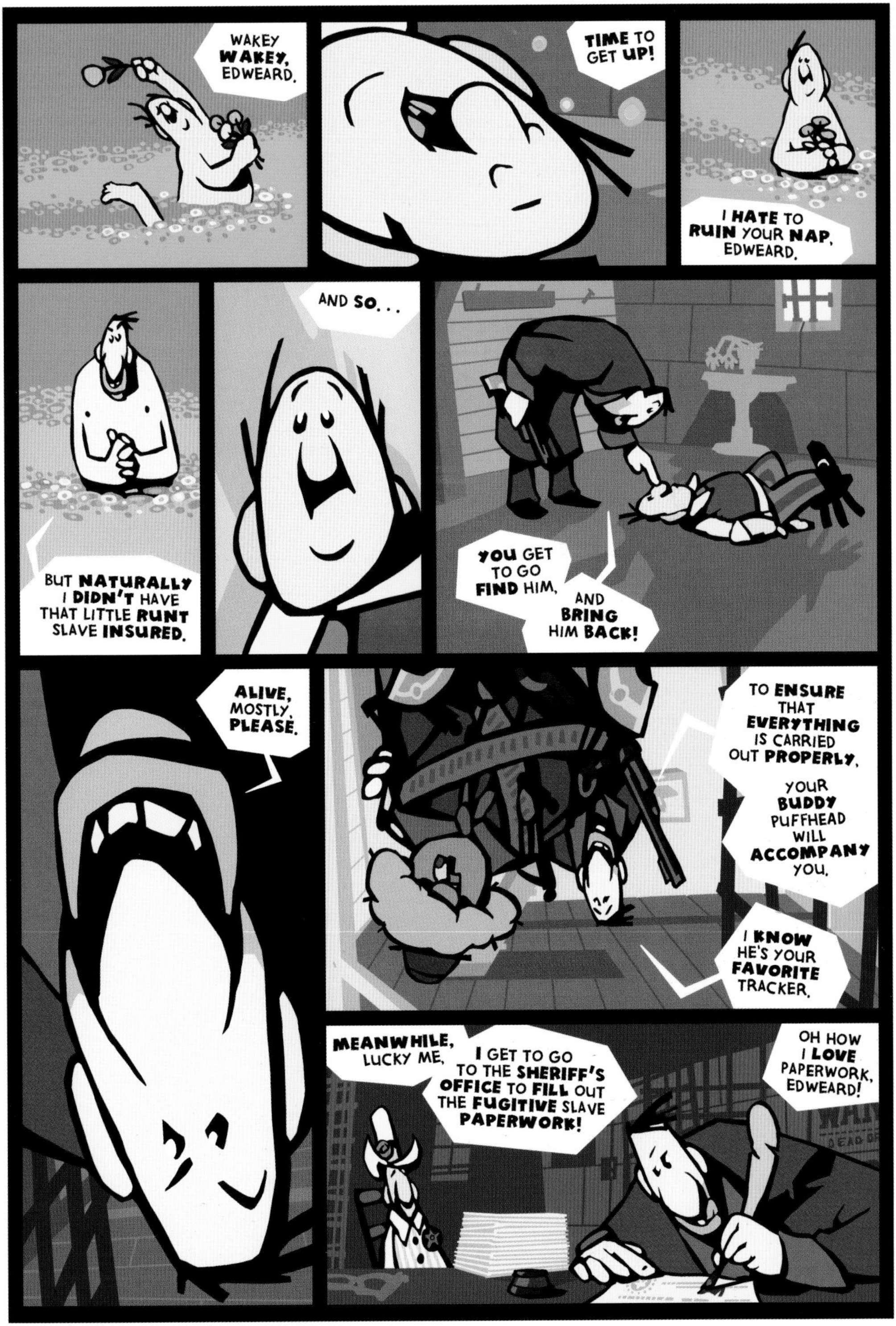

WAKEY WAKEY, EDWEARD.
TIME TO GET UP!
I HATE TO RUIN YOUR NAP, EDWEARD.
BUT NATURALLY I DIDN'T HAVE THAT LITTLE RUNT SLAVE INSURED.
AND SO...
YOU GET TO GO FIND HIM,
AND BRING HIM BACK!
ALIVE, MOSTLY, PLEASE.
TO ENSURE THAT EVERYTHING IS CARRIED OUT PROPERLY,
YOUR BUDDY PUFFHEAD WILL ACCOMPANY YOU.
I KNOW HE'S YOUR FAVORITE TRACKER.
MEANWHILE, LUCKY ME,
I GET TO GO TO THE SHERIFF'S OFFICE TO FILL OUT THE FUGITIVE SLAVE PAPERWORK!
OH HOW I LOVE PAPERWORK, EDWEARD!

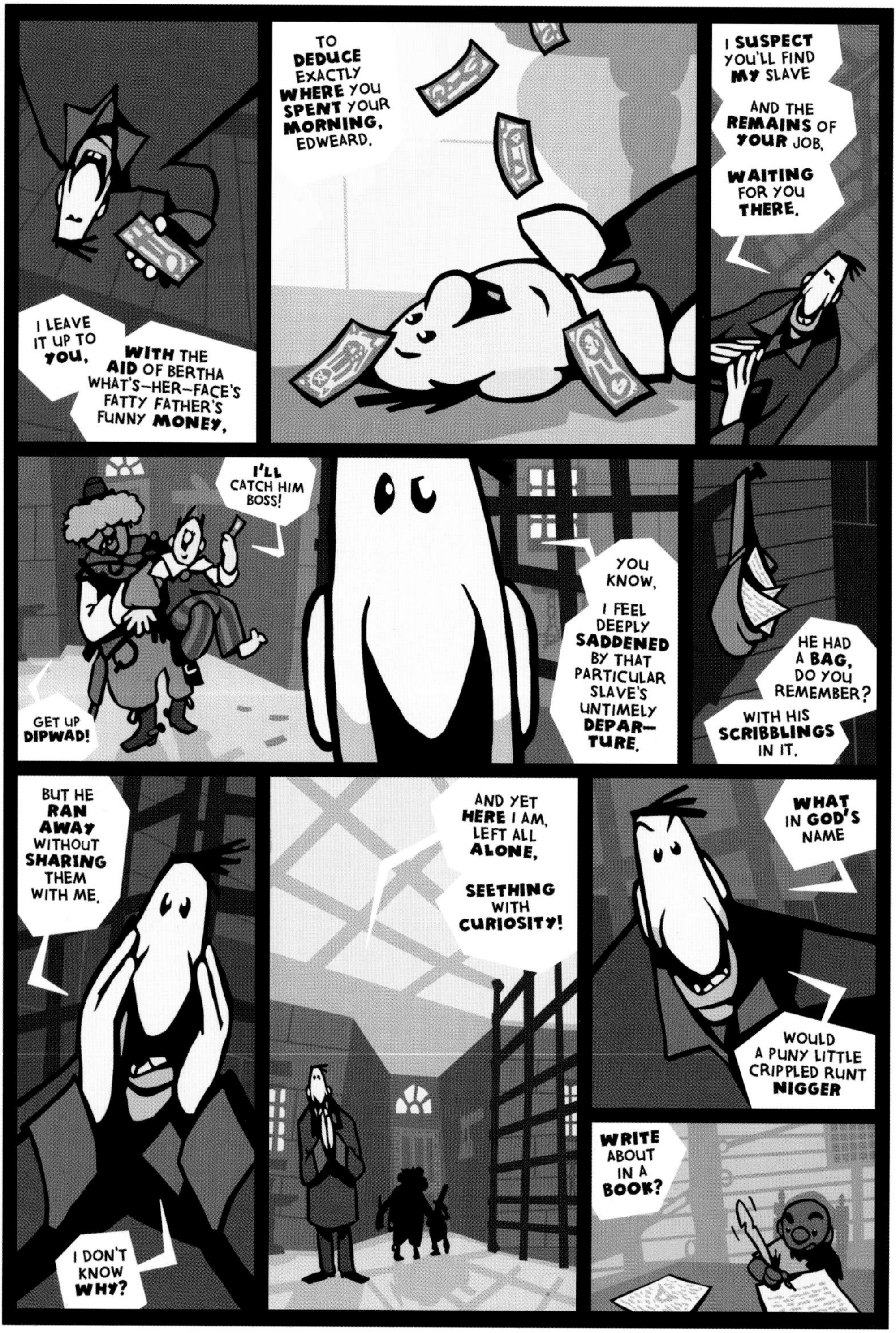
I LEAVE IT UP TO YOU,
WITH THE AID OF BERTHA WHAT'S-HER-FACE'S FATTY FATHER'S FUNNY MONEY,
TO DEDUCE EXACTLY WHERE YOU SPENT YOUR MORNING, EDWEARD.
I SUSPECT YOU'LL FIND MY SLAVE
AND THE REMAINS OF YOUR JOB,
WAITING FOR YOU THERE.
I'LL CATCH HIM BOSS!
GET UP DIPWAD!
YOU KNOW,
I FEEL DEEPLY SADDENED BY THAT PARTICULAR SLAVE'S UNTIMELY DEPAR-TURE.
HE HAD A BAG, DO YOU REMEMBER?
WITH HIS SCRIBBLINGS IN IT.
BUT HE RAN AWAY WITHOUT SHARING THEM WITH ME.
I DON'T KNOW WHY?
AND YET HERE I AM, LEFT ALL ALONE,
SEETHING WITH CURIOSITY!
WHAT IN GOD'S NAME
WOULD A PUNY LITTLE CRIPPLED RUNT NIGGER
WRITE ABOUT IN A BOOK?

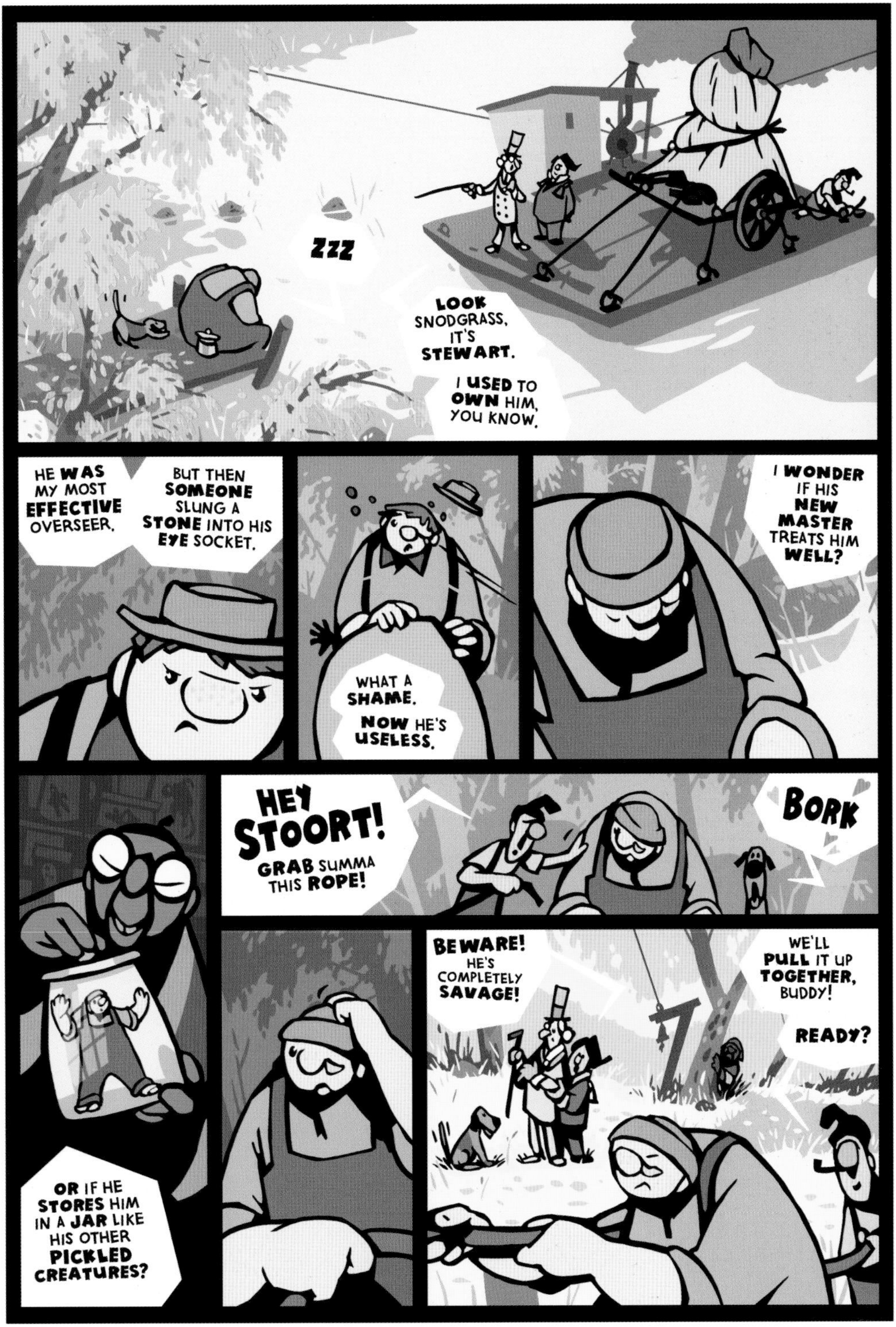
ZZZ
LOOK SNODGRASS, IT'S STEWART.
I USED TO OWN HIM, YOU KNOW.
HE WAS MY MOST EFFECTIVE OVERSEER.
BUT THEN SOMEONE SLUNG A STONE INTO HIS EYE SOCKET.
WHAT A SHAME.
NOW HE'S USELESS.
I WONDER IF HIS NEW MASTER TREATS HIM WELL?
OR IF HE STORES HIM IN A JAR LIKE HIS OTHER PICKLED CREATURES?
HEY STOORT!
GRAB SUMMA THIS ROPE!
BORK
BEWARE! HE'S COMPLETELY SAVAGE!
WE'LL PULL IT UP TOGETHER, BUDDY!
READY?

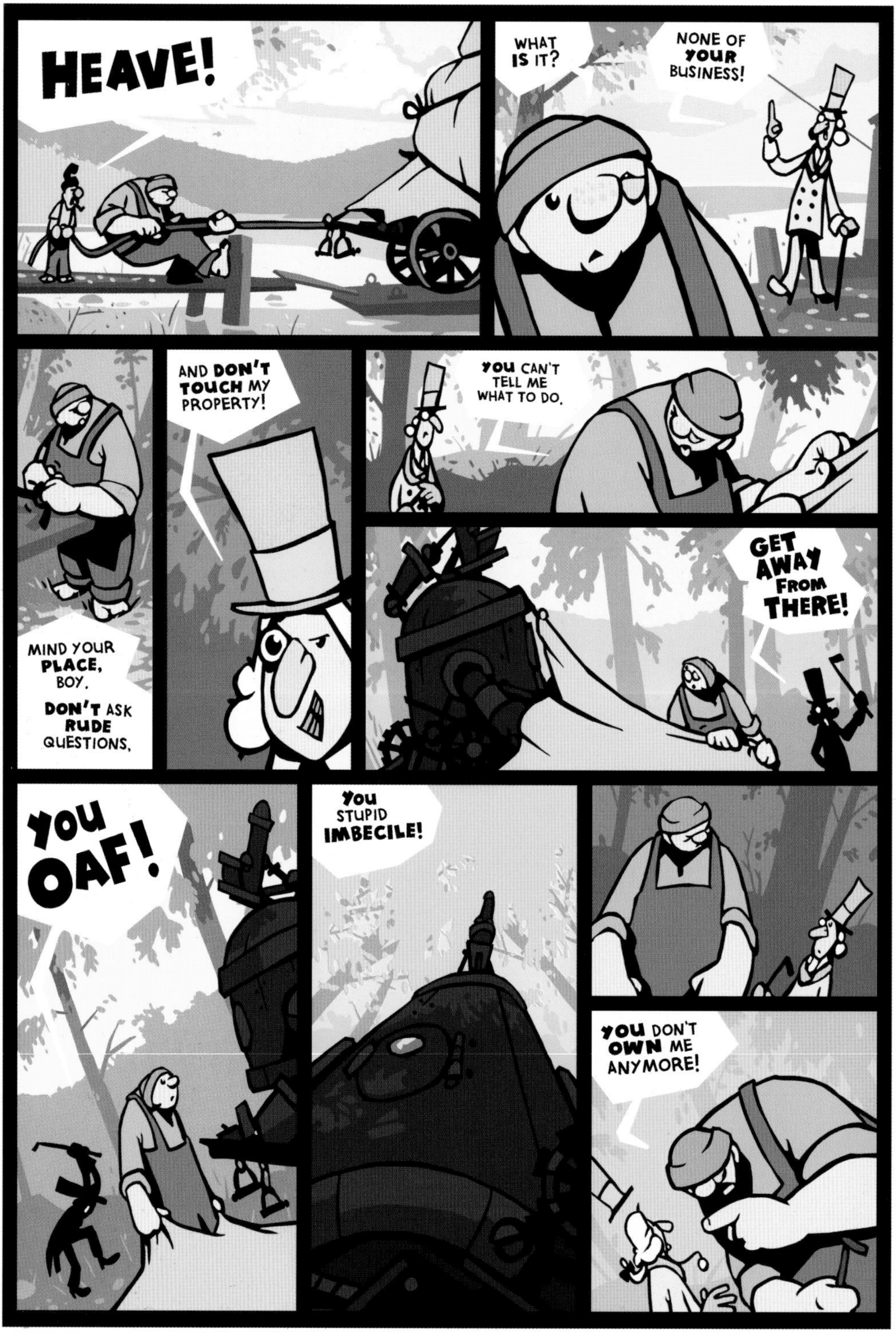
HEAVE!
WHAT IS IT?
NONE OF YOUR BUSINESS!
MIND YOUR PLACE, BOY.
DON'T ASK RUDE QUESTIONS,
AND DON'T TOUCH MY PROPERTY!
YOU CAN'T TELL ME WHAT TO DO.
GET AWAY FROM THERE!
YOU OAF!
YOU STUPID IMBECILE!
YOU DON'T OWN ME ANYMORE!

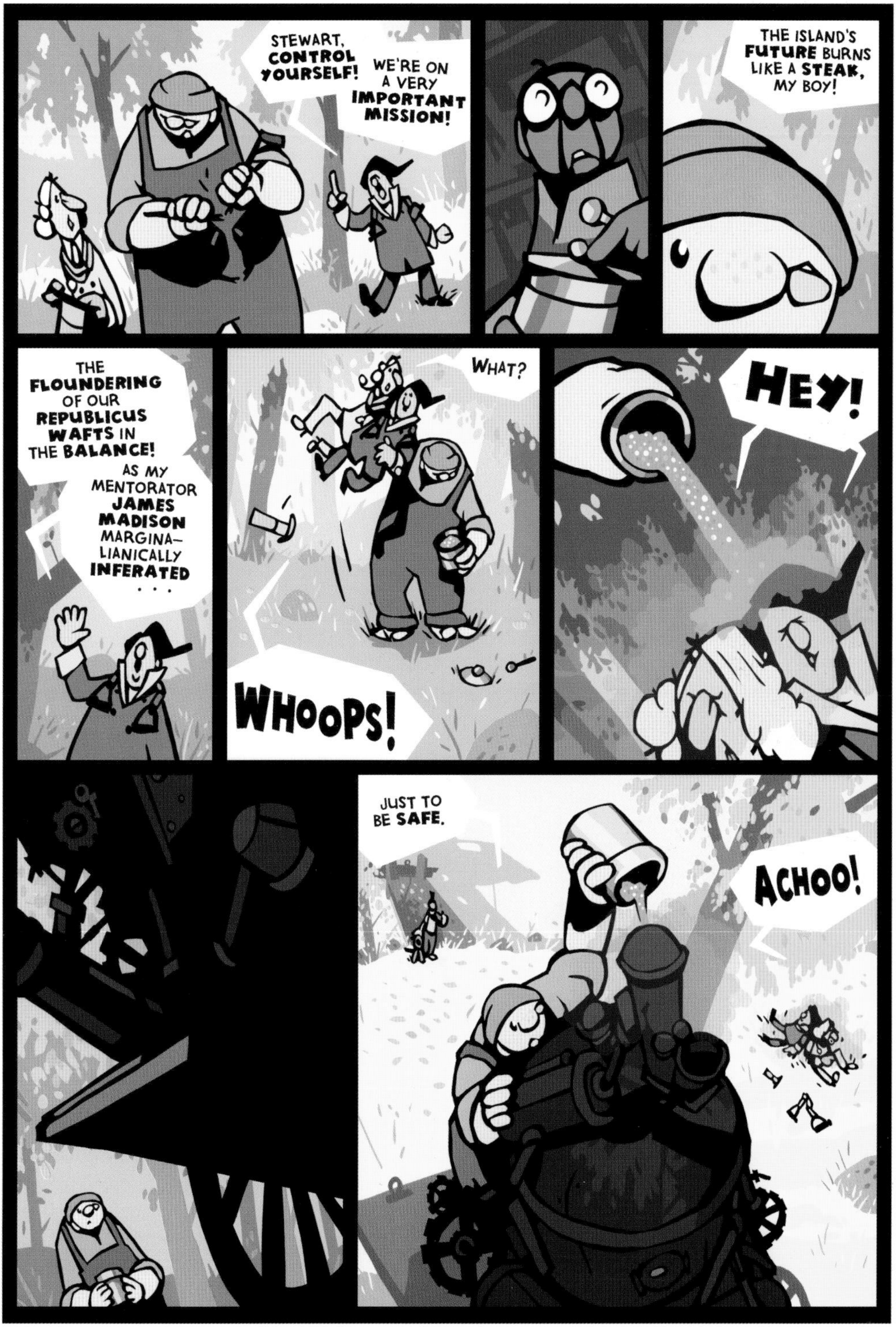
STEWART, CONTROL YOURSELF!
WE'RE ON A VERY IMPORTANT MISSION!
THE ISLAND'S FUTURE BURNS LIKE A STEAK, MY BOY!
THE FLOUNDERING OF OUR REPUBLICUS WAFTS IN THE BALANCE!
AS MY MENTORATOR JAMES MADISON MARGINA-LIANICALLY INFERATED . . .
WHAT?
WHOOPS!
HEY!
JUST TO BE SAFE.
ACHOO!

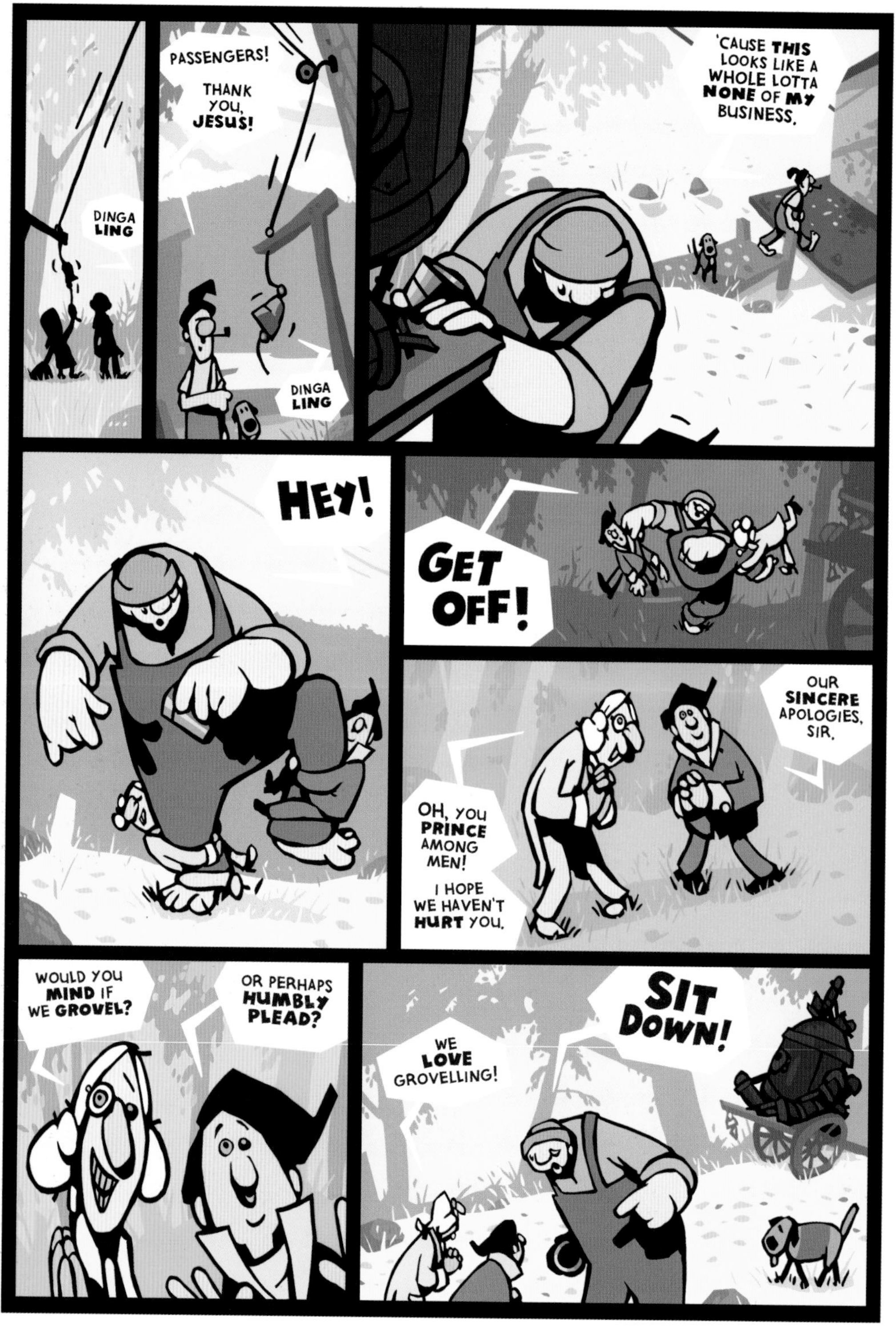
DINGA
LING
PASSENGERS!
THANK YOU, JESUS!
DINGA
LING
'CAUSE THIS LOOKS LIKE A WHOLE LOTTA NONE OF MY BUSINESS.
HEY!
GET OFF!
OUR SINCERE APOLOGIES, SIR.
OH, YOU PRINCE AMONG MEN!
I HOPE WE HAVEN'T HURT YOU.
WOULD YOU MIND IF WE GROVEL?
OR PERHAPS HUMBLY PLEAD?
WE LOVE GROVELLING!
SIT DOWN!

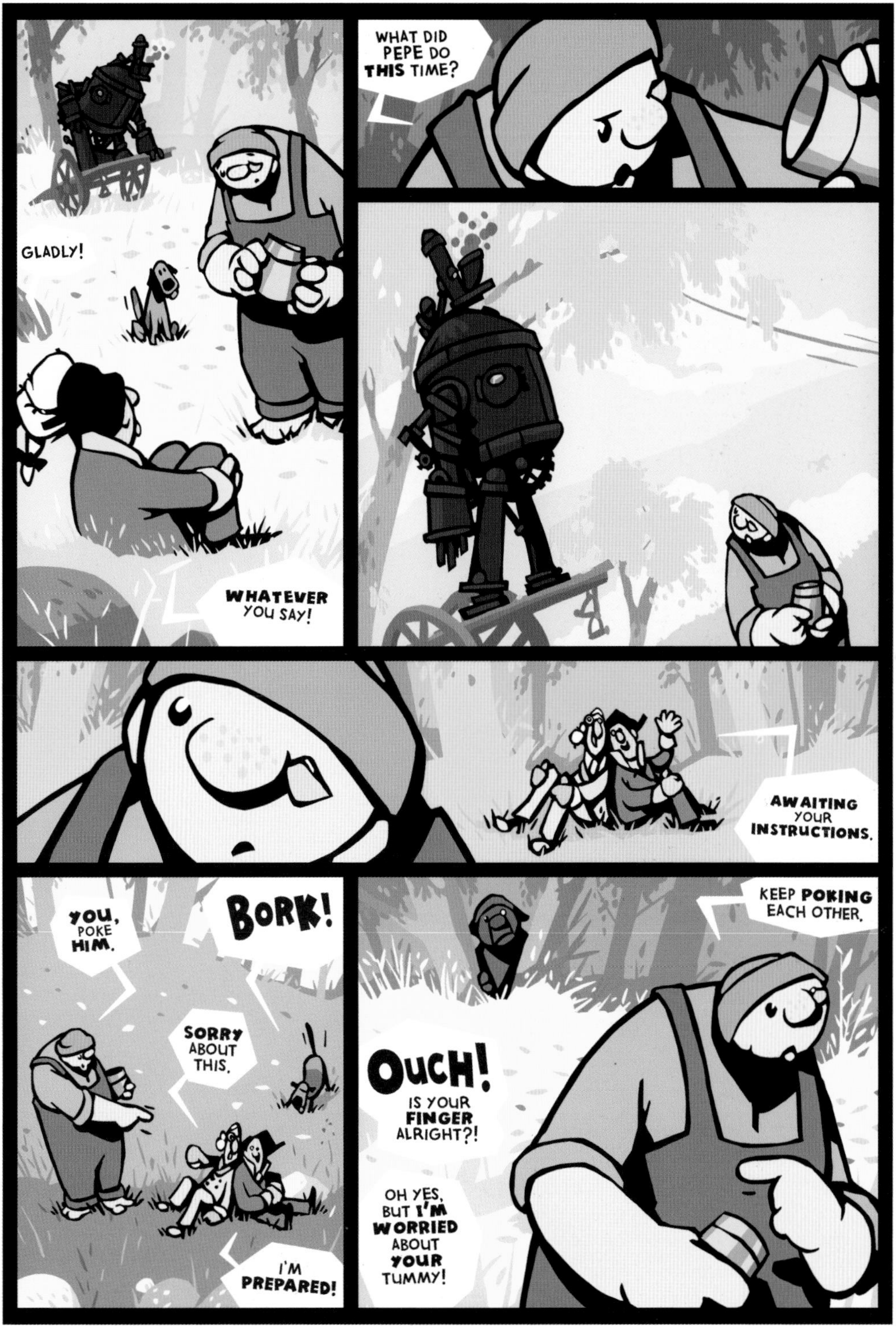
GLADLY!
WHATEVER YOU SAY!
WHAT DID PEPE DO THIS TIME?
AWAITING YOUR INSTRUCTIONS.
YOU, POKE HIM.
BORK!
SORRY ABOUT THIS.
I'M PREPARED!
KEEP POKING EACH OTHER.
OUCH! IS YOUR FINGER ALRIGHT?!
OH YES, BUT I'M WORRIED ABOUT YOUR TUMMY!

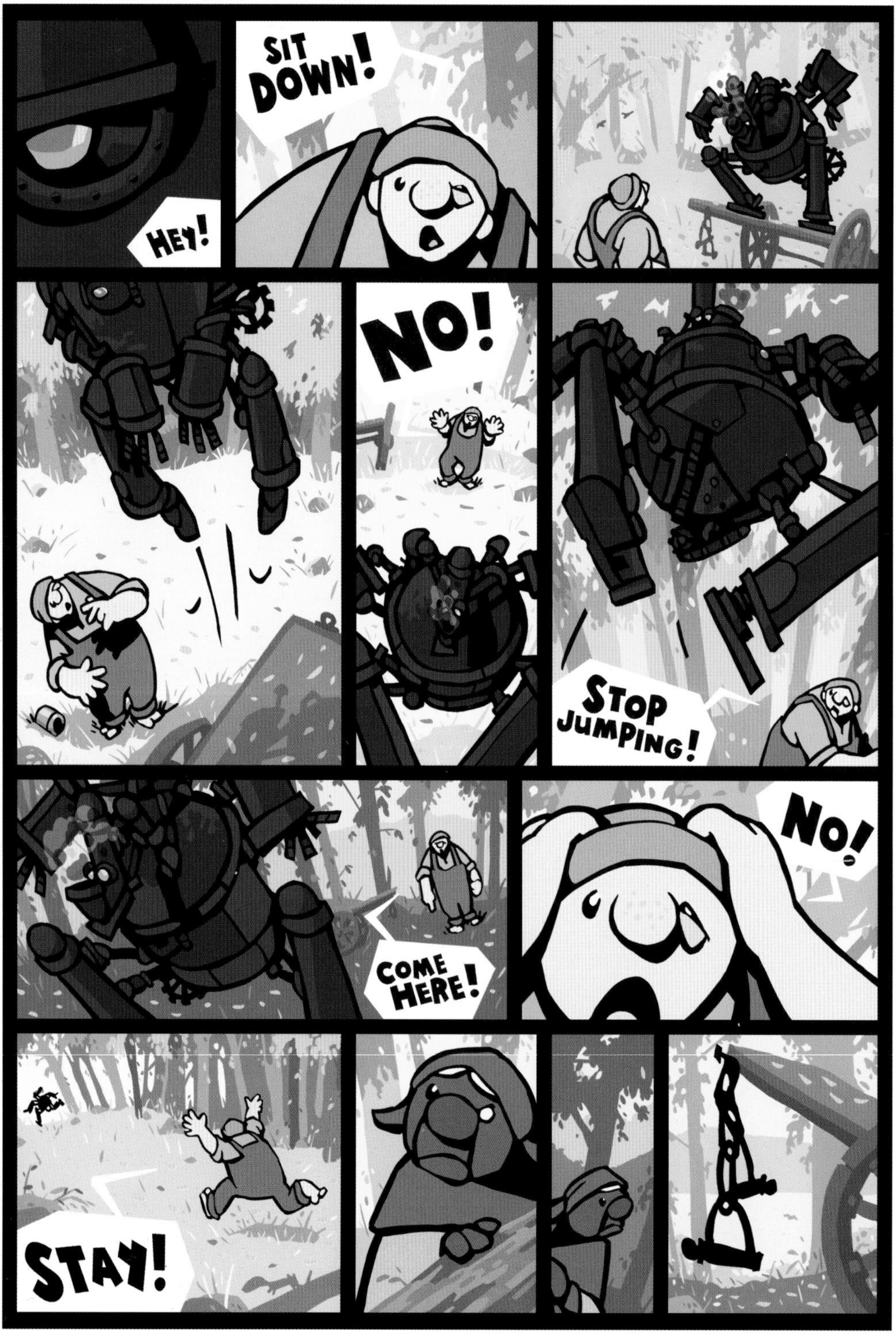
HEY!
SIT DOWN!
NO!
STOP JUMPING!
COME HERE!
NO!
STAY!

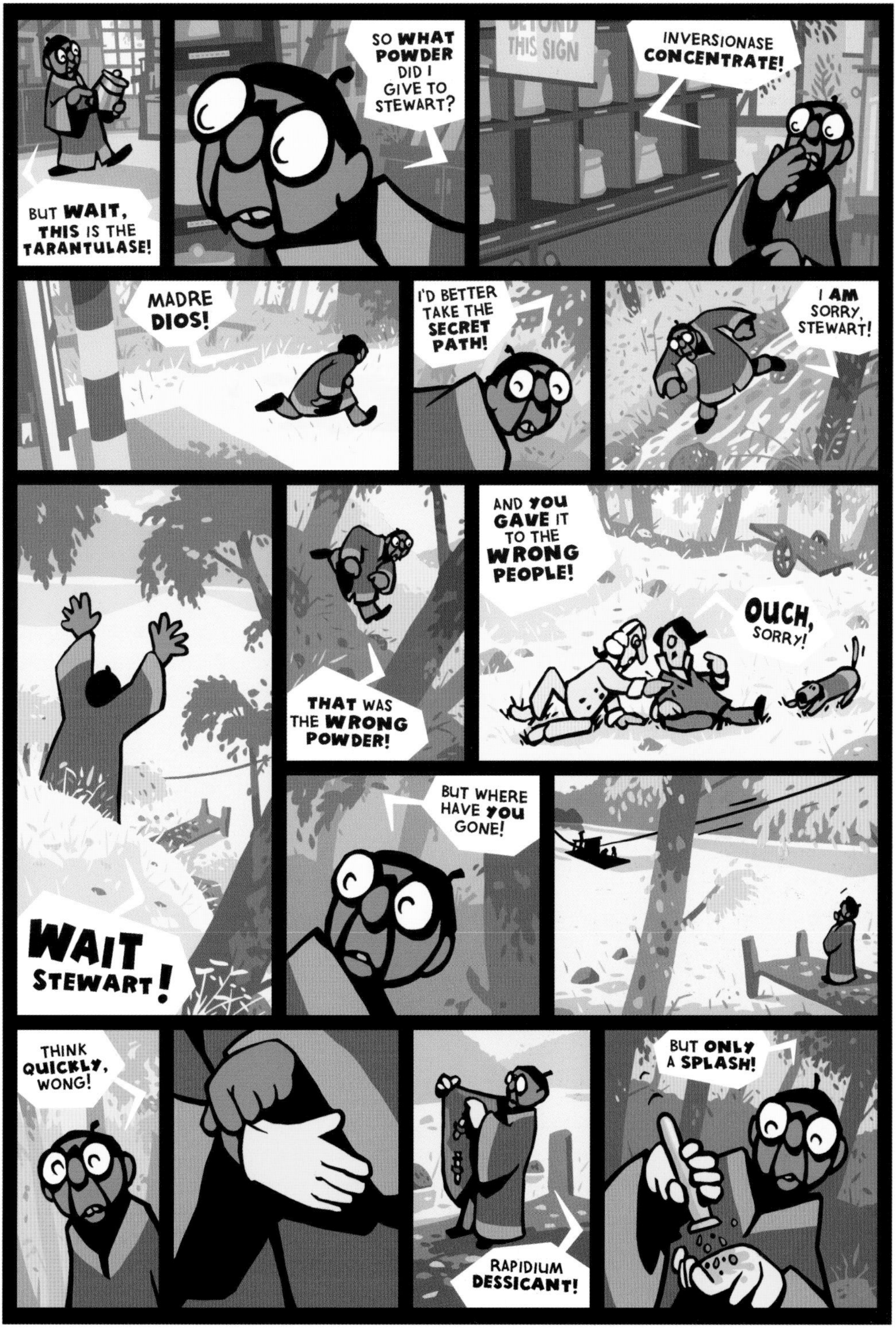
BUT WAIT, THIS IS THE TARANTULASE!
SO WHAT POWDER DID I GIVE TO STEWART?
BEYOND THIS SIGN
INVERSIONASE CONCENTRATE!
MADRE DIOS!
I'D BETTER TAKE THE SECRET PATH!
I AM SORRY, STEWART!
WAIT STEWART!
THAT WAS THE WRONG POWDER!
AND YOU GAVE IT TO THE WRONG PEOPLE!
OUCH, SORRY!
BUT WHERE HAVE YOU GONE!
THINK QUICKLY, WONG!
RAPIDIUM DESSICANT!
BUT ONLY A SPLASH!

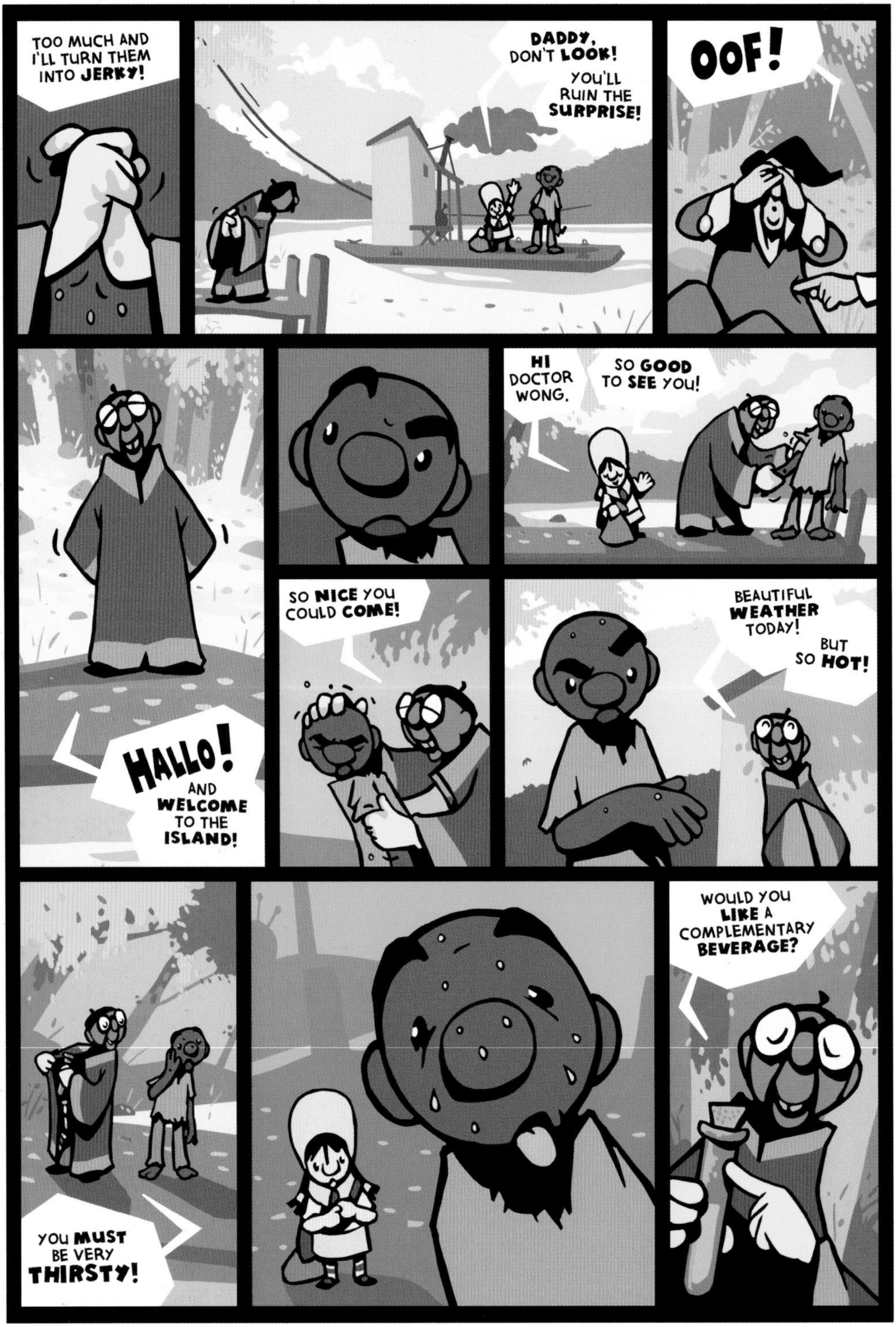

TOO MUCH AND I'LL TURN THEM INTO JERKY!
DADDY, DON'T LOOK!
YOU'LL RUIN THE SURPRISE!
OOF!
HALLO! AND WELCOME TO THE ISLAND!
HI DOCTOR WONG.
SO GOOD TO SEE YOU!
SO NICE YOU COULD COME!
BEAUTIFUL WEATHER TODAY!
BUT SO HOT!
YOU MUST BE VERY THIRSTY!
WOULD YOU LIKE A COMPLEMENTARY BEVERAGE?

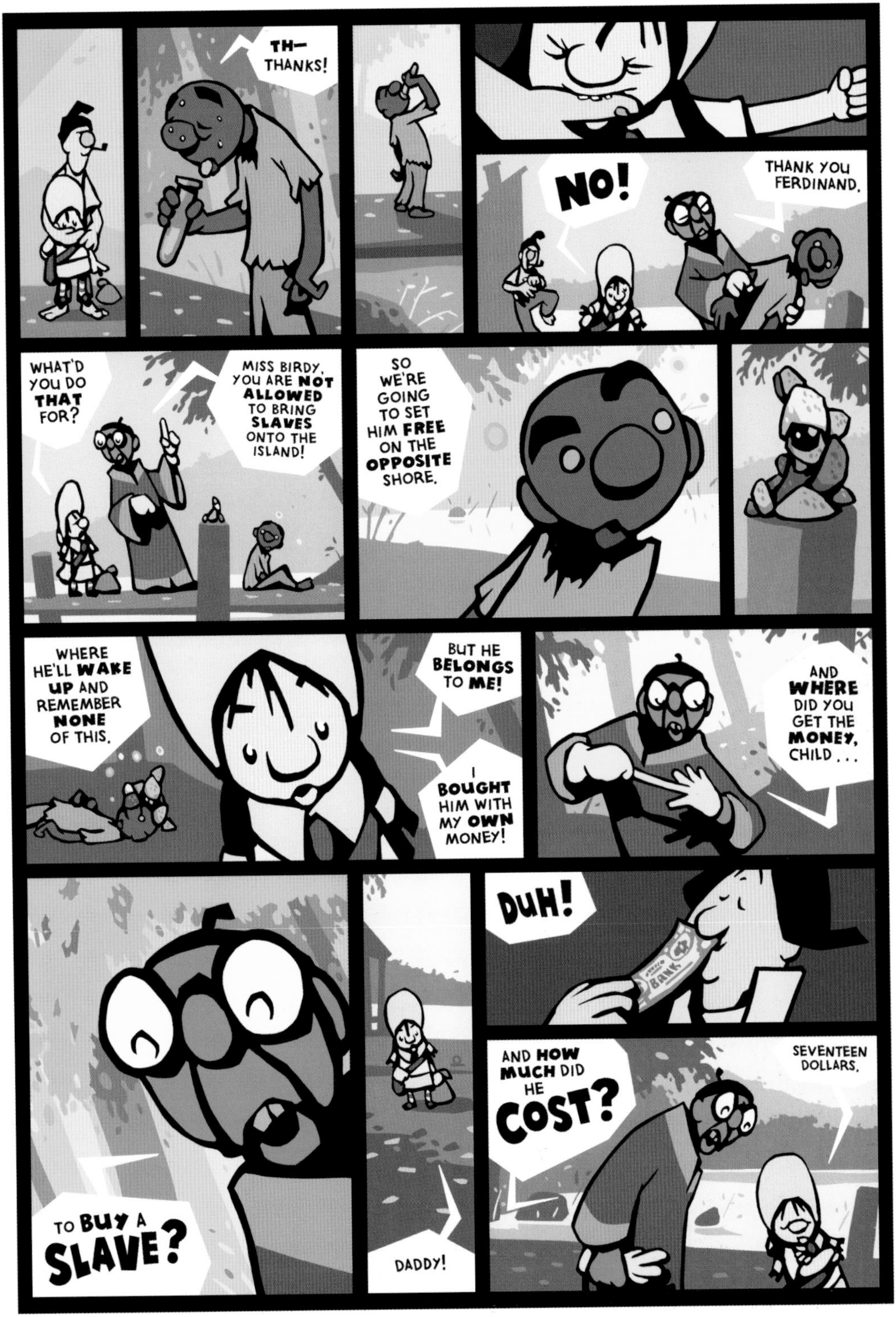
TH— THANKS!
NO!
THANK YOU FERDINAND.
WHAT'D YOU DO THAT FOR?
MISS BIRDY, YOU ARE NOT ALLOWED TO BRING SLAVES ONTO THE ISLAND!
SO WE'RE GOING TO SET HIM FREE ON THE OPPOSITE SHORE.
WHERE HE'LL WAKE UP AND REMEMBER NONE OF THIS.
BUT HE BELONGS TO ME!
I BOUGHT HIM WITH MY OWN MONEY!
AND WHERE DID YOU GET THE MONEY, CHILD . . .
TO BUY A SLAVE?
DADDY!
DUH!
BANK
AND HOW MUCH DID HE COST?
SEVENTEEN DOLLARS.

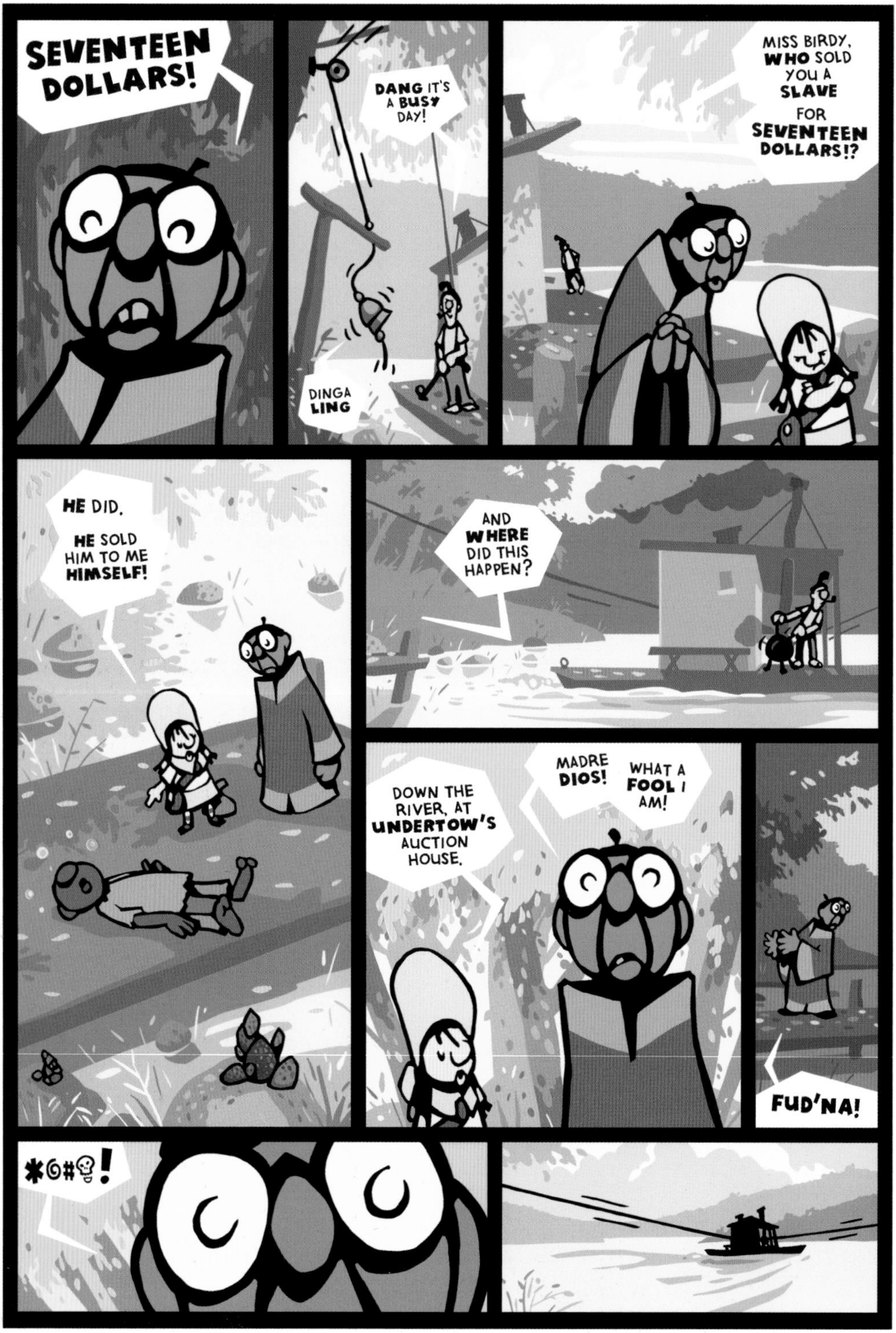
SEVENTEEN DOLLARS!
DANG IT'S A BUSY DAY!
DINGA LING
MISS BIRDY, WHO SOLD YOU A SLAVE FOR SEVENTEEN DOLLARS!?
HE DID.
HE SOLD HIM TO ME HIMSELF!
AND WHERE DID THIS HAPPEN?
DOWN THE RIVER, AT UNDERTOW'S AUCTION HOUSE.
MADRE DIOS!
WHAT A FOOL I AM!
FUD'NA!
*6#☠!

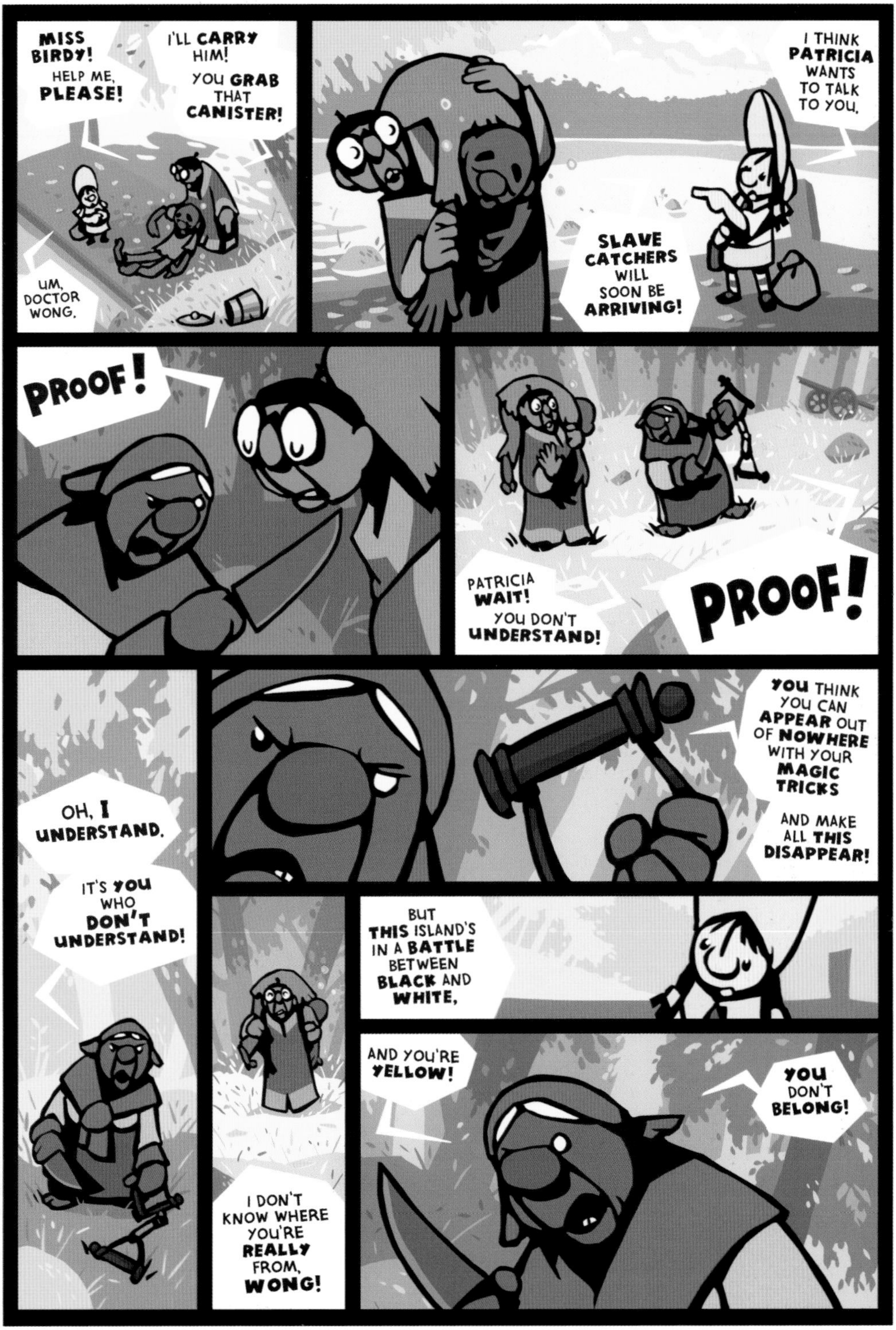
MISS BIRDY! HELP ME, PLEASE!
I'LL CARRY HIM! YOU GRAB THAT CANISTER!
UM, DOCTOR WONG.
I THINK PATRICIA WANTS TO TALK TO YOU.
SLAVE CATCHERS WILL SOON BE ARRIVING!
PROOF!
PATRICIA WAIT! YOU DON'T UNDERSTAND!
PROOF!
OH, I UNDERSTAND.
IT'S YOU WHO DON'T UNDERSTAND!
YOU THINK YOU CAN APPEAR OUT OF NOWHERE WITH YOUR MAGIC TRICKS
AND MAKE ALL THIS DISAPPEAR!
I DON'T KNOW WHERE YOU'RE REALLY FROM, WONG!
BUT THIS ISLAND'S IN A BATTLE BETWEEN BLACK AND WHITE,
AND YOU'RE YELLOW!
YOU DON'T BELONG!

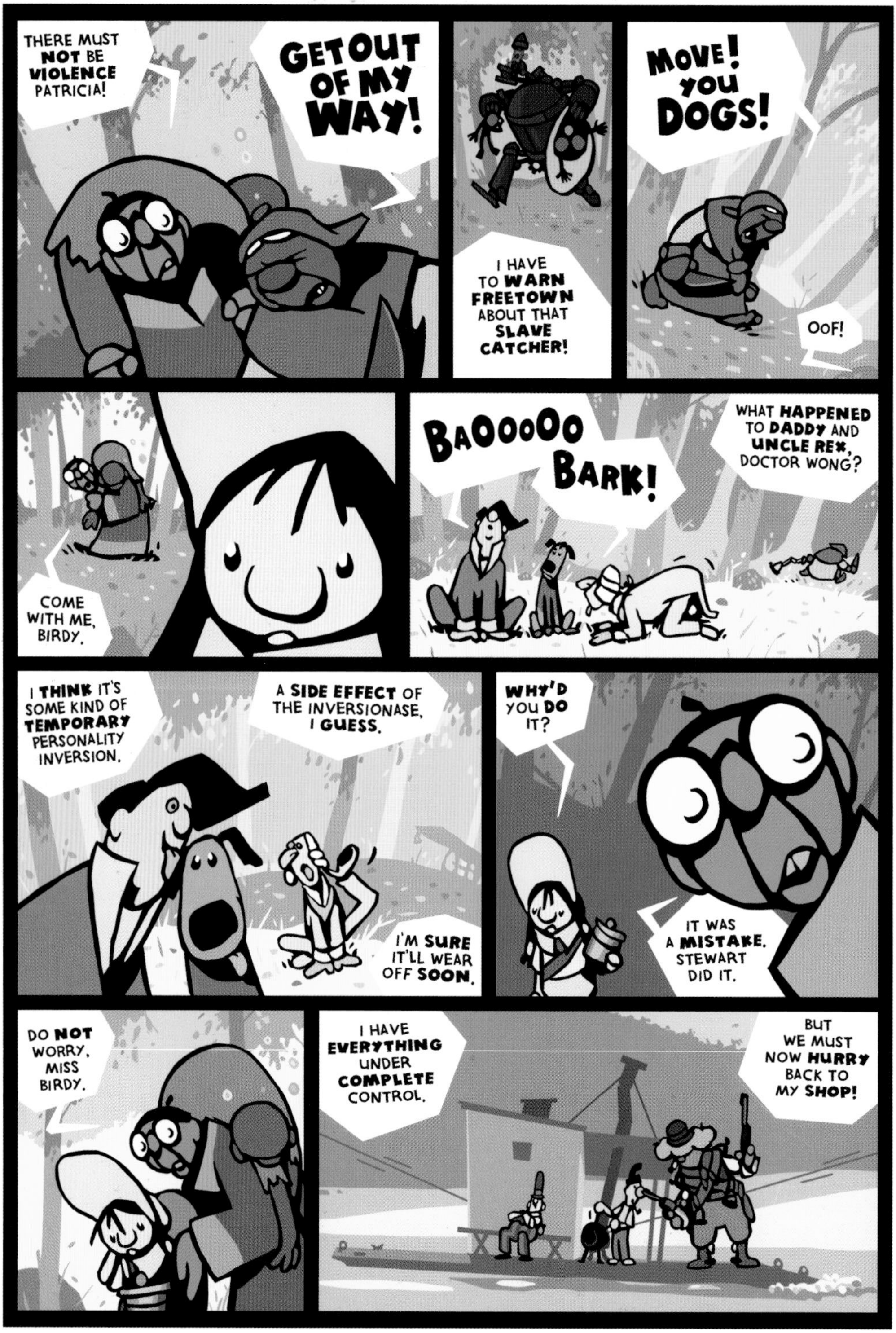
THERE MUST NOT BE VIOLENCE PATRICIA!
GET OUT OF MY WAY!
I HAVE TO WARN FREETOWN ABOUT THAT SLAVE CATCHER!
MOVE! YOU DOGS!
OOF!
COME WITH ME, BIRDY.
BAOOOOO BARK!
WHAT HAPPENED TO DADDY AND UNCLE REX, DOCTOR WONG?
I THINK IT'S SOME KIND OF TEMPORARY PERSONALITY INVERSION.
A SIDE EFFECT OF THE INVERSIONASE, I GUESS.
I'M SURE IT'LL WEAR OFF SOON.
WHY'D YOU DO IT?
IT WAS A MISTAKE. STEWART DID IT.
DO NOT WORRY, MISS BIRDY.
I HAVE EVERYTHING UNDER COMPLETE CONTROL.
BUT WE MUST NOW HURRY BACK TO MY SHOP!

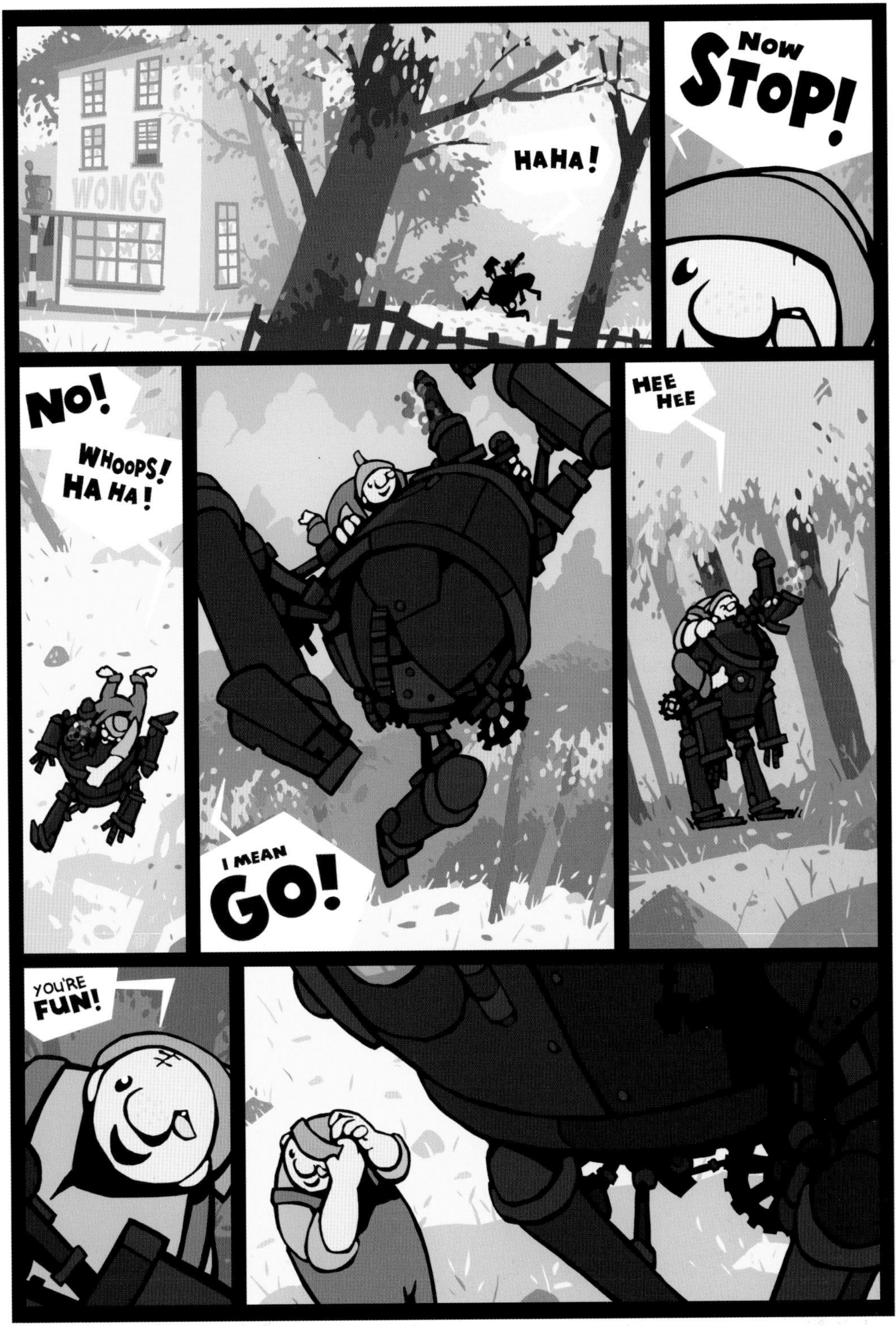
WONG'S
HAHA!
NOW STOP!
NO!
WHOOPS! HA HA!
I MEAN GO!
HEE HEE
YOU'RE FUN!

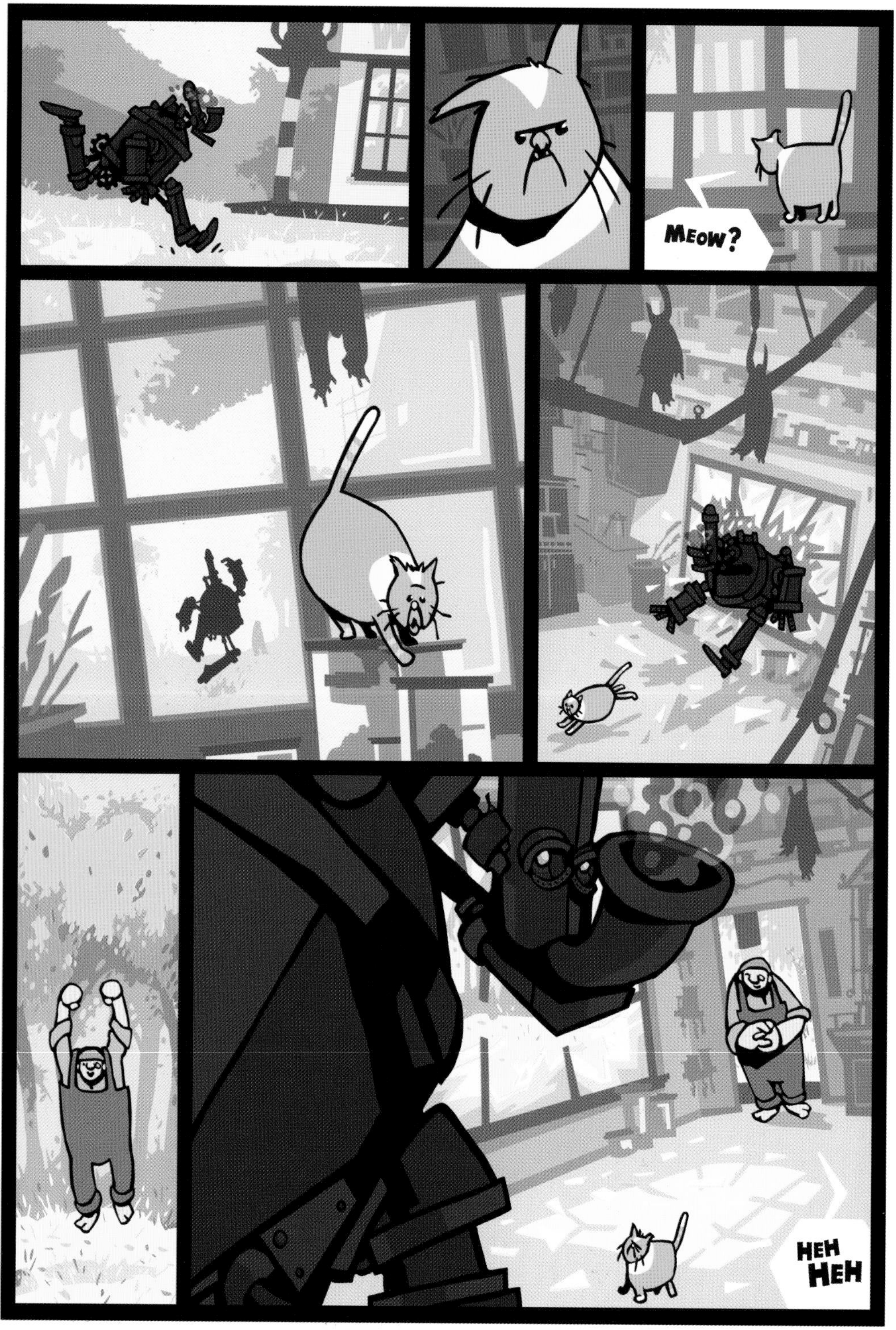
MEOW?
HEH HEH

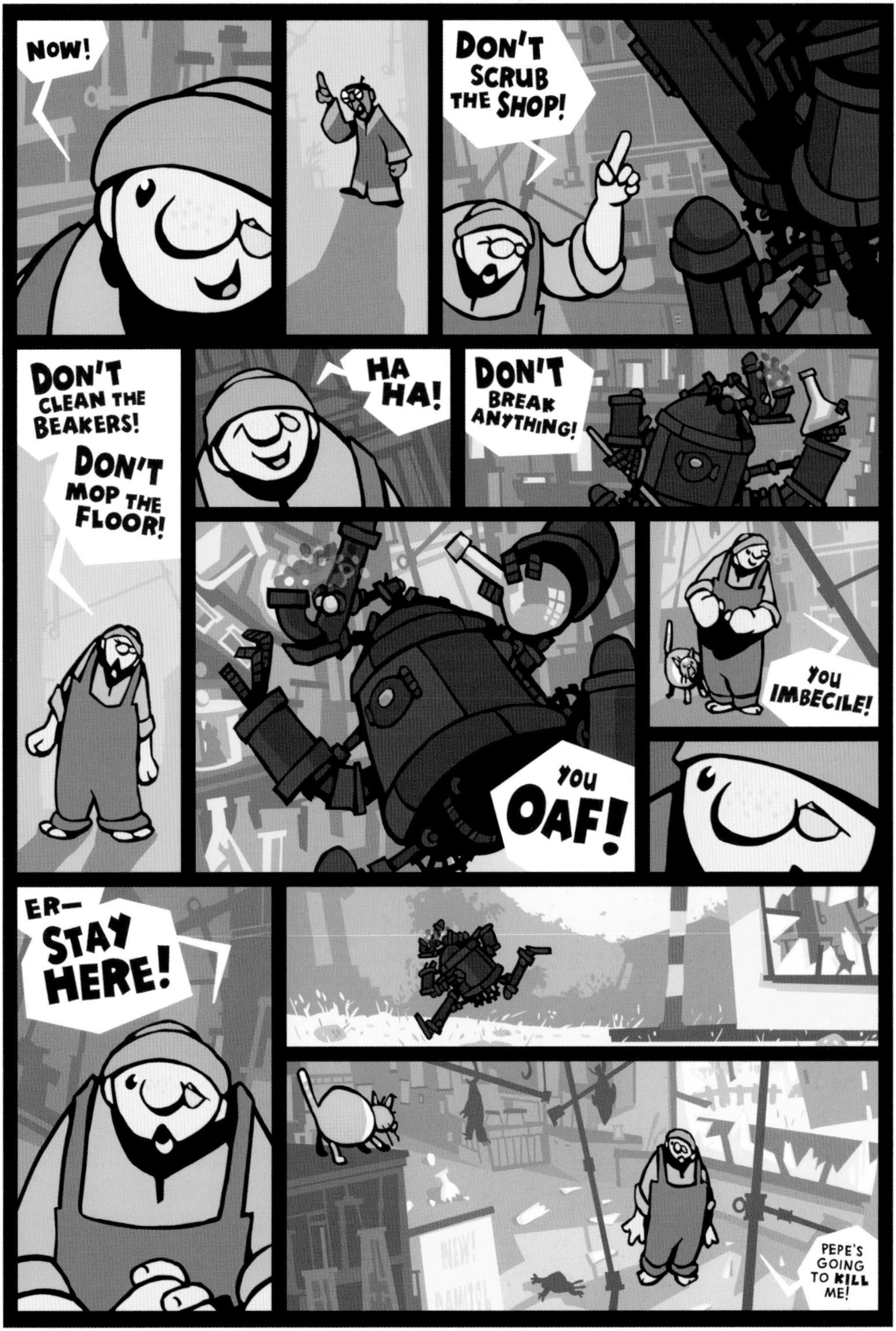
NOW!
DON'T SCRUB THE SHOP!
DON'T CLEAN THE BEAKERS!
HA HA!
DON'T BREAK ANYTHING!
DON'T MOP THE FLOOR!
YOU IMBECILE!
YOU OAF!
ER— STAY HERE!
PEPE'S GOING TO KILL ME!

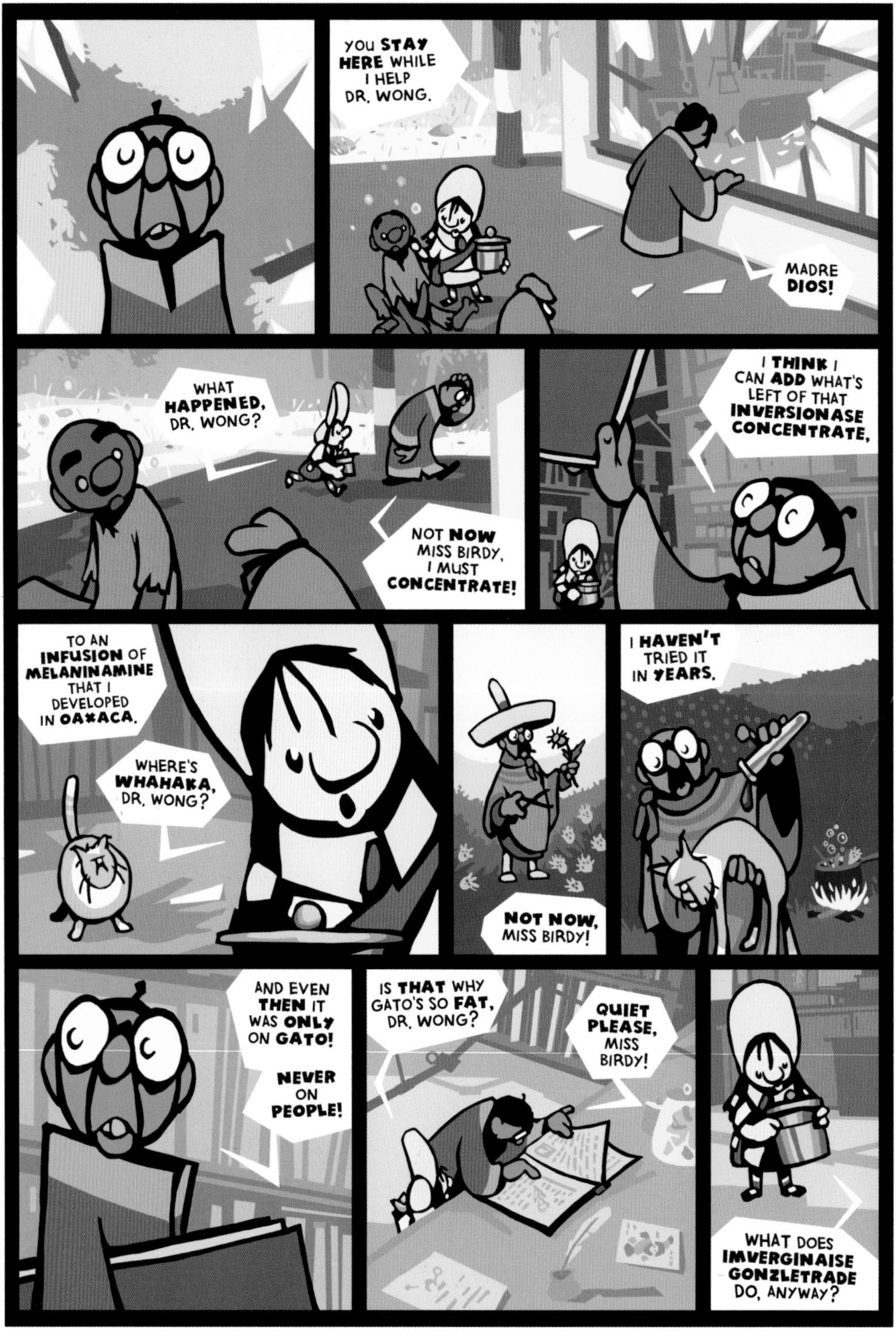
YOU STAY HERE WHILE I HELP DR. WONG.
MADRE DIOS!
WHAT HAPPENED, DR. WONG?
NOT NOW MISS BIRDY, I MUST CONCENTRATE!
I THINK I CAN ADD WHAT'S LEFT OF THAT INVERSIONASE CONCENTRATE,
TO AN INFUSION OF MELANINAMINE THAT I DEVELOPED IN OAXACA.
WHERE'S WHAHAKA, DR. WONG?
NOT NOW, MISS BIRDY!
I HAVEN'T TRIED IT IN YEARS.
AND EVEN THEN IT WAS ONLY ON GATO!
NEVER ON PEOPLE!
IS THAT WHY GATO'S SO FAT, DR. WONG?
QUIET PLEASE, MISS BIRDY!
WHAT DOES IMVERGINAISE GONZLETRADE DO, ANYWAY?

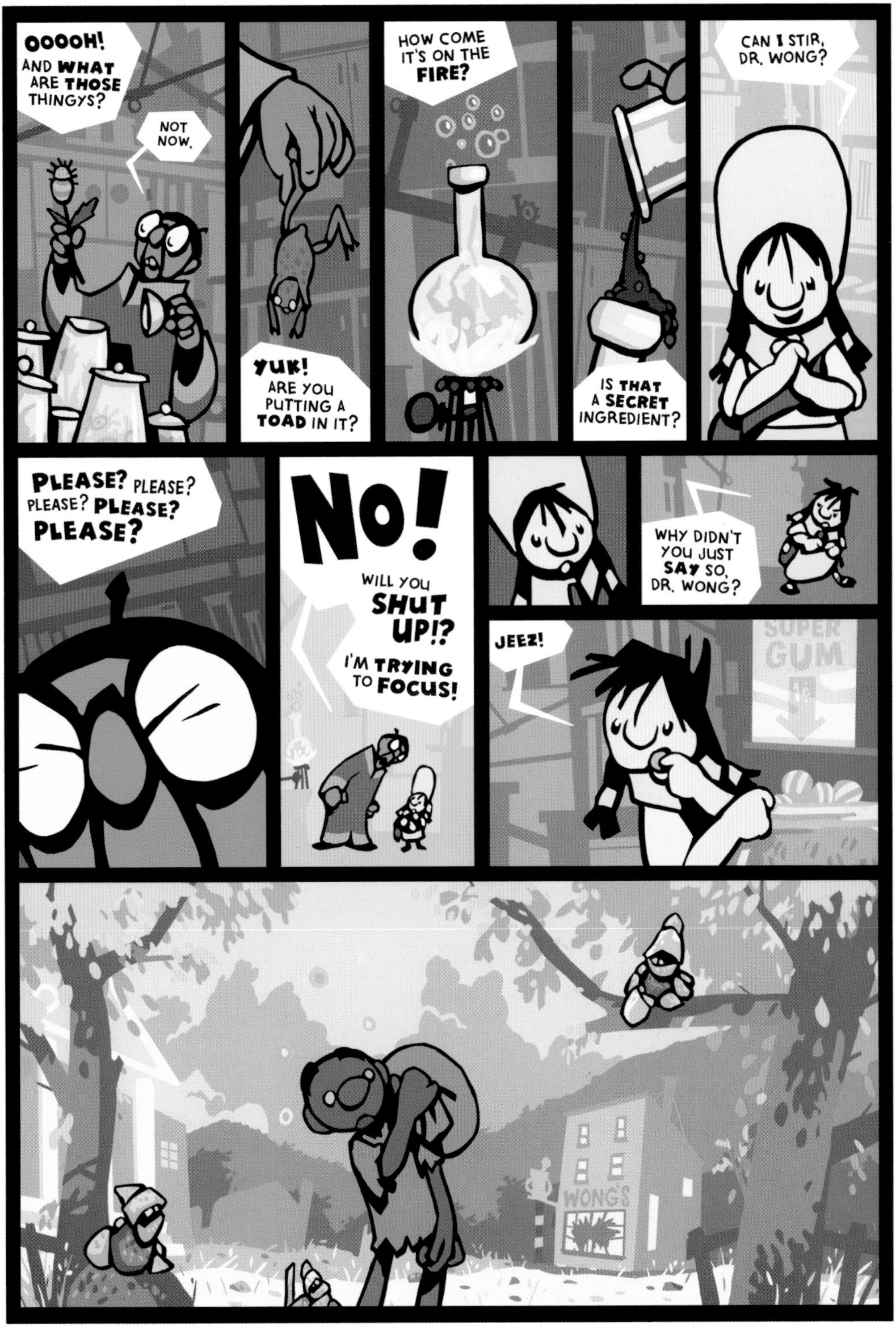
OOOOH!
AND WHAT ARE THOSE THINGYS?
NOT NOW.
YUK! ARE YOU PUTTING A TOAD IN IT?
HOW COME IT'S ON THE FIRE?
IS THAT A SECRET INGREDIENT?
CAN I STIR, DR. WONG?
PLEASE? PLEASE? PLEASE? PLEASE? PLEASE?
NO!
WILL YOU SHUT UP!? I'M TRYING TO FOCUS!
WHY DIDN'T YOU JUST SAY SO, DR. WONG?
JEEZ!
SUPER GUM
WONG'S

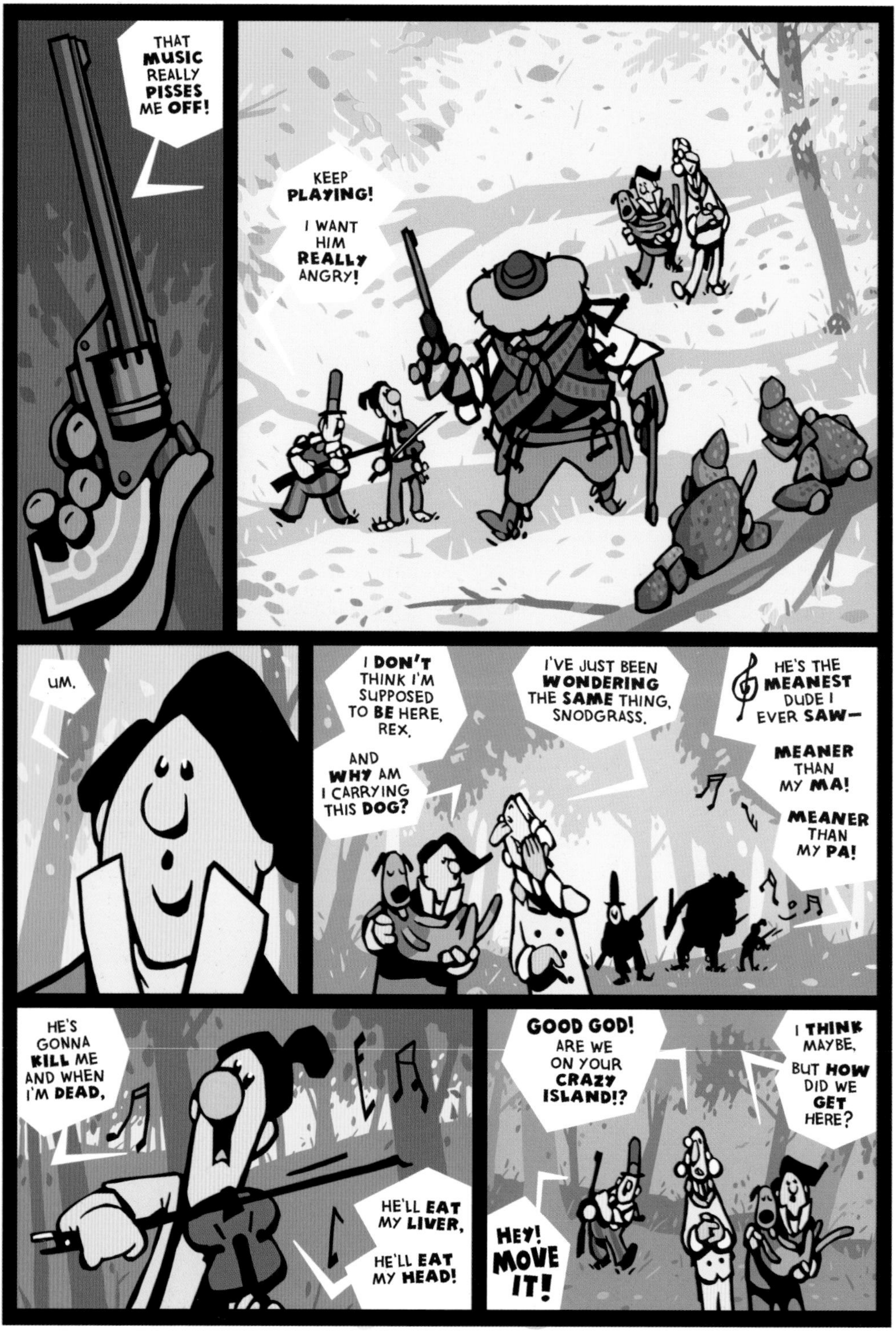
THAT MUSIC REALLY PISSES ME OFF!
KEEP PLAYING!
I WANT HIM REALLY ANGRY!
UM.
I DON'T THINK I'M SUPPOSED TO BE HERE, REX.
AND WHY AM I CARRYING THIS DOG?
I'VE JUST BEEN WONDERING THE SAME THING, SNODGRASS.
HE'S THE MEANEST DUDE I EVER SAW—
MEANER THAN MY MA!
MEANER THAN MY PA!
HE'S GONNA KILL ME AND WHEN I'M DEAD,
HE'LL EAT MY LIVER,
HE'LL EAT MY HEAD!
GOOD GOD! ARE WE ON YOUR CRAZY ISLAND!?
I THINK MAYBE,
BUT HOW DID WE GET HERE?
HEY! MOVE IT!

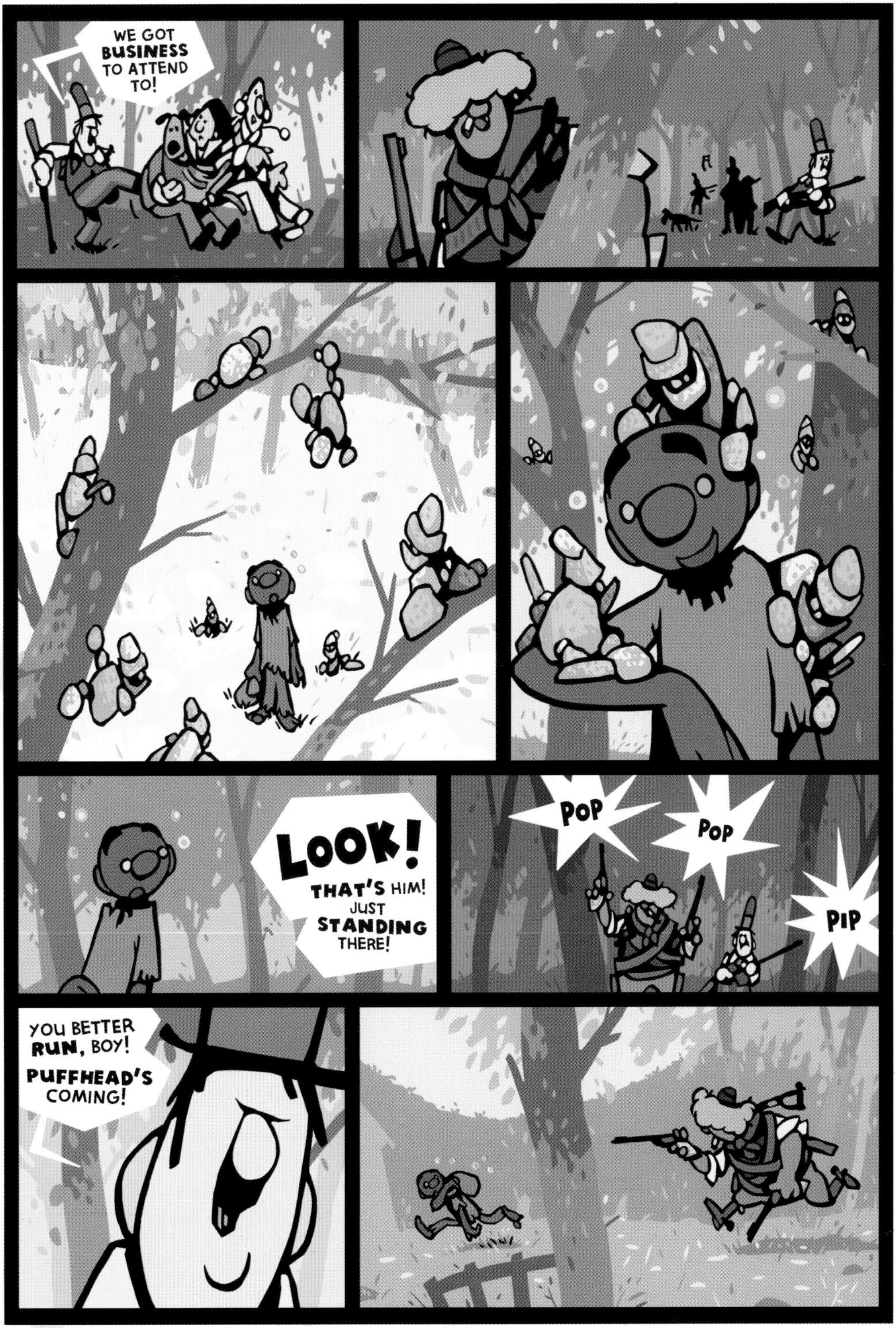
WE GOT **BUSINESS** TO ATTEND TO!
LOOK!
THAT'S HIM! JUST **STANDING** THERE!
POP
POP
PIP
YOU BETTER **RUN**, BOY!
PUFFHEAD'S COMING!

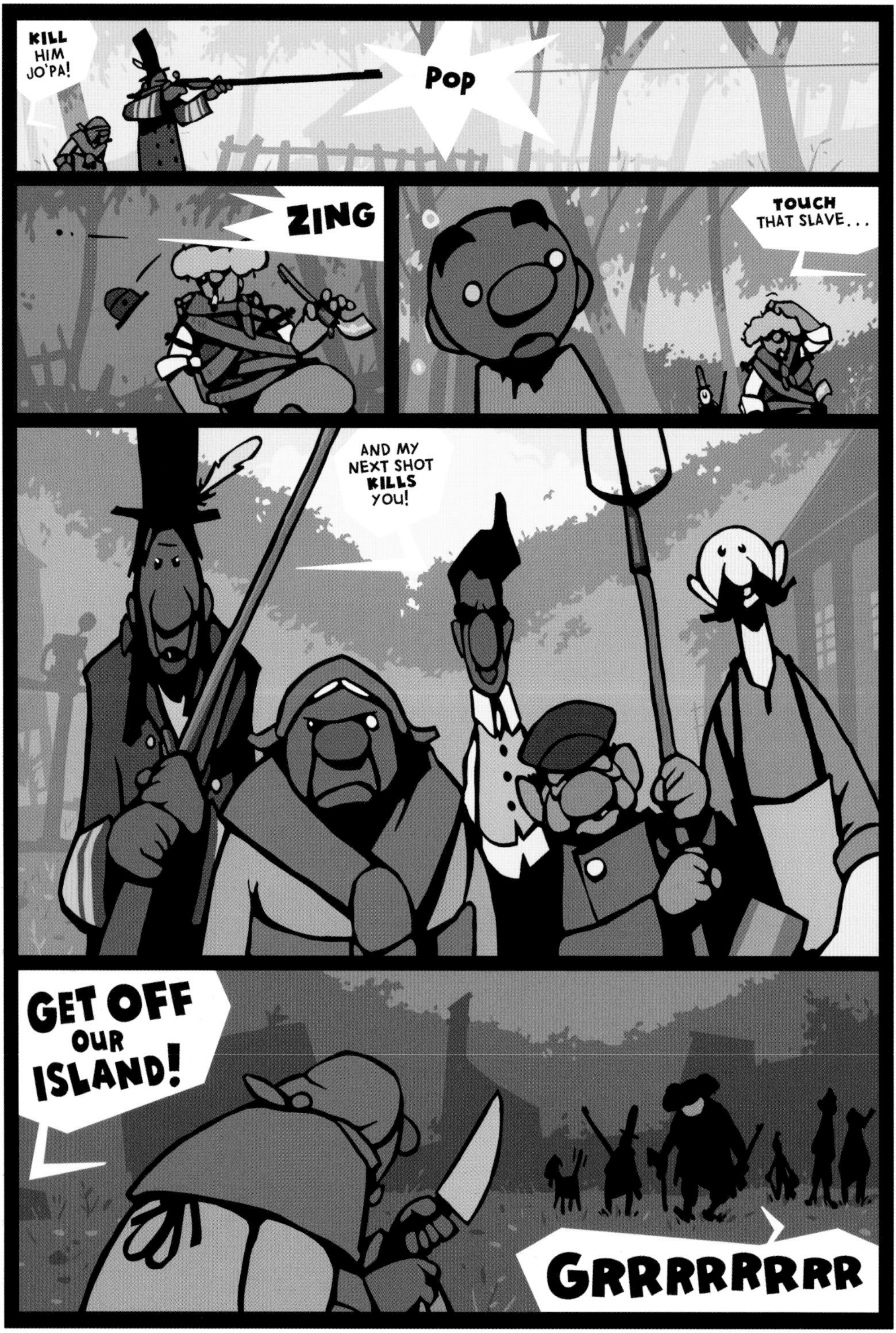

KILL HIM JO'PA!
Pop
ZING
TOUCH THAT SLAVE...
AND MY NEXT SHOT KILLS YOU!
GET OFF OUR ISLAND!
GRRRRRRRR

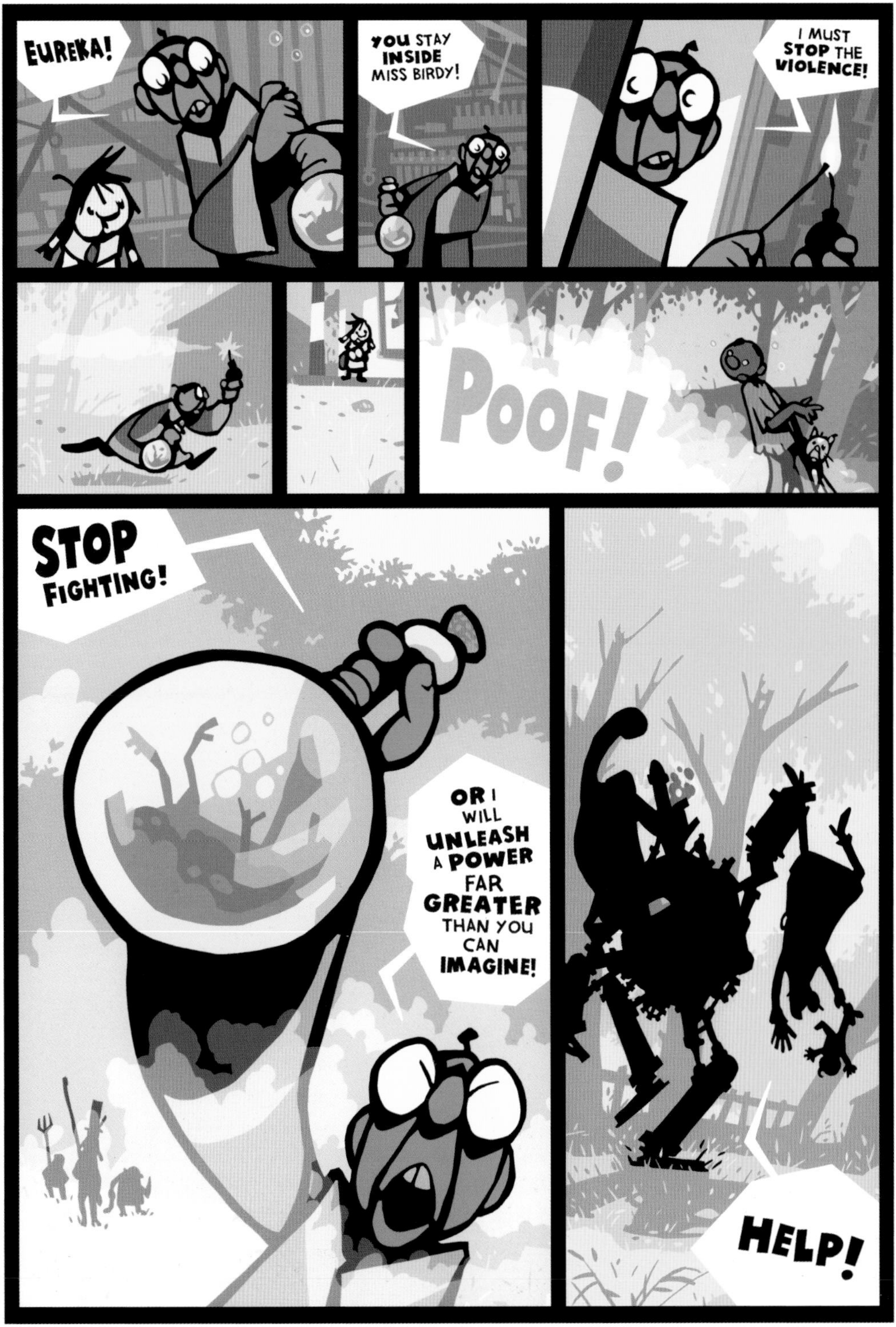
EUREKA!
YOU STAY INSIDE MISS BIRDY!
I MUST STOP THE VIOLENCE!
POOF!
STOP FIGHTING!
OR I WILL UNLEASH A POWER FAR GREATER THAN YOU CAN IMAGINE!
HELP!

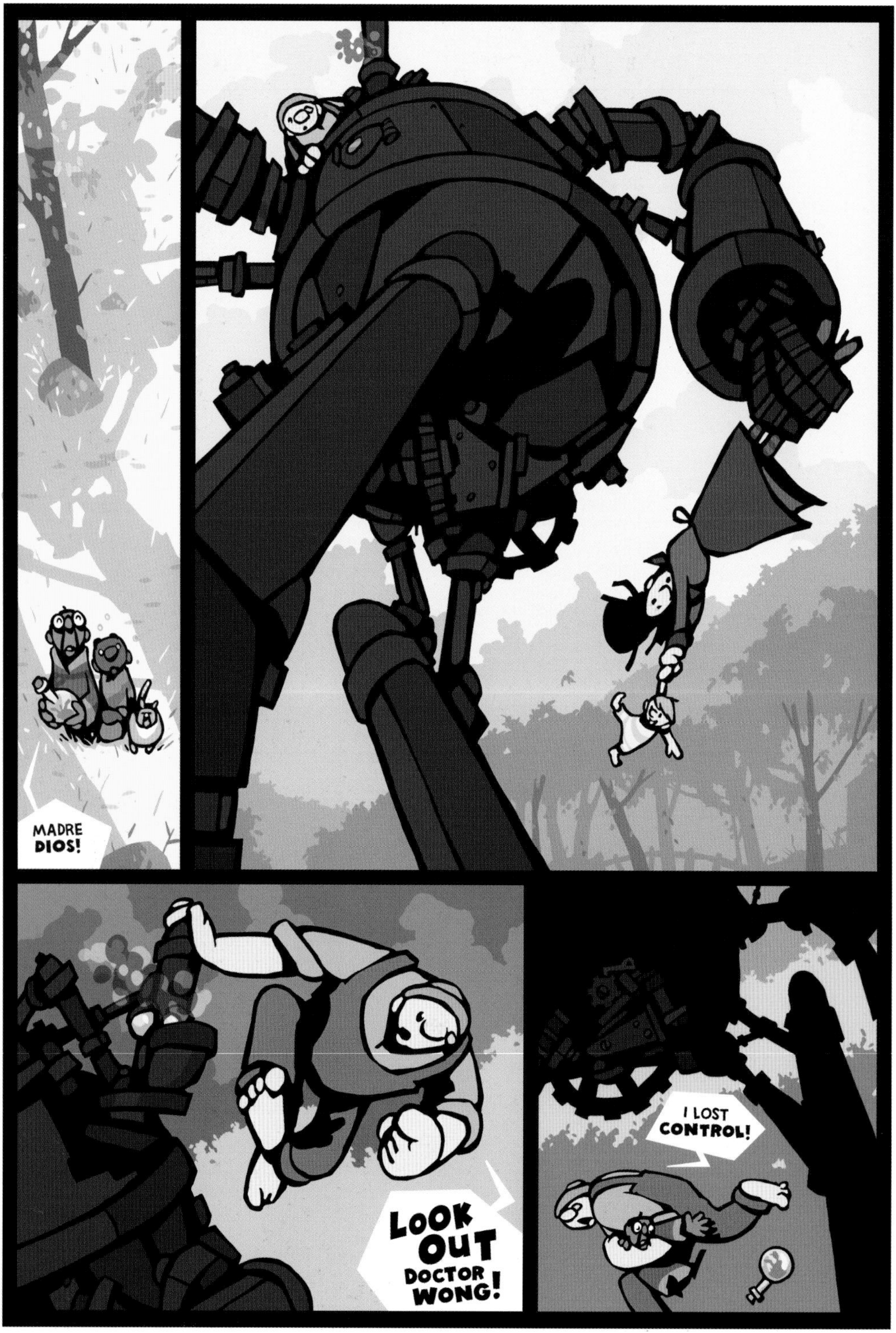
MADRE DIOS!
LOOK OUT DOCTOR WONG!
I LOST CONTROL!

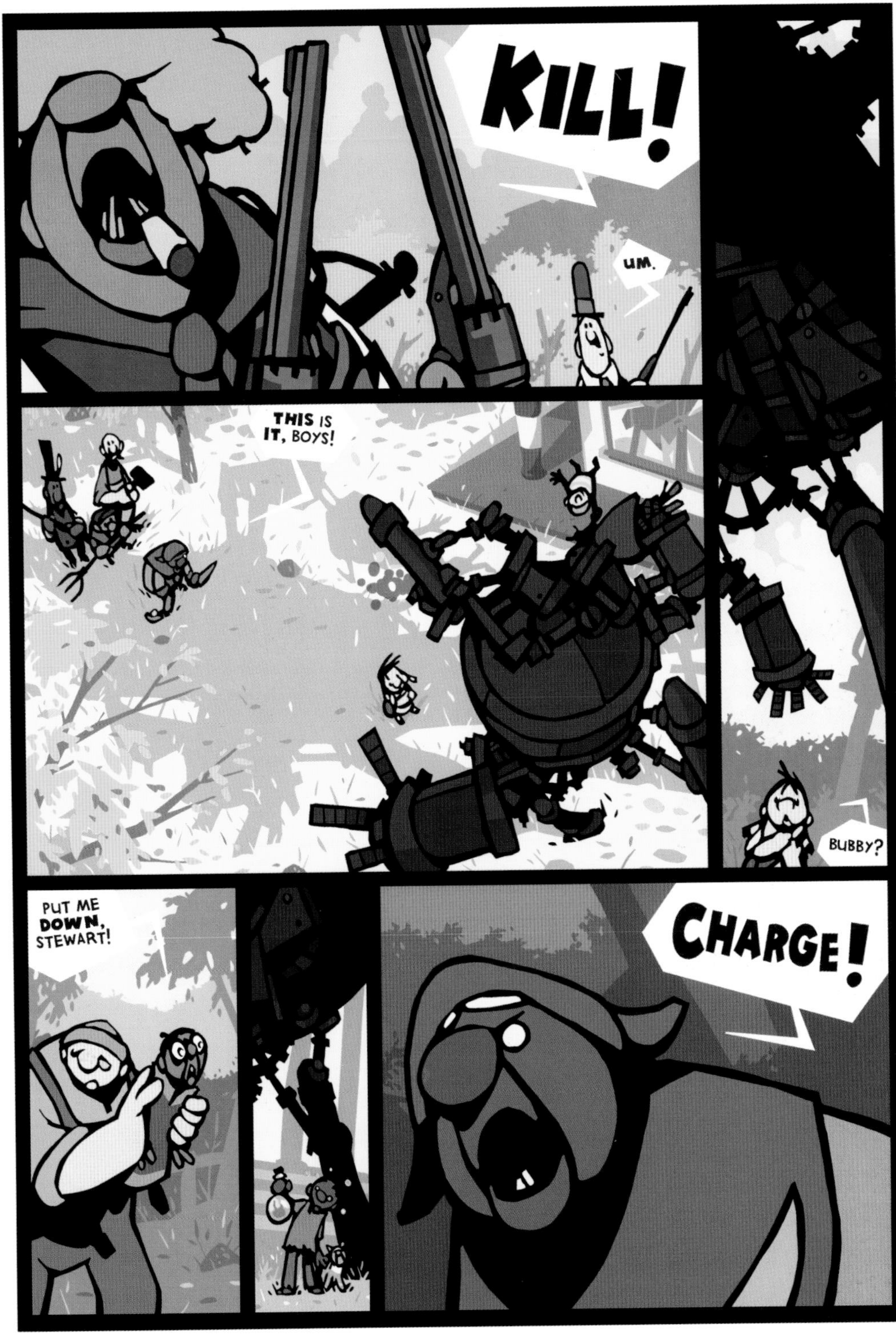
KILL!
UM.
THIS IS IT, BOYS!
BUBBY?
PUT ME DOWN, STEWART!
CHARGE!

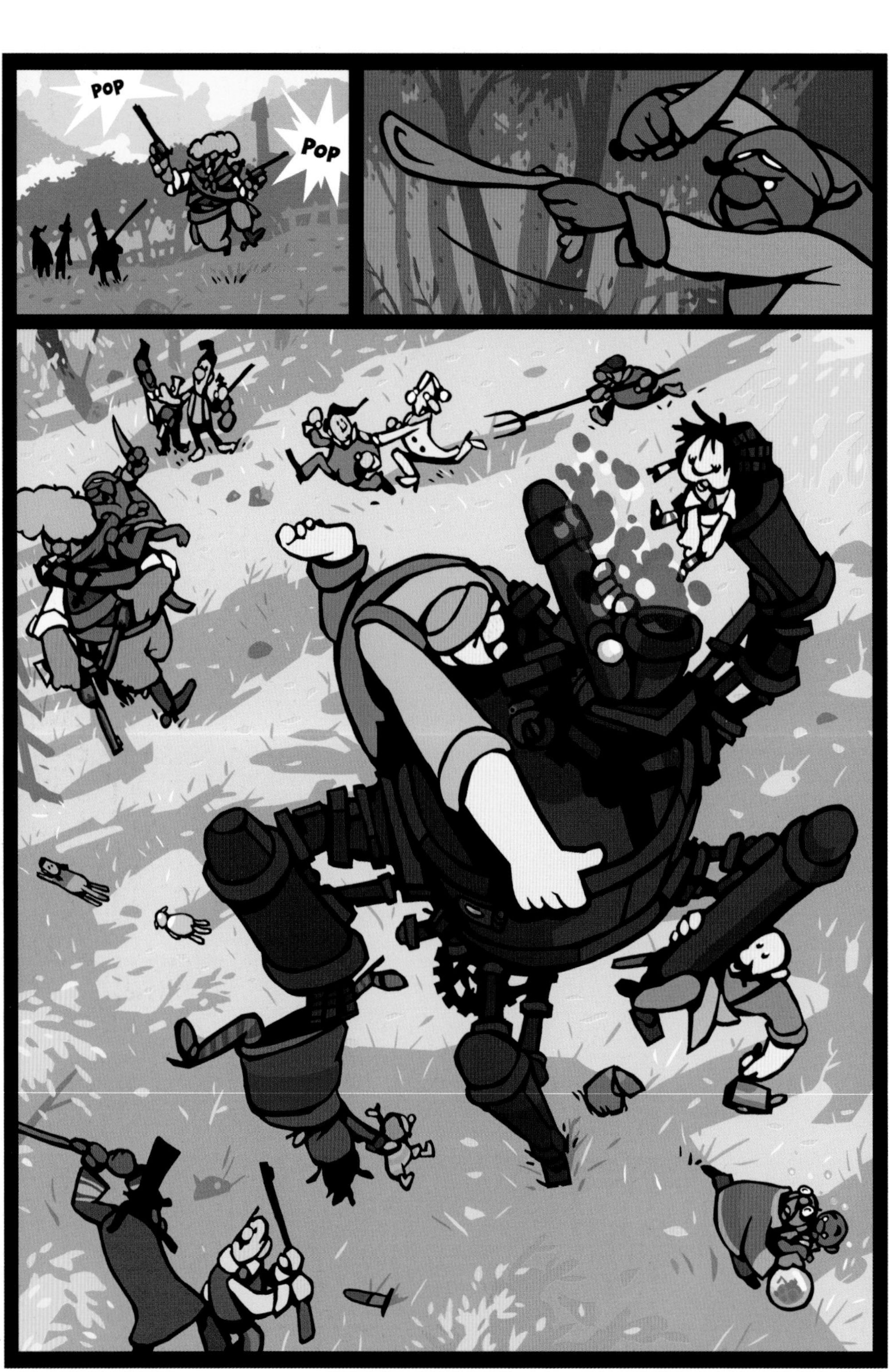
POP
POP

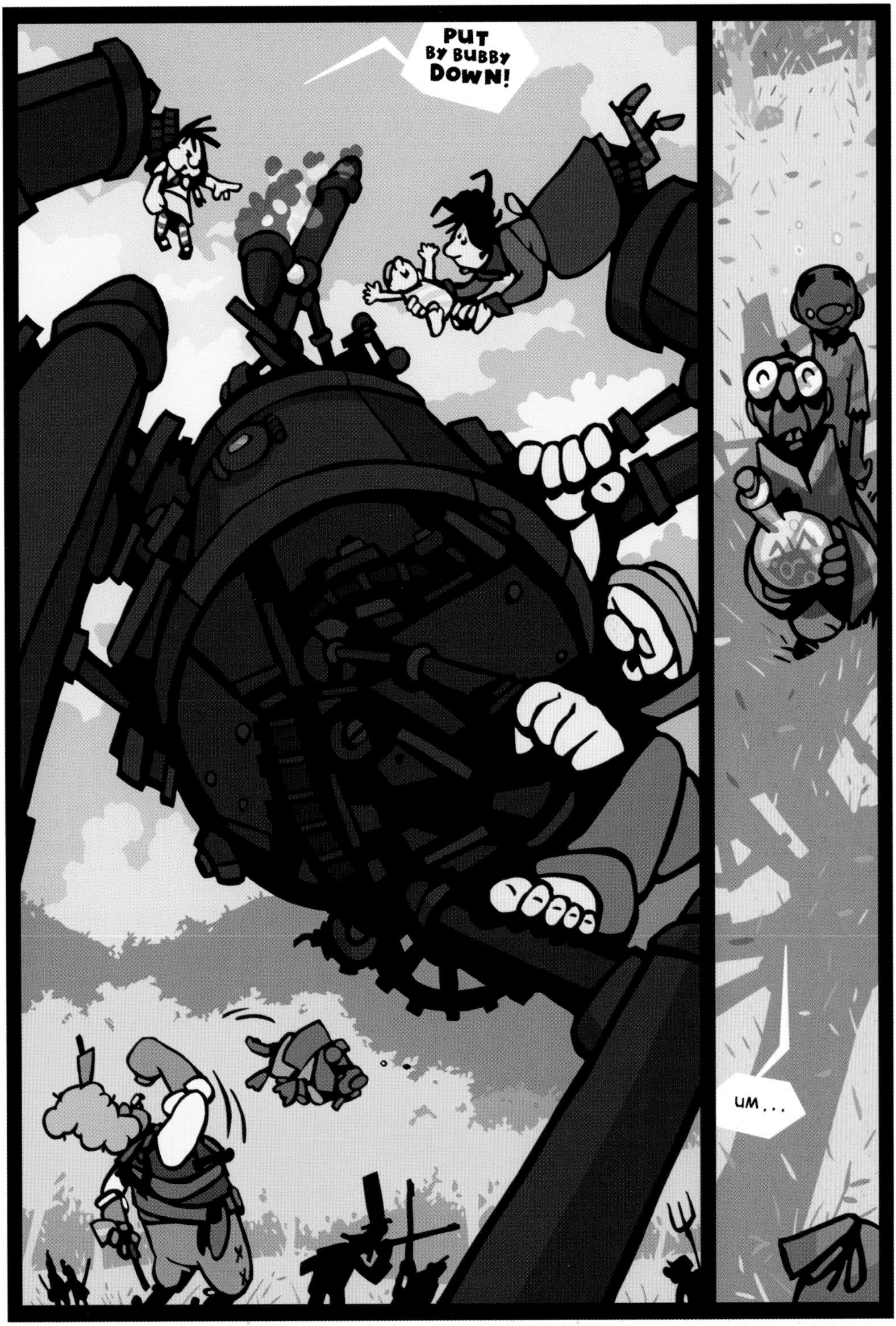
PUT BY BUBBY DOWN!
UM...

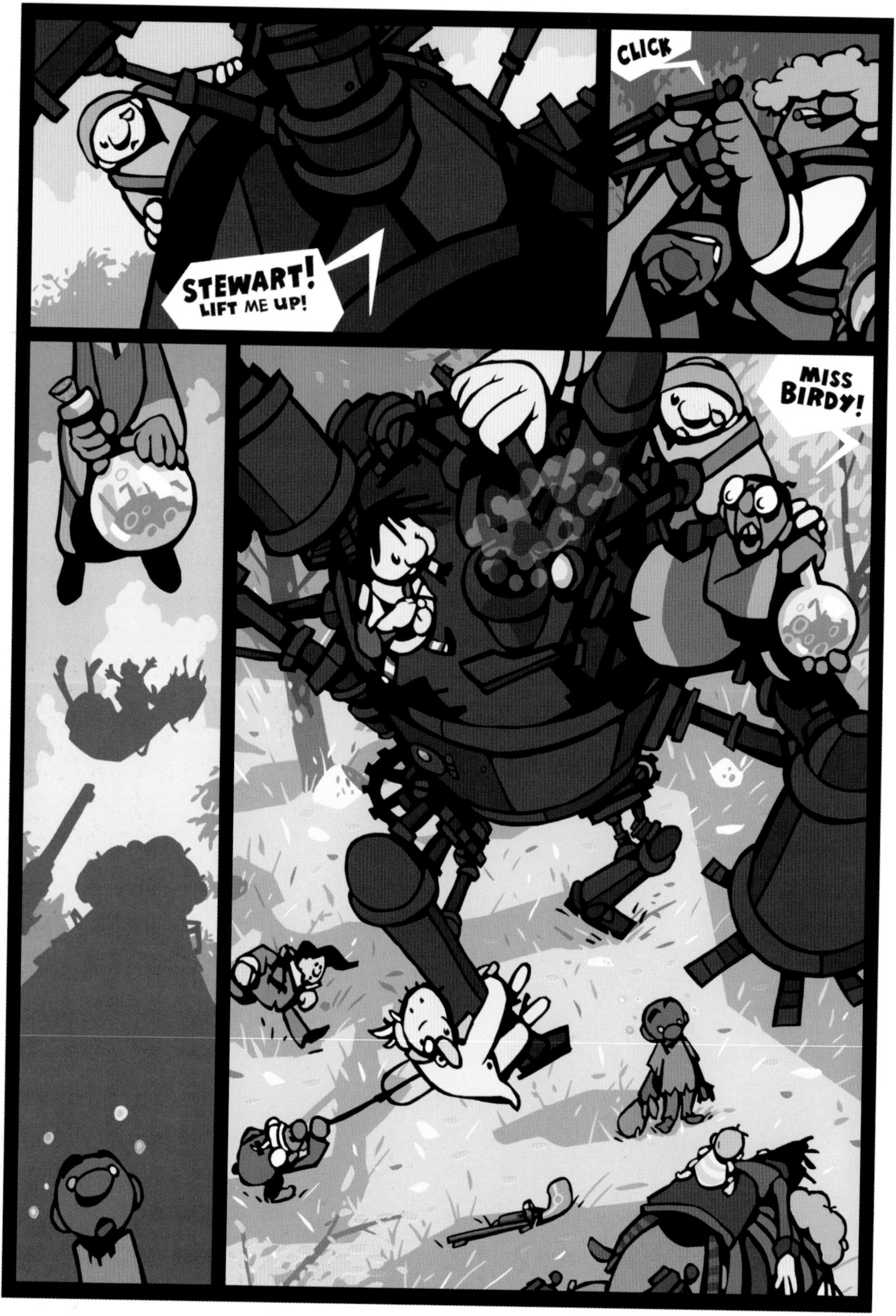
STEWART! LIFT ME UP!
CLICK
MISS BIRDY!

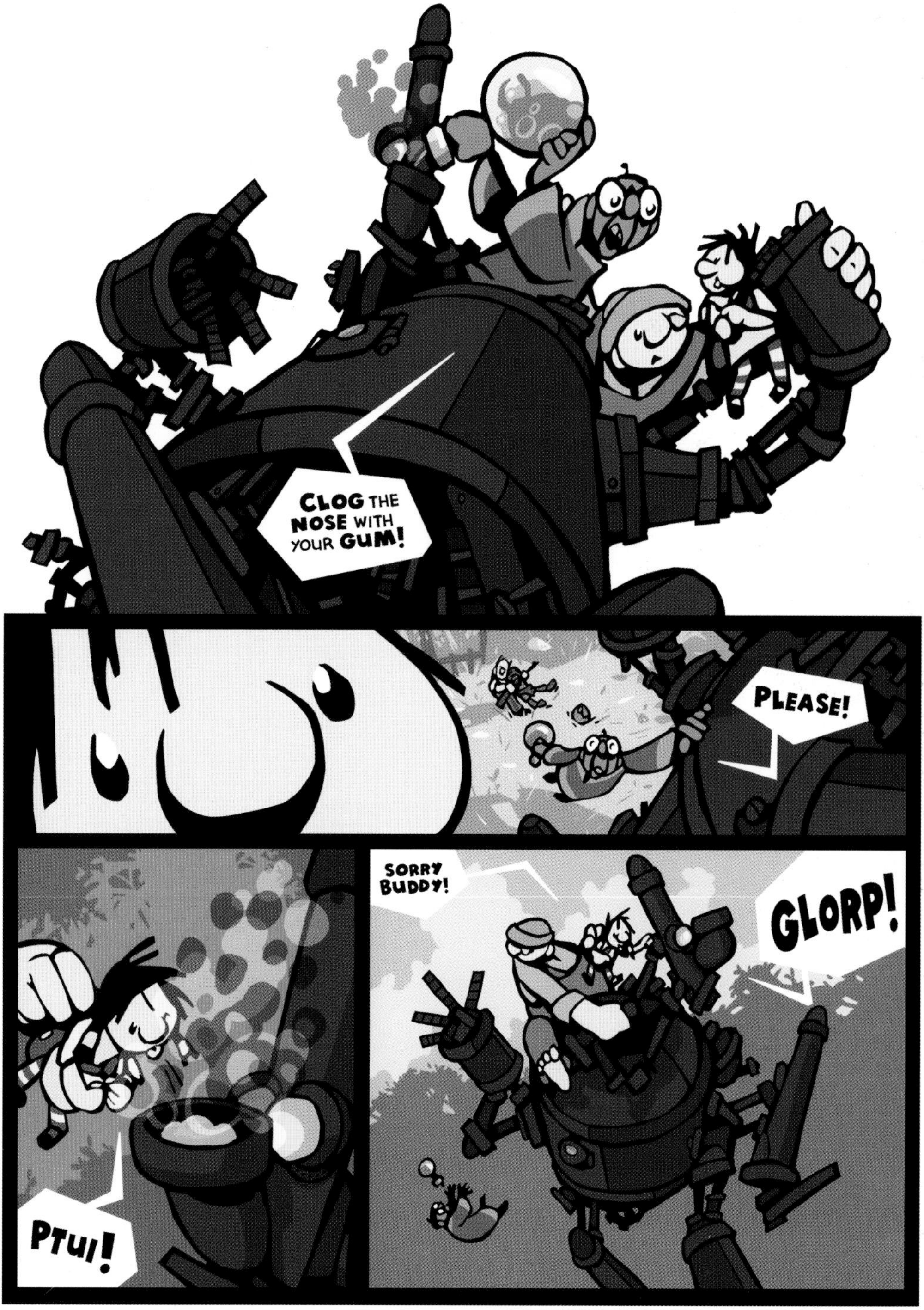
CLOG THE NOSE WITH YOUR GUM!
PLEASE!
PTUI!
SORRY BUDDY!
GLORP!

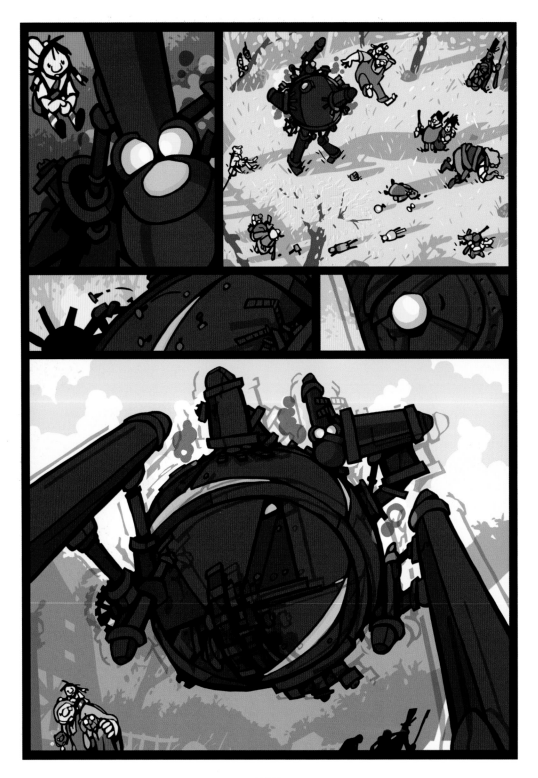

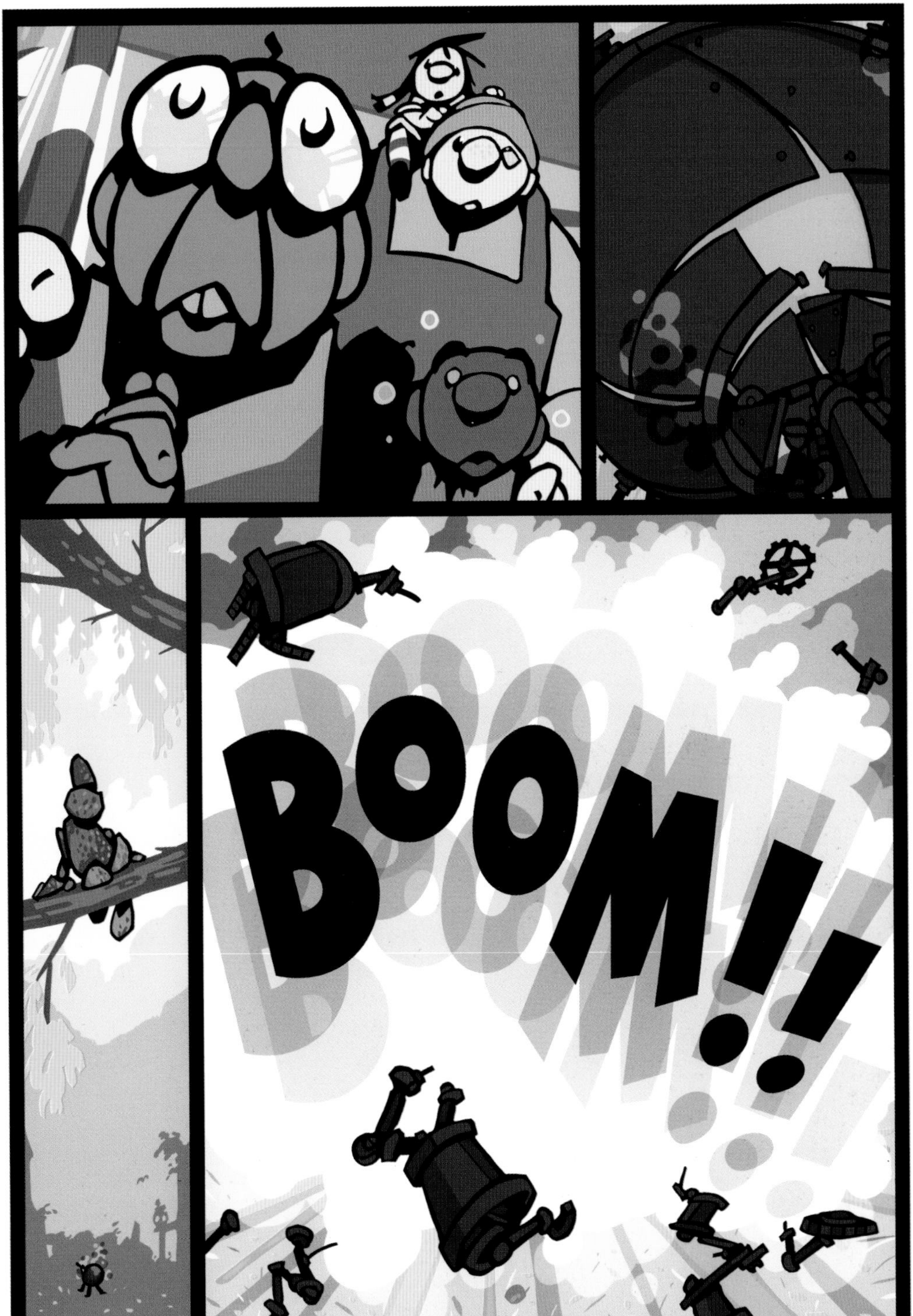
BOOM!!

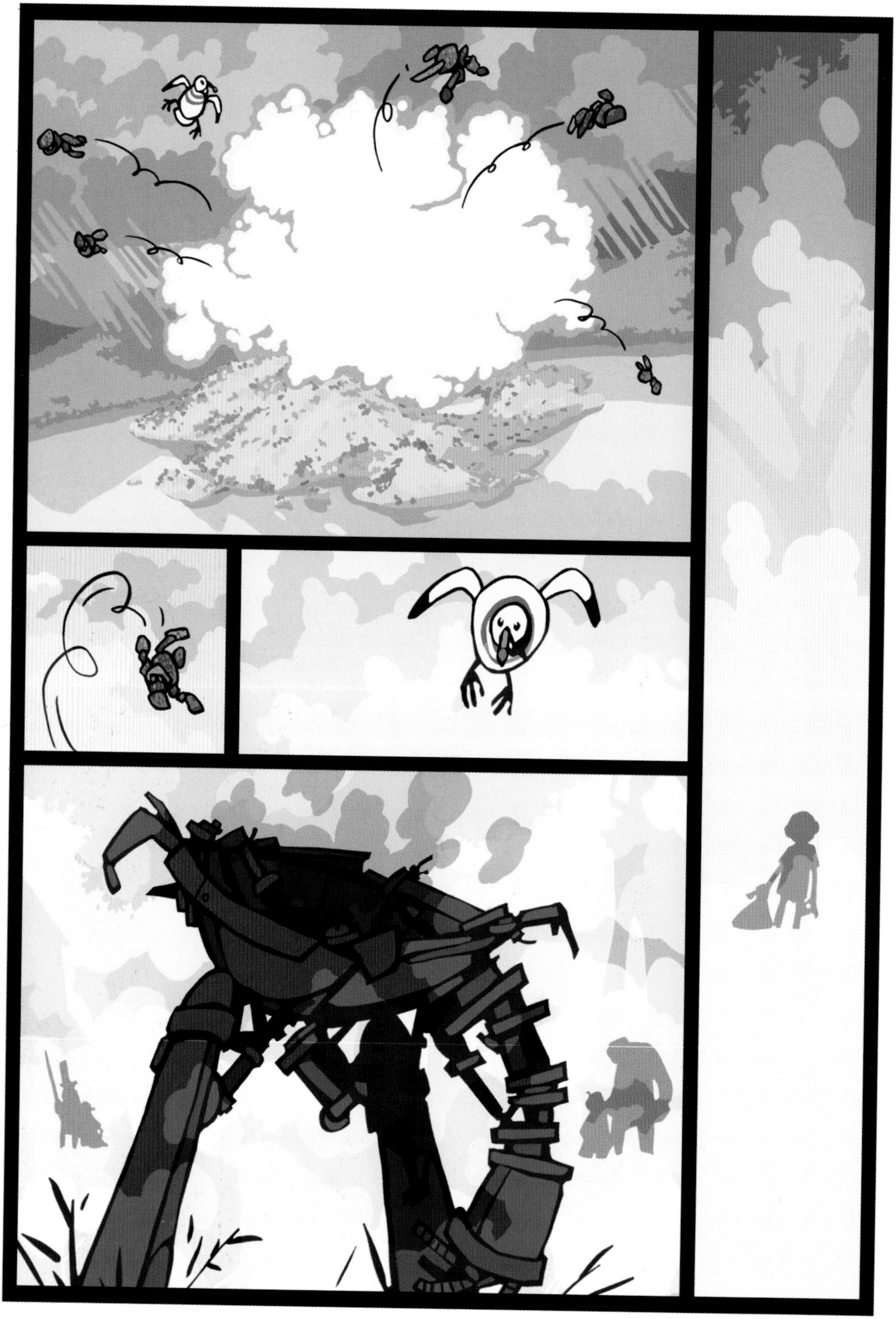

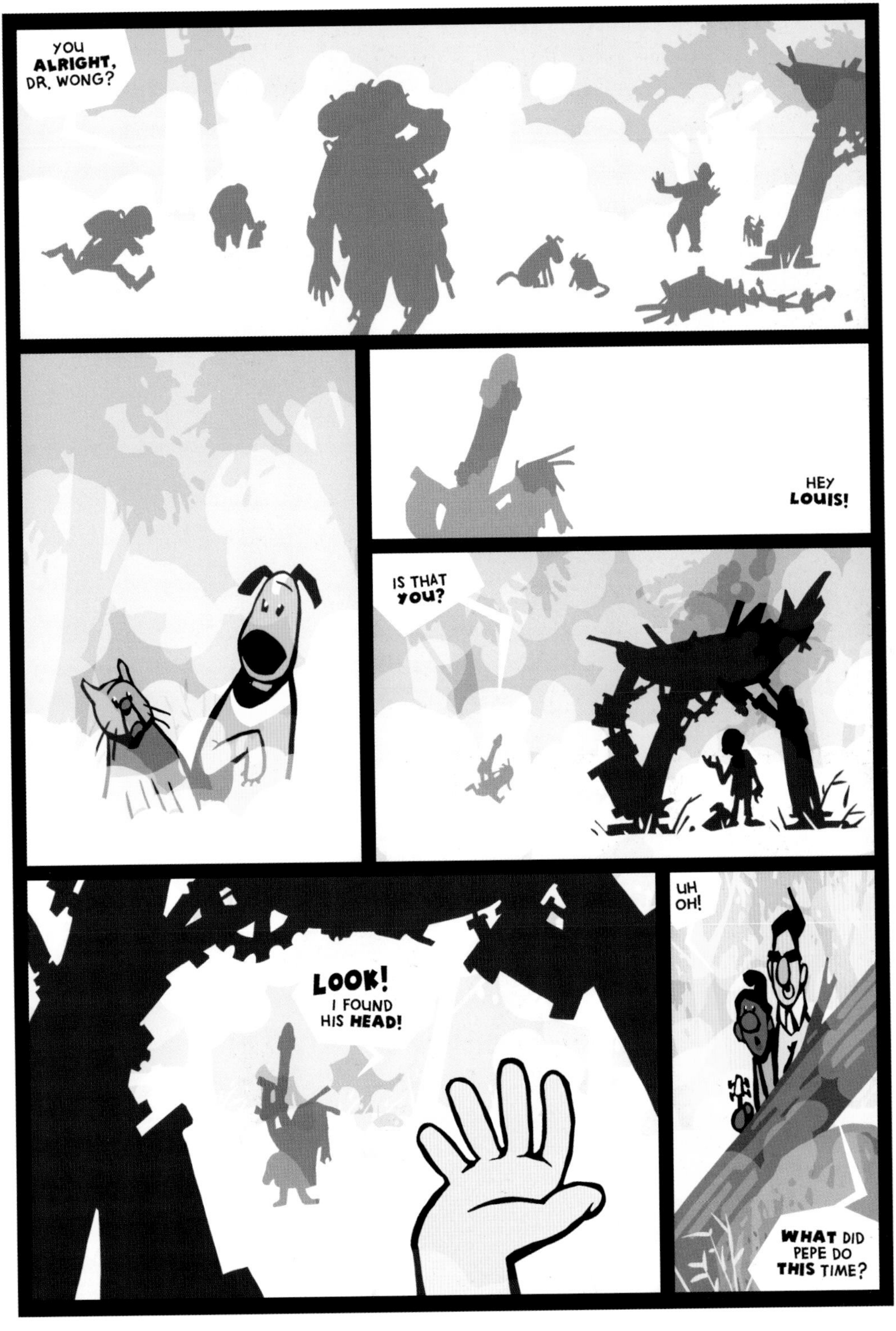
YOU ALRIGHT, DR. WONG?
HEY LOUIS!
IS THAT YOU?
LOOK! I FOUND HIS HEAD!
UH OH!
WHAT DID PEPE DO THIS TIME?

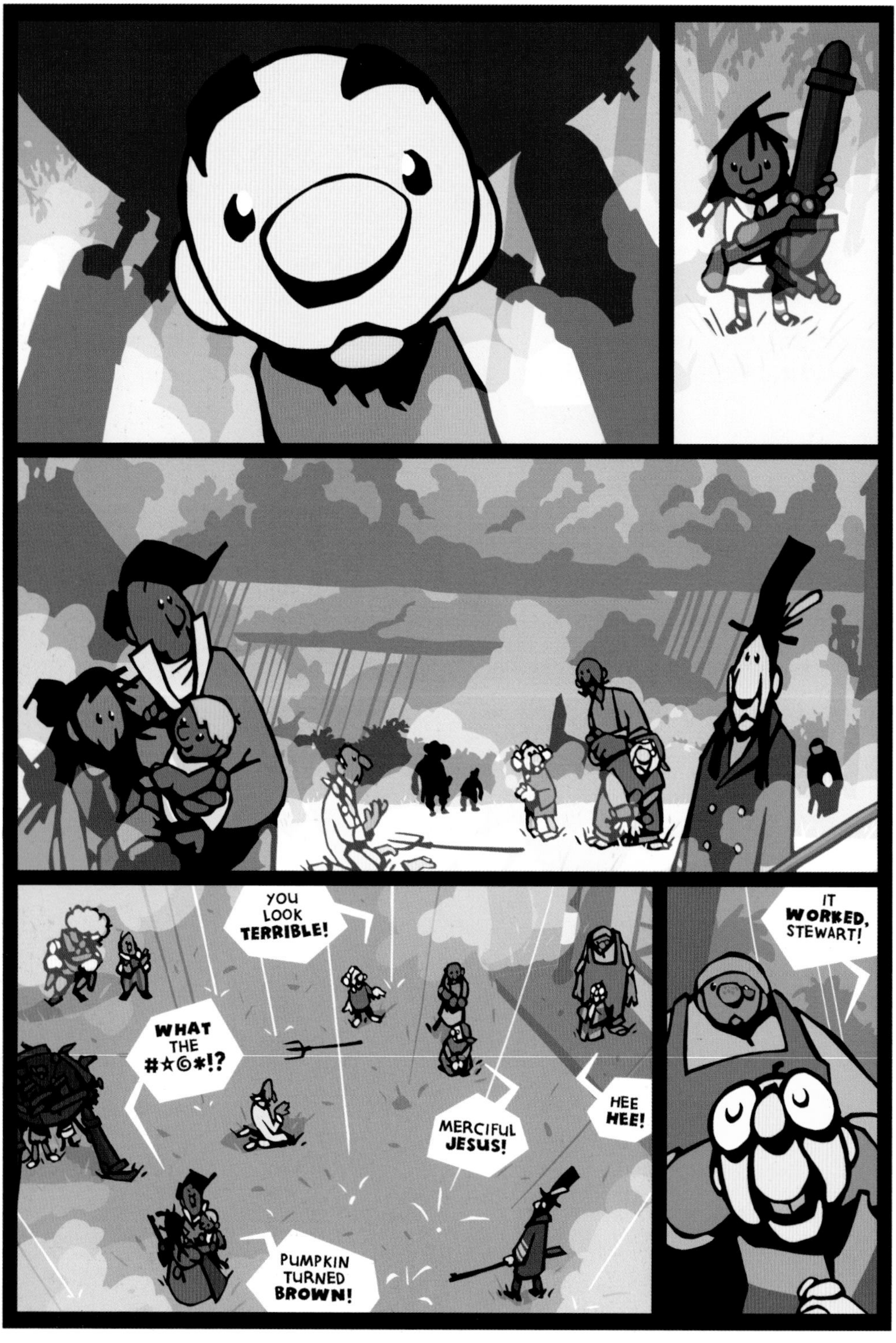
YOU LOOK TERRIBLE!
WHAT THE #☆©*!?
MERCIFUL JESUS!
HEE HEE!
PUMPKIN TURNED BROWN!
IT WORKED, STEWART!

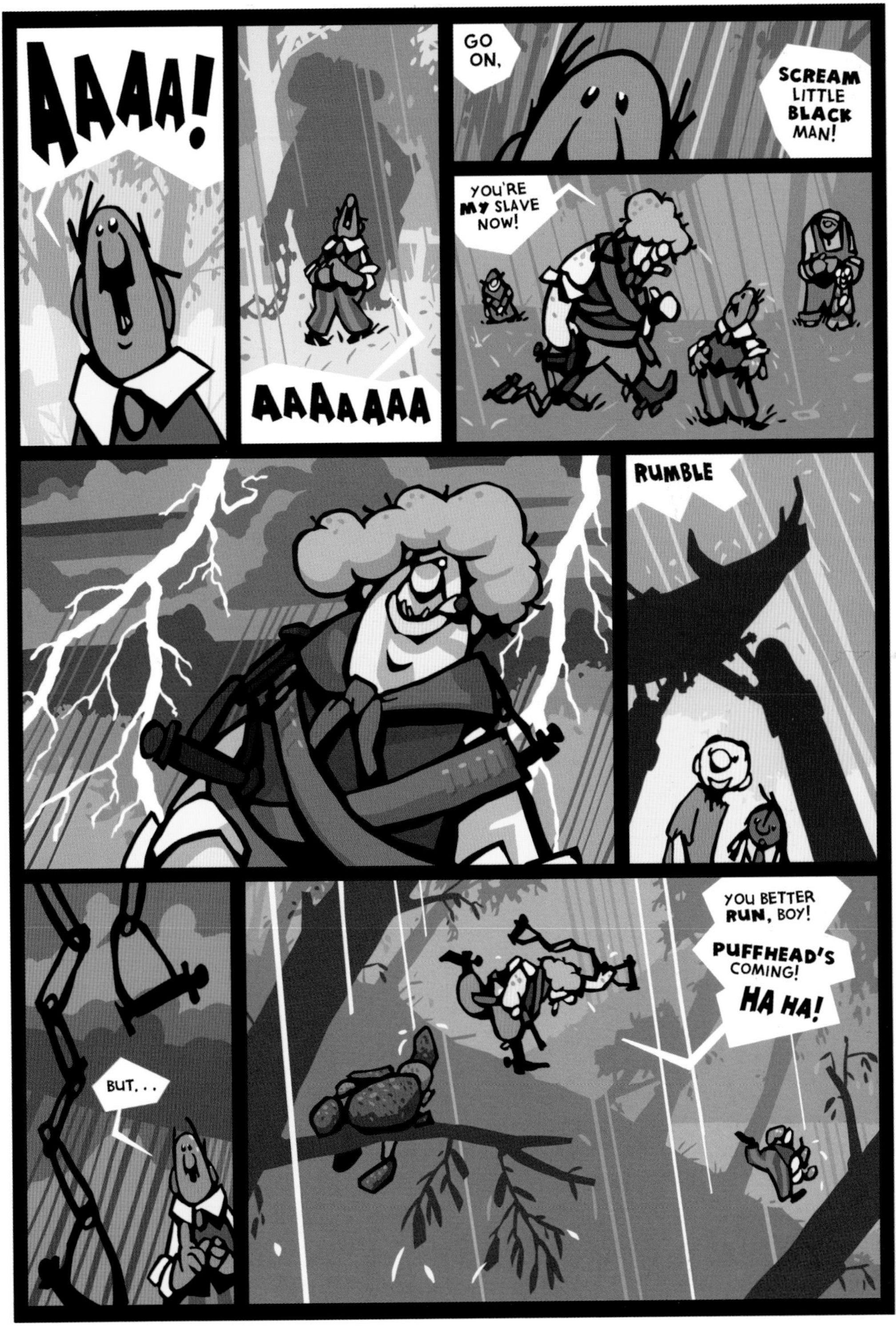
AAAA!
AAAAAAA
GO ON,
SCREAM LITTLE BLACK MAN!
YOU'RE MY SLAVE NOW!
RUMBLE
BUT, . .
YOU BETTER RUN, BOY!
PUFFHEAD'S COMING!
HA HA!

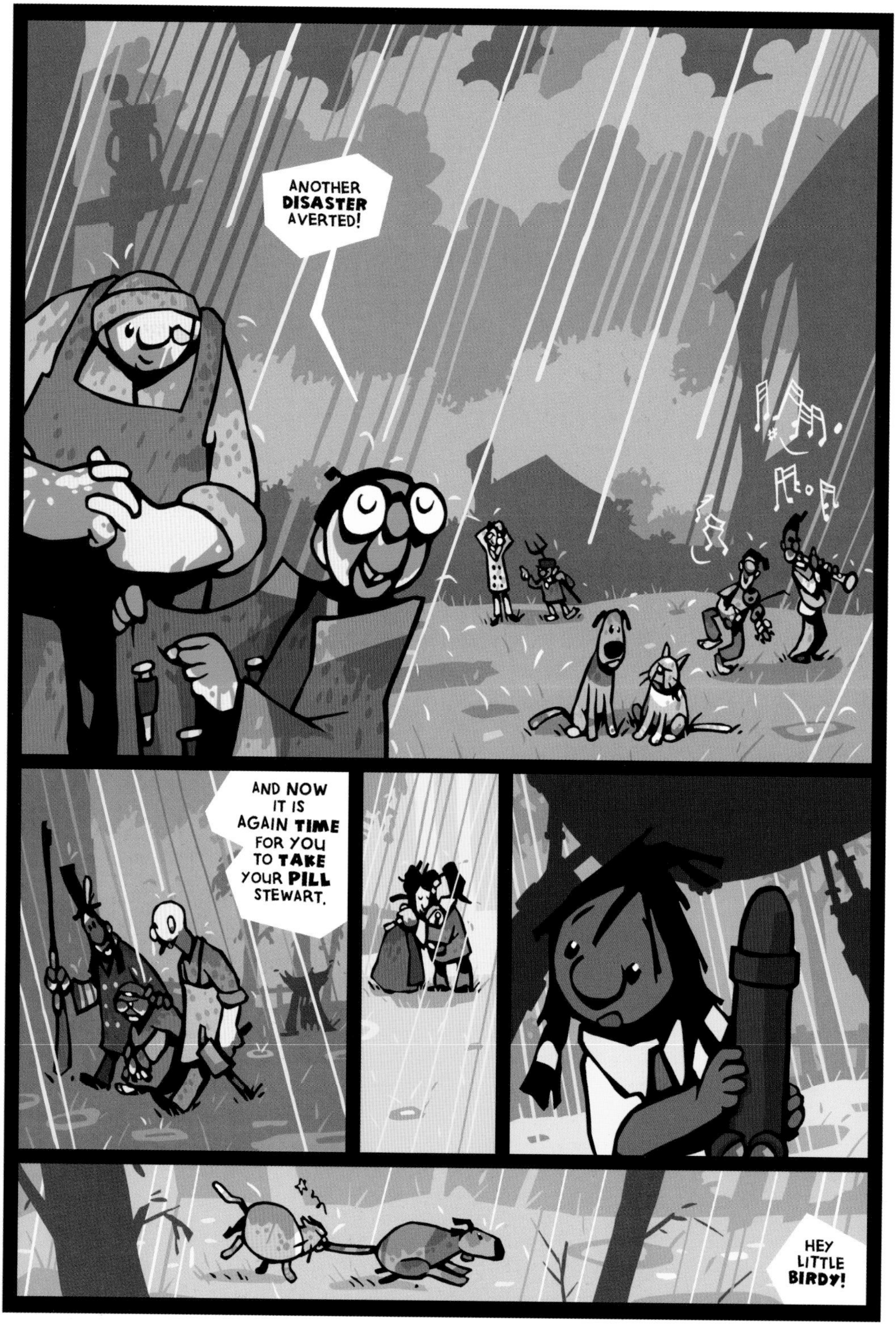
ANOTHER DISASTER AVERTED!
AND NOW IT IS AGAIN TIME FOR YOU TO TAKE YOUR PILL STEWART.
HEY LITTLE BIRDY!

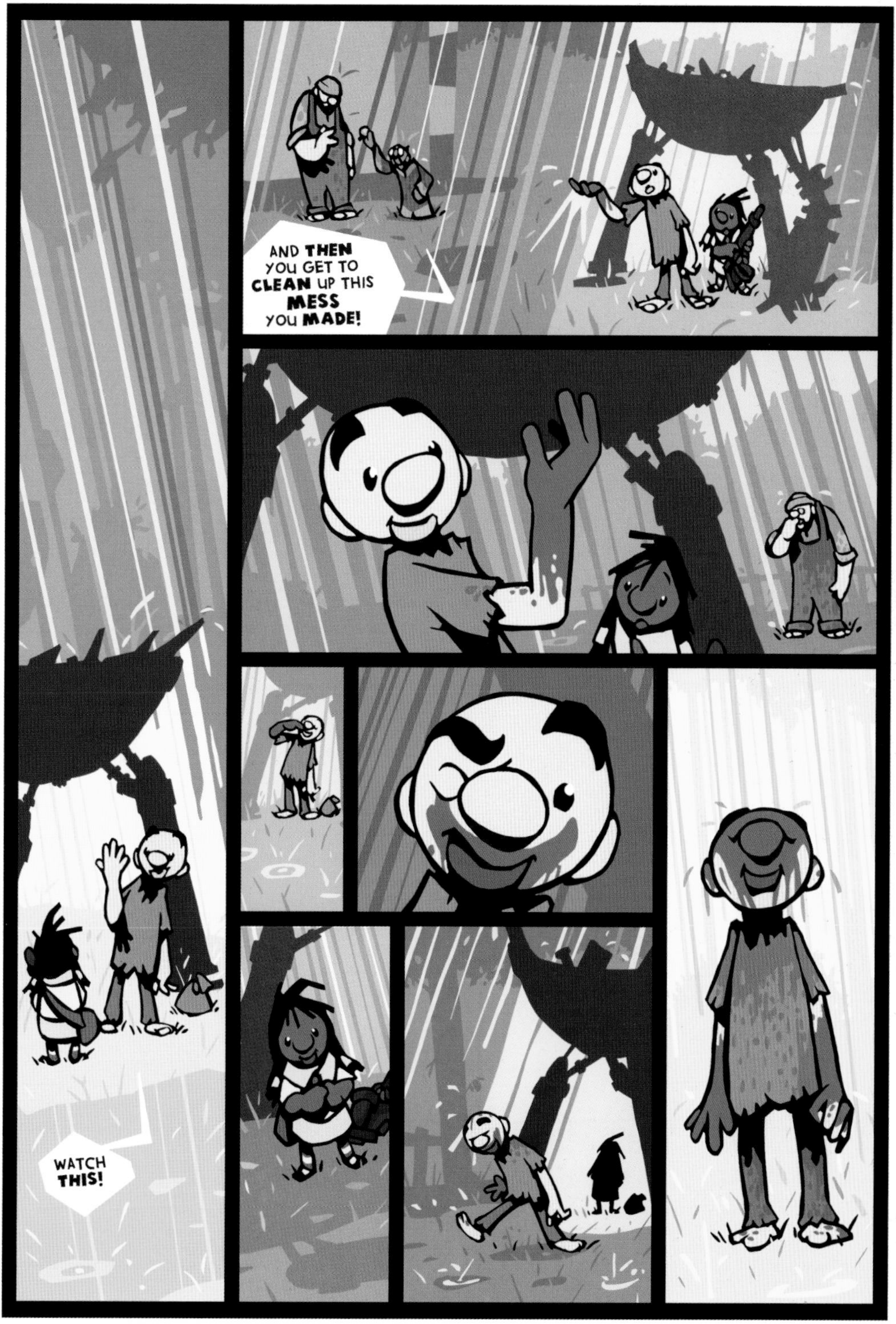
AND THEN YOU GET TO CLEAN UP THIS MESS YOU MADE!
WATCH THIS!

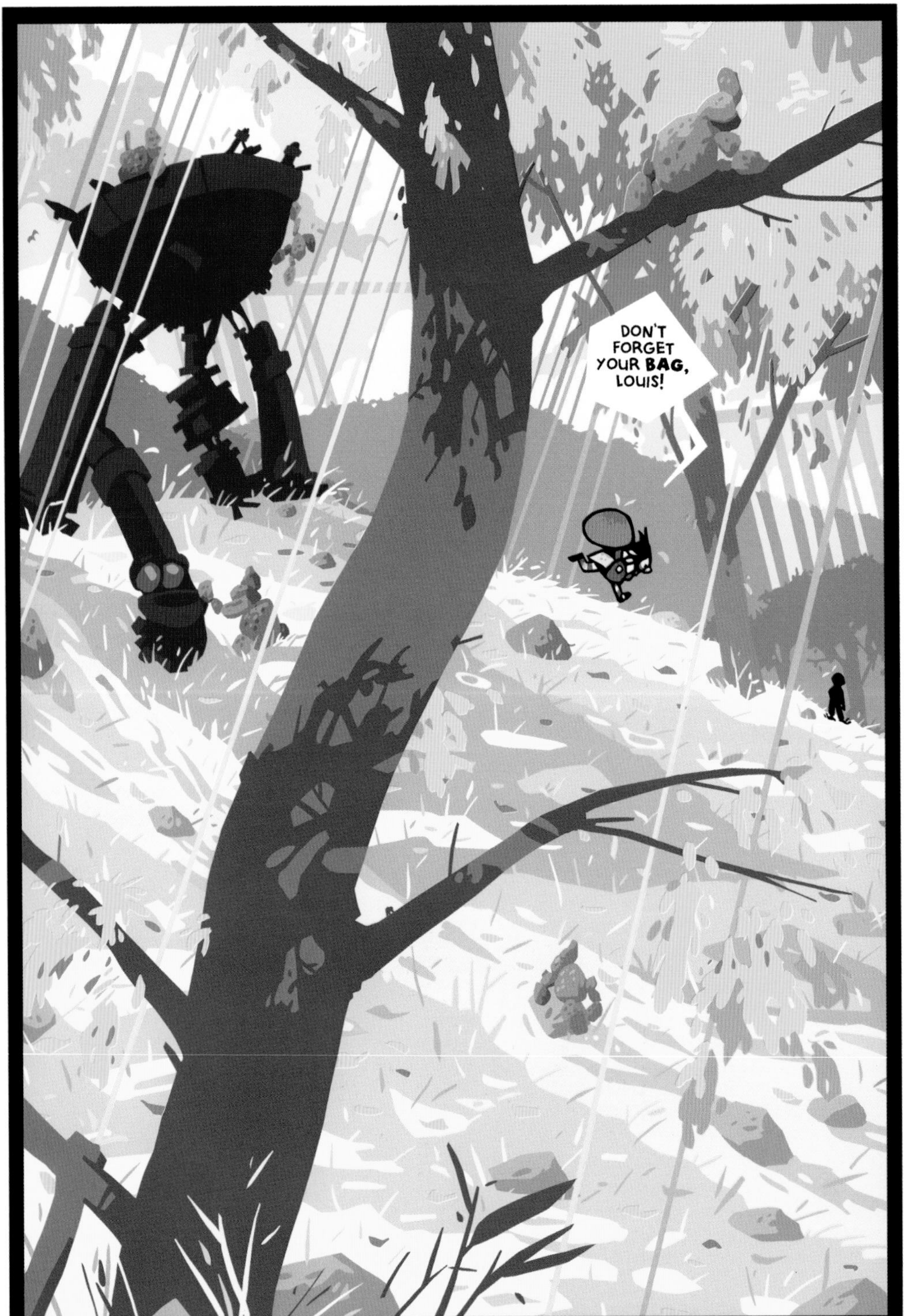
DON'T FORGET YOUR BAG, LOUIS!

For my grandma Louise, a truly inspirational woman.

First Second

Copyright © 2006 by Grady Klein

Published by First Second
First Second is an imprint of Roaring Brook Press, a division of Holtzbrinck
Publishing Holdings Limited Partnership
175 Fifth Avenue, New York, NY 10010

Distributed in Canada by H. B. Fenn and Company Ltd.
Distributed in the United Kingdom by Macmillan Children's Books, a division
of Pan Macmillan.

Cataloging-in-Publication Data is on file at the Library of Congress.

ISBN-13: 978-1-59643-097-6 (paperback)
ISBN-10: 1-59643-097-4 (paperback)

COLLECTOR'S EDITION
ISBN-13: 978-1-59643-172-0
ISBN-10: 1-59643-172-5

First Second books are available for special promotions and premiums.
For details, contact: Director of Special Markets, Holtzbrinck Publishers.

FIRST
EDITION

First Edition May 2006

Printed in China

10 9 8 7 6 5 4 3 2 1